Sc
ple

R
Er
Tex

L3

B 2009

A SISTER'S PROMISE

Anne Bennett was born in a back-to-back house in the Horsefair district of Birmingham. The daughter of Roman Catholic, Irish immigrants, she grew up in a tight-knit community where she was taught to be proud of her heritage. She considers herself to be an Irish Brummie and feels therefore that she has a foot in both cultures. She has four children and four grandchildren. For many years she taught in schools to the north of Birmingham. An accident put paid to her teaching career and, after moving to North Wales, Anne turned to the other great love of her life and began to write seriously. In 2006, after 16 years in a wheelchair, she miraculously regained her ability to walk.

Visit www.AuthorTracker.co.uk for exclusive information about Anne Bennett.

By the same author

A Little Learning
Love Me Tender
A Strong Hand to Hold
Pack Up Your Troubles
Walking Back to Happiness
Till the Sun Shines Through
Danny Boy
Daughter of Mine
Mother's Only Child
To Have and to Hold

ANNE BENNETT

A Sister's Promise

HarperCollins*Publishers*

HarperCollins*Publishers*
77–85 Fulham Palace Road,
Hammersmith, London W6 8JB

www.harpercollins.co.uk

Published by HarperCollins*Publishers* 2007
1

A catalogue record for this book
is available from the British Library

ISBN-13: 978 0 00 722601 6
ISBN-10: 0 00 722601 2

Set in Sabon by Palimpsest Book Production Limited,
Grangemouth, Stirlingshire

Printed and bound in Great Britain by
Clays Ltd, St Ives plc

This book is proudly printed on paper which contains wood
from well managed forests, certified in accordance with
the rules of the Forest Stewardship Council.
For more information about FSC,
please visit www.fsc-uk.org

Mixed Sources
Product group from well-managed
forests and other controlled sources
www.fsc.org Cert no. TT-COC-2139
© 1996 Forest Stewardship Council

FSC

To my eldest grandson, Kynan Wilkes,
with all my love

ONE

'Molly, they will come no quicker with you running to the window every five minutes,' Stan Maguire told his granddaughter.

'I know, but I can't help it,' Molly said, turning so quickly her dark brown plaits slapped either side of her face. Her large brown eyes were sparkling. 'Dad has been left for flipping ages and I'm dying to see Mom.'

'Well, think what it's like for young Kevin,' Stan said. 'Must be a sight worse for him, and your flitting about does him no good at all.'

Molly immediately felt contrite because she knew her grandfather had a point. Her mother, Nuala, had been in hospital for nine terrifying weeks, when the cold she was trying to work off turned into pneumonia in the middle of February. She had very nearly died.

When the hospital said she was well enough for visitors, Molly had been allowed to go because she was over twelve – in fact she had turned thirteen a few days before her mother had been taken to the hospital. She would go with either her granddad, Stan, her father, Ted, or Hilda Mason, their next-door neighbour and her mother's best friend. Not that anyone had been able to go often, for visiting was only allowed on Wednesday and Saturday evening for one hour, though her father could also see his wife for two hours on Sunday afternoon.

1

Still, Molly had seen her and rejoiced as she watched her improve though at first her recovery was so slight she would wonder afterwards if she had imagined it. And then one day she had gone in to find her mother propped up in bed instead of prone, her beautiful hair tied back from her face with a ribbon, and wearing the peach-coloured bed jacket her father had bought for her. She also wore a wide smile for Molly, despite the fact her face was as white as lint and her eyes heavy with fatigue.

When Molly felt her mother's arms encircle her and she had drunk in the familiar smell of her, she had sighed in contentment. She knew in that moment that she would recover and that was what she had told Kevin when she got home. He had let his breath out in a loud sigh and Molly realised he had been worried that he would never see his mother again. She knew he had missed her sorely. He had had his fifth birthday in March and when they had asked him what he wanted he said the best birthday present he could have was to have his mommy home.

However, from the day Molly assured him their mother was getting better, Kevin had marked the days off on the calendar and today, Tuesday 23 April 1935, was circled in red. He had been fizzing all day, like a bottle of pop. Molly thought it a shame that her mother hadn't been allowed home before Easter but the hospital hadn't thought her well enough. Kevin had been disappointed at first and he had saved part of the chocolate egg their father had given them both the Sunday before to share with her. Molly thought that really good of him because, like Molly, he had given up sweets all through the forty days of Lent anyway. He must have sorely wanted all that chocolate.

Molly was glad it was still the holidays though because she had been able to help Hilda make a big spread to welcome her mother home. While her mother had been ill, Hilda had taught her to make all manner of things, and it

2

was nice to be able to practise, but she just wished now they would hurry up.

Kevin came in from the kitchen with a mug of milk Hilda had poured for him and wiped the milk moustache from his upper lip before saying, 'Why d'you think they are so late, Granddad?'

'I don't rightly know, lad,' Stan said, for he had thought they would have been here more than an hour ago. 'Maybe they had to see a doctor before your mom could leave and there was a wait, like. But don't you fret, they'll be here as soon as they can be, I'm sure.'

Hilda was just as anxious as the family to see her dear friend Nuala back fit and well again, but she also had duties at home. 'I'll come in again when I see them arrive,' she said, as she covered the food on the table with clean tea towels to keep it fresh, before putting on her coat. 'Now I'm off to get the old man's tea, but don't fret, I'll be back before you know it.'

Molly smiled at the neighbour that she had known all her life. Hilda had been a great help to her when her mother had first become sick and had tended the whole family along with her own. And Molly often thought it was a good job that she had. Her paternal grandmother, Phoebe, had died when Kevin was just a baby and Molly had missed her very much. There was really no one else, for her father had been an only child.

She had thought then that maybe her granddad would make his home with them, and so had her parents, but he insisted on staying in the little two-bedroomed terraced house in Gravelly Lane that he and his Phoebe had moved into the day they were married all those years ago. Molly's house was in Osbourne Road, which was no distance away at all, and her grandparents had been a major part of her young life.

This didn't change essentially after her grandmother died. Ted would still take his father for the odd pint a couple of evenings a week and to watch the Blues play at St Andrews of a Saturday, and every Sunday he came to dinner. However, he was an independent man, who would allow the family to do no more for him. He looked after himself: cooked, washed for himself, kept the house like a new pin and grew much of the family's produce in his garden.

Molly knew there was family on her mother's side, on a farm near a place called Buncrana in Donegal, Ireland. Her mother had pointed it out on a map, but they never heard from them and she often said that the Great War had fragmented the family.

'I'll tell you now, Molly there was nothing great about it at all,' Nuala had told her daughter. 'Dear God! "Terrible War" might have been a better name for it. Almost every country in the world was fighting and men went in their droves to join up. I've never understood why. Even my own youngest brother, Finn, marched off with the rest and then lost his life at the Battle of the Somme in 1916. But, even before Finn's death the people in Ireland were starting to feel a bit cheated, I suppose, because they had been promised Home Rule if Ireland was to support Britain in their fight against Germany.

'When there was no sign of it, and the Irish boys began to die in large numbers, or were ferried home blinded or with severed limbs, there was that uprising in Dublin the Easter of 1916. Anyway, I've told you all this many times before.'

'I know, but tell it again,' Molly would say each time. 'It's like a fairy story. It was after this Great War, this Terrible War, you came to England, to Birmingham?'

'Yes. Well, things in Ireland were anything but stable after the uprising. There were troublesome years ahead. It began after the war with factions looting and burning down people's houses and shooting anyone they didn't like the look of. The mistress got a bit jumpy about it and, to be honest, I didn't blame her one bit. Anyway, the upshot of this was they decided to go back to England. They owned another large house in a place called Sutton Coldfield and they offered me the chance to go with them.'

Molly knew all about Sutton Coldfield. On occasions, she had been taken to Sutton Coldfield's park on the little steam train from the station at nearby Station Road. The park was enormous and even had roads running through it. Rippling streams fed the five large lakes, and there was also woods and pastureland. Unless a person actually lived in Sutton Coldfield, they had to pay to get into the park.

'I was nineteen years old by then,' Nuala would say. 'And of course mad keen to see England, but I didn't think for one minute that my parents would have let me go. But for the troubles, I think that would have been the case. As it was, they said I would be better out of Ireland for a few years.'

'And there you met Daddy,' Molly would usually shout at this point.

'Not just like that I didn't,' Nuala would say. 'I hadn't gone to Birmingham to net myself a husband and anyway, there was little opportunity. My employers kept a weather eye on me and in a way were stricter than my parents. Followers, which was what they called boyfriends then, were discouraged. It was the summer of 1921 before I even saw your father as I went walking with the kitchen maid in Sutton Park one Sunday afternoon and he asked If he might walk along with us.'

'He was a hero, wasn't he?' Molly would ask every time.

Naula would always shake her head and say sadly, 'Believe me, Molly, all of those poor men who had fought in that war were heroes.'

But Molly knew her father, Ted, had got a special medal because he had crawled into no man's land to save his commanding officer, a man called Paul Simmons.

'I couldn't just stand by and do nothing,' he had told Molly. 'We had been chatting before we went over the top and the man told me he'd had two brothers and both had copped it and he was the last, the only remaining son so, for the sake of his parents, as much as anything else, he would like to make it back. All that came back to me as I saw him lying there in the slurry of mud and blood of no man's land and I went out to get him. We both came through it, and all he had to show for it was a gammy leg. Though now he walks with a limp, many live with far worse.'

The point was too that when the war was over, Paul Simmons did not forget the soldier who had saved his life. Before the war, Ted had been a gun maker, working alongside his father from the age of twelve. It was a fine living then, for they exported their guns all over the world. When war broke out, the orders increased, although by then Ted was in the army.

After the war, though, no one wanted guns in any quantity any more and Molly's father and grandfather were out of work, like thousands of others. Stan said he wouldn't be bothered chasing the few jobs there were. He was getting older and had savings – for during the war he had earned well and invested wisely, and Phoebe had always been a good manager. Added to that he had the vegetables growing in the garden and a small pension, so they got by.

Molly's father, though, had been in dire straits until he was sought out by Paul Simmons. His own father owned a brass factory, but he wanted to retire and hand it over to his son. Paul had no objection to this, but he first set out to find the man that had saved his life and see how he was placed. The result of that was Ted was taken into the office and very soon became the young factory owner's right-hand man.

Molly knew that her mother liked Mr Simmons. She also admired him for paying the debt back, as it were. 'Oh, I know your father saved his life and all,' she often said, 'but that was different. It was a war situation. Once the war is over, such actions are often forgotten. We could never have married at all if your father had been unemployed. I mean, I doubt that I would have been let, for he said that he wanted no hole-in-the-corner courtship. He went to see my employers and asked their permission for him to walk out with me.

'I think they found out everything there was to find out about him before they agreed. They were only concerned for me, I knew that, for they were good employers and didn't want me sinking into poverty. Believe me, it was easy enough to do at the time.'

Molly knew it was, because her father had explained it all to her when she had asked him about the disabled and blind men that she had seen in the Bull Ring, selling all manner of things from trays fastened around their necks.

'They, Molly, are like flotsam from the Great War,' Ted had told his daughter. 'We were told that we were returning to a "land fit for heroes" and we found out it was a myth and that all most had to come back to was unemployment and poverty.'

And it wasn't just the soldiers either, for Molly had seen the many ragged and barefoot mothers and children with pinched-in faces, and arms and legs like sticks, skulking around the market. 'If it weren't for a quirk of fate and the integrity of Paul Simmons, you and Kevin could easily be like one of those children,' her father had told her. Molly had shivered at the thought.

'I bet your employers were glad that Daddy had such a good job,' she had said to her mother.

Nuala nodded. 'Yes, they were. Your father was driving by then, because he said Mr Simmons found driving difficult with one leg shorter than the other.'

Molly knew her father loved driving, which he said he had learned to do in the army. Each morning he would cycle over to Mr Simmons' house, which was in Edgbaston, and drive him to the factory or any other place he wanted to go to in his car. The car her father drove was called a

Phantom, which he considered was just about the best car in the world, and made by a firm called Rolls-Royce.

Earlier that day, just after lunch, he had driven it into the street to show them because Mr Simmons had given him leave to fetch his wife home in it. A crowd had gathered on the pavement to see this phenomenon, cars being uncommon then. Kevin had been pop-eyed with excitement.

Ted had winked at him and said, 'Might give you a ride in it later, mate, if you play your cards right, like. Might give you all a ride if I decide that I like the look of you, for Mr Simmons has given me the rest of the day off.'

Molly shivered in excitement because she would just love that. Ted caught sight of that shiver, grinned at her and said, 'What d'you think of it, Moll? Ain't she just the business?'

Molly had to agree that it was indeed a fine car – not that she had ever seen much to compare it with, but she knew that this was really something special. It was long and low, with a large bonnet on the front and painted glossy black with burgundy doors, its large headlamps and even the radiator sparkling like silver in the spring sunshine. Even the tyres were different and painted white on the sides.

Molly noticed her father's face full of pride as he ran his hand over the body of the car, which he looked after with such meticulous care. 'You must be a clever man to know how to drive that,' Molly praised him.

'Ain't nothing to driving, Moll,' Ted said airily. 'It's just the other silly buggers on the road that you have to be careful of. And,' he'd added, waving an admonishing finger at her, though his eyes had sparkled with amusement, 'when your mother comes home, don't you be letting on that I said the word "bugger". God, she would be at my mouth with the carbolic.'

Molly and Kevin laughed at that mental picture and Stan said with an emphatic nod, 'Aye, she would that.'

Stan was immensely proud of his son, landing such a

good job and being in a position to provide properly for his family, but cars scared the life out of him. In his opinion they were dangerous and went far too fast.

'Thanks for the offer of a ride, son,' he said to Ted, 'but I won't be taking you up on it. I prefer to keep my feet firmly on the ground.'

'So, you are too windy to come for a spin later?'

'Aye,' Stan said calmly, 'though I would prefer to call it sensible. A tram ride is exciting enough for me.'

Ted shrugged. 'Well, no one's forcing you. But the children will appreciate it anyway. And now I must be away to fetch Nuala, for she is desperate to be home again.'

They had all watched until Ted had driven out of sight.

'He must be a kind man that Paul Simmons,' Molly said, going back into the house. 'Fancy Mom coming home in such style.'

'Aye, fancy,' Stan said with a grin, lighting up a cigarette. 'Your father always says he's generous to a fault.'

'But Daddy always thinks the best of people,' Molly said. 'And he is always so nice and kind himself. Isn't it strange, Granddad, that Mom's parents didn't want her to marry him?'

'Well, we must assume they didn't,' Stan said. 'They had never met him, of course, because from Nuala writing that first letter, saying they wanted to become engaged, she never heard a word from any of them again.'

'Mom said it was because she is a Catholic and Daddy a Protestant,' Molly said.

'That's what it must have been, right enough,' Stan said. 'But it was so silly because Ted isn't even a Protestant. I mean, he's a nothing. Thinks religion is all eyewash, as I do myself. When we came here from Fermanagh, neither Phoebe nor me ever went near either church or chapel again. I sent Ted to Sunday school while he was a lad, like, because if he was to choose later, then he had to know what the options were. When he was about fifteen

9

or sixteen, he said he didn't want to go any more and that was that. But he would have never stopped your mother practising her religion.

'She wrote week after week, after the first letter, and never got a reply,' Stan said. 'She was all for going over once to see them face to face, but she was nervous. As she said, if her parents wouldn't even write to her, they wouldn't be likely to give her much of a welcome and indeed might not let her in through the door at all. Anyway, in the end, she never went.'

'I don't blame her.'

'I don't either, and Ted said he would abide by her decision, but the silence has just gone on and the family in Donegal, might as well not exist.'

However, none of them in Birmingham was aware that when Nuala's parents had received the first letter she had sent, her father had died of a heart attack, the letter still clutched in his hand as he toppled from the chair to the stone-flagged floor. Her mother, Biddy, was almost consumed with bitterness against her daughter, whom she felt was responsible for her husband's death.

She elected to cut Nuala off from the family. Not only did she not write, she also forbade any one else to contact her either and so Nuala knew nothing of the death of her father, whom she had loved so much. Nor did she know that her brother, Joe, unable to stand the atmosphere in the house any more, had taken himself off to America. That only left Tom, the eldest, still on the farm.

'It's sad, though,' Molly said to her granddad. 'Do you think she still misses her parents – or her brothers, anyway?'

'I reckon she is used to it by now,' Stan said. 'Ted told me that in the beginning she used to talk about them a lot. As the years passed, she would say she often wondered if her brothers had married, and that it was sad for you to maybe have Irish cousins that you would never ever know.'

'Well, I'm glad Mom didn't let her parents stop her getting

married, anyway,' Molly had declared stoutly, 'for me and our Kevin have the nicest and kindest parents anyone could wish for.'

'Oh I don't think either of them ever regretted it,' Stan said. 'Like me and Phoebe were, they are happy and easy with each other. Your father has been like a lost soul without your mother and now soon she will be here again and everything will be back to normal.'

But the minutes ticked into hours and there was still no sign of the car. Stan sat in the chair and smoked one cigarette after the other, anxiety tugging at him.

He opened his packet of cigarettes again and was surprised to find it empty. 'Will you pop down to the paper shop and get me ten Park Drive, Moll?' he said. 'I must be smoking like a chimney. I'm clean out.'

Molly didn't want to stir from the house until her parents came through the door, but it wasn't as if the paper shop was miles away. It was only in Station Road, which Osbourne Road led into, and it would take her no time at all, if she ran. So she said, 'All right, Granddad' and took the half a crown, he offered her.

Molly had scarcely left the house when Stan saw a policeman striding up the path, and his stomach gave a lurch. Telling Kevin to stay where he was, he went to the door, his heart as heavy as lead.

The young and very nervous policeman licked his lips before saying, 'I am looking for a Mr Stanley Maguire.'

'You've found him,' Stan said, in a voice made husky with apprehension. Policemen didn't come to anyone's door to impart good news.

When the policeman said, 'Could I come inside, sir?' Stan said, 'I'd rather not have you in just now. I have my grandson in there and he is only five years old. Perhaps you'd better state your business here.'

The policeman wasn't used to imparting such news and certainly not on the doorstep, but he could quite see the man's point of view. He gave a slight shrug of his shoulders and said, 'I'm afraid, sir, there has been an accident involving a Mr Edward Maguire and a Mrs Nuala Maguire. Your name was among their effects. I believe they are your son and his wife?'

Stan nodded solemnly and let his breath out slowly, while the news seeped into his brain. Hadn't he feared something like this when they were much later than expected? 'How are they?' he asked.

'I'm afraid, sir, the accident was a fatal one.'

Stan couldn't take that in. 'Fatal?' he repeated. 'You mean they are dead?'

'Yes, sir.'

'Both of them?'

'I am afraid so. They died instantly, so I believe.'

'But how . . . ? I mean, what happened?'

'They were in collision with a van,' the policeman said. 'The doctors think the van driver had a heart attack and died at the wheel and the van then crashed into your son's car.'

'Dear Almighty Christ!' Stan cried. Tears started in his eyes and began to trickle down his wrinkled cheeks.

'Is there anyone I could call for you, sir?' the policeman said, worried for the man, who had turned a bad shade of grey.

'There is no one,' Stan said, realising at that moment how alone he was. There was no one left but him and the children and the burden of responsibility joined that of sorrow and lodged between his shoulder blades weighing him down. But he faced the policeman and said, 'It's all right, I will be fine. I shall have to be fine, for my son and his wife were the parents of the wee boy in the room there and I shall have to break the news to him and his sister.'

'If you are sure, sir?'

'I'm sure,' Stan said, but he wiped his face with a handkerchief before he went in to face his grandson, who looked up at him bewildered and a little frightened.

Kevin had wondered who was at the door and normally he would have gone out to see, for in fact few people knocked in that street, but as he neared the door, the serious tone of the conversation unnerved him, though he couldn't hear what was being said. So, instead of going out to them, he stole up the stairs and into his parents' bedroom where the window was a bay and, even with the overhang of the door, a person could usually see who was there. Kevin could see the policeman clearly.

In Kevin's short experience of life, policemen spelled trouble. Even when you had no idea you were doing anything wrong, they could usually find something to tick a boy off for. He didn't associate them with breaking bad news, so when his grandfather returned he was back in the room and he asked apprehensively, 'What did the copper want, Granddad?'

Stan looked at the child and he wished with all his heart and soul he could protect him from what he had to say, but he knew he couldn't. He sat down beside Kevin and put an arm around his shoulders as Molly burst in. She had spotted the policeman leaving their door as she had turned the corner and sped home as fast as she could.

Older and wiser than Kevin, she knew that the police did other things than box the ears of errant and cheeky boys. She cried, What is it? What's up?'

She saw that tears were spilling from her grandfather's eyes and her hands were clenched so tightly at her sides that she was crushing the cigarette packet she hadn't been aware that she was still holding. 'Please, please,' she begged, sinking to her knees before her grandfather. 'Please tell me what's wrong.'

Stan tried valiantly to stem the tears and he lifted Kevin onto his knee and snuggled Molly beside him, his arm encircling her as he broke the news as gently as a person could, that their parents had been killed in a car accident.

Both children looked at him in shock. Molly thought

13

there must be some mistake, it couldn't be true, of course it couldn't.

It was the howl of sheer unadulterated agony, which preceded the paroxysm of grief that Kevin displayed, that started her own tears as she cried out for such terrible loss. The pain of it seemed to be consuming her whole body.

And that is how Hilda found them, as she told her husband later. 'Sodden with sadness was the only way to describe it and no wonder. Almighty Christ, how will they survive this, the poor wee mites? I feel the grievous loss of one of the best friends I ever had, but Molly and little Kevin. God Almighty! Isn't life a bugger at times?'

Many thought the same, for Hilda had not been the only one to spot the policeman at the Maguire's door, especially amongst those neighbours on the look out for the car, ready to welcome Nuala home. Now those same neighbours gathered in the house, feeling helpless at the sight of such heartbreaking grief, but feeling they needed to be there. The party tea all set out seemed such a mockery now.

Most of the rest of that day was a blur for Molly. She remembered people trying to get her to eat something, but she wasn't hungry. She was filled with sorrow and anguish, but she drank the hot sweet tea that they pressed on her, because it was easier than arguing with them.

Other people came – first the priest, Father Clayton, his own eyes full of sorrow. But he could do nothing for them and when he offered to pray with Molly because it might ease her, she turned her face away. She had no desire to pray to a God that allowed her parents to be killed in such a way. When her mother had been very ill with pneumonia and it was feared that she might die, Molly prayed night and day. She knew of families that said the rosary each night for Nuala's recovery, there were Masses said, and Molly was not the only one who started a novena. When Nuala passed the crisis and they knew that she would survive, everyone was praising the power of prayer and saying how good God was. Hilda even said, 'He didn't want to take your mom, see. He knows she is needed far more here.'

And she was. But now it was as if God had been playing one awful and terrifying joke on them all, letting them think it was going to be all right, that her mother was better and was coming home and then . . . not content with taking just her mother away, He had taken her father too. He had had the last laugh, after all. She wanted to ask the priest why He had done that, but she couldn't seem to form the words. All her thoughts were jumbled up in her head and she was also suddenly unaccountably weary and Kevin was shaking from head to foot.

The next thing she remembered was the priest was gone and Dr Brown was there, though Molly had no idea who had sent for him. He gave Kevin an injection and almost immediately he curled on the settee and went to sleep. No one, not even her granddad, suggested that he be put to bed, and a neighbour went upstairs and took a blanket from one of the beds to put over him.

Molly refused the same injection that Kevin had and the doctor left her some tablets. She didn't want to take those either but her granddad prevailed upon her to try. 'They may help, Molly.'

Molly just stared at him, for she knew that nothing would help the despair that she was filled with. But afterwards, when the pain became unbearable, she did swallow two of the tablets hoping they would blur the edges of it a bit. Within minutes, she felt as if she were one side of a curtain and everyone else was on the other and she was totally disconnected from all that was happening.

She could see through the curtain, so often knew people were speaking to her, but her mind couldn't seem to make sense of what was said and she was utterly unable to make any sort of response. So when Paul Simmons called in to express his deepest condolences, that much she knew only by the look on his face. She didn't understand a word he was saying and that was her last memory of that dreadful, terrible day.

TWO

When Molly awoke next morning, she felt like she was fighting her way through fog. Her eyelids were heavy and her whole body felt sluggish. She wondered for a second or two what was the matter with her. Then suddenly, how she felt was of no account, as the memories of the tragic events of the previous day came flooding back. However, she had no recollection of even mounting the stairs, never mind getting undressed and into bed. Pushing back the bedclothes, she realised that she hadn't a nightdress on at all, just her slip.

She glanced at the clock and saw with surprise that it was past ten o'clock. As she heaved herself out of bed, she heard Kevin give a sudden, harrowing cry.

Stan had refused medication, feeling he owed it to the children to stay alert and in full charge of himself and his emotions, but that meant he had slept badly and in snatches, and it showed in his drawn face and rheumy bloodshot eyes. He was the only one awake in the house when the policeman had called earlier that morning to ask if he could go down to the hospital to formally identify the bodies, and that he would send a car.

No way did Stan want to look on the dead bodies of his son and Nuala, but he knew there was only him and so he nodded. But the children had not woken and he explained that both of them had been sedated the previous evening.

There was no way he would go out without telling them, and so it was arranged for the car to come at half-past eleven when he was sure the two would be up and about.

Before either of the children were astir however, a bevy of neighbours were in the door, including Hilda, asking Stan if they could help in any way. Hilda readily agreed to mind the children while Stan went to the hospital. When Kevin woke up, though, and Stan told him of the arrangements, he had been distraught and it had been his cry of distress that Molly had heard.

'I don't want to be left behind,' Kevin was crying to his granddad as Molly entered the room. 'What if you don't come back either?'

Molly quite understood Kevin's concerns and so did Stan. He knew the time was gone when he could have heartily reassured his grandson that of course he would come back. Instead, he said, 'You are right, Kevin. We will all go up to the hospital and I will just pop round and tell Hilda that.' And Molly saw Kevin give a sigh of relief.

With the children deposited in the waiting room, Stan followed the white-coated doctor down the long hospital corridor to the mortuary, his heart hammering in his chest. At the door, the doctor said, 'Before you see the bodies, I think you ought to know that with the impact of the crash, they were both thrown through the windscreen, so their faces were very badly injured. Your son was not too bad, but your daughter-in-law's injuries are extensive. We have done our best to clean them up, of course, but there is only so much you can do.'

Stan swallowed deeply and then nodded. 'I understand.'

'Are you ready?'

Are you ever ready for such a thing? Stan thought, but he said, 'Aye, yes.' He squared his shoulders and again tried to swallow the hard lump lodged in his throat. 'Let's get it over with.'

Ted's face was a mass of small cuts and black-grey bruises, and he had one massive jagged cut that seared the whole length of his forehead and another running diagonally from the corner of his right eye, across the bridge of his nose to the left-hand corner of the mouth. But all the blood had been wiped away and, though it was upsetting, Stan was able to nod at the doctor and say, 'Yes, that is my son.'

Poor Nuala was a different matter all together. When they removed the sheet covering her face, despite the fact that he had been warned, Stan staggered and it was the doctor's arm that steadied him. Her face was just a blooded mass of putrefying flesh and he felt the bile rising in him even as he nodded at the doctor.

He barely reached the yard outside before he was as sick as a dog, vomiting over and over into the drain until his stomach ached and his throat was raw. Then he straightened up and wiped his face with his handkerchief, knowing he had to return to the children and pretend everything was all right, or at least as all right as it could be in the circumstances.

However, the policeman assigned to sit with the children, took one look at Stan's haggard face and said, 'Sit down for a while. You look all in. I'll fetch a cup of tea.'

Stan was glad to obey and more than glad of the reviving cups of tea the young policeman brought for all of them. He couldn't remember when any of them had last eaten, for he had not touched the party food and he knew the children hadn't either.

Some of it was stored away in the cupboards at home – the women had seen to that. Anything that wouldn't keep, he insisted the neighbours take, rather than it be thrown away. Although he had been too overwhelmed to do anything himself, he had been pleased that all sign of the welcome home party was gone by the time he had got up that morning. The children had wanted no breakfast and

19

Stan, who hadn't been able to eat either, had not insisted, and so was gratified to see that at least they were drinking the tea.

It was as Stan was draining the cup that he remembered Nuala's parents and knew despite anything that had gone before they still needed to be told. Of course they both might be dead and gone now, and Nuala's brothers off to pastures new, but he had to find out. He hadn't any idea how to go about this so he mentioned it to the policeman.

'I know so little about them you see other than their name, which is Sullivan, Thomas John and Bridget Sullivan. They have a farm in a place called Buncrana in Donegal. I'm sorry there's not any more to go on, but there was a falling-out when their daughter, Nuala, married my son, basically because he was a Protestant and Nuala and her family were all Catholic.'

'In these country districts it will probably be more than enough,' the policeman said. 'And, as they are Catholic, if all else fails the parish priest will know who they are. We'll see to that and without delay, so you don't worry about it.'

Later that day, there was a smile on Biddy Sullivan's face as she shut the door on the young guard who had come to the door to tell her of the untimely death of her daughter and son-in-law. She thought Nuala had at last paid for her father's death. It had taken some time, but since the day she had held her dying husband in her arms, she had prayed for something bad to happen to her daughter.

Tom, was nervous of his mother's smile. It wasn't an expression he saw often and it usually boded ill for someone, so he asked tentatively, 'What did the garda want?'

'He came to tell me the thing I have wished for many a year,' Biddy said. 'Your sister, Nuala, and her husband have both been killed in a car crash in Birmingham.'

20

Tom felt a momentary pang of regret and sadness. The eldest boy, he had been twelve when Nuala was born, had left school and was already working in the fields with his father from dawn to dusk. He well remembered the tiny, wee child and how she had grown up so slight and fine-boned she was like a little doll. Biddy had never let the boys play with their little sister, but she hadn't needed to say that to him, he wouldn't have dreamed of playing with her, he knew his hands were too big and too rough.

And now she was gone, killed in a car crash, and his mother saying it was what she had wished for years. His mother was a strange one, all right, but what she had said this time was just downright wicked.

Tom seldom argued with his mother, but this time he burst out, 'Mammy, that's a dreadful thing to say.'

'She killed your daddy.'

'You can't be certain of that,' Tom protested. 'And even if it was her news that hastened Daddy's death, she didn't know. It wasn't her fault.'

'Well, I think differently and I am glad that she has got her just deserts at last,' Biddy said with an emphatic nod of her head. 'And if you have eaten your fill, shouldn't you be about your duties and not standing arguing the toss with me?'

Tom knew there was no use talking to his mother when she used that tone – he would be wasting time trying – so with a sigh he went back outside. And when a little later, he saw her scurrying away from the house, he didn't bother calling out to her and ask her where she was bound for because he knew she probably wouldn't tell him.

And she didn't tell him until he had finished the evening milking and was sitting at the table eating a bowl of porridge his mother had made for supper and then her words so astounded him his mouth dropped open. 'You are going to Birmingham tomorrow,' he repeated.

'That's right.'

'But have you even got the address?'

'Aye, the guard gave it to me. I suppose I can ask for directions when I am there. I sent a telegram for them to expect me anyway.'

'But, Mammy, what are you going for?'

'Why shouldn't I go?'

'Because you never did when Nuala was alive,' Tom said. 'Why go now when she is dead?'

'I'm not going for her, numbskull,' Biddy snapped, 'but to see the set-up of the place.'

'Set-up of the place?' Tom queried. 'What are you on about?'

'There are children, more than likely,' Biddy said. 'And if there are children they are going to no Protestant to rear. They will come here to me and be raised in the one true faith.'

'Here, Mammy?'

'Well, where else?'

'I know but . . . well you have never cared for children,' Tom said, adding bitterly, 'at least you told me that often enough when I was growing up.'

'I don't care for children much,' Biddy said. 'But I think I know where my duty lies.'

Tom remembered his life as a child and young boy in that house and the scant attention and even less affection he, his brothers and his elder sister, Aggie, had ever received from their mother. The only one petted and spoiled was Nuala. However, after the letter and his father's death, bitterness against Nuala seemed to lodge inside his mother, where it grew like a canker, getting deeper with every passing year. Tom had little hope that any children Nuala had would receive any love or understanding from his mother. He could only hope there was no issue from that union.

*   *   *

22

Stan looked at the telegram in his hand and could scarcely believe that, after all this time, Nuala's mother was coming here. Like Tom, he thought it a pity she hadn't ever made the journey when Nuala had been alive.

However, he told himself maybe she was sorry now for the stiff-necked, unforgiving way she had been with her daughter. She must be indeed to want to show her respect by turning up for the funeral, set for Friday. It would be good too for the children to realise that he wasn't the only living relative that they had. He loved them dearly but he had worried what would happen to them if he was taken ill.

Maybe this woman, their own grandmother, would be a comfort to them, especially to Molly. It was important, he thought, for a girl to have a woman's influence in her life.

'Any answer?' the telegraph boy asked.

'Oh, yes,' Stan said, for he would not have the woman arriving without any sort of welcome, so in his reply he said that both he and the children were looking forward to her coming and if she gave him the time of her arrival he would be at New Street Station to meet her.

Molly too was pleased because it would be a link with the mother she still missed so very, very much.

'D'you think she is sorry now about the quarrel?'

'Aye,' Stan said. 'I'd say so. Why else would she be coming?'

'Mmm, I suppose . . .'

'What are you fretting about now?'

'What will happen to me and our Kevin, Granddad?'

'Why, you'll stay with me of course.'

'We won't have to go to no orphanage?'

'Not a bit of it,' Stan told her. 'Why should you do that when you have a fit and active grandfather up the road willing and able to see to the two of you? And now you have other grandparents too and your uncles are probably living there as well don't forget. Your grandparents live in the country, on the farm your own mother grew up on.

23

Wouldn't that be a fine place for you to go for a wee holiday?'

'I suppose,' Molly said again.

'There is no suppose about it,' Stan said firmly. 'Now you get on your feet and give me a hand cleaning up the house. It would never do for your grandmother to find fault, and anyway that Mr Simmons said he would come to see me this evening.'

Stan was very impressed with Mr Simmons, even though he was slightly awed by such a fine gentleman bothering with the likes of them. He quite understood how it had been between him and Ted, though his son had said it didn't work with many of the toffs at the front. They might be quite pally while they were in the trenches together, but once out of uniform, all that was forgotten and they'd hardly bid the ordinary soldier the time of day.

Stan knew that full well. That's how it was with toffs, and he thought that with Ted dead, any debt Paul Simmons thought he had owed to him had been paid and well paid.

However, Paul didn't see it like that at all. He had been terribly upset when he had heard of the double tragedy, and to honour Ted's memory he felt he should at least show some care for his children. He knew that the family would now be in dire straits with only Stan's pension and possibly the pittance given by the government to live on, and he was arranging for an allowance to be paid to the family, rising annually until the children should be twenty-one. That is what he told Stan when he called.

Stan was bowled over by such generosity, but too worried about how they would manage to think of refusing it. Now he knew financially, at least, they would get by and thanked the man gratefully.

Stan knew he had to be strong and practical for the children. There was to be no more crying, at least in front of them. The terrible, dreadful thing that had happened to their parents had to be put behind them because they had their whole lives yet to live and he knew Ted and Nuala would want them to do that. However, even by now, their grief and Kevin's dependence on him almost overwhelmed him. He looked forward to Biddy Sullivan's arrival and hoped she might stay on for a little while after the funeral and help him with them.

When he saw the woman alight from the train and stand uncertainly on the platform the following evening, Stan knew he didn't like the look of her. She was dressed in black from the hat perched upon the grey hair to the old-fashioned button boots on her feet. Stan had expected that the woman would be in mourning, but what he didn't much care for was the expression on her face.

He castigated himself soundly. Here he was making judgements on this poor woman he had never met, who had travelled over land and sea to see her daughter finally laid to rest. What did he expect, that she would leap from the train with a whoop of joy?

He approached Biddy with his arm outstretched and a smile of welcome on his face. Biddy watched his approach with a cynical smile that twisted her lips into a grimace, but Stan didn't see that, though he did note that the woman was very tall and very skinny. Everything about her was thin, so that her sallow cheeks, either side of her long, narrow nose, were sunken in. But it was her eyes that shook him, for they were as cold as ice. He plainly saw the malicious intent there and his heart sank. He doubted there would be any help forthcoming from this quarter.

She ignored Stan's hand and instead, in the sharp, shrill voice that Stan fully expected her to have, snapped out, 'Are you Stanley Maguire?'

'I am,' Stan said, extending his hand to her again. 'And I am very pleased to meet you at last, though I would have preferred it to have been on a more pleasant occasion.'

Biddy looked at Stan's hand as if it might be a snake that

25

would leap up and bite her, and Stan let it fall to his side as she said, 'I have no pleasure in meeting you, Mr Maguire. Indirectly, you were the cause of all this. If you had exercised full control of your son, you would not have let him marry my daughter.'

Stan was irritated and annoyed by Biddy's inference, but still he excused the woman and bit back the sharp retort that had been on his lips. She was likely tired, he told himself, and suffering still from grief. Certainly the lines running either side of her nose and pulling her mouth down in a sag of disapproval spoke of strain of one kind or another. And, he told himself, when a death occurs of a loved one, especially a death so tragic and unexpected, it is surely natural to want to blame someone. Anyway, it would hardly help things to have a slanging match with Nuala's mother only minutes after her arrival.

And so instead of the counterattack Biddy might have expected, Stan said gently 'Come now, this is neither the time nor the place to discuss such matters. Let us get you home, and rested and a cup of tea and a meal inside you, and then I will answer any question you wish to ask.'

Stan's reply took the wind out of Biddy's sails a little bit, for she had braced herself for an argument. She had no option but to follow Stan, because he had picked up her case and begun walking away with it. In actual fact, though she never would have admitted it, she was glad that someone had come to meet her. She had never gone further than her home town before and she'd been flustered by the throngs of noisy fellow travellers, strangers all to her, and the boat with its throbbing engines and hooters blasting out black smoke into the air, tossing about in the turbulent water until she had been dreadfully sick. And there were also the panting trains, with their screeching whistles and the noise of the wheels clattering along the rails and now she was glad to alight from the train and just as anxious to leave the noisy smelly platform.

26

However, once outside the station, Biddy was totally unnerved by the volume of traffic, the like of which she had never seen before, especially the clanking, swaying trams, careering up and down the road alongside the buses and lorries, vans and cars. And there was a smell – dusty, acrid, full of smoke and very unpleasant – that seemed to have lodged at the back of her throat.

The pavements too were filled with hurrying, scurrying people. She had told her son that she would ask for directions, but she knew she couldn't have easily asked directions of these serious-faced people, who all looked as if they were in a rush to be some place.

No one took the slightest notice of her and Stanley Maguire either, but then this was a city, Biddy told herself, and strangers were not a novelty, not like back home where every strange face was noted and the person interrogated gently until the townsfolk had ascertained what he or she was doing there.

She was glad to get out of the mayhem and into the relative quiet of the taxi Stan had hailed, though she commented sourly as she climbed into it, 'A taxi. Huh, you must be made of money.'

Stan said nothing for he wouldn't be drawn into a sparring match. Hoping to engender some sympathy for the grieving children at least, he told Biddy all about Molly and wee Kevin, and how upset they had been; how they were looking forward to meeting her. But she made no response of any sort. By the time they reached their journey's end, Stan was exhausted and filled with trepidation and knew he would feel happier when Biddy was making the return trip.

'Now,' Biddy said to Stan that night with the meal over, Kevin in bed and Molly left drying the dishes in the kitchen, 'you're telling me that this house is not yours at all?'

'No,' Stan said. 'This was Ted and Nuala's place. I moved

in to help Ted care for the children when Nuala went into the hospital. After the funeral, I am going to look into the legal position of keeping this on, transferring the tenancy while the children are dependant. I think it would be the best thing because my house has only two bedrooms, you see, and this has three. Apart from that, all the children's friends are around the doors, and the neighbours have been kindness itself.'

'You don't need to trouble yourself with any of that,' Biddy snapped. 'And you definitely don't need any more room, because I am taking both children back to Ireland with me.'

Stan felt as if the breath had suddenly left his body and he slumped back in the chair. It was the very last thing that he had expected and the very last thing he wanted. The woman didn't seem even to like children and had reduced Kevin to tears more then once since they had met, because of both her sharp tongue and her total lack of understanding of what the child was still going through.

'You can't do this,' Stan said. 'I am their grandfather and have as many rights as you – more in fact, because I know the children, whereas they are strangers to you and that was through your own choice.'

'That is neither here nor there,' Biddy said. 'The children had a Catholic mother and therefore they need a Catholic upbringing.'

Stan felt his heart plummet because he knew the power of the Catholic Church. Ted had refused to turn before marrying Nuala, and Stan had been proud of him for not bowing to the quite considerable pressure from the priests, but Ted had had to agree to marry in Nuala's church and to bring any children up as Catholics. He had no bother with this, and supported Nuala in her faith, though he had very seldom darkened the door of the place himself.

'They have had a Catholic upbringing,' Stan protested desperately. 'They have never missed Mass on Sundays or the Holy Days, and they have been baptised into the Church and attend Catholic schools. Last year Molly was confirmed, and has made her First Communion. What more do you want?'

'She did that because Nuala was alive and Catholicism was drummed into my daughter from the day she was born,' Biddy said icily. 'What chance have they got to continue that, living here with you, a Protestant?'

'I'm not a Protestant,' Stan said. 'Religion makes no odds to me. I went to Sunday school until I began work and then never went to church again until I married Phoebe, and we brought Ted up the same way.'

Stan was unaware that he had made things worse for himself, cooked his own goose, as it were.

An outraged Biddy spat, 'It just gets worse and worse. You, Mr Maguire, are a heathen and I will not have my grandchildren growing up with a heathen. Whether you allow them to practise their religion or not isn't the issue. It is a matter of example. Why should they go to church when you do not? No, I'm sorry, I would be failing in my Catholic duty if I left the children with you. I will have a word with the priest after the funeral and see what he says about it.'

Stan felt the blood in his veins turn to ice. He knew he could indeed lose the children if the priest backed Biddy. And why wouldn't he? In his experience, Catholics stuck together over religious issues and the Church's power was immense.

Molly, drying dishes in the kitchen, had no idea of the turn the conversation was taking in the living room, but she was disappointed enough anyway. She had had such high hopes of her maternal grandmother and hoped she would help her cope without the love and support of her parents. However, when Molly first saw her grandmother come in with her granddad, she thought that Biddy looked grim rather than sad.

But, she remembered her mother saying she shouldn't judge people by the way they looked. She had also said that although her parents had been cross with her for marrying her father, before that they had loved her very much, too much perhaps. And so, when Molly met her grandmother, she told her quite truthfully that she was pleased to meet her at last.

Biddy just gave a grunt, which was hardly encouraging but Molly was sure she would feel better with food inside her and she was proud of the casserole dish she had produced with the help of Hilda. But Biddy seemed not to like it at all. She said the meat was tough and the vegetables stringy, the potatoes should have been on longer and the gravy was tasteless.

This was the tone of the conversation around the table, broken only by the way she was continually finding fault with Kevin. She ordered him to sit up straight, use his knife and fork properly, to eat his dinner, not just move it around his plate, wipe his mouth and definitely not to talk with his mouth full. Really, Kevin couldn't seem to do right for doing wrong and it wasn't just what her grandmother said, but the snappy way she said it. Molly wasn't surprised to see her little brother's eyes brimming with tears more than once and he had seemed quite relieved to be going to bed.

Molly too was relieved to be away from the woman for a while and had readily offered to wash and dry the dishes. But once in the kitchen, she tried to excuse her grandmother: she was likely tired because she had had a long journey. Molly finished drying the dishes and put the things away, made a pot of tea for the three of them and took it out on a tray.

She didn't notice the uncomfortable silence, nor the stricken look on her grandfather's face, for she decided she would try harder to get to know her grandmother and concentrate on the one link they had, the one thing she would like to know about.

30

As she handed her a cup of tea she said, 'Can you tell me, Grandmother, what my mother was like as a little girl?'

Biddy's lips pursed still further and she almost spat out, 'Aye, I'll tell you – not that you'll want to hear it, for your mother was a bold and disobedient girl. She showed scant regard for her parents, was only interested in pursuit of her own pleasures and even went against the teachings of the Church and married a man of another faith, or as I have found out today, a man of no faith at all.'

The words were said with such malice that Molly recoiled. It was the very last thing that she had expected the woman to say, and she suddenly knew that her grandmother wouldn't be one bit sorry she hadn't made it up with her daughter before she died. She somehow doubted she had ever felt sorry about anything in the whole of her life.

'Of course,' Biddy went on, 'we only have ourselves to blame for the way Nuala turned out for we both spoiled her. When she wrote that letter saying that she wanted to marry a non-Catholic, Thomas John was so shocked he dropped dead of a heart attack. So that is your fine mammy for you, the sort who kills her own father.'

Tears were now pouring from Molly's eyes and Stan put his arm around her. 'Here, here, the child doesn't need this sort of carry-on. Have some compassion, woman. If you spoke the truth and what Nuala wrote in the letter caused your husband to have a heart attack, then I am sorry, but you must see that it was the last thing in the world that Nuala would have wanted or expected to happen.'

'She knew he would be upset. She wasn't stupid.'

'She wasn't cruel either,' Molly burst out. 'She wouldn't mean that to happen.'

'Your opinion wasn't asked, miss,' Biddy snapped. 'Nor is it welcome, and I will thank you not to speak until you are spoken to. To spare the rod is to ruin the child totally and I see that that is what has happened to both you and that brother of yours. Well, there will be none of that with me, I'll tell you. I will put manners on the pair of you if it's the last thing I do.'

Molly stared at her. What influence could she have on either of them? After the funeral this horrible woman would go back to her own life on the little farm in Ireland and Molly would live with her granddad and gradually come to terms with her loss and help her little brother to cope too.

'What do you mean?' she said, almost challenging.

Biddy heard the tone and it annoyed her. She would soon have that temper knocked out of her, she thought. 'I'll tell you what I mean, my girl,' she spat out. 'When you come to live with me over in Ireland, you'll find life no bed of roses.'

'Come to live with you in Ireland?' Molly repeated, managing to hide the shiver of distaste that ran through her. 'I don't know you. I'm not going to live with you. I'm staying here with Granddad and so is Kevin.'

'No, that's where you are wrong. You are a Catholic because of your mother, who at least started you off on the right road, and you must be reared as a Catholic.'

'I don't care about being a Catholic,' Molly shouted at Biddy. 'And there is no way I am coming to live with you,' adding, probably unwisely, but too upset to care, 'I don't even like you very much.'

'Your likes and what you want will not come into this at all,' Biddy snapped. 'And there is no good turning on the waterworks,' she went on, as tears of helplessness squeezed from Molly's eyes. 'You will find they don't work with me.'

Molly turned anguished eyes to her grandfather. 'Granddad,' she cried. 'Say this isn't true. We're going to stay with you. You promised.'

Stan's eyes slid from Molly's to Biddy's gloating ones and then back to Molly, and because she deserved the truth he said, 'I may find my hands are tied in this.'

32

'Oh, Granddad, no,' Molly cried, and flung herself into Stan's arms.

As he held the weeping child, he glared at Biddy and knew when she took the children from him she would also take away his reason for living.

THREE

Stan was astounded at the numbers who attended the funeral of Ted and Nuala on 26 April. Paul Simmons had helped him make all the arrangements and had insisted on paying for everything. He had closed the factory as a mark of respect, but even so, Stan was amazed by those from the workforce who attended. Ted, Paul said, was very well thought of by everyone who met him, and many of the men who'd shaken Stan by the hand and commiserated with him on his loss said similar things. So also, it seemed, was Nuala liked and the pews were packed with neighbours and special friends of hers, mothers she met at the school gates, and those from the Mothers' Union she used to attend regularly. Many were in tears.

Added to this, all of Paul's family came too – his father and mother, and two sisters and their husbands, all of whom still remembered what they had owed to Ted. They seemed genuinely shocked by his death and that of his young wife. Not that it was spoken of openly and certainly not in front of the children, who had both insisted on attending.

Molly had remained dry-eyed, her distress and sense of loss too deep for tears, though she held on to Kevin's hand to take comfort from the child as well as to give it, as the tears dribbled down his cheeks ceaselessly.

As they stood at the graveside, they were warmed by the bright sun shining down from a sky of Wedgwood blue, and somehow this made the tragic deaths even more poignant. As the clods of earth fell with dull thuds on the coffins they seemed to reverberate in Molly's brain. Dead! Dead! Dead! Kevin's sobs became more audible and Biddy moved towards the child purposefully, but he pushed her away and turned instead to his grandfather. Stan held the little boy's shuddering body tight. He didn't urge him to stop crying either thinking he had a good enough reason to break his heart.

He envied him in a way because he would have liked the opportunity to go home now and lock the door and cry his eyes out. Instead, he knew he had to lead the mourners to the room at the back of the Lyndhurst pub which Paul Simmons had booked, and make small talk with the people who had come to pay their respects.

When he'd first been discussing the funeral arrangements with Mr Simmons, Stan, who had thought the mourners would only amount to a handful, said he intended to invite them back to the house. Mr Simmons had said he thought a room at a pub might be better and Stan, not up to arguing and certainly not with a toff, had agreed reluctantly.

He had thought though the few people he had anticipated coming would look silly and maybe feel out of place, but it wasn't that way at all. He looked at the crush of people around him in the room the pub had allocated them and was glad he had agreed. Kevin still held tight to his hand as Father Clayton, who had said the Requiem Mass, approached them.

Father Clayton liked Stan, with whom he was not above sparring and joking, as he had liked Ted, and thought them fine men. He couldn't understand for the life of him why they hadn't turned Catholic and embraced the one true faith.

That day though, Kevin's large brown eyes still swam with tears as he turned them on the priest and demanded, 'What did God want with my mammy and daddy?'

Father Clayton didn't have an answer that would satisfy the child. 'We don't understand the ways of God, Kevin.'

35

'Not even you?'

'Not even me.'

'Well, then,' Kevin said. 'What's the point of it all? That means that God can go round doing what He likes and you just say we can't understand and that.' He stamped his foot suddenly and cried in a high voice full of hurt and confusion, 'I want to know. I think we needed Mammy and Daddy much more than He did.'

'Kevin!' The name was said like a pistol shot.

Kevin jumped and his eyes were full of foreboding as he watched his grandmother approach. 'Now you see the level of my concern that I explained to you this morning when I called in to introduce myself and arrange an appointment?' Biddy complained to Father Clayton. 'The child has not even been taught how to address a priest correctly, and as for questioning the ways of our Good Lord, well, words fail me totally.'

Before the priest had time to reply, Stan burst in, 'I think Kevin has a perfect right to ask what manner of God it was at all who allowed his parents to be taken away, and who else to ask but the priest? So you just leave him alone.' He turned to Father Clayton and went on before Biddy could speak, 'We're taught that God loves us, aren't we? Well, He sure as hell didn't show much love to poor Nuala and Ted. That's how I feel and so I know exactly what young Kevin means.'

So did Father Clayton, and he was glad he had been the one assigned to take the Mass and not Father Monahon, for he would have torn the child to ribbons if he had been silly enough to say those things in front of him. As for Stan, a non-Catholic, Father Monahon would have a total lack of understanding for his pain. To Father Monahon, Catholicism and the pursuit of it was all that mattered. He was like the maternal grandmother, just recently arrived from Ireland, no doubt a devout and ardent Catholic, but not a woman he could take to at all. Father Clayton turned to her now as she burst out, 'D'you hear that, Father? Blasphemy, and before the child too. As if I could leave a child in a home where such views are felt and, even worse, expressed. The sooner I get them both to Ireland the better I'll like it.'

'Come now . . .' the priest began soothingly.

He got no further, for what the women had said had penetrated Kevin's brain. He had been shocked into silence when she had shouted at him, but now he said, 'What do you mean about going to Ireland?'

'Just what I say,' Biddy almost hissed. 'You and your sister are coming to live with me.'

'Oh no I'm not! I ain't,' Kevin cried desperately. 'I'm staying with my granddad, I am. Aren't I, Granddad?' He appealed as Stan stayed silent. 'Tell her, Granddad. Go on, tell her.'

'Ah, yes, tell me?' Biddy mocked.

'Have you no shame?' Stan demanded of her coldly. 'We have just buried the child's parents. You might be holier than I am, but there isn't a kind bone in your body.'

'But it ain't true, is it?' Kevin cried. At the grave expression on his granddad's face, he felt suddenly cold, afraid and lonely as he insisted, 'Say it ain't true, Granddad. Tell her.'

'May your God forgive you,' Stan said, picking Kevin up in his arms, 'for I will struggle to do so.'

Father Clayton watched Stan stride across the room and knew he was going to go somewhere quiet and explain to the child that his suffering was far from over yet. That now he had to go to some alien place with a woman he was so obviously scared of and live there until he was adult and could choose for himself. And tell him too there wasn't a damned thing either of them could do about it. The priest felt suddenly terribly dispirited and heavy, as if his body was filled with lead.

'They're both wilful, those children,' Biddy said fiercely. 'Too fond of getting their own way and totally disrespectful.'

'You don't think it's just that they are both still in shock and missing their parents, and maybe a little afraid of the future?' the priest put in mildly.

'I don't go along with all this psychological claptrap,' Biddy said. 'Their parents are dead and gone, and that's that, and it is obvious they will have to live with me. I am putting myself out too, you know? Do you think I want to start rearing children at my time of life?'

'Then why do it?' The words were out before the priest could stop them.

Biddy stared at him coldly. 'I would have thought you of all people would not have to ask that question,' she said, 'I know my duty and do not approve of my grandchildren being brought up with a heathen.'

'Stan Maguire is no heathen,' Father Clayton said quite heatedly because the woman was annoying him greatly.

'I don't see how you can say that so categorically when the man worships nowhere and neither did his son,' Biddy said. 'As far as I am concerned that makes him a heathen and I do not want my grandchildren brought up by one such as him. I am surprised that you are not similarly concerned. I think I need to talk to your superior about this and I fully intend to do that.'

Father Clayton knew that Father Monahon would see things exactly as she did, and when she complained about his attitude, as he knew she would, he would be hauled over the coals himself. That in itself wouldn't matter if anything had been achieved by his interference, but he knew it hadn't. He sighed. Sometimes he found it difficult to follow the Church's teaching in blind obedience as they were taught they had to, for he often found issues were not so black and white. He couldn't help wishing that, regardless of Stan's religion, or lack of it, the children could be left with the grandfather they loved.

Molly had watched the altercation and knew by her grandfather's determined strides across the room with Kevin in his arms that he was hopping mad about something and the same something was making her brother cry. She sighed as she followed them, for she didn't have to be a genius to guess what it was all about.

On the way in, Stan had noticed a couple of chairs set against the wall in the foyer and he sat down in one of these and set about telling Kevin what was going to happen to him and Molly, and why, despite his promise to them, he would be unable to fight against it.

That is where Molly found them and her heart constricted in pity for her distressed little brother, who was weak from weeping.

He turned anguished eyes towards her and said in a voice almost broken with sadness and disbelief, 'Molly . . . has our g-granddad told you wh-where we've got to go and – live?'

Molly nodded, and knealed down beside Kevin and held his agitated hand between hers. Her heart hammered in her chest, her mouth was very dry and she felt the familiar lump in her throat, and willed herself not to cry.

'But . . . don't want t-to live with her,' Kevin said. 'Sh-she's horrible. I want to . . . stay with G-Granddad.'

'So do I,' Molly said fiercely. 'I hate her as much as you do, but I am not afraid of her and you needn't worry, because I will look after you, fight for you if I have to.'

Kevin looked at the sister who had always looked out for him before and said, 'Promise?' He didn't know if he believed in the power of a promise any more. Hadn't his granddad promised? But it was all he had.

Molly said without any hesitation at all, 'I promise, Kevin. I swear it on the Bible.'

'Ah, Molly,' Kevin said, and he leaned towards her with a sigh and she put her arms around him. As Stan's arms encircled both children he felt a sharp pain in his chest. So, he thought, this is what it feels like when a person's heart is broken in two.

*　　*　　*

After the funeral was over, Biddy made her way to the presbytery and Father Monahon who had been expecting her.
He listened to her proposals to take the children to Ireland
and fully approved. In fact, he couldn't see any viable alternative. In his opinion the sooner the children were removed
from the clutches of their grandfather the better. Their
immortal souls were at stake.

'I'm gratified that you feel the same as I do,' Biddy said.
'At my time of life it is not easy to tie myself down with
the worry and burden of raising children again, but I know
where my duty lies. I must say, I was surprised that your
curate didn't share your view on this matter,' she went on
as Father Clayton entered the room.

Father Monahon's cold eyes slid over to the younger
priest as he asked testily, 'Is this true?'

'In a way,' Father Clayton admitted. 'Mrs Sullivan has
just said she would find it difficult raising the children.
Added to that, they seem so happy with Stan. They have
both just lost their parents and are naturally distraught over
it. I thought perhaps taking them away from everything that
was familiar . . .'

'You thought,' Father Monahon mimicked mockingly.
'That's your trouble, you think too much. As a priest, you
don't have to think, but you do have to obey the teachings
of the Church. It might be good for the children to get away
from memories and get some healthy living and country air
into their lungs, but that is neither here nor there. If they
are upset, that is the very time when they would need the
comfort and support of the one true church and a loving
grandmother to bring them up correctly.'

Father Clayton knew there wasn't a loving bone in Biddy
Sullivan's body and he knew too that wouldn't matter a jot
as far as Father Monahon was concerned. If she lashed the
children mercilessly, verbally, physically or both, she would
still be considered a fine woman in his superior's book, if
she saw to it that they attended Mass and the sacraments.

40

Father Monahon shook hands with Biddy and said, 'I would suggest that you see the authorities as quickly as possible and set all this in motion. Rest assured, you will have my full support.'

Father Clayton said not a word. There was nothing left to say.

That night, Kevin had a horrific nightmare. As he was sharing his granddad's bed so that a room could be given up to Biddy, Stan was quick to comfort and reassure, but long after his granddad had fallen asleep again, Kevin had lain wide-eyed, for though he ached with tiredness and his eyes smarted from lack of sleep, he was afraid of closing them.

Next morning, Kevin was listless his face was as white as a sheet, his eyes were red-rimmed. But Biddy didn't believe in children having a lie-in. There was no time to lay about on a farm and the sooner they got to grips with that the better. Biddy had a host of jobs she wanted Molly to do and she listed these at the breakfast table. As well as the shopping and cooking, Biddy wanted her to tackle the family wash and then clean the house from top to bottom.

Molly said nothing, though she looked across the table to her grandfather and saw him purse his lips. He hated the thought of his granddaughter working so hard all day. The child was no slouch anyway and had been tremendous with her mother so ill in hospital, taking on a lot of the house-work and cooking. Both he and his son had given the child a hand. And then, of course, there was always Hilda, who had showed what a true friend she was.

Biddy, however, had taken an instant dislike to Hilda and told her firmly that her help was no longer required, not that she intended to fill this gap herself. She did nothing but carp and complain and find fault with everything and everybody. Often Stan found it hard to believe that this objectionable woman was the mother of the lovely Nuala.

So though he wanted to complain about this, he knew

41

his authority, as far as the children were concerned, was of no account, and so he said nothing. He had an appointment with the landlord that morning to tell the man of his changed circumstances. As soon as the children left with Biddy he would be returning to his own little house.

Stan was in the bedroom getting ready when Kevin sidled in. 'Can I come with you, Granddad?' he asked. 'I'll be good. I'll wait in the corridor for you. Please don't leave me behind.'

Stan looked at the child's white and frightened face and wished he could take him, but he knew for his own sake he had to get used to Biddy and so he said, 'No, it's better if you stop here. I'll likely not be long.'

'Please, Granddad?'

The expression on Kevin's face tore at Stan's heart, but he knew he wouldn't be part of the child's world for much longer and so he bent to his level and said, 'Kevin, you know what I explained to you the day of the funeral? Maybe you should try to get to know Biddy. I know the woman is not easy, but it would likely help you if you could get along together.'

'I don't like her, Granddad and I'm scared of her too.'

'I know that, Kevin,' Stan said sadly. 'All I'm saying is perhaps you need to try a little harder and maybe she will be better if I am not around.'

Stan didn't believe that for a minute and neither did Kevin, but there was no help for it. Once his grandfather had left, Kevin wanted to hide away in the bedroom, but Biddy found him there, hauled him out and set him to cleaning the family's shoes.

For some time the only sound in the house was Biddy's nagging voice. Kevin envied Molly escaping it when she went out with a list to do the shopping.

Molly was finding the day long and arduous, and not the work alone, but coping with all the complaints, however hard she tried.

By the time she carried the shopping back she was feeling weary, for she had already stripped the sheets off the beds, remade them and left the soiled linen in the boiler while she washed, rinsed, mangled and hung out the rest of the washing. Then she was sent out to do the shopping and knew after that she would have to tackle all the sheets and clean the house, for Biddy did nothing.

Biddy noticed how jaded Molly looked as she hauled the heavy bags into the house and was pleased. She would soon show the child who was the boss in this house.

'This is a rest cure compared with what you will be doing when I get you to my place,' Biddy told her. 'There, as well as housework, you will be expected to help on the farm. Your mother was never expected to do any of this and look where that got me. The Devil makes work for idle hands, people say, so you will not be allowed to be idle at any time, let me tell you. I have learned the error of my ways and you will not go the way of your mother.'

Molly was incensed by the disparaging way that Biddy spoke of the mother she had loved with a passion. She faced her grandmother and said, 'I would be pleased and proud to be like my mother. Don't you dare say bad things about her! She was a lovely person and much nicer and kinder than you.'

The slap across Molly's cheek was so hefty she was nearly lifted from her feet. She made no sound, though her hand flew to her cheek where she knew a large bruise would shortly form, and running her tongue around her mouth she knew her bottom lip was split. Yet she refused to show fear and she looked at her grandmother in defiance with her head held high.

'By God, girl when I get you home I will knock that spirit out of you,' Biddy almost snarled. 'I have a bamboo cane that I used to chastise the boys and you will feel the sting of it a time or two, I'm thinking.'

Molly saw Kevin looking at her, his eyes alive with panic and his fear so great his teeth began to chatter. She knew that for his sake, as well as her own, she had to stand up

43

to this woman and so, though her insides crawled with apprehension, she cried, 'I don't care a jot for you or your stupid cane. We will get along well enough if you stop saying bad things about my mother for there aren't any bad things that you can say. She was wonderful and so was my father, and you can bully me all you like, but you will never be able to make me say anything different.'

'I'll put manners on you, miss, if it is the last thing I do.'

'There is nothing wrong with my manners,' Molly contradicted. 'It is you who is being rude, not me.'

Biddy, furious at being spoken to in such a way, and because Molly was displaying no fear of her, administered a punch of such ferocity that it caused Molly to sink to her knees. She couldn't prevent a cry escaping from her nor the tears spurting from her eyes. Her whole face throbbed and she knew that her nose was pouring blood. She had the acrid taste of it in her mouth.

Kevin had given a scream at the punch and thrown himself against Molly. He remembered her saying she would protect him against his grandmother and realised suddenly the woman was stronger than both of them and the only weapon they had was to stick together. And so, despite his intense fear, he glared up at Biddy and yelled, 'Leave her alone you. Molly is right. You are nothing but a big bully.'

Biddy's face was red and contorted with temper as she said with disdain. 'And you are an insolent young pup who will get some of the same before he is much older.'

Molly put her arms around Kevin and said, 'Don't you dare lay a finger on him.'

'And who is to stop me?' Biddy asked. 'You?'

'I'm telling my granddad about you,' Kevin cried.

'Go ahead,' Biddy said. 'But remember that there will be no granddad in Ireland.'

And of course that was true. They would have no one to fight their battles for them there and both children were well aware of it.

44

So when Biddy said, 'And now, if that little tantrum is over I suggest you get that shopping put away and cook some lunch, for my stomach thinks my throat is cut,' Molly got to her feet, stanching the flow of blood from her nose with a handkerchief, because there was nothing else she could do.

They had scrambled eggs on toast because it was what Biddy wanted and Kevin looked at it with distaste. He had never liked his eggs scrambled and when he began to move them around his plate with his fork, Biddy snapped, 'Eat it!'

Kevin was filled with trepidation as he mumbled that he didn't like scrambled eggs.

'Don't mumble like that. Speak up!'

Kevin shot a look at his sister and she spoke for him, her voice sounding strange with her thick lips, 'Kevin isn't that keen on scrambled eggs.'

'What is this, "not keen" about?' Biddy snapped. 'From what I have seen since I have been here, he is not keen on a lot of things, for he eats nothing. I'll not stand such nonsense,' she said, glaring at Kevin. 'It's good food. Eat it, or I will make you eat it.'

Kevin looked at his plate and just the look of the eggs made him feel sick. 'I can't.'

'Oh, yes you can,' Biddy said, leaping from her chair. She pinned Kevin's arms down, holding his nose at one and the same time while she pushed a huge forkful of scrambled eggs into his mouth when he opened it to breathe.

Kevin kicked and struggled and cried, and Molly was pulling at her grandmother and shouting at her to leave Kevin alone, but it made no difference and Kevin was forced to swallow the egg. The minute he did, this was followed by another forkful and then another.

Suddenly, Kevin felt the nausea rising in his throat but he couldn't speak for another forkful of egg was in his mouth and he tried manfully to swallow. However, he couldn't, and he began to cough and choke and splutter, and then suddenly vomited with ferocity over the table, the floor and his grandmother.

'You bold wee boy,' she shrieked and, scooping him up from his chair, she laid him across her knee.

Stan came in then and took in the scene at a glance. The hateful woman paddling Kevin's bottom with her large hands and Molly trying to prevent her. It didn't need a genius to work out what had happened to Molly's face either. Stan felt unaccustomed rage build inside him as he yanked Kevin out of Biddy's grasp.

'You have no right!' she said angrily. 'The children are my responsibility and I was chastising the child.'

'Like you chastised Molly?' Stan said with scorn. 'Look at the state of that poor girl's face. Come here, Mol.'

Molly crossed to her granddad's side and he put his arm around her shoulder. Glaring at Biddy he said, 'There is to be no more of this chastising as you call it. Personally, I call it beating a child and that will not happen while they are under my roof. The children have already suffered enough and you are not to lay one hand on them.'

But Kevin, his arms around his grandfather's neck, still shaking and giving gulping little sobs, knew that it would only be a brief respite and his bleak eyes met Molly's and he knew that she was well aware of this too.

The next day, Kevin stuck like glue to his grandfather and the old man knowing of his fear never left him alone with Biddy and they kept out of the house as much as possible. He could do nothing about Molly for again she was kept hard at it. She told him she didn't want to go out anyway because she would be embarrassed with her face the way it was. The marks of Biddy's handiwork were clearly visible, though the woman seemed not a bit ashamed of what she had done. Molly, however, wanted as few people to catch sight of her as possible and so she had risen early and gone to the half-past seven

Mass. It was never well attended, that Sunday was no exception, and she had kept her head bowed throughout most of the service. She fervently hoped that the marks would be gone by the morning because she wanted to return to school. She badly needed to get away from her grandmother.

Despite his grandfather never leaving him alone with Biddy on Sunday, Kevin was in an almost permanent state of anxiety. He had another horrific nightmare that night that raised the house. The next morning, Stan looked at his grandson's thin and wan face and rheumy eyes, 'Kevin, you stay home from school today. You look far from well and I would like the doctor to take a look at you.'

'Kevin cannot stay at home today,' Biddy said. 'You forget that I am in charge now of the children and I will not tolerate laggards. There is nothing wrong with the child at all. He is seeking attention that is all, because you have utterly ruined him. As for the screaming and all last night, that was probably the reaction to something he ate.' Molly knew that wasn't it, because Kevin was eating practically nothing. In fact, she realised with a jolt, it had been some time since he had eaten anything properly. He had had no breakfast that morning either. She decided to tackle him about eating more when they were on their way to school and away from their grandmother hearing any of it.

FOUR

'How d'you feel, Kev?' Molly said as they made their way to school later that morning. 'Granddad's right, you know. You don't look at all well.'

'I'm all right,' Kevin said. 'And I would be better if that horrible old woman would go back to Ireland. But she won't and so I would rather go to school than stay at home. Anyroad, I like school.'

Molly knew he did. He was in the baby class, the Reception and had loved every minute of it since the day he had started. 'You might feel better too if you ate something,' she said. 'You must try. Not because of what that old bat will say and do, but because you will be ill if you don't.'

'I can't eat, Molly,' Kevin said. 'I do try, honest. It's just like I feel sort of full all the time.'

Molly knew what her young brother was full of: misery and despair. She suffered these emotions herself. In fact sometimes, the enormity of the tragedy, and the uncertain and fear-filled future dangled before her, were almost overwhelming. She took Kevin's hand, gave it a squeeze and said, 'I know how you feel, Kev, honest I do, but you've got to eat or you will be really sick. Do your best, eh, for my sake?'

Kevin nodded. 'I will, Molly,' he said firmly. 'I'll try really hard.'

* * *

48

Not long after the children had left for school Biddy donned her coat and went out. Stan didn't ask where because he didn't care and, despite his concerns about Kevin's health, in one way, he was glad he was at school and away from his grandmother.

Biddy was making for the Social Services for she wanted to get the plans for taking the children away to go as speedily as possible. The authorities were delighted that there was a grandmother willing to take on the care of the orphaned Maguire children.

However, it couldn't be done as speedily as Biddy would have liked as, even with the backing of the Church, there were certain formalities to attend to and the first thing was that the children would have to be seen by a social worker. Biddy was annoyed at the delay, but there was nothing to be done about it and she sent a telegram to Tom, telling him that the business was taking longer than she thought.

At least, she thought, as she made her way home, it will give me time to lick those children into shape and put some manners on them before I take them back to Ireland.

The next day, Kevin collapsed in the playground at play-time. A doctor was summoned and he arranged to have him admitted to the General Hospital.

'But why?' Stan asked the secretary who had come with the message.

She knew nothing further, though. 'That's all I was told, that he was being sent to the hospital.'

'I suppose no one has thought to inform his sister in the Seniors?'

'I should hardly think so, but that can be rectified if you think . . .'

'No,' Stan said. 'Leave it as it is until I find out what is wrong with the child.'

'I will come with you of course,' Biddy said as Stan closed the door.

'You'll go nowhere with me,' Stan thundered. 'You are probably at the root of any problems Kevin has.'

'You have no right. The welfare of the children is now my concern.'

'Not yet it isn't,' Stan snapped. 'And until it is official, I will decide what is best for them, and that, woman, is that.'

He swung his jacket from the hook behind the door as he spoke, jammed his cap determinedly on his head and was through the door and away before Biddy had time to draw breath.

She could have followed him, demand she go too. After all Stan had no right to stop her walking down the street, but she wasn't ready to go out yet. She hadn't even changed from her slippers and she decided to let the old fool go to the hospital on his own and find out that the child was just playing up, swinging the lead no doubt, to get more attention. By God when she got him to Ireland, he would soon find out what sort of attention he would get if he tried that caper.

The doctor summoned to talk to Stan a little later didn't think it was any sort of caper at all. Scrawny, undersized children were a common enough sight in most cities in those days, but Kevin wasn't just skinny, he was gaunt.

By the time Stan reached the hospital, the boy had regained consciousness and the doctor looked coldly at the old man coming to enquire about him. Most of the malnourished children he had treated had equally malnourished parents, but he noted that though the man before him was not fat, he looked robust and pretty healthy, and so he said quite scathingly, 'This child is just skin and bone, and this state of affairs has been going on for some time. You must have been aware of it.'

Stan nodded miserably. 'Yes, I know,' he said. 'Kevin hasn't eaten properly for days and to treat him properly, you need to know it all.' He told the doctor of the tragedy

50

that had befallen Kevin and his sister, and the arrival of Biddy, which had made Kevin worse.

The doctor nodded. He had known from the beginning that it wasn't malnutrition alone that dogged Kevin, but something deeper. 'That explains a great deal,' he told Stan.

'Biddy intends to take the two children back to Ireland with her when all the formalities are completed,' Stan said. 'And the thought of that, and without me around to protect him from the woman's viciousness, is terrifying Kevin.'

'Can you not fight this?' the doctor asked. 'As his grandfather you have rights too, surely?'

Stan shook his head. 'Normally, I would fight tooth and nail, because I don't mind telling you that when those children go, it will tear the heart from me, but I have come up against the brick wall of the Church.'

And then, at the doctor's quizzical look, he went on, 'Nuala, my daughter-in-law was a Catholic and my son wasn't, but both children were being brought up as Catholics. Now, with Nuala gone, their Irish grandmother is afraid they will backslide – or that is what she claims, anyway. And she has got the full support of the parish priest for her to take on the care of the children she seems to care not a fig about.'

The doctor knew all about the power of religion, and the Catholic Church in particular, but still he said, 'I am less concerned by your grandson's immortal soul and more about his physical and mental well-being, and for the moment at any rate I want him in hospital. And even after this,' he assured Stan, 'I would block any moves to try to remove the child from your care, if I thought it was detrimental to him.'

'I appreciate that, Doctor,' Stan said.

'And now I suppose you would like to see the child,' the doctor said. 'He has come round, but still seems a little bewildered. Maybe you can reassure him that we mean him no harm.'

'I'll do that, and welcome.'

51

Kevin was delighted to see the familiar face of his grandfather, and not at all worried when he told him he was in hospital. He was relieved, and more so when his grandfather told him he had to stay there for a little while and only one thing worried him.

'You won't let my grandmother come and visit me will you?' he pleaded.

'Well, now, Kevin, I don't know if I can rightly do that,' Stan said awkwardly. 'I mean, she is flesh and blood, after all.'

Kevin was so crestfallen at the news that even in the hospital he wouldn't be safe from his grandmother that Stan mentioned his request to the doctor before he left and was surprised by his response. 'If you are right, and this woman's arrival from Ireland has worsened Kevin's condition, then her visiting him could undermine any treatment that he might be undergoing. And, as the care of the patient is paramount here, if this woman visits the hospital she will be blocked from the wards.'

'You don't know how much better that makes me feel,' Stan said.

The doctor smiled at him. 'Your face gives you away,' he said. 'Don't fret. Your grandson is safe here.'

As the doctor watched Stan walk away, he felt a wave of sympathy wash over him. Sickness, tragedy, even death were part and parcel of his job and yet he felt that the little boy now in his care had suffered so grievously already he vowed to do all in his power not only to restore him to full health and strength, but also under the guardianship of his grandfather.

Stan couldn't quite keep the hint of satisfaction out of his voice as he told Biddy that she wouldn't be allowed to visit her grandson. She didn't believe it, said she had never heard anything so ridiculous in her life and set off for the hospital immediately to challenge this ruling. However she found herself face to face with Matron, a formidable woman, who had had her orders from the doctor and was carrying them out to the letter.

Biddy was outraged and went home via the presbytery where she complained bitterly to Father Monahon. He had known nothing about the collapse of Kevin, but assured Biddy there must be some misunderstanding and that he would go himself to the hospital to find out what was what.

The hospital staff had been given no instructions about the priest and so he was allowed to see Kevin. Even he was shocked to see how thin and wan the child looked. His eyes seemed huge in the gaunt, pinched face and they grew ever bigger and wider as he looked at the priest he had always been a little nervous of.

'Well now, Kevin,' the priest said heartily. 'What's all this?'

'Dunno, Father.'

'Collapsing at school I was told.'

'Yes, Father.'

'Did you feel unwell?'

Kevin could have said he had never felt right since the day he had learned that his parents had died, but he didn't know how to put that into words and he was too weary to try, so he shrugged and said, 'Not specially.'

'Had everyone worried, you know,' the priest said, as if it had been Kevin's own fault.

He didn't know what to say to that other than, 'Yes, Father.'

'Your grandmother in particular is very worried.'

He saw the shudder pass through Kevin's body and it irritated him. He went on, 'She came along to see you and they wouldn't let her in – some notion or other that it might disturb you. Well, I am going to see about that this minute, for I have never heard such nonsense.'

Kevin's eyes grew wider than ever. 'No! No!' he yelled.

'Kevin, don't be so silly,' the priest snapped. 'And really, this is not a matter for you to decide. You are just a small

53

boy and not equipped to make judgements. That is for your elders and betters, and whatever strange aversion you have to your grandmother, you will have to overcome it, for I'm sure when I speak with the doctor he will see how ridiculous the whole thing is.'

Kevin was sure he would too. Few adults seemed to care about the things that bothered children. There was a sudden roaring in his head at the dread of seeing his grandmother in the room, and he opened his mouth and began to scream.

The priest leaped up from the side of the bed crying, 'Stop this, Kevin! Stop this nonsense!'

The next minute he was almost knocked on his back as the doctor pushed past him, and when he saw the child in the grip of terror, he knew that whatever the priest had said or done had brought this on, and so while he prepared a syringe for the child, he said through gritted teeth, to the nurses that had followed him into the room, 'Get him out of here.'

'I assure you, I did or said nothing,' the priest said as he was led away. 'One minute I was talking to the child and the next he was yelling his head off.'

He was yelling no longer, for the sedative had done its work and Kevin had lapsed again into a drug-induced stupor. The doctor knew that from that point on, the priest would be another on the banned list of visitors.

Almost a week after Kevin's admittance to hospital, Molly was given the day off from school because it was the Silver Jubilee of King George V. She visited Kevin in the hospital, which was festooned in red, white and blue, and in festival mode.

'They say we're having a party and that,' Kevin told his sister. 'And a concert.'

'You going?'

'Nah. Don't think so,' Kevin said. 'I don't feel like it.'

Molly understood, for there had been things planned in

Erdington too. She had met Hilda on the road a few days earlier and she had advised her to go and enjoy herself. 'Your mom and dad wouldn't want you like this,' she'd said assuredly. 'You mustn't feel bad about having a bit of fun now and then.'

'I know that, Hilda,' Molly had answered. 'And maybe in time I will be able to do this, but just now I am too full of sadness to think of anything else. I really am poor company for anyone these days and I am best on my own learning to cope with everything. Anyway, if I had been breaking my neck to go, do you think for one moment my grandmother would let me? She has a poor view on anything that might spell enjoyment for me. God, I have to fight tooth and nail to visit Kevin.'

'What does your grandfather say of all this carry-on?'

'Very little,' Molly said. 'There's no point because it would do no good and anyway, if he does say anything she is worse to me afterwards.'

'I feel that sorry for you, bab.'

'Hilda, I feel sorry for myself and that doesn't help either,' Molly said candidly. 'And I am afraid that the Jubilee celebrations will have to go on without me.'

One Thursday afternoon over a week later, Molly returned home from school to find a social worker in the house, filling in forms with her grandmother. The visitor looked up and smiled as Molly entered the room.

'Aren't you the lucky girl then, going to live far from this dusty city?' she said.

Molly didn't feel the slightest bit lucky and she had to know whether there was any sort of viable alternative, even if Biddy punished her afterwards. Just lately she had begun to think an orphanage in Birmingham would be preferable to going anywhere with her horrid grandmother. At least then she might be able to see her granddad and Kevin sometimes.

'But, you see, I like Birmingham,' she said, 'Couldn't I stay in an orphanage here?'

The social worker laughed a little before saying, 'Well, you are a funny one and no mistake. Most children wouldn't choose an orphanage if they had any choice in the matter, but you wouldn't be offered a place anyway.'

'Why not?'

'Because our orphanages are already bursting at the seams,' the social worker said. 'They are for children who have no one. They have either been abandoned by their parents or the parents are dead and there is no one else to care for them, while you on the other hand—'

'Have a home waiting for you,' Biddy said, cutting in. She continued with a malevolent sneer, 'Get used to it, Molly. I'm stuck with you and your brother and you are stuck with me.'

Molly knew she was right and at first she told herself that she was the lucky one, because in a year she could be working and then she could save and get away from the woman, come back to Birmingham if she liked. But then, how could she leave Kevin totally unprotected? She knew that she could not do that. When they escaped her clutches they had to do it together. She sighed as she realised she was looking at years and years of putting up with verbal and physical abuse, scorn and ridicule.

However, when her grandfather came home from a meeting he had had with Kevin's doctor at the hospital, he had more news, which he told them over tea that evening. It had been decided that when Kevin was well enough to leave the hospital, he would be delivered into his grandfather's care and left there. The medical staff had said, in their opinion he needed people he knew and loved around him, and taking him from the familiar would be detrimental to his health. Not even the Catholic Church had the power to overturn that ruling and Stan was hard-pressed not to show his blessed relief at the decision, though he felt heartsore that nothing similar could be done to save Molly from Biddy's clutches.

At first Molly did feel slightly resentful and was saddened that she would be leaving her little brother behind, but then she decided it was better for both of them. She knew he would be all right with their grandfather. Meanwhile she only had to look out for herself and she was of the opinion that that would take all her time and energy.

Biddy had a momentary pang too that she wouldn't have the boy to bully, but then she told herself she had never liked boys much anyway. She did have Molly, who was the image of her bold and wilful mother, and she would make the child pay and dearly for her mother's transgressions until she wished she had never been born.

Molly and her grandmother were due to leave on 21 May and the time left in Birmingham passed in a blur to Molly, especially as Biddy kept her hard at it. Each morning she had to get up first. Biddy gave her an alarm clock to ensure she did this. Her first job of the day was to clean the grate and lay and light the fire. That had always been her father's job, even long before her mom took sick, and when he had lit the fire he would bank it with slack for safety. Then, when her mother got up, she would poke it well and put some nuggets of coal on it before calling Kevin and Molly, and so the room was always warm for them in the morning.

Molly decided very early on that she would rather clean the whole kitchen than the grate. It took skill to lay a fire that drew properly and lit first time. Biddy boxed her ears on a couple of occasions when the damned thing had gone out on her. The point was she couldn't watch it because she had to make the porridge for breakfast, which she could never linger over because she had to make the beds and wash up the breakfast things before she left for school.

After school, she would be presented with a shopping list and when she had hauled the stuff home, she had to cook the evening meal. How she missed Hilda at those times, for her lively encouragement, ready sense of humour and the way she could make Molly smile, even when she had been worried about her mother. Molly often wondered bleakly if she would ever smile again.

And when the meal that Biddy carped about and criticised had been eaten, Molly would clear away and wash up, and then Biddy would produce a basket of mending. She taught Molly to darn, sew on buttons and turn up hems, and there was always plenty for her to practise on in the long evenings.

Any homework Molly did secretly in the bedroom by the light of a candle. It meant she was almost constantly tired, but she didn't bother saying anything, knowing there would be little point.

Saturday was particularly tiring, for as well as a big shop, there were the beds to change and the washing to do. When the wet and heavy clothes were hauled from boiler to sink, and her fingers rubbed raw on the wash board, it all had to be put through the mangle and hung out on the line.

Molly hated the wet and miserable days when it had to be hung inside, for she knew it would take ages to dry and, as Biddy would not let her iron on a Sunday, there would pile of ironing waiting for her on Monday after school. On good days she would start this chore after she had given the house a good clean. Clothes for Mass, for Biddy and herself, had to be ironed and left on the picture rail to air if they were still not completely dry, and then the shoes had all to be cleaned. Molly would often be nearly sobbing with weariness by the time that she was able to seek her bed.

That last Saturday Biddy went into the station to see about the tickets and, despite the mountains of things Molly had to do, she said to her grandfather, 'I'm popping next door. I can't leave without bidding Hilda goodbye.'

'You do right,' Stan said. 'The woman is worried about

58

you. She stopped me in the street the other day and was asking about you. She would value a visit.'

Hilda was delighted to see Molly, though she saw the black bags beneath her tired, sad eyes in her bleached face, and her heart turned over. She made a cup of tea and produced a tin of biscuits, and Molly felt the saliva form in her mouth, for she was nearly always hungry.

Hilda saw her expression and she said, 'Tuck in, girl. You look as if you need feeding up. I know one thing: your mother would hate seeing you this way.'

'You have known Mom always, haven't you, Hilda?' Molly said.

Hilda nodded. 'From the day she and Ted moved in after the wedding.'

'Didn't they have a honeymoon?'

Hilda shook her head. 'Few people did then. Your father did have a few days off and used the time to do up the house a bit and get the garden tidied up, and Nuala and I were the very best of friends from that first day. I promised your mother that I would look after you if anything happened to her. She asked me just before she was taken to hospital.' Hilda went on, adding sadly, 'I feel right bad that I have been unable to keep that promise.'

'Don't worry about it, Auntie Hilda,' Molly said. 'There is no help for it, I know that now. At least Kevin is all right and I will survive it. It is only a year until I leave school and then once I have a wage, I will save, however long it takes, and come back here just as soon as I can.'

'You do that, ducks, and you knock on my door any time 'cos you will be welcome.'

'I know that, Hilda,' Molly said. 'Will you sort of keep an eye on Kevin? Granddad too, of course?'

'You don't really need to ask that,' Hilda said. 'A poor sort of neighbour and friend I would be if I just washed my hands of them now. Your mother and father were the best neighbours to have in the world, and your mother the kindest, sweetest person, and there isn't a day goes by when I don't miss her. Anything I can do for any of you, I would do gladly in her memory.'

There were tears in Molly's eyes as she said, 'I know how much you thought of Mom, in particular. I spotted you at the funeral, at the church, but when I looked for you afterwards, I couldn't see you.'

'No, I slipped back home,' Hilda said. 'I went to the church to say my goodbyes, but afterwards, I wasn't in the mood for any party, and anyway, your grandmother was looking daggers at me and I thought it best to make myself scarce.'

'That's her normal expression,' Molly said gloomily. 'It is the way she looks at everything and everybody. I don't mind the work that I have to do in the house really, though I would be grateful if she would lend a hand now and again, but it is the constant finding fault that gets to me.

'D'you know, Auntie Hilda,' she went on, 'when I think of Mom and Dad it's like there is a gaping hole inside me and sometimes it hurts me so bad. I sort of hoped that my grandmother might help fill it, give me a link with my mother when she was younger. But when I asked her, she said horrible things about her, hateful things. I can't think of my mother like that anyway, and I told her that. I know Mom would have done anything for me and I really can't think of any time when I might do something she disapproved of so much that she would never, ever forgive me.'

'No, of course not,' Hilda said. 'It isn't normal to do that either. I mean, children have to go their own way in the world. It is what it is all about. You might not like the decisions they make and the people they take up with, and yes, if you are concerned enough you might say something, but if they take no notice, you don't cast them out like some sort of avenging God.

'What you have got to realise, Molly,' she continued, 'is that your grandmother is a very unhappy woman, because no one could be happy with all that bitterness inside them.

60

You have got to develop the strength to rise above that. Don't let it bog you down and destroy you too.'

'I'll try,' Molly promised. 'I really will try hard 'cos I'd hate to turn out like her anyway. Now I'd better go back.'

'Yes,' Hilda agreed. 'Wouldn't do to give that old besom reason to berate you again.'

'She doesn't need a reason.' Molly said glumly. 'Honest to God, she doesn't.'

'I know, lass,' Hilda said. 'And this isn't goodbye, it's just farewell for now.' She enfolded Molly in her arms as she spoke and then pushed her away gently and said in a voice thick with unshed tears, 'Don't you go round forgetting us now. I'll want to know how you are getting on.'

'I will write to you,' Molly promised. 'I'd like to. Granddad has packed a paper, envelopes and stamps in my case already. He said rural Ireland is not like Birmingham, with a shop on every corner.'

'Dare say he is right there,' Hilda said with a slight smile.

Her hand suddenly shot into the biscuit tin and came out with a handful. 'Here,' she said, pushing them at Molly. 'Take these, and just for you, mind. Don't you go sharing them. You are far too thin.'

'Are you sure?'

'Course I'm sure, positive sure,' Hilda said with a sniff. 'Now get going before I end up blarting my eyes out.'

Everything stood ready, bags and boxes packed, for they were leaving early in the morning.

Molly and her grandfather went to the hospital to say goodbye to Kevin. As the day grew nearer to his grandmother's departure, and with his grandfather's continual assurance that he was going home with him, the child had improved dramatically. Stan had hoped the hospital might have allowed him to go with him to see Molly and Biddy off at the station.

'He may have a very bad reaction to seeing his sister go off like that,' the doctor said. 'Have they ever been apart before?'

'Not that I know of.'

'Well, from what I have seen, they seem remarkably fond of one another,' the doctor commented. 'I would rather they said goodbye here, where we are all on hand if we are needed.'

Stan could see the doctor's point of view, and Kevin was upset when it dawned on him that he probably wouldn't see Molly for a long, long time. Molly also cried bitterly. She had been eight when he was born and she had helped her mother bring him up. Though he was a nuisance at times, as little brothers go he wasn't bad, and she loved him to bits and really thought she should be there for him with both their parents dead.

However, for Kevin's sake, she tried to get a grip on herself. 'I will be working next year, Kevin,' she told the child. 'I will come back when I am sixteen and we will be together again, you'll see.'

'Do you promise?' Kevin said.

Molly looked at Kevin's eyes, sparkling with tears, and said firmly, 'Course I do.'

'What if our grandmother don't let you?'

'She won't be able to stop me when I am sixteen,' Molly declared. 'Anyroad, she can just go and boil her head.' She saw the ghost of a smile at the corners of Kevin's mouth. 'Look,' she said, and she licked her index finger and chanted, 'See it wet, see it dry,' then drew the finger across her neck, 'cut my throat if I tell a lie.' She saw Kevin sigh with relief. 'Three years, that's all, Kevin,' Molly said. 'And I promise we will be a family again.'

However, three years when you are five is a very long time indeed. Kevin clung to Molly at the moment of parting and when Stan eventually peeled the weeping child from her, held him in his arms and signed for her to go, she left the room rapidly, knowing that to linger would only make matters worse.

Stan held the child until the sobs ceased and Kevin lay

still. Then he said, 'Would you like to go fishing, sometime with me, Kevin?'

Kevin was so surprised at the question that he was nonplussed for a moment or two. Then he shrugged and said, 'I don't know, Granddad.'

'I used to take your daddy when he was a wee boy.'

'Did you?' Kevin found it hard to imagine his daddy as a young boy at all.

'I surely did,' Stan said. 'Would you like to give it a go?'

'Um, I think so.'

'And I think that you are old enough to go to the football matches now too,' Stan said. 'What do you say?'

Kevin's face was one big beam. 'Oh, yes, Granddad.'

'Right then, 'cos us men have got to look after one another, you know,' Stan continued. 'So you have to get well and out of here mighty quick, and look after your old granddad.'

'Yes. All right, I will,' Kevin said determinedly.

A little later, Stan came upon Molly waiting for him in the corridor and at the sight of her woebegone face, he wished he could cheer her up as easily as Kevin, but he couldn't think of a thing to say. Molly didn't seem to want to talk anyway; she was sort of buttoned up inside herself all the way back to the house.

FIVE

Molly knew she would never forget the sight of her grand-father standing on the platform waving until he became a small dot in the distance. She felt a sharp pain in her heart as if it had been split asunder just as when she had heard of the death of her parents. Granddad was the last link with all that was familiar in her life, and she cried silently as she leaned her head on the window of the carriage.

Stan felt almost as bad to see his granddaughter move out of his life. He was glad he had told Biddy nothing about the money for the children from Paul Simmons. His conscience had smote him about this at first, until he had really got to know Biddy. Then he realised that had she been aware of the money, it wouldn't have benefited Molly in the slightest – and Molly might have need of money some day. At least that was something he had done for her, he thought as, with the train out of sight, he turned sorrowfully away.

When Biddy, sitting beside Molly, realised she was crying, she was furious with her.

'Stop this at once,' she hissed, but as quietly as she could, mindful of the others sharing their carriage. 'Making a holy show of yourself.'

Molly saw the woman opposite look at her with sympa-thetic eyes, but she knew enough about her grandmother's character to know that it would be the worse for her if she were to engender any sort of interest from her fellow passengers. So she tried to swallow the lump of misery lodged in her throat and looked out at the landscape flashing past the windows, knowing that in any other circumstance she would probably have enjoyed the experience because she had never been further than Birmingham in the whole of her life.

She saw the buildings and houses at the city's edge give way to fields, dappled here and there by the early morning sun peeping from the clouds. Some of the fields were cultivated, set in rows with things growing in them; others were bare, the long grass waving in the breeze, or dotted with sheep, many with their lambs gambolling beside them. In another there might be horses, the lean racy sort, or the thick heavy ones with shaggy feet, the kind of horse the milkman and the coalman used in Birmingham. Sometimes, cows would lean their heads over the five-barred gates, placidly chewing and watching the train pass.

Now and again Molly would spy isolated farmhouses, and she realised suddenly she knew nothing about the farm she was going to. She asked her grandmother about it.

'We do a bit of everything,' Biddy said. 'We grow vegetables, have a few cows, a pig and chickens, of course. We used to have sheep, but after my man died and Joe hightailed it to America, Tom couldn't manage the sheep as well as everything else. Even as it stands now, it's a lot for one man. He will be glad of your help.'

'But won't I have to go to school?'

Biddy smiled her horrible, hard smile. She said with more than a measure of satisfaction, 'I think you have enough booklearning. Any more won't be any sort of asset on a farm.'

Molly's heart sank. For one thing, she had thought school would get her away from her grandmother's brooding presence for much of the day, and anyway she was good at her lessons. When her parents were both alive they had intended keeping her at school until she was sixteen and allowing her to matriculate. She told her grandmother this

65

and went on, 'Dad said it would help me get a good job in the end.'

Again there was that sardonic smile. 'You have a job,' Biddy said. 'Like I said before, you'll be on the farm alongside Tom, and all the book-learning in the world won't make you any better at that.'

Molly felt suddenly cold inside and she held out little hope that she would get on any better with this Uncle Tom she had not seen, who was probably just as nasty as his mother. Her heart plummeted to her boots.

She saw her plans for any sort of life she might have imagined for herself crumble to dust, but she knew that to say any of this would achieve nothing. So she was silent, and mighty glad later to find her grandmother had fallen asleep.

If it hadn't been for the other people on the train, Molly would never have managed at Crewe, where they had to change trains, for they also had to change platforms and other people helped carry the bags up the huge iron staircase, along the bridge spanning the line, and down the other side. Molly was immensely grateful, especially when those same people helped her board the ferry at Liverpool.

It was called the *Ulster Prince*, and she thought it magnificent, towering up out of the scummy grey water of the quay, with its three large black funnels atop everything, spilling grey smoke into the spring morning. She was on deck, the sun warm on her back and sparkling on the water as she watched the boat pull away. Her knuckles were white, she was gripping the rail so tightly. She remembered the promise she had made to Kevin and she vowed, but silently, 'I will be back. However long it takes, I will be back.'

'Come along,' her grandmother said, just behind her. 'They are serving breakfasts in the dining room until noon, and it is turned eleven already.'

Molly followed Biddy eagerly. They had been travelling for many hours and she had been too nervous to eat much before they left the house.

The dining room was delightful. Its windows were round, and when she queried this, she was told they were called portholes. In the dining room they were decorated with pretty pink curtains.

They could have creamy porridge with as much sugar and hot milk as anyone wanted, followed by toast and jam and a pot of tea, all for one and sixpence. Molly ate everything before her, and took three spoons of sugar in her tea, just because she could, and afterwards thought how much better a person felt when they had a full stomach. She kept this thought in her head just a little time. It certainly wasn't there when she stood alongside her grandmother and a good many more and vomited all her breakfast into the churning waters.

By the time they alighted in Belfast, Molly was feeling decidedly ill. Her stomach ached and her throat burned from the constant vomiting that continued long after she had anything left, and made her feel wretched for the entire crossing, which took three and a half hours.

By the time they disembarked and were aboard the train, she was also feeling light-headed and had a throbbing pain behind her eyes. Her grandmother's voice, berating her for something or other, seemed to be coming from a long way off and she was too tired and disorientated to distinguish what the woman was on about anyway. Her eyes closed almost by themselves, and the next thing she remembered was her grandmother shaking her roughly as the train pulled in to Derry.

She knew her uncle would be there to meet them with a horse and cart, to save them having to take the train the last step of the way. Molly was so travel worn and weary that she was immensely glad when she saw the man waiting for them, the shaggy-footed horse standing patiently between the shafts of the farm cart.

Tom knew he would never forget that meeting. It was like his sister Nuala had returned to him, but never had he seen his sister so disheartened and sad, nor her eyes with blue smudges beneath them and her face bleached white.

He felt suddenly very sorry for the girl and went towards her with a smile.

'Welcome to Ireland, Molly,' he said, taking her limp hand and shaking it vigorously. 'It is a pity that we are not meeting under happier circumstances. I was sorry to hear about the death of your parents and I'm sure you will miss them very much.'

Molly's eyes filled with tears at her uncle's words and the compassion in his face, and she knew that he was the antithesis of his mother.

Then Biddy, watching this scene, commented sarcastically, 'Very touching. Now stop your stupid blethering, can't you, and get this luggage into the cart.'

Molly saw the sag of her uncle's shoulders at his mother's words. 'And welcome home to you too, Mammy,' he said with a sigh, throwing up the bags and cases as he did so. He helped his mother up on to the seat beside him and then he turned to Molly with a smile. 'Now you,' he said, lifting her with ease. 'And Dobbin here will have us home in a jiffy.'

It wasn't quite a jiffy, for the horse wasn't built for speed, but Molly took the opportunity to look around her. Once outside of the town, most of the farmhouses seemed to be white, squat, single-storey dwellings, with thick dark yellow roofs, and all the protruding chimneys had smoke curling upwards from them.

'That's your typical Irish cottage,' Tom said, seeing Molly's preoccupation.

'Mom described them to me,' Molly said, 'but I've never see roofs like those. We had grey slate.'

Tom smiled. 'That's called thatch, Molly,' he said. 'It's made of flax that we grow in the fields and then weave it together.'

They passed small towns and villages, and Molly noted the names of them. Springtown was the first, and then Burnfoot. It was as they neared a place called Fahan that Tom said, 'Did your mammy tell you much about this place?'

'Some,' Molly said. 'I mean, I knew she lived near Lough

Swilly and that it was a saltwater lough because it fed out to the sea. In Birmingham most people have never seen the sea. It is just too far away. When we were on the boat was the first time I had seen it and then I was too sick to take in the expanse of it really.'

She stopped and then went on more hesitantly, 'I once asked Mom if she missed the place, because she always said how beautiful it was, but she said that it was a funny thing but seldom does a person really value where they are born and reared. Anyway, she always said people were more important than places.'

Tom, noting Molly's exhausted face and her eyes glittering with tears, said, 'Not long now, at any rate. Buncrana is next, but I will skirt the town this evening because the farm is beyond it in a district called Cockhill, and we will pass St Mary's, the Catholic church, this way.'

St Mary's was quite an impressive place, though it wasn't that large. It was made of stone and had a high and ornate belfry to the front of it. The church was approached through a wrought-iron gate and along a gravel path with graves either side.

'Why was the church built so far out of Buncrana?' Molly asked as they passed it. 'It seems silly.'

'That was because at the time when St Mary's was built, the English said all Catholic churches had to be built at least a mile outside the town or village, and England controlled Ireland then,' Tom told her.

'That was what the Troubles were over that Mom spoke of?' Molly said. 'To get rid of English rule.'

'Aye,' Tom said, 'that was it right enough. Anyway, while the English could tell the Catholic Church where to put the building, they couldn't tell them what to put in it. In that church, above the altar is the most amazing picture of the Nativity painted by an Italian artist who was specially commissioned. You'll see it on Sunday and be able to judge for yourself how lovely it is.'

They went on a little way past the church, past hedges bordering the fields, and then the horse determinedly turned into a narrow lane almost, Molly noticed, without her uncle needing to touch the reins at all.

'Old Dobbin knows the way home, all right,' Tom remarked, seeing her noticing. 'I really think he could do it blindfold.'

Molly looked about her with more interest, noting that the narrow lane was just wide enough for the cart to pass down with thick hawthorn hedges in both sides. She could see beyond the hedges because of the height of the cart seat. Fields stretched for miles, some cultivated, others with cows in them, and some of these were milling around the five-barred gate set into the hedge.

'Waiting to be milked,' Tom explained with a nod. 'Bit early yet, though.'

Molly looked at the cows' distended udders and, though she knew that was where milk came from, because her mother had told her, she would have preferred to get it from the Co-op milkman.

The lane led to a cobbled yard that seemed full of pecking chickens. Tom drew the horse to a halt in front of a thatched whitewashed cottage with the dark red door that looked as if it opened in two halves.

'This is it,' he said to Molly, hauling the luggage from the cart. 'What do you think?'

Before Molly was able to reply, two black and white dogs, which Tom greeted as Skip and Fly, came to meet them, barking a welcome. Molly was not used to animals, for she and Kevin had had no pets, and the dogs unnerved her a little.

'They're saying hallo just,' Tom said reassuringly, seeing that Molly was a little edgy. 'Let them sniff your hand and then they'll know you are a friend.'

Molly would rather not have done any such thing, but she knew that dogs were an important part of any farm and she would have to get used to them. So she extended her hand and let the dogs sniff. When she met her grandmother's malevolent gaze, she said in a voice she willed not to shake, 'My mother was always saying that what can't be cured must be endured and I suppose that is what she would think about this situation. I haven't chosen to come here, but now I have arrived, I suppose I will like it well enough in time.'

She saw her grandmother seemed almost disappointed, but Tom clapped her on the shoulder. 'Well said, young Molly. Come away in and see the place.'

In all her life, Molly had never seen anything quite like it. She stepped into a low room, the flagged floor covered with rugs. To her left was a door that she learned later housed the two bedrooms, hers first and then beyond that Tom's. Next to a dresser displaying plates and bowls and cups was a large bin that she was to learn was where the oaten meal was stored. A cupboard and a sideboard stood against the back wall next to a heavily curtained area that Tom told her closed off the bed her grandmother slept in.

To her right was a stool with one bucket of water standing on it and one bucket of water beneath it. There were no taps here and all water had to be fetched from the spring well halfway up the lane, which Tom had pointed out to her as they passed. Beside that was a large scrubbed wooden table with chairs grouped around it.

'That doesn't look very comfy,' Molly said, pointing to the wooden bench seat bedecked with cushions and set beneath the window.

'That's a settle,' Tom said. 'It opens to a bed that the children can sleep in when the house is full. I have used it a time or two, but you are right, it is very uncomfortable to sit on. The easy chairs before the fire are better.'

There were two, and when Tom said, 'We'll have to think about getting another for you,' Biddy snapped, 'You won't need to bother. I aim to see to it that that girl isn't going to have much time for sitting resting herself and for the times she is allowed to sit, a creepie will do her.'

'A creepie is way too low for her, Mammy,' Tom said. A creepie, Molly was to learn, was a very low seat made of bog oak. 'And if you want Molly to work hard, then she has to have time to rest too. I have an easy chair in my room and as it is only to put my clothes on, a wooden kitchen chair will do the job well enough.' And at this he gave Molly a wink.

'Molly and I understand each other,' Biddy said with a sardonic smile. 'She knows that if she doesn't work effectively, then she doesn't eat – and thinking of eating, I am famished. The meal on the boat I have brought back up. What have you in?'

'I bought ham and tomatoes in the town,' Tom said. 'And I have the potatoes scrubbed and in the pot, ready to be put on.'

'Well, put them on. What are you waiting for?' Biddy snapped, and Molly wondered how the potatoes were to be cooked, because she had seen no cooker. Tom, however, went towards the open fire and pulled out a bracket with hooks on of different lengths. He hung the black pot he had ready on one of these hooks before giving the fire a poke and throwing something on it that looked like little more than lumps of dirt.

When her grandmother saw Molly staring, she shrieked, 'Don't just stand there, girl. I told you this was no rest cure. Away to the room and take off your coat, then lay the table at the very least.'

It was one of the most uncomfortable meals that Molly had endured. While eating it, Biddy regaled Tom with tales about Birmingham. She hadn't a good word to say about it, and fairly ripped into the character of Molly's parents and her grandfather. Many times, Molly was going to leap to the defence of those she loved, but the first time she opened her mouth to do this, she felt the pressure of Tom's foot on hers and when she looked up quizzically, he made an almost imperceptible shake of his head. So she let her

72

grandmother's words wash over her, because really she was too tired to argue.

After the meal, Tom fetched the chair from his room as he had said he would, then said, 'Right, that's that, then. Now, I'll bring the cows in for milking.'

'Wait,' said Biddy. 'Molly will go with you.'

Both Molly and Tom looked at Biddy as if they couldn't believe their ears. Molly was so weary she was having trouble functioning and she had been wondering how soon she would be allowed to go to bed, but now this. She couldn't do this. She barely knew one end of a cow from the other and hadn't dreamed that milking them would be part of her duties.

Tom had no idea of Molly's rising panic, but he had noted her exhausted state and said. 'There is no need for this, Mammy. I don't need anyone to help me. Haven't I been doing it alone for a fair few years anyway?'

'Aye, but there is no need for you to do it alone now. You have help.'

'Can't you see the child is worn out?' Tom said. 'She has been travelling all the day.'

'I have told Molly there is no place for passengers on a farm, and the sooner she is made aware of this, the better it will be for everybody,' Biddy said with some satisfaction.

Molly wanted to say she had never had any desire to milk a cow and didn't particularly want to learn either, but she had already decided that she would show no weakness in front of this woman. So, turning to Tom, she said, 'You will have to show me how it is done.'

Biddy may have been disappointed with Molly's response, but Tom was full of admiration. 'There is nothing to it,' he said. 'You'll pick it up in no time. Let's whistle up the dogs to help bring them down.'

Tom was patient and kind, and his voice so calm that Molly could never imagine it raised in anger, or indeed anything else, and it was like balm to her bruised and battered soul. He seemed to understand her initial distaste, but he was so gentle and reassuring that Molly battled to overcome this because she knew it would please him.

She was quick to learn generally, and soon got the hang of milking. She even began to enjoy it, finding, like many more, there was something incredibly soothing about sitting astride a three-legged stool, her face pressed against the velvet flank of the cow, and gently but firmly squeezing the udders and seeing the bucket fill with the squirts of milk.

'Molly,' said Tom after a while, 'let me give you a word of warning. Don't rise to Mammy's bait. Let her rant and rave and all, and you say nothing. Eventually, she will have to stop.'

'Yes, but when she says thing about my family . . .'

'She says that because she knows it upsets you,' Tom said.

'She told me that my mother killed her father,' Molly said. 'Was that true?'

Tom sighed. 'When Daddy read the letter Nuala sent, telling of how she met your father and wanting to become engaged, and about his being a Protestant and all, Daddy had a heart attack.'

'So she did then, in a way?'

'Yes and no,' Tom said. 'Not long after Nuala left for England, Daddy developed pains in his chest and he was diagnosed with a bad heart. He knew he was on borrowed time – we all knew. The doctor said he could go any time, but Mammy said that Nuala wasn't to be worried about it. If she had known maybe she would have come over in person and told him herself more gently, so I don't think she can be blamed.'

'She wasn't told anything,' Molly said. 'Surely she should have been told her own father died?'

'Of course she should,' Tom said. 'I blame myself. I should have stood against Mammy. She was just so adamant.'

Uncle Tom was soft, a fact Molly had realised within a

few minutes of meeting him. She would take a bet that he hated confrontation of any kind so, much as she liked him, she doubted that she could depend on him for support.

He did try objecting when, on their return to the house, Biddy told Molly to wash the pots and to be quick about it, because she had to be up early in the morning for milking.

'Mammy, for God's sake, let the girl lie in tomorrow at least.'

Biddy continued to Molly as if Tom hadn't spoken, 'And first you will kindle up the fire from the rakings, clean out the ashes and fill the kettle, and put it on before joining Tom in the cowshed. Oh, and you can leave your lah-d-dah city clothes in the wardrobe. They will do for Mass, but are not suitable for work on the farm. While you were at the milking I fashioned you a couple of working shirts and a pair of dungarees from things I had in the house. Put them on in the morning.'

'You'll kill the girl before you're done,' Tom commented morosely, and Biddy smiled as if that would be a quite acceptable outcome.

The next morning Molly rose before five o'clock, put on the clothes her grandmother had given her and surveyed herself in the mirror. She supposed the shirts and dungarees were more serviceable, but she didn't like them much, and they were rather big for her – so big that she had to roll up the sleeves of the shirts and the legs of the trousers over and over. Tom had already left to collect up the cows, and so the first time he saw the clothes was when Molly appeared in the cowshed a little later.

He laughed his head off. 'God Almighty,' he said. 'You'd fit in them twice over. They were probably Finn's once, or Joe's even, and both were a sight bigger than you.'

Molly knew who Finn and Joe were for she had asked many questions about her mother's family though Nuala had known nothing about them from the day she had left.

Molly had known about Finn's death, of course, but nothing of Joe.

She said now, 'What happened to Joe? Mom always thought he would be here on the farm with you, but my grandmother told me that he had gone to America.'

'Aye,' Tom said, 'and, God's truth, I couldn't blame him. With Finn gone and Nuala too and Daddy dying, the place was not the same at all. In the end he could take no more. Anyway, as he said, what was he doing working his fingers to the bone on a farm that would never be his?'

'Is he still there now?'

'Aye, and he didn't do badly at first,' Tom said. 'Well, he ended up marrying the boss's daughter, a girl called Gloria, and probably thought he was set for life, but then there was something called the Wall Street Crash and . . .'

'What was that?'

'Oh, it's to do with stocks and shares,' Tom said. 'And I have never had any truck with them. But it meant the boss, Joe's father-in-law, lost a heap of money and ended up killing himself.'

'Golly!'

'Joe was left with the debts the man had rung up,' Tom said. 'The house and fine way of living had to go, and he had a wife and mother-in-law to support and no means of doing so. I asked him to come here, but he can't because the mother-in-law refuses to leave the land where her husband is buried and so they live in a downtown tenement, surviving on handouts or the odd day's work Joe gets in a factory or down at the docks. It was worsened by the birth of their son, Ben, last year.'

'Sad, isn't it?' Molly said wistfully. 'You think your life will just go on the way it always has been and then something happens and the whole thing goes up in the air. Your brother is stuck just like I am.'

'That's about it,' Tom said. 'You won't be stuck here for ever, though, young Molly, don't fret. But if you don't

76

want Mammy giving out to us both for wasting time, we'd best be away back to the house, now we have finished the milking.'

Molly soon found that there is an art to filling a kettle from a full bucket of water and that it took time to acquire it. The first time she tried she swamped the floor and she knew if she hadn't been able to clear away the evidence of this before Biddy got up, then she would probably have joined Tom in the cowshed with a thick ear.

She was always more than ready for her breakfast after milking, which was a boiled egg or porridge, and she ate her fill. She was aware almost from the first day that once she rose from that table it would be a long time before she had the opportunity to rest her legs again. Her grandmother saw to that.

Once she had put the water on to boil for the washing-up, Tom would fill up the buckets again. A large pan of water would be needed to scald the drinks for the two calves in the byre and to boil up the potatoes and turnips to feed the indolent, smelly pig and her litter of squealing piglets. Then Molly would feed the dogs and the hens, and collect and wipe the eggs.

After the Angelus bell had rung at twelve o'clock, they would stop for dinner. Sometimes this would just consist of potatoes and shallots, though Tom told her there was fish most Saturdays after they had been to the market, and other days in the week if there was ever the occasion to go into the town again and the fishing fleet was in.

'I bag the odd rabbit as well,' he said. 'And of course when a pig is killed we might enjoy a bit of pork, and if there is an old hen not laying at all well, then she might just find herself with her neck wrung.'

'Ugh!'

Tom laughed. 'I suppose you got all your meat from the butchers all nicely packed and packaged,' he said. 'Well, this is where it all starts, and I'll tell you, we are glad enough to see a bit of meat or fish when we have had potatoes and just potatoes for time and enough.'

After dinner that first day, Biddy took Molly on one side to teach her how to make soda bread and bread with oaten meal. 'This needs to be done three times a week,' she said. 'On Saturdays, of course, you will also make scones, barnbrack and potato cakes for Sunday, and in addition to this on Thursday, you will do the churning and Monday is, of course, wash day and that will take some time. And remember whatever other duties you have, you will go with Tom to do the milking twice a day.'

Molly knew the workload would be a heavy one, but after only a day or so she found that she valued those peaceful times with her uncle in the cowshed. Biddy never went near it and so it was sort of a special place, where she could get away from her grandmother's whining, complaining voice and the clouts that she seemed to find necessary to administer for the most minor things. But Molly was no fool, and she never, ever showed how much she enjoyed, even sometimes looked forward to, the milking. She knew that it was her grandmother's intention to make her life as miserable as possible.

On Thursday afternoon, Biddy prepared the churn, while Molly washed up the dinner dishes and then showed her what to do.

'Up and down for twenty minutes,' she said, handing her the paddle. 'And without stopping.'

Molly tried valiantly, but after a few minutes her arms felt like lead weights and she laid down the paddle with a sigh.

Biddy cuffed her on the side of the head, sending her senses reeling. 'Twenty minutes, I said.'

'I can't.'

'You can if you want to eat tonight.'

Molly knew that was no idle threat, but even then she

could only manage a few minutes at a time, and every time she stopped, Biddy would clout her. But she hardly cared, for the pain in her arms and her back was worse than anything Biddy could do. When eventually Biddy called a halt and began to scoop the butter out and shape it, Molly's arms continued to shake.

They still ached when she joined Tom in the cowshed later, and when Tom saw the stiff way that she was working, he asked her if she was all right. He was angry when he learned that she had done the churning all on her own. She was so slight, for one thing, and she hadn't been brought up to it, but he knew that there was no point in him saying anything about it.

'There was so much butter too,' Molly said. 'What do you do with it all?'

'What nearly everyone does,' Tom said. 'We have a stall in the Market Hall in Buncrana on Saturdays and we sell the surplus there.'

'Oh,' Molly said, delighted at the prospect of leaving the farm. 'Do you go every Saturday?'

'Aye,' Tom said. 'But I doubt that you would be let go.'

'Why not?'

Tom shook his head. 'I have given up trying to understand my mother, but she said you are to be left here.'

There was a flash of disappointment, but Molly knew there was no point worrying about a situation she couldn't change. At least this way she was going to be free of her grandmother for a few hours.

'What I was going to suggest,' Tom said, breaking in on her thoughts, 'was that if you wanted to write to your grandfather and all, I could post the letters for you in Buncrana.'

'Oh, Uncle Tom that would be great,' Molly cried. 'Granddad packed everything that he thought I might need – paper, envelopes, he even managed to get hold of some Irish stamps – but I couldn't imagine how I would post any letters and so I haven't used anything yet.'

79

'Well, that is one problem solved,' Tom said. 'You just get the letters written and I will do the rest. Now, sit you up on that milking stool and rub your arms to get the feeling back and leave the rest of the milking to me tonight.'

Molly was grateful to her uncle and sat back with a sigh of relief. For once, she didn't mind that Biddy roared at her as soon as she was in the door, to get on the porridge for supper and not take all night over it, because her head was full of the letters that she intended writing that night.

Feeling sure that Biddy would object and make disparaging remarks, Molly left the writing of the letters until she was in her room. Normally, she was so tired when she went to bed that she fell into a deep sleep as soon as her head touched the pillow, but that night excitement drove sleep from her and she sat in her bed and wrote feverishly by the light of a candle.

Knowing that neither Hilda or her grandfather could do anything to change the situation she was in, she didn't tell them that she didn't attend school any more, and very little about her grandmother at all. She did tell them of Tom and how welcoming he had been, how kind and patient he was teaching her things about farming life, and how she enjoyed helping him out on the farm. She knew that they would be pleased by that and she urged them to write back soon for she was desperate for news of them all.

SIX

Molly couldn't believe the relief she felt when she watched Biddy drive off with Tom that first Saturday – and that was despite the long list of jobs awaiting her. She had hoped that they would stay away the whole day. However, Tom had said that their business would probably be completed by dinner-time, and when she caught a glimpse of the cart turning in the head of the lane, about half-past twelve, she felt her heart sink.

Molly knew that it was too much to expect her grandmother to be pleased with anything she did and this was just as well, because that way she wasn't either surprised or disappointed with Biddy's reaction. In fact, she was far more interested in the fresh fish that Tom had brought home. He gutted it and had it in the pan above the fire in no time at all, and it tasted so delicious when they sat down to eat it.

The house had to be spotless and a batch of baking done for Sunday, so Molly was run off her feet all afternoon, glad after washing up the tea things to escape with Tom to the cowshed.

Molly had already got the Mass clothes ready for them all for the following morning and cleaned the shoes as her grandmother had bade. Now, as she emerged in the door after the milking that evening, Biddy said, 'Time you had a bath, girl.'

Molly, used to an indoor bathroom, had wondered about that. Her grandfather had had no bathroom either, and had told Molly that he, Phoebe and Ted too, before he was married, would bath in front of the fire. Molly had presumed she would have to do the same here, and this was proved when Biddy ordered Tom to fetch the bath in from the barn while a large pot of water was put over the fire to heat.

The galvanised bath Tom brought in looked neither large, nor very comfortable, but Molly was less concerned about that than she was about where Tom would go, for she had no intention of taking one stitch of clothing off in front of him. Fortunately, he stayed only long enough to mix the hot water and cold water together before leaving to tramp the hills while Molly washed herself.

Despite the fairly primitive conditions, Molly would have enjoyed her bath, if it hadn't been for the presence of her grandmother, sitting in the chair watching her. She wondered at the ability the woman had of changing the atmosphere of a room just by being in it, and so she had no intention of lingering over her wash, which was just as well because she had barely rinsed the soap off before her grandmother was urging her to hurry up.

She was, however, dressed in her pyjamas and slippers and her towelled hair in plaits before Tom put in an appearance. Then he emptied the bath into the gutter in the yard, despite Biddy telling him to leave it to Molly.

'She is too slight for this, Mammy,' he told her. 'She will do herself an injury. Besides, what sort of a man would it make me to sit idly by and see a child struggle? Molly is worn out. Anyone with half an eye can see it. She needs to seek her bed.'

Molly looked at Tom gratefully, as her grandmother said, 'I will say when she goes to bed.'

'Is that so?' Tom snapped, suddenly and uncharacteristically angry as he faced his mother across the room. 'No one is any use to me who is sluggish through lack of sleep. They are more a liability than anything.'

'I told you, if Molly doesn't work then—'

'She doesn't eat,' Tom finished. 'Don't start on about that again.'

'But I do work,' Molly protested. 'I do the very best I can.'

Tom nodded in agreement. 'You do, Molly, but if you are to continue to help me effectively on the farm, then you need proper rest and good food. Surely, Mammy, you can see that yourself?'

Molly was grateful and surprised at her uncle's intervention but, she noted, not as surprised as her grandmother, whose eyes were narrowed in discontent.

Biddy was almost astounded. Tom had never gone against her before; he always had been easily cowed. She knew what had changed him, however. It was all the fault of that girl. He couldn't see what a troublemaker she was.

In a way his mother was right, for Tom had only challenged her because of pity for Molly.

He was glad, though, that his mother didn't know how his legs were shaking and his heart thumping almost painfully against his chest. He had always secretly been afraid of her and he was annoyed and a little ashamed of himself for feeling that way because he was a grown man.

Biddy hadn't spoken and Tom said, 'Well, Mammy? What about it?'

'She hasn't even said the rosary yet,' Biddy said.

Tom answered, 'I'm sure God will understand the one night.' And then he turned to Molly and said, 'Get yourself to bed. You look all in.'

Molly gave a sigh of relief. She knew that for her grandmother this issue was not resolved and that she might suffer for it in the morning. That was another day, however, and not one that she was going to worry her head over.

She lay in bed and realised she was ridiculously excited

to be going to Mass in the morning. For one thing, she would wear a dress, and then she would leave the farm, which was starting to feel a little like prison, and meet other people. Her toes curled in pleasurable anticipation of it.

Everyone at the church was interested in seeing Molly Maguire the next day. They had known she was coming. It was too small a place for anyone to keep anything secret for long. With the guards at the door of the cottage, and then the sending and receiving of telegrams, the whole community knew of the death of Nuala née Sullivan and her husband, and of the grandmother off to see to things.

When Tom had told Nellie McEvoy, the postmistress, his mother would be returning, first with both children and then just the girl, she had been amazed. Other women that she told felt the same way and a collection of townswomen had gathered in the post office to discuss it.

'Didn't think she'd be that bothered about any child of Nuala's,' Nellie said.

'Well, no. I mean, she never even sent a scribe to her since her man died that time.'

'Aye, and before that wouldn't you have thought the sun shone out of young Nuala?'

'You would,' one said emphatically, and added, 'Spoiling is good for neither man nor beast, and she had the child ruined altogether.'

'Aye,' another commented. 'I own that she was a pretty enough wee thing and so kind and thoughtful, almost despite Biddy and all, but—'

'It wasn't the child's fault,' Nellie said. 'She was a lovely wee thing, like a little doll, but you'd think there wasn't another child in the universe to hear the mother talk.'

'That's right,' agreed the first woman. 'Blowing on about her all the time, till she would make a body sick.'

84

'That's why she took it so bad, likely, when the girl went off and married a Proddy, as Joe was after telling me before he took off for the States,' another woman said. 'Further to fall, see.'

The others nodded sagely and then Nellie commented, 'Maybe that is why she taking the child in. Making it up to her, like.'

'D'you think that she feels sorry for the way she went on – is that what you are saying?' one woman asked, adding, 'From what I know of Biddy, feeling sorry for something she does or says is not part of her make-up at all.'

'Aye,' Nellie said, 'but this is death. Very final, is death, and that changes a lot of things.'

'And,' said the first woman, 'she has taken the child in, there is no getting away from that.'

There were nods and murmurs of agreement.

'So let's all wait and see, and not have her tried by judge and jury beforehand,' Nellie said.

'Aye, you're right,' said another of the women. 'Let's all wait and see.'

And they did see, that first Sunday morning. Everyone saw, in fact. Those who could remember Nuala saw the resemblance to her in Molly, and they also were soon well aware, from the malice-ridden eyes Biddy turned on the girl and the brusque way she spoke to her, that she had not brought the child to live with her because she felt sorry for her. It was for other reasons altogether and not ones that were making the young orphaned girl happy.

Molly sensed the people felt sorry for her, and indeed many expressed this as they shook her by the hand, the priest, Father Finlay, amongst them.

'In the midst of life there is death, Molly, and we must remember that,' he told her predictably.

'Yes, Father.'

'And I am sure your parents are now reaping their reward in Heaven.'

'Her father won't be,' Biddy said harshly and with satisfaction. 'He'll have descended to the fiery pit by now, where all sinners go.'

Ashamed at her grandmother saying that about her lovely father, Molly burst out, 'He's not. My father was no sinner.'

'No sinner,' Biddy repeated, and turned to the priest. 'Went nowhere to worship, Father, neither church nor chapel. That's why I took the girl. Couldn't have left her there with the heathen of a grandfather, for he was the same as his son.'

The priest was embarrassed and whispered something noncommittal. Those close enough to hear what Biddy had said were looking askance at her and could clearly see how upset the poor girl was. Molly was, in fact, angry, and she wondered why her grandmother thought she had the right to judge her father. She knew not the slightest thing about him; didn't know what a good kind man he had been. He didn't go to church, that was true, but she knew a fair few who never missed Mass who were not half the man her father had been. And she knew that if God was the loving Father they were taught He was, then she was sure that He would treat her father fairly.

She didn't attempt to say any of this, however, because she knew she would cry if she tried. Tom, who had stopped at the gate to talk to neighbours, had not seen any altercation and was unaware of any undercurrent until he saw the tears glistening in Molly's eyes.

'You all right?' he whispered as he got closer.

Molly gave a brief nod.

'You sure?'

Molly, seeing her grandmother was now out of earshot, said quietly, 'I sometimes wonder if I will ever be right again, but it's nothing that can be fixed here and now. But I'll tell you one thing,' she added fiercely. 'I don't care how sensible it is. I am not going to let my grandmother say what she likes about my parents and say nothing in their defence ever again.'

'Molly—' began Tom warningly.

'No, Uncle Tom. I know what you are going to say,' Molly said. 'You must do as you see fit, but I will not let her or anyone else destroy the memories I have of my parents, for they were the best parents in the world to me and Kevin.'

She walked away from her uncle then and he watched her with worried eyes, knowing that if she stuck to her guns she was heading for extremely choppy waters.

When Molly entered the church and saw the painting of the Nativity scene, she could understand her uncle's enthusiasm, because it was magnificent, especially with the sun glinting on the vibrant colours so that the whole thing looked almost lifelike. Somehow, the sheer beauty of it soothed her a little, and this was helped by the familiarity of the Mass, so that she let it all wash over her and give her a measure of peace.

After a very good dinner, Molly washed up while Tom took his ease by the fire with his pipe and the Sunday paper, but really he was watching Molly and as she put away the last plate he said, 'I don't suppose you would fancy a tramp amongst the hills this fine afternoon?'

Molly turned to her uncle with her eyes shining, for there was nothing, absolutely nothing, that she would like better. The baking for the Sunday tea had been done the day before and she could conceivably be free for an hour or two.

Biddy didn't think so. 'Don't you offer to take the girl off out without as much as a by-your-leave.'

'I wasn't under the impression I had to ask permission of you to take a walk with my niece,' Tom said mildly. 'Come along with us if you like?' He caught the look of distaste that flitted across Molly's face at his words and the slight shiver to her body and hid his smile. He knew he was on safe ground.

'You know full well my gallivanting days are over,' Biddy snapped.

'All right, Mammy,' Tom said. 'But Molly's are just beginning, do you see? She's young and well up for gallivanting. Isn't that so, Molly?'

There was such a broad smile on Molly's face as she answered in like manner, 'I am, Uncle Tom.'

'So, are you ready?'

'Quite ready.'

'Then what are we waiting for?' Tom said, catching up her arm.

Only when she was a little way from the house did she say to her uncle, 'Did you see the look? Crikey, by rights I should be lying dead now on the kitchen floor.'

'I should say you're not that easily killed, Molly,' Tom said.

'People are very easily killed when you think about it,' Molly murmured quietly.

Tom felt immediately contrite. 'Oh, my dear, I am so sorry.'

'No, I'm sorry,' Molly said. 'For bringing such sadness into this lovely afternoon. It wouldn't be something my parents would have approved of at all. They were always telling me to take joy in every day.'

'You are a privileged girl to have such memories,' Tom said. 'Your home sounds as if it was once a happy one.'

'It was, very.'

'Well, no one can take those memories away, and they will help sustain you during the bad times.'

Molly nodded. 'I know, but sometimes I am sad that those times will never come back.'

'You are not alone, Molly,' Tom said. 'You'll always have me.'

'I know I am not alone, Uncle Tom,' Molly commented grimly, but with the ghost of a smile playing around her mouth. 'I have your blooming mother as well.'

Tom laughed as he said, 'By God, young Molly, with that spark of humour, I'd say you'll do all right. You are one of life's survivors.'

Molly gave a definite nod of her head. 'I fully intend to be,' she said.

Tom caught up her arm. 'Come on then, Molly. Let's you and me stroll out with the best of them and you can tell me all about your life in Birmingham.'

'Only if you tell me about my mother when she was a girl.'

'It's a deal,' Tom said.

Afterwards, Molly was to see that walk she undertook with her uncle as a sort of turning point in her relationship with him. The tentative talks that had begun in the cowshed had opened the way for them and that day each found out more about the other's life.

Molly could see how it had been for them all growing up on the farm, the three boys and the baby, Nuala, spoiled and petted by them all. She tried to paint the picture of her life before the tragedy. She wanted him to see how the adult Nuala had fared, of the fine man she had married and what a marvellous mother she was.

'It wasn't always easy for her, either,' Molly said. 'She wanted a houseful of children, she told me herself, but she lost three babies before Kevin was born. Then she was so ill giving birth to him that the doctor said there were to be no more.'

'Ah, that must have been a disappointment for her.'

'I'm sure it was,' Molly said. 'In fact, she said it had saddened her at first, but then she got over it and took pleasure in the children she had. That was the type of person she was, you see, someone really special. She said often people hanker for things they can't have, until it takes over their lives and they miss enjoying the things they have got. I know that she would want me to always remember them, but not let their loss destroy my life totally.'

'A wise woman, I'd say,' Tom said. 'And I regret the fact that I ever lost contact with her.'

'So do I,' Molly said. 'I had thirteen years of loving care from my parents, while my little brother only had five. He never even knew his other grandma because she died just after his first birthday and it would have been nice for him to know – both of us, I suppose, but him especially – that there were other people that cared about us.'

'I see that,' Tom said. 'Pity we can't roll back the clock and have another go at the things we know with hindsight we did wrong. Was your other grandmother kind to you?'

'She was lovely,' Molly said, smiling at the memory. 'She was round and cuddly, and her lap just the comfiest place to sit. Her house always smelled nice too, of cooking mainly, because she was always baking. When I would go and see her she always had cakes or something for me. Mom liked her too and they got on well. Granddad used to laugh and say the pair of them weren't normal, that it was written in the rule book that they should be at it hammer and tongs.'

'You must all have missed your grandmother when she died.'

'We did, and it was so sudden,' Molly said, casting her mind back. 'I mean, she hadn't been ill or anything. She was fine one minute and had a massive heart attack the next. I was nine then, and I didn't think people just died like that. I was so shocked that for a while I didn't believe she was really dead and, in the end, Granddad took me to see her and there she was lying in a coffin. I knew she was dead then. She didn't look bad or anything, she looked just as if she was asleep, only you see I never saw my grandma so still before. She was always on the go – "on the batter", Granddad used to call it.'

'Does it upset you to talk about it?' Tom asked, noting the reflective tone that had crept into Molly's voice.

'No, not upset really,' Molly said. 'It helps in a way. I mean, I wish none of it had happened, that my life with my parents and grandparents had gone on uneventfully for

90

years and years and we would all live happy ever after. But life isn't like that and you have to take the bad times with the good times and learn to cope with it.'

She smiled and looked up at Tom and said, 'Your mother is about as bad as it gets, and for now, while I am a child, I have to put up with it, but she will have to chain me down when I am grown, for I will not stop here one moment longer than necessary.'

'And I will not blame you one bit,' Tom said earnestly.

'Hilda was our next-door neighbour and Mom's great friend,' Molly said. 'And just before I left she said that your mother was a very bitter and unhappy woman and I had not to let it drag me down; that I had to rise above it or it would destroy me too. She was lovely, Hilda, and I am dying to hear how they are all getting on. I'm sure they will write straight back.'

'Look who is ahead of us,' Tom said suddenly. 'I knew we wouldn't be the only ones out walking today. Good day, Nellie. Lovely afternoon.'

The postmistress stopped and smiled at them both. 'Couldn't be better,' she said. 'Hello, Molly. Lovely to see you enjoying the fine weather. You need more of it, get some roses in your cheeks, for you are far too pale. Not like my girl, Cathy here,' she said, indicating the girl by her side, whose cheeks were like two rosy apples either side of her nose.

'Huh, and when I go out in the sun,' said the girl with a toss of her head, 'all I get is more freckles.'

Molly saw the girl, who looked a similar age to herself, was right, for merry eyes danced in a face covered in little brown spots. She had glimpsed her in the chapel that morning, but her grandmother had seen to it that she had no chance of a conversation with anyone.

Tom smiled at the girl. 'Ah, will you give over, Cathy,' he said. 'Sure, aren't freckles just sun kisses?'

'Kisses I can well do without,' the girl said. She turned

to Molly. 'I saw you at Mass earlier and I really envied you your hair, for it is beautiful, while mine is dull brown and like a frizz in comparison.'

'If you ask me, miss, you think too much about your appearance,' Nellie told her daughter sharply, but Molly knew from her twinkling eyes that she wasn't really cross. 'And in Mass too, when you should have your mind on higher things.'

Cathy made no reply to this, though she looked not the slightest bit abashed and when she glanced across at Molly and surreptitiously gave her a wink, Molly decided that she liked Cathy McEvoy very much.

It seemed that the McEvoys liked her too, because Nellie said, 'You must come and see us so that we can get to know you better. I am tied up with the post office through the week, but what about next Sunday for tea?'

Molly knew she would love it, but she also knew her grandmother would more than likely not allow it, but before she could open her mouth to say this, Tom said, 'That would be lovely. You'd be delighted, wouldn't you, Molly?'

'Yes, but—'

'So, shall we say four o'clock?' Nellie said. 'We eat about five so that gives you some time together first.'

'Perfect,' Tom said. 'And I will come up later to leave Molly home.'

As they made their goodbyes and were on their way again, Molly said, 'Uncle Tom, my grandmother won't let me go there.'

'Why not? What is wrong with going to tea with someone your own age?'

'She doesn't have to have a reason, you know that,' Molly said. 'And what about the tea and the milking and all?'

'Molly, we managed fine before you came,' Tom said. 'And believe me, the house won't fall to pieces because you are out of it for an hour or two next Sunday. I will ask you one question: do you want to go to tea at the McEvoys?'

'I'd love to, but—'

'Will you stop saying "but",' Tom said with a grin. 'If you want to go then you shall go, or my name isn't Tom Sullivan.'

SEVEN

First thing on Monday morning, Molly had to tackle the washing. All the time her mother had been ill and then in hospital, Molly had helped Hilda, who had done the bulk of the Maguire wash until she had been banished by Biddy. Molly had found the load a heavy one when placed totally on her shoulders, despite the big gas boiler and wringer above it, not to mention running water and big sinks.

Molly gazed at the mass of things to be washed that first morning in dismay, and Biddy watched her in almost gleeful satisfaction. She told her there was more washing than usual because while she had been away, Tom had just swilled out things as he needed them and she had better get on with it, and quickly. Nothing would get done by staring at it.

Tom had already filled three buckets of water, which he tipped into the big pot hanging above the fire while Molly put all the clothes into the pot with the soap powder, before joining her uncle in the cowshed.

Once the milking and breakfast was over, Molly had to ladle the water from the pot to the maiding tub, pounding the poss stick up and down like she had done at home, with stubborn stains rubbed against the washboard. Then the tub had to be emptied panful by panful until it was light enough for her to push to the doorway and let it drain into the gutter in front of the cottage, before filling it up again with the clean water for rinsing. Tom was in the fields by this time, so Molly had to fetch the water from the well herself. She found this a back-breaking enough job at the best of times, and however carefully she carried the water, some of it always slopped out and soaked the side of her dungarees.

The collars and cuffs on Tom's shirts for Mass were detachable and had to be starched in a basin and then strung out with the rest of the mangled wash on the line that stretched across the yard. Then Molly, who felt as if she had done a full week's work, emptied the tub again and replaced it and the mangle back in the barn and fetched another pail of water from the well as Biddy was roaring at her to wash the potatoes for the dinner.

Tom noticed Molly's face glistening with sweat and the damp curls around her face at dinner, but said nothing about it, for it would achieve no purpose and could make his mother even more vindictive. But when Biddy told Molly to hurry up with her dinner because she had the beds to make up yet and the bedrooms to clean before she tackled the ironing, Tom said, 'Give the milking a miss this evening, Molly. You have enough to do.'

'She will not give the milking a miss,' Biddy said. 'And she had better not dawdle either, because she has the supper to make after it.'

Tom opened his mouth to protest, but Molly forestalled him. She would not beg, or even show weakness before this woman whom she was beginning to despise, and besides, she enjoyed the milking. It would be great to be able to sit down, even if it was only on a three-legged stool and lean her aching head against a cow's flank. And her uncle, she was finding, was such an easy man to be with.

'It is far too much for you,' he said that evening as they began.

Molly ached everywhere it was possible to ache and was too bone weary to dispute this. 'I'll likely get used to it.'

'You shouldn't have to,' Tom burst out. 'Almighty Christ,

there is nothing to you and you are not full grown yet by any means.'

'Well, I am not going to ask for favours that she will take pleasure in refusing,' Molly said. 'And another thing: I know in a way that she is making me pay for my mother's so-called mistakes and the indulgent way she brought her up – she even said as much – but I reckon that she'd be more or less like that anyway. I mean, how harsh was your upbringing? According to you and what my mother said, she was the only one spoiled. I bet you were made to work hard when you were young.'

Tom remembered back to the time that he had tilled the fields when, because of his tender years, even an empty spade was a strain to lift. 'You're right,' he said. 'We all had precious little childhood, even Finn, though he was much younger than us. In fact, that was one of the reasons he joined up, if the truth be told. He told me straight he was going somewhere where he would be given a measure of respect and a wage for the job he did, and that a trench in France could be no worse than an Irish one, and if he popped off a few Germans along the way so much the better. Course, he never knew what he was letting himself in for. None of us did at the time, not really, and when people did realise, there was an uprising and the beginnings of the Troubles in Ireland.'

'Mom told me that was one of the reasons that she was allowed to go to England with her employers,' Molly said.

'Aye,' Tom replied. 'They had a big house just outside Derry. Protestants, of course, virtually the only ones to have big houses in Ireland at that time – or in Donegal, at any rate. Nuala had worked there as nursemaid since she was fourteen, and the children knew her and loved her, but if Ireland had been a more stable place there would have been no question of her going with them to England. But it wasn't and so our parents let her go. I wasn't to know that from the day she climbed on the train at Derry station I would never see her again.'

'Sad, isn't it?'

'I'll tell you what I think is worse,' Tom said, almost bitterly. 'And that is the fact that it was my own fault that I didn't see her. When the letter came and Daddy died with it still in his hand, Mammy said that, as far as she was concerned, Nuala was no longer a daughter of hers and that was that. I can scarcely believe now that Joe and I just went along with it.

'I mean, what Mammy said was probably when she was in a state of shock, and though I know neither of us could have gone at the time, with her so upset and all, never once in the intervening years did I try to keep in touch with my wee sister, get to know her husband and children, or even try to help Mammy cope with her loss and deal with her stiff-necked resentment.

'You coming here has shown up my shortcomings all right. The tragedy of losing your parents might still have happened, but by then you might have known me better, maybe already have been here on holiday. Mammy isn't too great with children anyway, and never has been, but without really trying she could have given you a far warmer welcome than she has so far.'

'Yeah,' Molly said. 'I agree with everything you say and, knowing the kind of woman your mother is, how are you going to get my grandmother to allow me to go to Cathy McEvoy's on Sunday? If I thought it was actually going to happen then I would be excited, for all it's days away, but every time I think of it my stomach curls up in knots because I know she will try to spoil it.'

Tom smiled. 'Leave Mammy to me and you get just as excited as you want to be.'

'That, of course, is if I survive till then,' Molly said grimly, handing her uncle another bucket of milk.

'There is that to consider too,' Tom commented laconically.

When Molly opened her eyes the next morning, she thought her survival might be in doubt, for there wasn't one bit of her that didn't hurt in some way. When she got to her feet her taut muscles throbbed in protest but she suppressed the groan she would have liked to give voice to, lest her grandmother hear it. She dressed with difficulty and then went stiffly from the room to see to the fire.

When the milking was done and the breakfast eaten and tidied away, Biddy said, 'Now I hope that you are feeling good and strong, Molly, for you have to churn for butter today.'

Molly just stared at her and so did Tom. The butter was churned on Thursdays. Molly's arms still ached from the washing and ironing of the day before, and her body recoiled at the thought of more pain to come. However, when she looked into the old woman's eyes and saw that she was enjoying her discomfort, she straightened her aching back, met her gaze levelly and silenced Tom, about to protest, with a small shake of her head.

Within minutes of starting the churning, the stabbing pains began, running from both shoulders to her fingertips. The ache between her shoulder blades grew in intensity, as did the one in her back, until even her legs were trembling with the effort of keeping going, up and down, up and down. Molly wanted to lie on the floor and weep, but she bit her lip to prevent any cry escaping her.

Biddy watched her, expecting that any minute she would say that she couldn't go on, beg to be excused. Then she would really make her suffer.

Molly herself didn't know what kept her upright and her arms moving as if of their own volition, but she went on and on, like some sort of machine.

When, in the end, Biddy tried to take the paddle from Molly she had to almost wrest it from her fists closed over it, and then Molly's pain-glazed eyes met those of her grandmother before she sank to the floor in a faint, just as Tom came in the door.

Concern for his niece threw caution to the wind as he

fixed his mother with a glare, demanding, 'What have you done with her now, you malicious old witch?' He crossed the room as he spoke and lifted Molly into his arms with ease.

'Kindly don't speak to me in that way,' Biddy said. 'And for your information, I did nothing to her. I had just taken the paddle from her when she collapsed.'

'When you tried to work her half to death, you mean?' Tom said contemptuously, kicking open Molly's bedroom door as he spoke. He laid her unconscious form on the bed, where he took her small, limp hands between his own, rough and calloused though they were, and rubbed at them solicitously as he said, 'Well, there is to be no more of it – not today at least, and not at all until she is fully recovered.'

'And who, pray, is to do all the jobs around here?'

'I should imagine the same one who did them before,' Tom said. 'Tell me, Mammy, when did you lose the power of your arms and legs, because since Molly first came here you have scarcely lifted a finger?'

'I can't do everything. I'm not as young as I was,' Biddy said.

'I know that,' Tom said. 'And I'm sure Molly would help you, but not this way, working her into the ground.'

Biddy was incensed, but at that moment Molly eyelids fluttered open. She was at first alarmed to find herself in bed in the middle of the day and her uncle and grandmother standing over her. She cast her mind back to the events of that morning, but could only remember the interminable churning.

'What happened?'

'You fainted,' Tom told her. 'From exhaustion, I would think, and so I want you to stay in bed today at least.'

Molly knew, though, who wielded the power in that house and so her eyes sought her grandmother's, who after a nudge from her son, said grudgingly, 'I suppose the one day would do no harm, as long as you don't make a habit of it.'

Inside, Biddy's mind was saying something entirely different. It was not to be borne, her son telling her what

99

to do and criticising the way she was bringing up her grand-daughter, when all she was doing was stopping her going the same way as her mother.

Molly felt quite strange when she woke the next morning and more rested than she had ever been since she had arrived at the house. She slipped quickly out of bed. Tom had already gone out to attend to the cows and, unusually, her grandmother was up. Immediately Molly felt flutters of nervousness begin in her stomach.

'So,' said Biddy sarcastically, 'you have decided to arise from your bed today, have you?'

'As you can see,' Molly said, and saw Biddy nip her lip in annoyance at the way she had spoken to her.

'Don't think that you can get away with that tack every few days either,' Biddy said. 'I will not have you slacking.'

Molly stood up from the fire she had been poking into life and feeding with turf and said, 'I have seldom had a free moment since I stepped over the threshold of this house. I do my share and more.'

The blow knocked her against the fireplace and this was followed by a hefty slap across her face as Biddy hissed, 'You watch how you talk to me, girl. Your uncle is not here to fight your corner now, and I will knock that temper out of you if it is the last thing I do.'

Without a word, Molly hung the kettle above the fire and walked across the room. Once there, she looked back at her grandmother and said, 'Pity the same thing wasn't done to you,' before escaping to the cowshed.

Her grandmother didn't follow her and Molly imagined that was partly because Tom would be there. She knew, though, that Biddy wouldn't forget and that she herself would probably pay dearly for that last remark. But she didn't care. It had been worth it to see the look on her grandmother's face.

She knew too that she couldn't go running to Tom with a list of complaints every five minutes. For one thing, he would hate it, and for another, she could guess then her grandmother's punishment, when Tom wasn't around, would probably be worse, for she would be hitting out at him too, through her. So she said nothing about the altercation that morning and was glad the cowshed was dim enough to hide her cheek, which was stinging so much she knew it would be scarlet.

Molly's assessment was right: the more Tom attempted to stick up for her, the greater was Biddy's anger and subsequent retribution when they were alone.

But by Friday evening something else was playing on Molly's mind, and that was the fact that she had had no reply to either of the letters she had sent. She never saw the postman for he always came when she and Tom were in the cowshed and sometimes when they went in for breakfast the post would be there on the table. It was mainly catalogues for feed stuffs or farm equipment, and Molly had also seen a letter from Joe in America.

'I just can't understand it,' she said to Tom as they were at the evening milking. 'I mean, they'd know I would be anxious for news of them. I expected an answer by return.'

Tom agreed. 'I did think they would have written back by now,' he said. 'I caught the post last Saturday so, all things being equal, they would have received the letters on Monday, Tuesday at the latest. But then maybe we are being too hasty. Maybe they will come tomorrow, or early next week. Have you asked Mammy if any post has come for you?'

'I speak to your mother as little as possible, Uncle Tom. You know that,' Molly said. 'Anyway, if she had any letters for me, wouldn't she have told me, given them to me?'

The silence was telling and Molly burst out, 'You think she might have kept them from me, don't you? Is she really capable of that?'

'You can bet that if my mother has withheld your letters she will have convinced herself it was for your own good,' Tom said. 'The only way to clear it up is to ask her.'

Molly decided that she had to bite the bullet, so to speak,

so as soon as they were in the door she said to her grand-mother, 'Has there been any letters come for me?'

Biddy remembered the two letters she had thrown into the fire the day before, but still said, 'Why should there be letters for you?'

Molly stared at her. 'Well, because I thought Granddad at least would want to know how I am. Anyway, I asked him questions in my letter about Kevin.'

'Your letter,' Biddy repeated. It was obvious that she hadn't known about this, but Molly hadn't been secretive on purpose. It was just that she had as little to do with Biddy as possible and she hadn't thought to mention it. 'When, pray, did you write a letter?' Biddy demanded.

'Nearly a week ago,' Molly said. She thought her grand-mother was looking at her strangely, but then she often did. Tom, however, had seen that expression before. He knew Molly was heading straight into trouble, and there was not a thing he could do about it. Molly went blithely on, 'Granddad packed the paper and envelopes and all in my case.'

'And how did you post it?'

'Oh, Uncle Tom did that for me.'

Biddy's cold and accusing eyes slid towards Tom and it was when he said in a bumbling apologetic voice, 'Ah, Mammy, sure I saw no harm in it,' that Molly felt the first feelings of unease.'

'No harm in the child writing to heathens?'

'Heathens!' Molly cried. 'Who are you calling heathens?'

'Don't you take that tone with me, my girl,' Biddy snapped. 'You shouldn't have to ask who the heathen is? Your grand-father, for one.'

Molly was incensed. 'Don't be stupid!' she cried. 'My granddad is not a heathen.'

The slap knocked her off her feet and Biddy said to Tom, 'Fetch the stick.'

'Ah, no, Mammy,' Tom said. 'Sure, Molly didn't mean to say you were stupid.'

Molly's blood was up, however, and she was too angry to be in any way conciliatory. 'Oh yes I did mean it,' she cried. 'I meant every bloody word.'

Biddy hauled her to her feet and shook her as if she was a rag doll, then dragged her across to the fireplace where the stick was. Molly was writhing and screaming like a stuck pig, especially when the stick sliced through the air and made contact with her skin. She braced herself for another blow, but it didn't happen, for Tom not only wrenched the stick from his mother's hand, he also broke it in two and threw the pieces into the fire.

'I had more than enough of that bloody thing when I was growing up,' he growled out. 'It's past time it was burned.'

Biddy was incensed, but she said sneeringly, 'I can always get another. Besides,' she added, 'there is more than one way of killing a cat than by drowning it.'

'Mammy, for heaven's sake . . .'

'I will not tolerate the way Molly spoke to me,' Biddy declared.

Tom had pulled Molly away from his mother and she faced her, anger overriding any fear she might have as she said, 'Well, I won't tolerate you saying horrible things about my family. My father and grandfather and even Hilda have more kindness and goodness in their little fingers than you have in your entire body, and as for my mother—'

'Don't dare speak your mother's name.'

'I will if I like because she was wonderful, and I am glad I had thirteen years of her love before she died, and I will say so to anyone who asks me,' Molly said firmly, adding goadingly, 'So what are you going to do about that? Cut out my tongue?'

'You see,' Biddy said to Tom. 'To spare the rod is to spoil the child, and this wayward streak Molly has in her is the result of too little chastisement in her formative years.'

Tom didn't answer his mother. He had spent a lifetime studying her and scrutinising her face and now he suddenly

103

knew that letters had arrived for Molly. He said, 'All this anger has come about because Molly asked you a simple question. I think letters did come for Molly and I want you to tell me what you did with them.'

'Yes, they came all right,' Biddy said defiantly, 'and they went on the fire. And if any more come, they will receive the same treatment.'

Molly stared at her, almost refusing to believe that the woman in front of her had done such an horrendously cruel thing. She yearned for news of those she had left behind and tears rained down her cheeks as she burst out, 'How dare you burn letters addressed to me? You have no right.'

'You forget,' Biddy said. 'I have every right.'

'Mammy, surely to God you will see—' Tom began.

'Your opinion wasn't asked for and is not needed,' Biddy snapped. 'Kindly keep out of this altogether.'

'But, Mammy—'

'Is your hearing affected, Tom?' Biddy said, her words as brittle and cold as drops of ice. 'I said this is not your concern and that is exactly what I meant.'

Molly saw her uncle almost flinch and fall silent, beaten by his mother's iron will, which had dominated him since he was a child, and knew that she was on her own. She brushed the tears from her cheeks with her fingers and willed her voice not to shake as she faced her grandmother. 'You must allow me to write and receive letters. These are the people that are dearest in the whole world to me.'

Biddy looked at her implacably and said, 'That makes them even more dangerous.'

'Dangerous!'

'These are the people whose influence I removed you from,' Biddy said. 'For the good of your immortal soul I cannot allow you to communicate with them.'

'D'you think they might contaminate me or something?' Molly remarked sarcastically.

Biddy nodded her head sagely. 'We cannot run that risk.

However,' she went on, 'I don't think we will have many more letters arriving, for I have written to your grandfather and that neighbour you seem so fond of, telling them there is to be no further correspondence with you. I have the letters already written for posting tomorrow.'

Molly thought how comforted she would have been by reading her grandfather's words, reaching across the Irish Sea to the granddaughter he had had to relinquish. Maybe she might even get the odd wee note from Kevin when he had been at school a little longer, and she was in great need of the homespun wisdom and humour of Hilda. She knew that now her life would be harder and lonelier than ever.

EIGHT

With the business of the letters, Tom felt he had failed Molly, yet he knew there was no way on God's earth that he could have changed his mother's mind in the slightest degree. But one thing he was determined on was that she would keep her date with the McEvoys. So the next day in Buncrana, without saying a word to Molly about it and also unbeknownst to his mother, Tom had had a word with the postmistress.

Knowing her to be a kindly woman and one who could hold her own counsel if she had to, he put her wise to the situation at the house. Nellie wasn't surprised because she had had Biddy in already that morning with the two letters for Birmingham and she had told Nellie straight out that she had written to Molly's grandfather and the neighbour Hilda, saying that they were to have no further contact with Molly. Nellie thought it extremely harsh, but when she tried saying this, Biddy nearly bit her head off.

'I can't have her consorting in any way with those heathens in Birmingham. I would have thought you, as a good Catholic, would understand that.'

'But they are the people she has always known, Biddy, and she is so alone in the world. Surely to God a few letters would do no harm.'

'I will be the judge of that,' Biddy had snapped. 'The girl is in my care and I will do as I see fit.'

Nellie had said nothing further, knowing it anyway to be futile, but took the two letters from Biddy with a heavy heart and so, as she listened to Tom, she wasn't unduly surprised.

'I thought there was something not quite right when I saw the harsh way she treated her outside the church last Sunday,' she said. 'We were all looking forward to meeting Nuala's daughter and my, when I saw how she resembled her mother, it was like taking a step back in time. And then the priest came over to greet them and your mother spouted it out about Molly's father. I could hardly believe it, and you could see young Molly was upset. Everyone was on about it after.'

It was the first Tom knew of any of this. 'What about her father?'

Nellie told him what his mother had said. Tom was angered and understood Molly vowing that she would not let anyone denigrate her parents and go unchallenged ever again. He burst out, 'Do you know, I don't give a tinker's cuss whether the man was a Catholic, a Protestant or a Hindu. He was a good father to Molly and that, as far as I am concerned, is that. You should hear how she talks of him – of all of them. It would break your heart, especially as she is so brave, yet her loss was surely a grievous one. And it must have made things worse to be then ripped away from all that was familiar to her, including her grandfather, who seemed such an important part of her life.'

'It must be hard for her right enough,' Nellie said. 'I would say a little understanding and compassion wouldn't come amiss.'

'Nor would I,' Tom said.

'Molly needs time away from the farm,' Nellie said. 'She needs to meet and mix with people her own age and that was one of the reasons I asked her to tea at our house. You don't think your mother might forbid her to come?'

'Oh, yes I do,' Tom said. 'But I have been puzzling over

a way to get around this and I think if you were to ask her in front of people before church in the morning, as if you had just thought of it, and get the priest to endorse it, as it were, we just might get my bloody mother to agree and without too much of a row and ruction.'

'God, Tom, how did you ever get a mother like Biddy?' Nellie asked with a laugh. 'You are one of the nicest and most nonconfrontational people I know.'

'Even the mildest worm can turn,' Tom said. 'And even if I won't do it for me, maybe I will for Molly.'

'Well, that is a sight I would like to see anyway,' Nellie said. 'But don't you worry about this Sunday. I will prime the neighbours as well as the priest, and between the lot of us we will have Biddy eating out of the palm of our hands.'

'Hah, I doubt that very much.'

'And so do I really,' Nellie said with a grim little smile. 'However, for Molly's sake we will do our best.'

As soon as they reached the church that Sunday morning, Cathy pounced on Molly and spirited her away, saying she wanted to introduce her to her friends. And Molly went without asking, or even giving Biddy a look of any sort. Biddy could see her now in a group of young girls like herself, laughing and talking fifteen to the dozen as if she had known them all her life, and she vowed she would make Molly pay for that act of wilfulness when she got her home.

Then to cap it all, Nellie was by her elbow, asking if Molly could come to tea with them that evening. Before Biddy had a chance to say that she couldn't, everyone else took up the conversation, saying what a great idea and how grand it was for young people, like, to be together. Even the priest joined in.

'Molly has duties at home,' Biddy said through tight lips.

'Ah, but less on Sunday, surely?' said the priest. 'The Good Lord did not labour on the seventh day, on the Sabbath. It's not just for resting either, particularly for the young. It is for doing things you can't do on the other days of the week, like taking a walk perhaps, or visiting a friend. I can't think of anything nicer than Molly calling for tea with Cathy McEvoy.'

Biddy could think of a host of things she would rather have the girl do, but she felt as if she was caught in a corner. She would have said she hadn't a whit of interest in the townspeople and their opinion mattered not a jot to her, but Nellie McEvoy was the postmistress and that position meant power. It wouldn't do to make a real enemy of her. And then, of course, there was the priest. Biddy knew that this time, anyway, she would have to let the bloody girl go to tea with Nellie and her family, and she would wish her joy of it because if she had her way it would be for the last time.

However, Biddy was no fool. She knew that the fiasco had been engineered and could have an educated guess as to who was behind it too: the son she had once thought she could count on. The thought that she might be losing her influence over Tom put her in a filthy temper, and so she scowled her way through the Mass, and once it was over, she scurried from the place, pushing Molly in front of her and calling for Tom to hurry up. She looked neither to the right nor to the left and addressed no one as they made their way home. That gave the townsfolk something else to discuss over their dinner.

Tom and Molly had to put up with Biddy's ill humour all day. Her nagging and complaining reached new heights and Molly got more than one unwarranted slap. But she didn't care, not that day, when, with the dinner eaten and the dishes washed and put away, she took up her coat. Tom whistled to Skip and Fly as they crossed the cobbled yard, and together they walked across the fields to Buncrana and Cathy's place above the post office.

'I'm so glad that you could come,' Cathy said.

'And me,' Molly said fervently. 'I had my doubts I'd be let when your mother asked me last week.'

109

'I know,' Cathy said, and she giggled. 'I think Mammy and your uncle hatched something between them yesterday. I was going to go into the post office and saw them with their heads together. I couldn't hear what they were saying and all, but then this morning, as we set off for Mass, Mammy said for me to get you away from your grandmother with some excuse. Well, that was easy because all the other girls wanted to meet you. I tell you, Molly, you have been the subject of many of our conversations. I thought you would be joining us at the school, tell you the truth.'

'I would rather be at school any day in comparison to the drudge I am fast turning into,' Molly told Cathy firmly. 'Anyway,' she added, 'I should be there. I'm not fourteen and won't be until February.'

'Then why . . . ?'

'My grandmother said I had enough book-learning and that more of it would not fit me any better for life on the farm.'

'And you would rather be at school?'

'Much rather.'

'I can't wait to leave.'

'Yeah, but what are you leaving to?' Molly said. 'Your mother runs the shop and post office so I suppose there will be some employment for you?'

'Oh, aye,' Cathy said. 'It's what she wants for me, now I am the only one left. I have two sisters and two brothers, but they have all left home now and are, anyway, much older than me. Really, it was like being an only child in many ways.'

'It was the other way round in our house,' Molly said. 'I am eight years older than my brother, and yet my parents, particularly my mother, made us both feel very special in different ways.'

There was silence in the room for a few moments and Molly felt the changed atmosphere and said a little apprehensively, 'What's up? What did I say that was so wrong?'

'Nothing,' Cathy said. 'I mean, look, Molly, I was warned not to say one word about your mother and you just came out with it so natural.'

'I suppose you were told that in case it would upset me?' Molly said.

'Aye, that's what Mammy said.'

Molly thought for a second or two and then said, 'You know, I think that it is far better to talk about my parents, even if it does make me a little sad. Not talking about them at all makes it seem as if they really didn't exist and they very much did.'

'I just can't imagine how you have coped with it all.'

'Don't even try,' Molly advised. 'It is really so very painful, but I would rather talk of the things we did when they were alive than how and when they died.'

'Right,' Cathy said. 'You are absolutely right, and we won't go down that road unless you want to.'

Molly was surprised, when Nellie called both girls down for their tea, to find it was a quarter-past five. Never had time passed so quickly. She wished that they could have eaten their tea in the very comfortable bedroom where she could have relaxed properly with Cathy. Although she knew Nellie to be kindly to invite her to tea, she was still nervous of sitting up to a meal with her and Cathy's father, Jack, whom she had only glimpsed at Mass.

She was worrying unduly, though, because both adults went out of their way to make Molly feel at home and more than welcome. They were like chalk and cheese to look at, Molly noted, for while Nellie was a thin and neat little woman, with eyes the same brown as her daughter's and the same shape to her mouth, and her grey hair caught up in a bun, her husband was a bear of a man. He was about as tall as Molly's uncle, but much broader, from his barrel

111

chest to his more than ample stomach. His face was red, his eyes blue, and the hair that he had left on his head light brown.

He was constantly urging Molly to 'eat up', and offering her plate after plate of delicacies from the beautifully made sandwiches to the cakes and scones.

'Mostly shop bought, I am afraid,' Nellie said apologetically. 'I am too busy with the shop to bake as well.'

Molly didn't care. She seldom had food so fine and she tucked in with relish.

'That's the way, young Molly,' said Jack approvingly. 'I love to see a girl with an appetite.'

'If we all ate enough to please you, Daddy, we'd be the size of a house,' Cathy said.

Jack's eyes twinkled as he gazed at his daughter. 'Not at all, at all,' he said. 'Molly at least knows that the only thing to do with good food is eat it.'

Molly immediately wondered if she had eaten too much, been greedy. Nellie noticed her slight hesitation and urged, 'You eat away, Molly. Nothing vexes a woman more than preparing food that people just pick at.'

Cathy hooted with laughter. 'No danger of that here, Mammy. Anything anyone leaves is eaten by Daddy, shown clearly by his girth.'

'You cheeky young rip,' Jack said, but there was no menace in his voice, even when he added, 'You are not too old for a good hiding, you know.'

'Oh, that would be the day,' Nellie said. 'You have never laid a hand on any of them, even the lads, who could sometimes have done with a father's hand. All the chastising was left to me.'

'I am too big a man and my hands too large and rough to be hitting weans, sure,' Jack said. 'And you must have done the job right, for the children made a fine turn-out, the boys too.'

'Even me?' Cathy asked impishly.

112

'No,' Jack said. 'Not you, for you are the worst of the lot.' And he winked at Molly as he went on, 'Completely ungovernable. Still, there is usually one bad apple in every barrel.'

'Cheek!' spluttered Cathy indignantly, while the laughter swelled around the table and Molly thought that the love apparent between Cathy and her parents reminded her of how it had been in her own home. She refused to let herself be sad and spoil this happy atmosphere, but Nellie had seen the shadow flit across Molly's eyes and could guess her thoughts. 'I think that we should have a bit of decorum when we sit down to a meal, particularly on a Sunday,' she said, with a smile for Molly. 'I would say that Molly is shocked to the core, are you not, child?'

Molly could see by the smile on Nellie's face that she didn't believe this for a moment, and without a trace of self-pity, she said, 'No, not at all. I like it. It reminds me of some of the meals we used to have at home.'

There was a sudden silence and before it could become uncomfortable, Nellie said gently, 'Can I say, my dear, if it won't upset you too much, how like your mother you are?'

'I know,' Molly said happily. 'And I am glad. My little brother looks more like my dad did. And no, it doesn't upset me to talk about them. I don't want anyone to think that there were so many things they couldn't say to me that it was safest to say nothing at all, or skirt around the subject as if they were treading on eggshells.'

'Well said, Molly,' Jack said, clapping her on the back. 'I think that that is the very best way to look at things. Now can I tempt you to take another cake?'

Molly shook her head. 'I couldn't eat another thing. I am almost too full to move already.'

'I hope you're not,' Cathy said. 'I want to show you the town.'

'Oh,' Molly said, 'I would like that, but shouldn't we help with washing-up, first?'

113

'Not today,' Nellie said firmly as she began collecting the plates. 'Maybe when you are a regular visitor here I will let you put your hands in the sink or wield a tea towel, but today make use of the fine evening.'

'And try and work off that lovely tea.'

'That as well,' Nellie said with a smile.

The post office was situated almost at the top of a hill on a wide and straight street with the hills visible in the distance ahead. It was as they walked to the top of it that Molly saw the cinema and she exclaimed in amazement. It was a sizeable cinema too, made of honey-coloured brick with arched doors at the entrance.

'Why the shock?' Cathy asked. 'I'm sure they have cinemas in Birmingham.'

Molly laughed. 'Yes, of course. The Palace cinema was just up the road, on the High Street of Erdington and there were any number if you went as far as the town, and music halls and theatres, but somehow I thought—'

'That backwards old Ireland couldn't have such a thing; that we share our hovel with the pigs.'

'Cathy, I never said such a thing, or thought it either.'

'Good job too,' Cathy said with a grin and added, 'Some people do, you know – English people, of course. Actually, Buncrana is a thriving little place. We have factories and mills and all sorts. In fact,' she went on, pointing down the other side of the hill to the large grey building at the bottom of it, 'that's the mill my father works at. We'll go and take a look, if you like.'

'Oh,' Molly said as the two of them began walking down the hill past the numerous little cottages that opened on the street, 'he doesn't work in the post office then?'

Cathy laughed. 'Daddy would be no great shakes in the post office; more a liability, I think, for he can't reckon up to save his life. Mammy is going to train me up for it as soon as I am sixteen. Till then, once I leave school for good,

114

I will man the sweet counter and deal with the papers and cigarettes. Mammy has someone to do this now but she is leaving to get married next year, which couldn't be better timing.'

As they walked, they met others out, some standing on their doorsteps taking the air like themselves, or groups of children playing, and most had a cheery wave or greeting for the two girls. Molly felt happiness suddenly fill her being. It was the very first time she had felt this way since that dreadful day that the policeman had come to the door, and she gave a sudden sigh.

'What's up?'

'Nothing, nothing at all,' Molly said. 'That's why I am sighing.'

Cathy smiled at her and then said, without rancour, 'You're crackers, that's what. Clean balmy.'

Molly nodded sagely. 'I know it,' she said. 'It isn't so bad if a person is aware of it.'

Cathy began to laugh, and her giggle was so infectious that Molly, who had once wondered if she would ever laugh again, joined in.

'Did you see the faces of those we passed?' Cathy said, when their hilarity was spent a little and she was dabbing at her damp eyes with a handkerchief. 'If we are not careful, they will have the men with the white coats carry us away to the mental home in Derry.'

'Rubbish,' Molly said with a grin. 'It made them smile too. Laughter is like that.'

'My mammy always says it's good for a body,' Cathy agreed. 'She says she had read somewhere that if you have a good belly laugh it can lengthen your life.'

'Goodness!' Molly said. 'Can it really? I wonder by how much.'

'Maybe we should have a good laugh every five minutes and live for ever,' Cathy suggested.

'Now, who is the fool?' Molly smiled.

Cathy didn't have time to answer this, for then they passed under the bridge carrying the railway line and there was the mill in front of them.

It was built on three levels, the largest of these having a tall, high chimney reaching to the sky. It didn't look a very inspiring place to work in, but Molly reminded herself there were probably worse places in Birmingham, and she supposed that if it was work there or starve to death, one place was as inviting as the next.

'Awful, isn't it?' Cathy said. 'Daddy always said he didn't want any of his children near the place but my brothers, John and Pat, had to work there for a bit. Then the place went afire four years ago. No one knew for a while if anyone was going to bother rebuilding it, and anyway, the boys didn't stay around to find out. They both took the emigrant ship to America from Moville and Daddy said he didn't blame them. They are in a place called Detroit now and, according to their letters anyway, have good jobs there in the motor industry.'

'Didn't your mother mind them going so far away?' Molly asked.

Cathy nodded. 'It was worse, of course, when my sisters left just a year after the boys to work in hotels in England. They say it is great, the hotel provides the uniforms, a place to stay and all their food, and all they need to do with their money is spend it, though they do send some home, and the boys too. It's not the same, though. It isn't that Mammy isn't grateful for the money, she just says it's hard to scrimp and scrape, working fingers to the bone raising children only for them to leave as soon as possible. She was married at seventeen, you know?'

'Was she?' Molly said. 'It seems awfully young.'

'I'll say,' Cathy said with feeling. 'I certainly don't want to go down that road at such an early age. My sisters don't either. They say they are having too good a time to tie themselves down with a husband and weans, and that is what happens, of course, as soon as you are married. I mean,

116

Mammy had my eldest brother, John, just ten months after they were married and he's twenty-six now.' She smiled and went on, 'Mammy was glad that it was ten months. She always said the most stupid people in all the towns and villages of Ireland have the ability to count to nine.'

'You can say that again,' Molly said, for the girls were well aware that to have a baby outside marriage was just about the worst thing a girl could do, and to *have* to get married was only slightly better.

'Anyway, Mammy hates my sisters writing so glowingly about their lives in England,' Cathy continued. 'She's thinking, I suppose, that I might be tempted to join them.'

'And are you?'

'Not at the moment, certainly,' Cathy said. 'I like it here and I am set to have a good solid job helping to run the post office and probably going to take it on in the end. I don't want to throw that in the air now, do I?'

'Only if you were stupid,' Molly said. 'I really envy you to have your life so mapped out. But I will not bide here for ever. I will leave here as soon as I am old enough and be reunited with my young brother. I really miss him.'

'Well, there in front of us is the railway station you will have to start from,' Cathy said. 'But you probably know that already.'

'No. Why would I know that?'

'Didn't you come in there on your way from Derry?'

'No,' Molly told her. 'Uncle Tom brought us home in the cart.'

'Oh, I didn't know that,' Cathy said. 'It was probably just as well, for Derry is only six miles away from here, and the trains are far from reliable. They carry freight as well, with the passengers in a sort of brake thing behind them, and of course stop at every station to unload.'

'I would have travelled in anything at that time,' Molly said. 'I was so worn out. We had been on and off trains and boats since early morning.'

'Were you sick on the crossing?'

'I'll say.' Molly added with a grin, 'It was a bit of a waste too, because we had both had breakfast on the boat and we brought it back just minutes later and everything else that had the nerve to lie in our stomachs.'

Cathy nodded, 'My sisters said they were the same, and my younger brother, Pat, was so ill, John thought he would die on him. I bet he was more than glad to reach land, because they were at sea for ten days.'

Molly gave a shiver. 'Poor thing,' she said. 'I had three and a half hours of it and that was enough.'

'I bet,' Cathy said with feeling. 'Well, this now is the station. The roof looks bigger than the building. And I know where you get the tickets, because I came to see my sisters off.' She led the way to a two-storeyed, flat-roofed building housing the ticket office, adjoining the main body of the station, and then past that and on to the platform. Molly followed and looked about her with interest. She tried to imagine the time when she would board a train from there to take her home.

'What's that mass of green in front?' she asked Cathy.

'The golf course.'

'Golly, don't they lose their golf balls in the water ever?' Molly asked, because she could see the glistening waters of the Swilly just beyond the course.

Cathy smiled. 'Probably lots of times.'

'And what's beyond that on the other side of the Lough?'

'Rathmullen,' Cathy said, pointing. 'And just a bit further up, Glenvar. Come on now,' she urged. 'I want to show you the harbour where the fishing boats come in.'

Molly was impressed by the harbour and all the fishing vessels vying for space at the dockside, and she was charmed by the Lough, which she thought was just as good as the stories she had heard about the seaside because, just along from the harbour, she could plainly see large rocks and sandy beaches.

Cathy hailed two friends, Bernadette McCauley and Maeve Gilligan, whom Molly had met at Mass. Then Cathy pointed out the diving board and chute on the far side of the Lough. 'My brothers learned to swim there,' she said. 'Most boys did, but of course we girls were forbidden to go near.'

'Why?'

'Well, some boys swam with no clothes on,' Cathy said. 'Not my brothers – Mammy wouldn't let them – but some, and that is not a sight I would like to see.'

'Oh, I don't know,' murmured Bernadette. 'That surely would depend on the boy.'

'Bernadette McCauley,' exclaimed Cathy and Maeve together.

Cathy went on, 'Confession for you, my girl. Impure thoughts and all.'

Bernadette just laughed. 'I am telling no priest the thoughts that pop up in my head,' she declared. 'The poor man couldn't stand the excitement. God, I'm sure his hair would stand on end.'

The girls exploded with laughter at the image conjured up, and then suddenly Cathy noticed how low the sun was. She said to Molly, 'We'd best get on if you want to see Swan Park, for your uncle will be waiting for you,' and with a wave to the other two girls, she led the way.

'This sort of goes back the way we came,' Cathy said. And we will go a little bit along here to show you and then make for home. All right?'

'You bet.'

'We have to go across Castle Bridge, which you can see in front of you now. It spans the Crana River where the town got its name from.'

'And what's that wall on the other side of it?'

'Part of the grounds of the castle, which you will see once you are on the bridge.'

As they stepped off the bridge, to the side was a crumbling

tower, which Cathy said was called O'Dohery's Keep, dating back to the Middle Ages, but the building that Cathy had referred to as a castle was just a three-storeyed, slate-roofed house. It was made of brick and had a protruding wing on either end of it. Wide steps led up to the front door with ornamental railings either side, but it still wasn't Molly's idea of a castle.

'Well, I know,' Cathy said. 'Not officially, it isn't. I meant it was only built in seventeen something, but it's a sort of custom in Ireland to call large houses castles. Now, if we take this pathway through here, then we can get to the Swilly and there is a walkway that we can take.'

The path was overhung with trees, heavy with leaves and blossom, and the hedgerows alive with flowers. Molly felt very much at peace with the world as she followed behind her new friend. And then the Lough was before them, shimmering like gold in the waning sun.

'Let's see if we can get as far as the fort before we turn back,' Cathy suggested. 'We can do it if we put a spurt on.'

They hurried on, greeting those they met, but not stopping to chat, and in no time at all they had passed the boathouse where the lifeboat was kept, and then the fort.

'Built in Napoleonic times,' Cathy said as they surveyed the massive structure. But they had no time to linger, for the sun had sunk lower still. They retraced their steps and were soon on Main Street again.

'Plenty of pubs along here,' Cathy said as they climbed the hill, 'and they have all been here as long as I can remember, so they obviously do good enough trade, but then,' she said, wrinkling her nose, 'as Mammy said, any number of pubs would do good trade in Ireland, the only business where you would be sure to make money.' And then she laughed and said, 'Daddy goes to the pub sometimes – Grant's Bar usually – and he says he goes not as often as he would like, yet far too often in my mother's opinion.'

120

'Do they argue over it?'

'No,' Cathy said with a smile. 'It's just an ongoing theme, you know? Anyway, here we are home again and I hope your uncle isn't cross if he has had to wait ages.'

'Oh, Uncle Tom won't be cross,' Molly said with confidence. 'He never is.'

Tom and Jack were sitting chatting and drinking deeply of the malt whiskey that Jack had produced. Molly had never seen her uncle drink anything but tea, water or buttermilk before. She had thought maybe he didn't care for alcohol and she asked him about it as they walked back together.

'Oh, I suppose I like a beer as well as the next man, and I love a drop of whiskey now and then,' Tom said after a minute or two's thought. 'But it all costs money, and apart from that, when I have done a full day's work, I am not up to trudging over to Buncrana, especially when I have to get up early for the milking. Sunday is the one day when I take things easier. What about you? What sort of a day have you had?'

'Wonderful,' Molly said, and even in the dusk, Tom saw a light behind Molly's eyes that he had never seen before and he vowed he would do all in his power to keep it there at least once a week. 'I really like Cathy,' Molly told her uncle, 'and I wish I had been let go to school.'

'So do I,' Tom said. 'And Mammy would be in big trouble if the authorities got to hear about it. I can't do anything about that, but you can still be friends with Cathy. How would you like to go to the McEvoys' for tea next Sunday too?'

'I would love it if I am asked, but your mother—'

'Leave my mother to me,' Tom said. 'Nellie and Jack said you are welcome every Sunday evening. You made quite an impression, and I will come over to fetch you home.'

'There is no need,' Molly said.

'There's every need,' Tom maintained. 'Anyway, the walk

will do me no harm at all and give me the chance to sink a few pints with Jack in Grant's Bar while I wait for you. It will do me good as well to get out and meet people. A person can be too much on their own and this will be a fine opportunity for the pair of us.'

NINE

The following day at tea-time, Tom saw that Molly was exhausted. He had done what he could to help her that wash day, hanging around the cottage, doing jobs near at hand so that he could help bring any water she needed from the well. Later, he had helped her turn the mangle and put up with his mother's sneering comments that he was turning into a sissy, doing women's work.

He knew, however, that his mother had been particularly vicious that day and rightly guessed that it was her attitude that had worn Molly down so badly. While Molly had sort of expected some backlash for her visit to Cathy, she soon found that expecting such censure and dealing with it all day were two very different things.

In the end, while they were eating the last bowl of porridge before bed, she suddenly felt as if she had stood more than enough and she looked at her grandmother and asked candidly, 'Why are you always so horrid? I sort of expect you now to find fault with everything I do, but you have been worse than ever today.'

Biddy was astounded and outraged. She had never been questioned in this way before. 'How dare you?' she burst out. 'I have no need to explain myself to you, miss.'

Molly showed no fear, though her stomach was tied in knots. 'I need to know, if I am on the receiving end of it.

123

The point is, I can't see that I have done that much wrong today anyway.'

Tom hid his slight amusement as he watched his mother open and shut her mouth soundlessly for a few seconds, too stunned and taken unawares to make any sort of reply. He was absolutely astounded himself at Molly's temerity.

'Are you going to sit there like a deaf mute and let this brazen besom talk to me like this, Tom?' Biddy screeched, turning her malevolent eyes on her son. 'What manner of man are you at all?'

Listening to his mother's disdainful whine, it was suddenly clear to Tom why Molly could speak with such assurance and courage and that was because of the confidence she had in herself. He would guess that that confidence was gained by being loved and valued by her parents, while he, on the other hand, had been verbally and physically abused almost since he had drawn his first breath and so now he said, 'I am the manner of man that you made me, Mammy, and as for Molly, she has not been disrespectful to you in any way.'

'I will act as I see fit in my own house,' Biddy said mutinously. 'No one has the right to refute anything I say.'

'Dad used to say if everyone was able to do just as they liked, we would have something called anarchy and those who were more powerful or violent would rule over the others.'

'God, I wish I still had my stick,' Biddy ground out. 'You would find the sting of it this day.'

'That would just prove the point, though, wouldn't it?' Molly said.

'It's not right for a young girl to be speaking in such a way – and especially not to her elders and betters,' Biddy snapped. 'I only took you in because there was no one else suitable, but I dislike you intensely, and have done since the day we met.'

Molly shrugged. 'I honestly don't mind about that because,

124

as I said before we left Birmingham, I feel the same way about you.'

The slap knocked her from the stool and she lay on the stone floor. Tom was by her side in a moment. 'Mammy, I told you there is to be no more of this.'

Molly got to her feet and faced her grandmother, her gaze steadily, enraging the old woman further.

'You deserved that and more,' Biddy growled out.

'You can get away with that now because you are bigger and stronger than me, but it won't always be that way,' said Molly, glaring.

Biddy looked at the two ranged against her and deeply regretted bringing Molly to Ireland. She had thought she would easily break her spirit, but there was no sign of it so far, and Tom was taking her side at every turn.

'Tom,' she thundered, 'I will not tolerate this. Where is the respect you have always shown me in the past?'

'That wasn't respect, Mammy,' Tom said mildly. 'It was fear, and it gives me no pleasure to admit that. However, this is not about me, but Molly, and you may as well know here and now that Nellie McEvoy asked Molly to tea this Sunday as well and she has already accepted the invitation.'

Biddy glared at her son, hardly able to believe her ears. 'You take her part at your peril, Tom,' she said. 'For the girl is a born troublemaker and you can't see it.'

'How can you say that?' Molly cried. 'What have I done?'

'You have brought dissension to this house. That is what you have done, my girl,' Biddy shrieked.

Tom laughed. 'This was never a happy place, Mammy. All my life you shouted the orders and I jumped to it, but it was never a real home. Molly couldn't destroy what wasn't there in the first place.'

Molly wished she could tell her uncle to be quiet, for she knew her grandmother was storing all this in her head and it might come out in every blow she would administer her way at the earliest opportunity. And yet she couldn't totally regret the fact that Tom was beginning to stand up to his mother.

The next day, Molly lay in bed and faced what she had said to her grandmother the evening before. She didn't regret a single word, though she knew that, if anything, things might get worse for her because of it. She had valued her uncle's support, but she knew that defying his mother was an alien way for him to behave and she mentioned her concerns about this in the cowshed the following day.

'Every word you have just uttered is right,' Tom said. 'Neither of my brothers was as eager to please Mammy as I was. She seemed to strip me of any shred of self-confidence I had.'

'But now you are a grown man,' Molly said, 'and can take pride in yourself despite her.'

'D'you know, for a wee girl of thirteen, you speak very well,' Tom said, and added with the ghost of a smile, 'Argue well too. Were you good at the book-learning at school?'

'Pretty good,' Molly said. 'I was due to stay on until I was sixteen and matriculate. Daddy really would have liked me to go to university, but he wasn't pushy or anything. He just said we would take each stage as it came and see how well I did and also how far I wanted to go. I really enjoyed school.'

'That's where you should be,' Tom said.

'Maybe,' Molly agreed. 'But you know, Uncle Tom, there is so much I would like to change about the life I have now that staying on at school is just one more thing to resent your mother for. Crikey,' she added with a ghost of a smile, 'that list is so long now, it is like a roll of wallpaper.'

Tom laughed. 'You keep that outlook on life, young Molly, and you'll manage just fine, I think.'

'And what about you?'

'Don't you worry your pretty little head about me,' Tom said. 'I have managed this long and will cope, no doubt.'

'I can't help feeling that I have made life more difficult for you.'

Tom paused before saying. 'In a way, I suppose it was your fault that I said anything at all. Not that I am blaming you. I know I should have done something a lot earlier than I did. The point was, while it was just me she was having a go at, I didn't want to stir things up further and possibly make her worse. Then you arrived and Mammy was so unreasonable in her demands and expectations of you that she angered me. I knew I couldn't just sit there and let you take it all on your own.'

He grinned at Molly and went on, 'I had no idea then of the feisty little lady you were. You look so frail and slight, as if a puff of wind would blow you away. To tell you the absolute truth, you made me ashamed of myself when you stand and face Mammy and seem so unafraid.'

'That is just an act,' Molly admitted. 'I am scared as the next. Sometimes I'm surprised that she can't hear my heart banging against my ribs and my stomach is often tied in knots.'

'Well, you show no evidence of it,' Tom said admiringly. 'And now if you have no objection, we will go inside for breakfast before I collapse on the floor with starvation.'

Tom surprised everyone, not least Molly, the next Saturday by announcing that she was to accompany him and Biddy to Buncrana.

'Impossible!' Biddy said dismissively. 'Molly has a host of jobs to get through.'

'Well, they will have to wait.'

'Since when did you begin giving out the orders?'

'Not long,' Tom admitted with a sardonic grin. 'Some might say, better late than never.'

'Oh, don't start that again,' Biddy said. 'You always needed to be told. You're useless at taking responsibility for anything. You were the same, even as a boy.'

127

'So you say, Mammy,' Tom said mildly, 'but in this case I am telling you that Molly has to come with us to Buncrana today.'

'And why is that?'

'Because she needs wellingtons,' Tom said. 'I must start getting in the peat and Molly won't be able to help me unless she has suitable footwear.'

'Do you need her to help you?'

'It was you who said I needed help,' Tom pointed out. 'Anyway, it isn't only the peat you need wellingtons for on a farm. You may have saved money on her work clothes, though they would look better if they fitted her anywhere, but there isn't a pair of boots in the whole place small enough for her feet. And she is ruining the shoes she has – I noticed it just the other day – and soon she will have nothing suitable to put on her feet for Mass.'

Molly, listening to this interchange, wanted to hug herself with delight. She knew that though Biddy took pleasure in the fact that, weekdays, she was dressed worse than some of the beggars she had seen on the streets of Birmingham, when it came to Mass she had to be respectable. It was a matter of pride.

This was proved when Biddy said grudgingly, 'All right then, she needs a pair of wellingtons, but there is still no reason for her to come with us. We'll bring her a pair home.'

'You know that it is hard for one to buy footwear for another,' Tom said, 'even in the case of boots – maybe more especially in the way of boots. Molly will be wearing these most of the time that she is outside with me and I would be happier if they fit her well enough.'

And so Molly got to go to Buncrana. She fair rattled through the jobs beforehand. She sat in the back of the cart that early summer morning, with the sun just peeping over the hill to light up the pale blue sky with the clouds scudding across it, blown by the wafting breeze, and felt the beginning of happiness steal over her. She couldn't believe that she could be so excited over a simple shopping trip.

She had been used to a vast array of shops virtually on her doorstep in the shape of Erdington Village, and the city centre itself only a short tram journey away, and though she had been shown around Buncrana by Cathy, that had been on a Sunday when everywhere was shut up. What a different and vibrant place it was on Saturday. She drank in the noise, the chatter and laughter, and the shouts of the men on the market.

Molly helped Tom unload the surplus eggs she had collected, butter she had churned and the vegetables she had helped Tom lift from the ground. They stacked them on a trestle table in the Market Hall.

Then Tom said to his mother, 'All right, Mammy? I'll take Molly for those boots and then pop down to the harbour and see if there is any fish for sale there.'

He gave Biddy no chance to say anything to this, but swung Molly away and down the side street, and didn't miss the sigh of relief she gave at being away from his mother. Tom grinned at her and said, 'Damned if I don't feel the same way myself,' and Molly gave a little laugh.

The boots were bought and wrapped in no time at all, and then Tom set out to introduce Molly to some of the townsfolk, many of whom she had glimpsed at Mass. All seemed pleased to see her, and those who remembered her mother all remarked on the likeness between them, and added what a tragedy it was that she and her husband had been killed. It was said with such sincerity and sadness that tears would sometime prickle the back of Molly's eyes, but she didn't let them fall.

Any crying she did now was in the privacy of her own room. Not that she cried that much any more, but the aching loss of her parents was always there. She had little control over her dreams, though, and sometimes when she woke up, her pillow would be damp.

The townsfolk didn't see this, of course. They saw a wee strip of a girl, a beautiful girl too, with the large brown eyes and hair the colour of mahogany, so like her mother, coping stoically. That was one of the reasons the baker handed her a currant cake with a knowing little wink and then a little later, the greengrocer tossed her a red apple.

When she saw Cathy coming up the street with her father, Jack, Molly thought her happiness almost complete.

Cathy was just as delighted to see her, and after the families had greeted one another, Jack said to Tom, 'Let's leave the young ones to it. I'm away to the harbour to see what the catch is, and then I have a mind to sink a Guinness or two at the Lough Swilly Hotel and watch the world go round. How about it?'

Molly saw Tom hesitate and guessed that this wasn't something he normally did on Saturday mornings. Then he said, 'Aye, Jack, that sounds a grand occupation.'

'Good man, yourself!' Jack exclaimed as he clapped Tom on the back.

Tom bent to Molly. 'I would keep out of Mammy's way for an hour or so at least,' he said.

'You sure?'

'Positive,' Tom said definitely. 'We'll catch it when we get back whatever time it is, you likely more than me, and I'm in no rush to experience that.'

'Nor me,' Molly agreed with a shudder, and Tom smiled and pressed a thrupenny bit into her hand. 'Oh, Uncle Tom!' Molly cried in surprise.

'Nothing worse than looking round the shops without a penny piece in your pocket,' Tom said. 'Away now and enjoy yourself, for it is no sin at all.'

And how Molly enjoyed that first day, walking about arm in arm, chattering non-stop, greeted by this one and that, stopping for a few words with some of Cathy's school friends. When Tom first gave her the money, Molly's first reaction had been to save it, because it was the first time

130

that anyone had given her any money. Not, of course, that there was any occasion to spend anything on the farm, but she was worried how she would ever leave her grandmother's clutches without any money at all and she knew whatever age she was and whatever she did, there would be no sort of a wage coming her way.

However, while she was debating this in her head, Cathy, who had been given the same by her father, said, 'Let's go to the sweet shop,' and Molly's mouth had filled with saliva at the thought. She had never been allowed to be a great sweet eater in Birmingham – her mother had been particularly strict about that, and Molly was wise enough to keep quiet about the odd things her granddad used to pass her – but now, the thought of a bag or two of luscious sweets was very tempting.

After all, she told herself, what good was thrupence in the grand scheme of things? And so she turned to Cathy with a broad smile and said, 'Yes, let's.'

They had finished all the tiger nuts, by tacit consent leaving the bull's-eyes for another time, when they decided to go down to the harbour. 'We'll see if they are done with their pints of Guinness now and are ready to come home,' Cathy said.

'I'm all for that,' Molly said, 'because I am going nowhere near my grandmother without my uncle beside me.'

The men were standing outside gazing across at the Lough and as soon as Jack saw them, he said jovially, 'Now this is a sight for sore eyes: two visions of loveliness.'

Tom turned to look and Molly saw that he wasn't quite sober and she wondered if he would be any sort of protection at all between her and her grandmother, but Jack was speaking again. 'Now, what will you have, girls, a lemonade each?'

Molly thought a lemonade sounded lovely, for the sweets had made her thirsty, but she looked towards her uncle first. 'It's all right,' Jack said, taking Tom's empty glass from him. 'It's my round anyway.'

131

'Uncle Tom, you're tiddly,' Molly whispered when Jack had gone into the hotel bar, taking Cathy with him to give him a hand.

'I know,' said Tom. 'I'm not used to it, you see.'

'But your mother—'

'My saintly mother will give out to me all the way home,' Tom said. 'The same way she gives out to me every other Saturday when I am stone-cold sober. Maybe today I'll mind it less.'

'Well, I'll wish I had some of the same if you do,' Molly said. 'I don't think that lemonade will have the same numbing effect.'

'Maybe not, but there is nothing to stop you enjoying it here and now,' Tom said.

And then Jack was there with two pints of Guinness, and Cathy with two lemonades.

Tom lifted one of the foaming tankards. 'Might as well be hung for a sheep as a lamb, that's what I told myself today,' he said to Molly with a broad wink as he lifted the glass to his lips.

Later, Molly thought Biddy was going to kill the pair of them and more so when she found that Tom had not only been drinking but doing so 'to excess', as she put it.

'You have no right to leave me at all,' she screeched. 'Left alone for hours on end. Stuck here like a stook.'

'And why were you?' Tom asked amiably. 'If you got rid of the produce early, then what was to stop you parading the town, maybe taking tea with neighbouring women, only too glad of an excuse for a good gossip? That's what other women from the outlying farms often do on Saturday.'

'I am not other women,' Biddy almost snarled. 'I am me and I have no desire other than to go home, and where were you but tipping ale down your throat? And where,' she said suddenly grabbing Molly's arm, 'were you in this, miss?'

'With me, of course,' Tom said. 'Helped me choose the fish, didn't you, Moll?'

Molly nodded heartily, glad that she had the bull's-eyes safely hidden, and hoped that her grandmother wouldn't ask her what fish she had chosen, for she wouldn't have a clue.

However, her grandmother hadn't finished with Tom. Seeing him stumble as he helped her up into the seat at the front of the cart, she said sharply, 'And you are far from steady on your feet. Are you sure you are capable of driving this horse home?'

Tom gave a short laugh. 'Don't worry, Mammy, you are in safe hands. I am quite capable, but even if I were paralytic and passed out in the flat of the cart, old Dobbin would still get you home in one piece.'

'I'd rather not put it to the test,' Biddy replied with spirit.

'No need to,' Tom said with a flick of the reins. 'Hie up, Dobbin.'

All the way home, Biddy berated both Tom and Molly. Molly was so used to this now she let her grandmother's voice go over her head while she relived the last couple of hours. She thought her uncle was taking as little notice as she was because since they had left the town he had said little and listened to his mother with an inane smile plastered across his face. That was, until Biddy went on about the money that Tom had spent in the pub.

'What odds to you?' he commented mildly. 'It's money honestly earned.'

'Not earned to be wasted.'

'If I earn it then I can spend my share of it on what I choose, surely?'

'Your share of it?' Biddy repeated.

'Aye, Mammy, my share of it,' Tom repeated 'And there lies the rub, you see. I am forty-seven years old and I have been working this farm full time since I left school at twelve, and I have never had a penny piece to call my own. I have money doled to me as if I were a wean, like today. You decide when I need a new suit for Mass, or a shirt. I am consulted on neither style nor colour, and it is the same for my everyday

133

clothes. God, you even tip up the money for the collection at Mass. Well, it has to stop now. I will work out how much I do and how much I can legitimately take from the profits and pay myself a proper wage each week.'

'You will not.'

'Oh, yes, I will, Mammy,' Tom said, and Molly noted the steely edge to his voice with surprise. 'For there is nothing to stop me dropping you at the farmhouse door, putting all my clothes in a case, taking my share from the farm and hightailing it to England, or across the Atlantic to Joe.'

'Joe!' Biddy said scornfully. 'Living hand to mouth, reliant on handouts and soup kitchens.'

'Joe has no proper job, that's why he has to do that for now,' Tom said. 'Whereas I have a job and one I am at every day, and aren't I reliant on my mother for handouts for food and clothes and all else? It isn't right and the sooner you accept that, the better it will be for all of us. I want some money of my own.'

'What do you need money for?' Biddy asked testily, unwilling to let go of the purse strings that she had held for so long. 'To get drunk every night?'

'If I want,' Tom said defiantly. 'What I do with my money in my own free time is my business, but I'm warning you, Mammy, that there are going to be a few changes around here that are long overdue.'

Molly wanted to cheer. Even though she knew her life was not going to change drastically and that she might actually suffer for the stand that Tom had made, she couldn't regret he had made it. As he said, it was long overdue.

TEN

The next afternoon, on the way to the McEvoys', Tom admitted to Molly that he didn't think he would ever have spoken to his mother the way he had done if he hadn't been drinking.

'Maybe you should have taken to the drink years ago then,' Molly told him.

'I hate unpleasantness,' Tom said.

'Not when you're drunk you don't,' Molly said. 'You fair went for your mother yesterday and at least she put up little objection to me coming here today.'

'Well, that is because she is barely talking to either of us.'

'Personally, I prefer it that way,' Molly said with feeling. 'And you really don't have to walk all the way with me, unless you want to, especially as you are coming back to fetch me later. After all, it's broad daylight and I know the way.'

'Even on a day as overcast as this one, it is far preferable to be out in the fresh air than in with my mother,' Tom said.

'Well, I can't argue with that,' Molly said, 'for the look on your mother's face today would sour cream. And the dogs seem to appreciate the walk,' she added, indicating Skip and Fly cavorting in front of them. She was getting on well with the two dogs now and she always spoke to them and gave them a stroke when she took them out their food. 'I bet they are as pleased to get away from the farm as we are.'

'Man or beast, it is good to have a break, and I am only just beginning to realise that myself,' Tom said. 'Now you can go on from here and I will take to the hills with the dogs.'

'When will you come for me?'

'Well, I'll walk over when I have finished the milking and had my tea,' Tom said. 'No need for you to be ready then, though, for I'm going for a few jars with Cathy's father before we set off back home.'

'Oh, Uncle Tom, your mother will not be best pleased.'

'Is she about anything now, Molly? Answer me that.'

And she wasn't, that was the problem, Molly thought as she watched her uncle striding away, whistling to the dogs to follow him. Hilda was right: Biddy was a very unhappy woman. As Molly walked on she tried to imagine what it would be like waking up each morning, knowing that nothing that happened that day or any other day would even satisfy, never mind please. She wasn't sure she would want to wake up at all.

A few days later, Tom took Molly to the bog to cut the turf and there was an unseasonable chill in the air. The sky was gunmetal grey and heavy black clouds were shrouding the tops of the hills.

'Could rain,' Tom commented, looking out at the sky anxiously. 'But the only spare oilskin we have belonged to Joe, and I'd say that would be a mite big on you.'

Big was an understatement, for it reached Molly's feet, and even with the bottom cut off and the sleeves cut down, it was still ridiculously large. But as Tom said, few would be seeing what she looked like and it was better than nothing at all.

There were a fair few other farmers at the bog that day, as Molly could see from a distance. Some had lads with them, though Molly estimated that the boys were slightly older than she was. As they drew closer, she saw that most of them had their trousers rolled up and were barefoot. 'I used to go barefoot too throughout the whole summer,' Tom told her, seeing her watching this. 'We all did. In fact I used to hate to be forced into boots again to begin school in September, though I was glad enough of them when the snow and frosts were about. I thought you wouldn't like to go barefoot, though, not being brought up to it.'

'You're right,' Molly said. 'I wasn't brought up that way and neither was Kevin, and that was because my father was in work, but there were plenty in Birmingham not so lucky. I saw many thin, undernourished and barefoot children there, and that was the same summer and winter.'

'It is a terrible thing all right for a man to have no job.'

'That was what my father often said,' Molly said. 'The point is, he might have been in the same boat if it hadn't been for what happened in the war.' She related the story of the rescue of Paul Simmons and what happened because of it, when the war was ended.

Tom was impressed, Molly could see, and when he said, 'I would say that you had a hero of a father,' she nodded happily.

'I know,' she said. 'And he was lovely as well, but when I said that to Mom she always said all the men who fought in the war that they call "the Great War" were heroes, and some never came back from it. I mean, some of the families are so poor because they have no provider at all and some of those who did come back, were so badly injured they were totally unable to work.'

'You still miss your parents a great deal, don't you?' Tom said gently.

Molly nodded. 'It's like a nagging pain that is always there, but it helps to talk about them sometimes and remember how things used to be, and it is nice to hear things about my mother as a girl and everything. Was she ever taken to the bog?'

137

'No,' Tom said, smiling at the notion as he pulled the horse to a halt. 'Few girls, particularly those of your age now, are taken to cut the peat, in actual fact,' he said. 'And, God above, if I had ever suggested taking Nuala, my mother would have beaten the head off me.'

Molly laughed at that image, and at the sound the other farmers noticed their arrival and greeted them. Tom smiled as he saw that many of the boys were more than interested in Molly, and he couldn't blame them, for while most people would have looked ridiculous in the oversized clothes, Molly looked very fetching indeed. Tom thought her beauty was such that if she had been clothed in a sack she would still look good. She seemed totally unaware of it herself and oblivious to the boys' interest in her too, which Tom thought a good thing. She was very young yet.

He leaped from the cart and helped Molly down before saying, 'First the bog is cut into lines. See where the others have started?'

Molly nodded and Tom continued, 'So if I start marking out the lines could you come after me and do the cutting into the brick shapes you have seen at home?'

'Yeah,' Molly said. 'It doesn't seem so hard.'

It wasn't hard, but it was backbreaking, though Molly didn't find that out straight away. She soon realised why the terrain was called a bog. Because no rain had actually fallen for some time, the thin grass covering the bog was dry but as soon as she sliced through the earth with her spade she saw and smelled the black slurry seeping through it. The bog seemed not to wish to relinquish its sod either, and tried to suck it back into the earth, but Molly persevered and eventually withdrew the brick almost triumphantly, threw it into the cart and bent to cut another.

She thought she was working incredibly slowly and ponderously, but when Tom, thinking he had drawn enough lines for the time being, came to join her, he said she was doing just fine. 'There is a knack to it, as there is to most things,' he said. 'You will pick it up eventually, but considering this is your first time, you're not bad at all.'

They went on hour after hour, until the ache in Molly's back became unbearable and she stretched with a grimace of pain that Tom noticed. He decided enough was enough for now. 'How d'you fancy a breather?'

Molly barely kept the relief out of her voice as with a shrug she said, 'If you like.'

They sat a little way away from the bog on Tom's waterproof spread on the earth. They ate the bread and cheese that Molly had put up before they left, and they washed it down with cold tea, which revived them both. Molly sat back thankfully and surveyed the cart a little way from them.

'Isn't that turf too wet to burn?' she asked.

'Aye,' Tom said. 'It is surely at the moment. We'll take it back to the barn and stand the bricks up like little houses leaning against one another till the water has drained out of them and they can be stacked and then we will come back for more.'

'How often do you come?'

'Until I judge I have enough to last us the winter,' Tom said, withdrawing his pipe from his pocket. 'Now I am away for a wee smoke and a jaw with the neighbours. You can either come with me, or stop and rest yourself.'

Molly looked across at the now quite sizeable knot of men and boys, because more had come as they had worked, a fair few of them taking their ease as they were, and she felt suddenly shy to be the only girl amongst them.

'I think I will stop here, Uncle Tom,' she said. 'I am quite tired.'

She *was* thoroughly weary and when Tom left her she lay back on the waterproof, closed her eyes and in a few minutes was fast asleep. Tom, returning later, did not wake her but just carried on working in the bog alone. Molly woke an hour or so afterwards, disorientated first, and then guilty as she saw the sizeable amount of bog Tom had cleared

139

while she had slept. He waved away her apologies and she set back to work with a will.

That was not the last time Molly went to the bog. As one day slid into another, she got more into the routine of the work, both on the farm and in the house, and usually let Biddy's word wash over her, for the silent treatment didn't last nearly long enough in Molly's opinion. Biddy was especially bad on Sundays, and Molly knew that this was because she resented the fact that so many greeted her warmly, both before and after Mass.

Biddy particularly disliked it when Molly and Cathy got together and began chattering about what they would do later that day. Molly went to the McEvoys for Sunday tea every week. Biddy would have liked to have forbidden the girl, but she sensed that if she did, everyone would be against her. Nellie had enthused about Molly, saying that they all loved having her in the house and that she was no trouble at all, and the two girls got on famously. Then there was Tom, insisting she needed time with other young people and the town's folk agreeing with that, and the priest beaming in approval.

Biddy would have liked to tell them all to go to hell, that she would make any decisions about the girl. She was, after all, in her charge, but she had to live amongst these people afterwards. She didn't really understand why the townsfolk should seem to like the girl so well, for she had done all that she could to blacken her name. So, she contented herself with making Molly's life particularly miserable on Sundays, and if Tom was out of the way she was given many a clout that she kept quiet about.

Biddy blamed Molly's arrival totally for the sea change in Tom, yet in Molly's opinion he was acting in a more normal way now. He would go for a drink on Saturdays with the other men when they were in the town and then on Sunday evening before bringing Molly home. Molly often wondered why Biddy found this such a problem and why she would go for him as she did. It was hardly what a person could term excessive.

Her own father used to like a drink a couple of times a week and always after the match on Saturday, and her mother had never minded. Biddy, however, seemed to want Tom never to leave the farm, or seek any other company but hers. God, what a prospect!

As for Molly, she lived for the time spent with Cathy. Sometimes, they went out, maybe met up with friends, and other times it was just the two of them either outdoors or indoors. Molly barely minded which way it was, though if pressed she would have had to say that she liked best the company of Cathy on her own.

Molly had had friends in Birmingham, but she had sort of got out of the way of going about with them when her mother had been so ill. She had very little free time, anyway, at that time, as she shouldered much of the housework. But, in this place, where she had never wanted to live, Cathy was her life-saver.

The school holidays beginning made little difference to Molly, except the summer heat made the work more tiring, especially inside the house, for however hot it was, the fire had to be kept on. Sometimes there was so little breeze that opening the door and windows made no difference and she was glad of the light showers that took some of the heat from the days.

The farmers, though, watched the weather anxiously, knowing that heavy rain then might mean a poor harvest, but by and large the summer was hot and dry, and by the middle of August the harvest had begun. Molly and her uncle were soon hard at it from dawn till dusk because, as he said, their survival through the winter depended on it.

The flax was the first to be harvested. Once pulled and put into bunches, or 'beets' as Tom called them, it had to

141

be soaked in the water butt for about three weeks and then spread out to dry before the fibres would be any good for thatching. So while the flax was being soaked, Tom turned his attention to the hay, which was cut with scythes. He was very wary of letting Molly do that at all.

'It is not something you were brought up to,' he said. 'You are likely to slice the legs off yourself.'

Molly laughed. 'Why am I? Look, Uncle Tom, I might have been born and raised in a city, but I have got a brain in my head and I do know how sharp the scythes are. You show me what to do and I will copy you. And don't worry, I will keep my legs well away.'

There was, however, an art to scything, and Molly soon found wielding the scythe, heavy for someone of her build, hard, hard work that made her arms and then her shoulders and then her whole back ache almost unbearably. She watched her uncle slicing his way through the hay fields, seemingly with little effort, and felt quite useless.

Tom told her that however little she did, it would be less for him to do and not to worry about it, but seeing what an effort it was for Molly, he suggested after a little while that she leave the cutting to him and he showed her how to make the little hay cocks instead, which she then dotted about the field to make sure the hay was totally dry before the haystacks were built.

In the potato fields, Dobbin pulled the reaper that brought the potatoes to the surface. Molly went after, collecting them up in metal buckets, as she did with the turnips and swede, and she and her uncle collected the cabbages from another field together.

The corn was cut last and then taken to the mill to be threshed into meal, which Tom explained was used for oaten bread and porridge. The harvest was a tough time and general weariness and aching limbs encouraged Molly to fall into a deep sleep as soon as her head touched the pillow every night. Despite this though, she could quite see the satisfaction a person would feel knowing that by their labours there was enough food collected in for everyone throughout the winter, including the animals, and more than enough turf for the fire.

Of course, harvesting the crops meant she had been out of the house for days, working alongside her uncle a lot of the time. She knew without doubt that she would far rather be out in the fields with him, however arduous the work, than anywhere at all with her grandmother.

Just before the winter really set in, Tom brought quicklime back from the lime kiln one day, and he and Molly cleared out the well together, and lined the inside with the quicklime, which they had mixed with water, before allowing the well to fill up again. The quicklime was also used to make the whitewash for the outside of the cottage, and Molly found she liked doing that. Tom also checked that any poor thatch was replaced to keep the place weatherproof, but though Molly had climbed on to the roof with him, she was no good at the thatching itself – all fingers and thumbs, as her uncle said.

As the autumn rolled on, Molly realised how much she was dreading this first Christmas without her parents and guessed that there would be little festive cheer in that house of misery. She was right, for Christmas at the Sullivan house was almost a nonevent. No streamers festooned the house in the run-up to Christmas, there was no tree, no wooden Nativity scene decorating the mantelshelf and no cards at all.

Molly tried to push down the memories of the many Christmas days she had enjoyed at home, but she couldn't help thinking nostalgically about them. She cried herself to sleep on Christmas Eve, feeling her loss especially poignantly, and yearning so much to be with those still left to her in Birmingham that it seemed to spread all over her body, making her nerve ends tingle and ache.

Tom listened to the anguished sobbing of the young girl,

frustrated that he was so helpless to deal with such pain and sorrow, and hoped to God his mother wasn't roused. He was so disturbed that he lay with his eyes smarting with tiredness, long after Molly was eventually quiet.

Molly woke heavy-eyed and sluggish, and dragged herself from the bed into the cold black early morning, pulling on her dungarees, for even on Christmas Day cows have to be milked. She went into the room to rake up the fire and put on the kettle. While she was doing that, Tom stopped beside her at the hearth, on his way to the cowshed.

He was pleased that his mother's even breathing behind the bed canopy indicated that she was still asleep as he almost whispered, 'Happy Christmas, Molly,' and pressed a parcel into her hands.

Molly had expected no present, so she was stunned when she opened the packaging to find gloves, a scarf and a jaunty tam-o'-shanter, all of the softest wool in a myriad pastel colours. She was almost too overcome to speak, though she gasped in delight, and Tom saw her moist eyes and knew just how pleased she was. He was glad that he had asked Nellie's advice.

'I don't know what to say,' Molly said eventually. 'You have taken me so much by surprise and you couldn't have got anything better. My hands have been like blocks of ice some days, so thank you, Uncle Tom. Thank you so much. I can't tell you how this has pleased me.' She stood on tiptoe and kissed her uncle's cheek, and he flushed bright pink with embarrassment.

''S all right,' he said gruffly. 'I've given the gift to you now so that you can wear them to Mass if you have a mind.'

'Oh, I have a mind all right,' Molly said. 'I would be proud and pleased to wear them.'

Biddy, of course, tried to spoil it all, and laughed at Tom for what she called his stupidity. She wasn't even mollified with the shawl he had bought her, but Molly refused to let Biddy's sourness spoil her pleasure, and the people going into Mass that morning more than made up for it anyway. Nellie was so pleased the things suited her and Jack told her she was as pretty as a picture.

She so wished she could go home with the McEvoys after Mass, but it was no good wishing for things she couldn't have, and she knew that as well as anyone. At least, she told herself as they made their way home, they had decent food in the house for a change, for Biddy had wrung the neck of a hen that was no longer laying the day before and Molly had drawn the innards from it and it was now ready to be cooked.

Molly hated preparing the hens to eat. In Birmingham they had bought them from the butcher ready just to put in the oven. The very first time Biddy had made Molly draw out the bird's innards the sight and smell had caused her to be sick in the gutter in the yard afterwards, and Biddy had laughed at her. She couldn't help feeling nauseous every time, but she would never allow herself to be sick again and give Biddy any reason to gloat over her.

Despite the food, though, the day was as gloomy as Molly thought it would be, and though she did go for a tramp with her uncle and later played cards with him, she was glad when the day was over and she could look forward to seeing Cathy and her parents the following day.

The next day, though, she wasn't sure she would be allowed to go, for her grandmother kicked up shockingly. A tantrum of such magnitude used to terrify Tom to the extent he would give in to anything she wanted, and he felt his innards quail at the vitriol pouring from her mouth. Even Molly was unnerved.

And then Biddy's temper got the better of her and she lashed out at Molly. The first punch causing her nose to spurt blood and the second, administered before Tom could get to her, split her lip. Anger replaced the fear coursing through Tom's vein and he helped Molly to her feet because the power of the second punch had knocked her over.

He said to his mother through gritted teeth. 'You have cooked your goose right and proper now. Why in God's name would anyone want to stay with someone like you one minute longer than was necessary? And I'm warning you, Mammy, if you can't keep your hands to yourself, you'd better watch out I don't do the same to you one of these days.'

'How dare you?' Biddy shrieked. 'Let me tell you—'

'No,' Tom said firmly. 'I don't want to hear it. I am off for more congenial company and so is Molly, and we will see you later.'

Both Nellie and Jack McEvoy looked askance at Molly's face when she arrived at their door, but didn't ask any questions. Cathy, on the other hand, barely waited until they were in her bedroom, before she said, 'Your face is a right mess. What happened to it?'

Molly felt she owed Biddy no loyalty so she said, 'My grandmother wasn't that keen on me coming here today.'

'So, she did that to you?'

'That's right.'

Cathy was shocked to the core. 'That's awful.'

'I agree,' Molly said. 'In fact, I think it is so awful that I don't want to think about it any more, never mind talk about it.'

Cathy knew she was right. What was the point of going on and on about something dreadful that she had no power of changing? So she said, 'Let's talk about Christmas instead, because it is my favourite time in the whole year.'

'It used to be mine too.'

'Sorry,' Cathy said, wincing at her tactlessness. 'That was stupid of me.'

'It's all right, really,' Molly said. 'Though I must admit, I have missed my parents very much this year.'

'You were bound to,' Cathy said gently. 'I bet your grandfather sent you a card, though, and your brother.'

146

Molly stared at Cathy. 'I thought you knew, that your mother might have said or something.'

'What about?'

'No one from Birmingham is allowed to write to me.'

'Why on earth not?'

'Because my grandmother considers them heathens.'

'That's rubbish!' Cathy said. 'Anyway, she can't stop them.'

'She can, you know, and she does,' Molly said. 'I don't have a penny piece of my own, for a start. My granddad thought of that and gave me a writing pad and envelopes and some Irish stamps, and I wrote to him and Hilda just the once. Uncle Tom posted the letters in Buncrana. I never thought of asking permission – didn't think I would need it – but my grandmother went mad when she knew. Replies would have come for me, I know that, but I never saw them. She confiscated all the stuff my grandfather gave me and wrote and told them not to write to me again, that she was severing all communication between us.'

'That is perfectly dreadful,' said Cathy, distressed.

'I thought your mother might have told you,' Molly said.

Cathy shook her head. 'Mammy never talks of things like that,' she said. 'She said it isn't nice to bandy gossip about, and particularly because she does know, or could probably guess, a lot of what goes on in people's lives because of the job she does and things people say when they confide in her. She can keep things pretty close to her chest, can my mother when she wants to.'

'Would she tell me things if I asked her directly?' Molly asked.

'I don't know,' Cathy said. 'But personally I think you have a right to know if letters came for you and you never got them. We'll be having dinner soon and we'll bring it up at the table.'

Cathy did bring it up and Nellie looked decidedly un-comfortable. She knew of the letters that had come for Molly as she knew of the missive Biddy had sent banning them, though at first, despite that, the letters came thick and fast. She hadn't thought to mention any of this to her daughter, though as she watched the friendship develop between them, she had thought the day might come when she would have to explain herself. So when she was asked so directly she said to Molly, 'There were letters that came for you, at first anyway, but your grandmother obviously thought that it was better you didn't see them.'

Nellie looked into Molly's eyes, so sad they were like pools of pain in that battered face, and her stomach contracted in pity for the young girl.

'I don't know if you were aware of the letter Biddy sent, banning all communication, Molly. I only know myself because she told me. I thought it was the wrong thing to do then and I told her so, and I haven't changed my opinion. Anyway, those in Birmingham took no notice at first either because for a time the letters continued to come.'

Cathy was perplexed. She looked at her friend and recognised her suffering as she burst out, 'But why did you give them to the postman, Mammy, knowing that Molly wasn't going to be allowed to receive them?'

'I didn't know that absolutely at first,' Nellie protested. 'It was only when Molly never mentioned anything about them that I had my suspicions. After that, every time I put the letters for you in the sack, my heart would sink. It was almost a relief when they eventually stopped coming.'

'I still don't understand why you gave letters to the postman when you realised that?' Cathy insisted.

Nellie bit back, 'I did it because I had to.'

Cathy shook her head. 'You could have just left them all here and Molly could have had them when she came over on Sunday.'

'If only you knew just how often I have been tempted to do just that,' Nellie said. 'But withholding mail is a serious offence, and one I would be in really hot water for if it were brought to the authority's notice.'

'But isn't Molly's grandmother withholding her mail?'

'Yes, but Molly is a minor and under her grandmother's care,' Nellie said. She felt burdened by her part in all this, and in an effort to explain she addressed herself again to Molly.

'If I was to do this and your grandmother was to find out, she could make trouble for me because of it, and you know, don't you, Molly, that she would delight in doing that?'

Molly loved Nellie, the woman who had shown her nothing but kindness from the very first, and she saw immediately her dilemma.

'It's all right,' she said. 'I do understand, and you are right, my grandmother would love to get you into trouble – I know that as well as you – and I would hate it and feel responsible.'

'If only we could find a way around this,' Cathy mused.

Jack had taken no part in the discussion so far, but now he said sharply to his daughter, 'Cathy, stop this at once. Your mother has explained it to you. Let that be an end to it.'

'But what if Molly was to write from here and they could write back, addressing their letters to me?'

Nellie stared at her daughter. In fact, they all stared at her. Nellie knew she shouldn't agree to this, but Jack said, 'Don't see any harm in that, Nellie. After all, there is no law in the land that says Cathy can't write to anyone in the world if she takes a mind.'

'The postman will wonder,' Nellie said.

'Yeah, he might, but he won't connect it with Molly, will he?' Cathy said. 'You can tell him that I have a couple of pen friends in England, if you like. They are always advising us to do that at school, to broaden our horizons or something. Some of the others already do it, so it won't seem all that strange.'

'Do you know,' Jack said, 'it may just work. What d'you say, Molly?'

Molly turned her eyes on Jack and he saw the little flame of hope that had suddenly burned within her go out. She knew writing to her people was as remote a reality as ever, because she couldn't afford writing pad and envelopes, never mind stamps every week. Jack, though, guessed what was troubling her and, excusing himself, he left the table, coming back a few minutes later with a writing pad, a stack of envelopes and two pens.

'Here you are, Molly,' he said. 'Merry Christmas, and don't you worry about stamps, for I will buy them for you myself and will be glad to do it.'

Molly looked around the table at those good, kind people, so eager and willing to help her, and suddenly it was all too much, and she laid her head on the table and cried her eyes out.

ELEVEN

When Stan had first received the command from Biddy that he stop writing to Molly, he went to see Hilda to find that she had received a similar letter. Even knowing Biddy's character as he did, he didn't think that she really and truly intended to totally cut the orphan child off from those who loved her and that when she had thought about it, she would relent. Hilda agreed with him and for a while they continued to write, until it was obvious from the silence that the letters were not getting through.

Stan had been so concerned that eventually, as Christmas was approaching, he had screwed up his courage to see Paul Simmons to tell him of his anxieties and ask his advice. Paul Simmons said he had reason to be concerned and admitted to Stan that he hadn't taken to Biddy Sullivan when he had seen her at the funeral. He said he had been worried and a little dismayed when he realised that Molly was going to live with the old harridan in some godforsaken hole in Ireland.

'There was nothing else for it,' Stan said. 'Even without the influence of the Church – though it would never do to underestimate the power that has – they couldn't let her live with me, her being a girl and all, without a woman's presence in the house.'

'I crossed my mind to make her my ward,' Paul said. 'But then I thought I have a job of work to do, so she would be in the care of servants and that wouldn't be any good either. I was advised by a Catholic friend not even to bother mentioning the idea, because the Church would shoot it down in flames.'

'That's the very devil of it,' Stan said. 'We were both helpless.'

'Yes, we were,' Paul said. 'However, this situation cannot be allowed to continue. Unfortunately, I am tied up all over Christmas and into the New Year, but in the spring, when the weather is a little more conducive to crossing the sea, I will go over and see the situation first-hand.'

Stan had been so relieved, but before that plan could be put into action, he received another letter from Molly at the very start of the New Year.

She never mentioned her grandmother, though she said a lot about Tom, the kindness of the townsfolk, her friendship with the McEvoys and particularly her best friend and ally, Cathy, who had devised this plan on how to keep in contact.

When Molly received the first letter back from her granddad she felt his love and concern for her could almost be lifted from the page. Kevin had drawn her a picture he had obviously signed all on his own and it was of their old house and all of them in it, including their parents. It saddened Molly and she was glad to turn to Hilda's letter. The woman always had the ability to make her smile and, as she wrote as she spoke, it was just like having her in the room.

In rural Ireland, particularly on the farm, one day seemed very like another to Molly, and it was hard for her to visualise what was happening in other places, particularly the city she had been born in. When Molly had left Birmingham it had been a very depressed city in many ways, and from what her grandfather told her in his letters in 1936, it was in no better shape.

And then, in late January, the King died. Molly remembered the dour, bewhiskered King, whose picture had been

152

plastered everywhere in Birmingham in the weeks prior to his Jubilee celebrations the previous year.

No one in Ireland was the least bit bothered about which king or queen would be sitting on the throne in England, but it seemed that those in Birmingham at least had a lot to say about it. They weren't that concerned about the old King dying so much as who was to succeed him and that was to be his handsome and flamboyant son Edward, who would then be known as Edward VIII.

'Handsome is as handsome does, I always say,' Hilda wrote in her letter.

> The point is he is too flippant in my opinion to be a good ruler. Never taken his duties that serious, like, and now that he is the King he will have to show what he is made of. The first thing he will have to do is dump that American divorcee Wallace Simpson that seems intent on hanging on to his coattails. His days of gallivanting around the world with her are gone and the sooner he realises that the better it will be for everyone.

Molly's granddad said much the same, but it seemed the new King had no intention of knuckling down like people expected him to. Even the Irish papers had got hold of the story in the end.

'He is handsome, you have to admit,' Cathy said one Sunday in early February. She had the *Irish Times* spread out on her bed and both girls had been scrutinising it.

'Oh, I think everyone agrees with that,' Molly said. 'But as Hilda said, being good-looking doesn't mean he will be a good king. And he can't have that woman as the Queen,' she said, jabbing her finger at Edward's escort who was gazing up at him with adoring eyes, though, even through the grainy newsprint, Molly thought her eyes looked calculating. 'I mean, she's another handsome one. Beautiful, in fact, and up to the minute with fashion, might even be really nice, but none of that will matter because the British people will never accept her. Queen Wallace, can you imagine?'

Cathy laughed. 'Doesn't sound quite right, I must admit, but we could talk about it till the cows come home and it won't make a bit of difference. And meanwhile, there is something else happening next week that I think will prove to be far more entertaining – like your birthday, for instance.'

'Yeah, and thanks to you I will have cards from everyone,' Molly said. 'I know I can't put them up or anything, but I will get them and that is more than I had at Christmas. I'm so grateful for you all doing this, Cathy, you having the idea in the first place and your parents providing the wherewithal. I don't know if you realise how much I appreciate it.'

'Course we realise,' Cathy said. 'You have told us enough times. Didn't Daddy say last time you started on that if he heard one more thank you from you then you could buy your own stamps.'

Molly smiled. 'Yes, he did.'

'Well then, think on,' Cathy said, jumping to her feet. 'Come on, let's go to Swan Park and see if the snowdrops and crocuses are out yet like Bernadette said they were.'

'You're on,' Molly said, knowing that in the main it was always wiser to fall in with Cathy's plans.

However, Molly had a surprise awaiting her the following week. Stan had been to see Paul Simmons on receipt of Molly's letter outlining the new arrangements to ensure that she received her mail, and Paul was irritated by the subterfuge and thought it sounded draconian to deprive an orphaned child of letters from family and friends.

'She says nothing about that,' Stan said. 'But I know she is not happy. I have known my granddaughter for nearly fourteen years and she can't fool me. I reckon she will be back here as soon as she is able.'

'She will need money for that.'

'There is the fund you set up for her,' Stan said. 'I told

the grandmother nothing about it for I know whose pocket it would have lined, and Molly knows nothing about it either, of course.'

'Maybe she should be told now then,' Paul said. 'From what I remember she is a mature and sensible girl. Ted was always on about her, on about you all. Great family man, was Ted.'

'Aye, he was.'

'Tragic loss.'

'Aye.'

'This will never do,' Paul said impatiently. 'Going all melancholy when it should be Molly we are thinking of. You say she is nearly fourteen?'

'Aye, twelfth of February.'

'Yes, well,' said Paul. 'While it is good for her to know that there will be money accrued for her for when she is twenty-one, that can seem an age away when you are fourteen. I think I will arrange for her to have some money of her own and a fourteenth birthday seems just about the right time to do that.'

'It is so very kind of you,' Stan said. 'There just aren't words.'

'You don't need any words,' Paul said. 'I am a rich man and it pleases me to do this. And I wouldn't be here to enjoy those riches and gladden my parents' hearts if it hadn't been for Ted. That debt will not be repaid while one of his family is in any sort of need, and that is Molly at the moment.'

'Paul Simmons is the most generous, open-hearted and genuine man I have ever met,' Stan said to Hilda later. 'I tell you, it would have been a terrible tragedy if he had died on the battlefield.'

'I agree,' Hilda said. 'Thank God he didn't.'

Molly was excited as she made her way to Cathy's house the following Sunday because she was looking forward to seeing the cards she knew would be waiting for her. Since the system had begun she would have her letters written by the time she arrived for Sunday tea so that she might not waste any of the time she spent with Cathy. Cathy would post the letters first thing on Monday morning so that they would arrive in Birmingham on Tuesday or Wednesday. Hilda and her granddad would write straight back and they would reach Buncrana post office by Friday or Saturday at the latest.

Molly was so glad to receive the replies, though they often reduced her to tears. If she could, she would wait till she reached the farm to read them and then she would then reread them over and over until she could repeat them word for word.

She was surprised to find four envelopes and one in a handwriting she didn't recognise waiting for her that day, and as it was a special day she decided to open the letters there. Nellie and Jack had come to watch. Kevin's card, which she opened first, was homemade and showed a girl on a hillside dotted with sheep and underneath the girl he had written 'Molly' and inside the card he had written in his wobbly hand, 'Miss you. Lots of luv, Kevin.'

Inside the cards from Hilda and her granddad there were letters, which she put in her pocket for later, and then drew the mystery card towards her. The envelope was of the best quality and she caught a whiff of the scent on it as she slit it open. The card itself was silk and depicted a beautiful girl in a flowing dress in a garden awash with flowers.

'Golly, who's that from?' Cathy breathed in admiration.

'Mind your own business, Cathy,' Nellie said reprovingly.

'Oh, I don't mind,' Molly said, looking up from reading the card with a smile. 'Anyone would want to know. It's not the normal run-of-the-mill card, after all, and it is from Dad's old employer, Paul Simmons. You remember I told you about my father saving his life in the war and how he got a job working with him?'

'Kind of him to send you a card, and all.'

'Oh, he sent more than a card,' Molly said, pulling out a five-shilling postal order. 'He has written a little note here. Apparently he has set up a fund for me and Kevin to mature when we are twenty-one, but he says twenty-one seems a lifetime away when you are only fourteen and so from now on there will be five shillings a week coming from his solicitors.'

There was a gasp from the family. 'Isn't that the very devil's own luck, Molly?' Jack said.

'Aye, and about time some good fortune happened to you,' said Nellie sincerely. 'And I am as pleased as if it was myself, for it couldn't have happened to a nicer person.'

'Yes,' said Cathy in impatient excitement. 'But what are you going to do with all that money?'

'Save it,' Molly said decisively. 'You know I intend to leave this place and I think Mr Simmons maybe knows that. He didn't like my grandmother one bit – anyone could see that – but it didn't surprise me because most normal people don't.'

'I don't blame him either,' Nellie said. 'He sounds a wonderful man, so he does.'

'He is,' Molly agreed happily. 'I knew nothing of any fund until this moment, and it will be lovely to have a bit of money when I am an adult, but I will not bide here until I am twenty-one. But to move anywhere, you need money behind you and I will save up all these five-shilling postal orders.'

'Will I open you an account with the Post Office, Molly?' Nellie said. 'It will be safest, especially if I keep the book for you.'

Molly nodded. 'I was going to ask you, because it wouldn't be wise to keep anything at the farm.'

'Do you destroy the letters or keep them?' Cathy said.

'I can't bring myself to destroy them yet,' Molly admitted, 'though I know it would be safer. I daren't keep them in

157

my room either; my grandmother isn't above snooping around. But I have found a box behind all the bales of hay right at the back of the barn where my grandmother never goes. I keep all the stationery items there too and just smuggle in what I need, but I wouldn't like money kept out there as well.'

'Does Tom know about it?'

'I've told my uncle nothing.'

'Why?' Nellie said. 'Surely you know that Tom would never betray you?'

'He wouldn't mean to,' Molly said. 'But even though he has broken out a little and does stick up for me and himself a bit, he is still very much under his mother's thumb in many ways. He is unnerved by her rages and when you are not fully in control of yourself, you can sometimes let things slip out. If he doesn't know, then he can't tell.' She hesitated and then went on, 'I don't intend to tell him about the money either. I mean, I am really fond of Uncle Tom, but what if we should be talking about it and she overheard or something? I know with absolute certainty that if my grandmother got one sniff of this money she would have every penny piece off me. This will be my passport to freedom and I'd really rather no one but us in this room knew anything about the postal orders.'

'You needn't fret yourself, Molly,' Nellie said 'It is your business and that's how it will stay.' Cathy also promised and Nellie said, 'Jack, you hear that?'

'Course I hear it, and don't you be pointing the finger at me,' Jack said. 'I can keep my own counsel the same as the next man.'

'Even when the beer loosens your tongue, I mean?'

'Even then,' Jack said. He turned to Molly. 'No one will hear a dicky bird from me of the events of this afternoon, I promise you faithfully.'

Molly sighed in relief. 'Thanks, Jack – thanks, all of you. The first letter I shall write will be to Mr Simmons to thank him. But,' she added playfully to Jack, 'I can afford my own stamps and all now.'

'I should think so,' Jack said, matching her mood. 'And about time too, I think.'

'Come on,' Nellie said. 'There is a party tea awaiting us set out in the room. Let's go in and do it justice.'

Father Finlay was becoming worried about Molly and he was not the only one.

'It dates back to what happened years ago,' Nellie told the priest, who called at the post office, knowing that she probably knew more about the girl and what was going on in the home than anyone else in the parish. Nellie told the priest all about Nuala and the father's heart attack when he received the fateful letter.

'I think she is making Molly sort of pay for what her mother did,' Nellie said. 'The child is nearly a prisoner on that farm, and from what Tom tells me, does far more than the lion's share of work on it. And . . . I hesitate to say this, Father, for I deplore gossip, and had I not seen it myself I would not say a word about it, but Biddy is far too free with her fists.'

The priest frowned a little, disturbed by what Nellie said. Normally, he had no problem with physical punishment and he knew of many bold children – usually boys, he had to admit – that had been stopped from going off the rails altogether by the power of their fathers' belts, or a few strokes from a stick. Molly, however, didn't seem the type of girl to need such stringent punishment, certainly not at the age she was. 'You are sure of this?'

'I have seen it with my own eyes, Father.'

'Dear, dear. What is to be done?'

'Nothing about that, Father, I fear,' Nellie said. 'For knowing the type of woman Biddy is, I feel that if anything were said, things might be worse for Molly later.'

'What of Tom in all this?'

159

'Molly is very fond of Tom,' Nellie said. 'It would be hard not to be, but sure, the man cannot be everywhere.'

'No, indeed.'

'What Molly would really like, Father, for she has told my own daughter Cathy, is to come to Buncrana perhaps on a Saturday a time or two. Tom and Biddy come every week, but Molly is never allowed after the one time she was here.'

'Why not?'

Nellie shrugged. 'You must ask her that, Father, because to my knowledge she has been given no explanation.'

'If she was to come in with them, it would solve another problem I have and that is confession,' the priest said. 'There are weeks between each one Molly makes, and she comes to the church either Thursday or Friday evening, when the chores are done at home and Tom has time to bring her down, for her grandmother forbids her to go alone. This much she has told me when I asked her. The point is, I hear Biddy and Tom's confession every two weeks on Saturday morning when they are in Buncrana anyway, and surely it would do the child good to do the same thing.'

'You'd think so, Father,' Nellie said. 'Maybe you could use that as a lever.'

'Maybe I could indeed. I will certainly give the matter some thought.'

Before the priest had much time to give to thought at all, in fact that same evening, Molly entered the confessional box and kneeled down. 'Bless me, Father, for I have sinned. It is six weeks since my last confession.'

The priest decided, much as he trusted Nellie's judgement and assessment of the situation, he would get the child's viewpoint on it as well, and so he commented again that he would like to see her more often.

'I can't, Father. I have told you how it is.'

'But your uncle and grandmother attend regularly when they come to town with their produce on Saturday.'

'I know, Father.'

'So, why don't you come with them?'

'I'm not allowed,' Molly said. 'I think it is something to do with the fact that my grandmother would not like me to have fun of any sort.' She saw the sharp movement of the priest's head behind the screen and said, 'It's true. Come and talk to her yourself, Father, if you don't believe me. She sees sin in laughter and enjoyment. I can't understand it. My mother was forever saying that God wouldn't have given us the gift of laughter if he didn't want us to use it.'

'A wise woman,' the priest said. 'There is no harm at all in honest laughter and indeed, it lightens the load for many. I think it will be good for you to come to town and meet people, and I can't see any sin at all in that. I will come and have a word with your grandmother.'

Molly knew that priests were a law unto themselves and they had immense power, so she smiled and said, 'I'd say "best of luck", but that's not the thing to say, is it? Not in the confessional, at any rate.'

She heard the answering smile in the priest's voice as he commented, 'Let's say that I will endeavour to change your grandmother's mind with the help of God.'

You might need God and all the saints marshalled together, thought Molly later as she left the confessional box, and yet the priest had their immortal souls in the palm of his hand and even her grandmother listened to him.

As it was a fine evening, Tom was waiting for her outside, leaning against the wall, and he was amused by the large smile on Molly's face as she left the church.

'What's up with you?' he said. 'You look like the cat that got the cream.'

'What's wrong with being happy?'

'Nothing,' Tom conceded. 'It's just that most people don't come out of confession with a dirty great grin on their faces, but no one should be forced to share their thoughts if they don't want to, so you keep yours to yourself and no harm done.'

Molly was glad her uncle didn't press her. If the priest did what he said he would do and visited the house, then Tom and her grandmother would know soon enough and she resolved to think no more about it.

So when, just a few days later, Biddy opened the door to the priest, Tom caught sight of the look on Molly's face as the man entered the room. He suddenly knew that the priest's visit was linked in some way to what had been said to Molly at her last confession, which had put her in such good humour. Biddy was unsuspicious, for it wasn't completely out of the way for the priest to call, though he would usually mention on Sunday morning that he might call around one evening that week. He hadn't to be more specific than that, because the priest was the one person always sure of his welcome.

Biddy smiled as much as she was able, and bade the man come in and sit by the fire and rest himself. She helped the priest off with his coat as she spoke and then roared at Molly to put the kettle on to make the priest a cup of tea.

The priest did not broach the subject of confession straight away. He drank the tea Molly gave him and helped himself to a piece of barnbrack and another of oaten bread, which Biddy pressed on him. They talked of farming matters and the vagaries of the prices at the livestock market. Molly listened to the voices rise and fall as she waited in an agony of impatience, thinking maybe she had misinterpreted the reason for the priest's visit and that any minute he would get to his feet, thank her for the refreshments and be gone.

'Get Father Finlay another cup of tea,' said Biddy, her strident voice cutting through Molly's thoughts. 'Where are your manners?'

It was as Molly handed the priest the cup that their eyes

162

met and she felt he was saying that he hadn't forgotten the reason for being there. Then Molly began to relax a little. The priest took a sip of the tea before saying, 'I was glad to see young Molly at confession a few days ago.'

'Oh, yes, Father, I make sure she goes,' Biddy said self-righteously. 'Packed full of sin, she is.'

The priest bent his head for a moment to hide the smile as he remembered the small misdemeanours that Molly had recounted to him. Packed full of sin was definitely not the way he would have described her, but it maybe worked to his advantage and he said, 'That being the case, I am surprised that she doesn't come more often.'

Biddy flushed. 'It's time, so it is, Father. Tom is busy and indeed so is Molly.'

'I understand that,' the priest went on soothingly. 'And that is why I don't know why she doesn't come with you to Buncrana on Saturday as you and Tom do.'

'Isn't this what I have told you, Mammy, over and over?' Tom cried.

Biddy ignored her son and instead said to the priest, 'I don't approve of the young ones in the town. I see them laughing together and carrying on, and I don't want Molly up to any of that sort of caper.'

The priest remembered Molly's word in the confessional and knew she had spoken the truth. He said, 'There is nothing wrong with laughter, Biddy, nothing at all.' Then, paraphrasing Molly, he continued, 'Sure, if the Good Lord didn't want us to laugh then surely he would have not given us the ability to do so. As for the carry-on, well, there was nothing I liked better when I was young. High spirits is all it is. There is no harm in the majority of young people in Buncrana.'

Biddy gave an impatient toss of her head. 'Molly cannot be spared on Saturdays. She has duties at home.'

Father Finlay regarded Biddy gravely and shook his head as he said, 'I don't believe that I am hearing this. We are talking here of Molly's Catholic duty. Would you have her

163

immortal soul imperilled? Isn't that why you removed the girl from Birmingham, to ensure she had a proper, Catholic upbringing?'

Tom saw that Molly was sitting with her head bent and he knew that was to prevent Biddy seeing her face, which he guessed would have a smile on it, for he was having a similar problem adjusting his own features. Once he had heard the expression 'hoist with his own petard', and it seemed to fit this situation very aptly indeed.

Biddy knew it too. 'Yes, well, Father . . . you see, the thing is . . .'

Father Finlay took advantage of her confusion. 'I will expect to see Molly at confession at least once a fortnight from now on,' he said firmly. 'How you arrange it is your business, but I think it would do Molly no harm at all – indeed, a great deal of good – to meet with young people of her own age. I feel I would be failing in my duty if I didn't tell you this and if I allowed this situation to go on any longer.'

He got to his feet as he spoke. Biddy looked as if she was suffering from extreme shock, which was causing her mouth to open and close like a fish's.

It was Tom who got up, shook the priest by the hand and said, 'You have eased my mind, for this is what I wanted to happen from the beginning.'

'Well, we all have to avail ourselves of the sacraments,' Father Finlay said as Tom helped him with his coat. 'They are, after all, the very backbone of the Catholic Church. Good night to you all.'

Biddy didn't speak, but Molly said, 'Good night, Father.'

Tom put in, 'Wait, Father. I'll get a torch and go along with you to the head of the lane, for it's like pitch out there. I'd not want to find you in a ditch in the morning.'

Molly watched her grandmother's malicious eyes swivel to meet hers and she wanted to beg Tom to stay in the cottage, to let the priest make his own way, for she knew

164

that falling into a ditch would be nothing to what was going to happen to her once the men left.

She was right. Barely had the door closed behind them than Biddy, her face close to Molly's, hissed, 'You put the priest up to this.'

Molly was so scared her insides were jumping about and her heart was thumping against her ribs. She knew she was going to catch it and there wasn't anything she could do about it. She tried protesting, however. 'I didn't. I swear I didn't. The priest asked me. He said—'

'Liar!' The punch that accompanied the word, landed square between Molly's eyes. It knocked her from the chair on to the floor, and for a second or two she thought she had been blinded. And then she screamed as her grandmother yanked her to her feet by her hair and pounded into her again and again. Molly's knees had buckled beneath her, but her grandmother had Molly's hair twisted around her fingers and was holding her up as she laid into her.

A white hot fury had taken hold of Biddy and in the forefront of her mind was the picture of her husband lying dead on the floor. Each punch she levelled at Molly was because she was the daughter of the one who had caused that death and because she had gone whining to the priest. So out of control was Biddy that she wouldn't really have cared if she killed Molly. She pummelled her face and body, ignoring her gasps of pain, the screams and cries, and eventually Molly sagged unconscious. Biddy let her fall to the floor just as Tom came in the door.

'What have you done to her now?' he demanded, falling to his knees by Molly's side. It was only too obvious what had been done to her, and he could barely look down on that face as he reached across to her neck for the pulse. He sighed in relief when he felt it throbbing beneath his fingers.

But she had been so badly beaten her face was just a pulpy and bloodied mess and her eyes mere slits. Tom looked from his niece to his mother almost in disbelief. He castigated

165

himself for leaving Molly at all to accompany the priest and then to stand chatting with him as if neither had a care in the world, while this carnage, this brutality was going on just a few yards away.

It was not the first time his mother had behaved like an untamed, out-of-control animal. His childhood had been a harsh one anyway, but there were times when his mother seemed to lose all self-control, as if a form of madness had taken over. Tom had suffered from this more than either of his brothers, and it was only the intervention of his father, often alerted by one of the others, that had sometimes prevented his mother flaying the skin from his body with the bamboo cane.

'You deserve to be locked up, you bloody maniac,' he ground out as he lifted Molly in his arms. 'And it may come to that yet.'

'Don't you—'

'Don't even try talking to me,' Tom said. 'There are no words you could say I would want to hear. Do you know, I regret even breathing the same air as you and suggest you get to your bed and quickly, before I forget that I am your son and am tempted to give you a taste of your own medicine.'

The look in Tom's eyes was one that Biddy had never seen before, and she decided that she might be better in bed after all. Tom lifted Molly into his arms, laid her gently on her bed, and took off her boots. His hands were tender as he bathed her face gently. But her eyes remained closed, even as he eased her dungarees from her, though he left her shirt on. Then he settled himself in the chair beside the bed for the long night ahead, determined not to leave her, lest she need something.

He watched her laboured breathing and resolved to get the doctor in if she had not recovered consciousness by the morning. His mother would kick up, but what odds whatever she did now? God Almighty, she had nearly killed the girl, and showed not a hint of remorse at what she had done. By Christ, if there was any repeat of this, or anything remotely like it, he would kill the woman with his own hands.

When Molly woke up, she felt as if she was in the pit of hell, only she couldn't wake up, not properly, because she couldn't open her eyes fully. Her head was pounding. She remembered the events of the evening before, and she gingerly touched her face with her fingers, feeling the cuts, grazes and bruises.

She had the acrid taste of blood in her mouth and her probing tongue found her split lips, lacerated cheeks and torn gums. She groaned and the slight sound disturbed Tom, who was in a light and uncomfortable slumber in the chair with all his clothes but his jacket still on.

'Molly,' he whispered, gazing at her in the light of the lamp he had left on all night. 'How are you feeling?'

Molly shook her head and then gasped, for even such a slight movement hurt her almost unbearably and her words sounded muffled and indistinct through her damaged mouth and thick lips. 'I hurt.'

'Oh God,' Tom cried. 'I am sick to the very soul of me that this has happened to you. Sorry seems so inadequate, but I am sorry – more sorry than there are words for.'

'I am afraid,' Molly said.

She had been wary of her grandmother before and of the clouts, punches and slaps she would dish out, usually where Tom wouldn't see, confident that Molly would say nothing, but the attack the previous evening had been savage. Molly had felt deep and primeval fear, for she had truly believed that Biddy had wanted to kill her, was trying to kill her.

'Don't be,' Tom said. 'Please don't, because I promise she'll never lay a hand on you again.'

Molly shut her eyes then, so that Tom shouldn't see the disbelief in them and be upset, for she knew, with the best will in the world, he was no protection if his mother was bent on destroying her. He couldn't guard her twenty-four hours a day.

The tears seeped from her eyes because she felt so helpless. Tom patted her hand, but said nothing, for he couldn't think of any words to say that would help.

TWELVE

Molly stayed in bed for four full days and Tom tended to her every need. During that time she never saw her grandmother at all, but she knew that that way of life could not continue for ever and so the fifth day, though her face still bore evidence of the attack and her body was painful and stiff, she got out of bed and was dressed when Tom came in to see how she was.

He was pleased, taking it as evidence of her improvement, though he did urge her to take it easy.

Molly shook her head. 'It's not the workload that worries me, Tom. It is coming face to face with your mother, but I know that it's got to be done. I know that I can't skulk in my room for the rest of my life.'

'You're right, Molly,' Tom said. 'And once more I admire your courage. And I'll be right behind you, remember that.'

The knowledge should have made Molly feel better, but it didn't and she was full of trepidation. Her mouth so dry she could barely swallow when she stepped into that room. She knew that the only way to deal with her grandmother was to stand up to her, but she didn't know if she had the courage this time.

When she saw Biddy's eyes slide over her face, she felt her whole body start to quiver, especially when she saw her eyes held no remorse; rather they had a gloating look about them. Biddy wasn't sorry, not even one bit. She had felt sure that once she had the girl in Ireland she would soon lick her into shape, show her who was master, as she had her own children.

However, Molly had upended the whole house, and in her defiance and insolence had not only got Tom's support, but the McEvoys' and now even the priest's. It was not to be borne. But Biddy knew this time she had thoroughly frightened the girl and she was still so full of fear that Biddy could almost smell it emanating from her.

Tom watched Molly's reaction to his mother with worried eyes. He could well understand it. It had been that same fear that had dogged his own life and made him the soft, malleable man he was. From the arrival of Molly, his life had begun to change. For her sake he had to speak out, learn to criticise and even defy his mother sometimes and stand on his own feet more.

Molly's tenacity had astonished him at times, yet he acknowledged this latest vicious attack had really seemed to unnerve her. Maybe it was down to him this time and so he said, 'Haven't you something to say to Molly, Mammy?'

Biddy's eyes slid to those of her son. 'I don't think so,' she said.

'I was thinking of an apology, at least.'

'There will be no apology. The girl asked for everything she got.'

'No I did not,' Molly yelled, sudden anger replacing her fear. 'You hit me because you wanted to and kept on hitting me, even when I couldn't feel it any more. You are not even human, because it isn't normal to go on the way you did.

'Now you listen to this,' she went on, 'my face is a mess and my body a mass of bruises, but they will heal, but your mind I doubt will ever be right. Next time you hit me, because the notion takes you, I just might feel like hitting you back, so I should consider that, if I were you. And you can bring the priest, bring the goddamned bishop for all I care, and I will tell them what you did to me and that it was no cold kept me from Mass and the McEvoys, which is what I gather you told them. And at least now I know exactly where I stand.'

She walked across the floor as she spoke and took her coat from the peg behind the door.

'Where are you off to?' Tom asked.

Molly answered, 'I don't really know. Just somewhere out of this house, where the air is cleaner.'

Molly followed Tom to the cowshed that evening because she refused to be left in the house with his mother, but Tom said she was to sit on the stool and watch and she was still so full of pain she was glad to do so.

He had had no chance to talk to Molly alone all day, and they had barely closed the door, when he said, 'I couldn't believe it the way that you stood up to Mammy today. You must have nerves of steel. You looked scared to death when you first went into that room. I thought I would have to be the one to fight for you.'

'In my rational moments I am still scared,' Molly said. 'But what she said was so unjust I was incensed and that sort of overrode the fear. I never complained to the priest, Uncle Tom. He asked me all the questions and when he said he would come and talk it over with my grandmother, I was pleased. No one could have predicted that she would go off her head the way she did. I honestly didn't know what she is capable of, how brutal she can be.'

'The point is,' Tom said, 'what are we going to do about it, because there will be occasions when you are in the house together and I am nowhere around?'

'My father said fear had to be faced head on,' Molly said. 'He told me that everyone is scared at some time in their lives and if you don't learn to cope with it, then it will control you. He freely admitted he had been terrified that day he had crawled out to reach Paul Simmons. I know he would agree with my stand against your mother because

171

she is a bully and he was always adamant that no one should let a bully win.'

'That is all well and good, Molly, but—'

'You are always complaining that I am too fond of that word, "but",' Molly said with a smile. 'I really think your mother is not right in the head and I will never let myself be such a victim again. I imagine I could give a good account of myself if I had to.'

'And no one would blame you,' Tom said. 'God! When I saw what she had done to you, I wanted to kill her. If she hadn't got out of my sight, I really think I would have hit her and that would have been the first and only time, and changed something between us for ever.'

'Maybe it needs changing.'

Tom shook his head. 'Not in that way. God, I would feel even less of a man than I do already if I raised my hand to any woman, let alone my mother.'

'I can understand that,' Molly said. 'Just don't expect me to feel the same.'

'I don't,' Tom said. 'As I have already told you, no one will blame you, and for what it's worth, you will have my support. Not that you seem to need it.'

'I do,' Molly said. 'Maybe not to fight my battles, but in championing me in other ways. It is really very hard to live with someone who hates you so much. Without you I don't think I would be able to cope.'

'Molly, that makes me feel so much better,' Tom said.

'Good,' Molly said. 'And now if you are finished here, then let's go inside and face the old dragon.' But she was glad her uncle couldn't see her insides turning somersaults.

'I can hardly believe it,' Cathy said, taking hold of her friend's arm as they came out of the church the following Saturday morning. 'I could scarcely credit it when I saw you come into the pew. How did you get your grandmother to agree? Thought you said she was dead set against it?'

172

'She was – still is, probably,' Molly said. 'But this is all the priest's doing.' And she recounted what had happened when the priest called.

'And she agreed just like that?'

'No, not quite,' Molly said, and was unable to prevent the shudder that ran through her body.

Cathy was no fool. 'She hit you, didn't she?'

'You could say that,' Molly said. 'She thought that I had gone complaining to the priest, though I hadn't. He asked me why I wasn't at confession more.'

'And I suppose that cold you had . . .'

'Was no cold at all,' Molly finished for her. 'My face was too battered to be seen and my body so stiff and sore I could hardly move.'

'Poor you,' Cathy said sympathetically. 'What has she been like since?'

'Well, it has been pretty fraught, as you might imagine, and I stayed in the bedroom for four days,' Molly said. 'In the end, though, I had to get up. I knew eventually I would have to face her, and the longer I left it, the harder it was going to be.'

'God, you're braver than me,' Cathy said. 'I would be a crumpled heap, and I think that's how I would stay.'

'If I had been, then she would have won, for it was what she wanted,' Molly said. 'I know now that from the moment she saw me, her intention was to bend me to her will as she did Uncle Tom. She isn't right in the head, and reacting the way she does to things is crazy. Now, when we are in the house together and Tom not there, we seem to spend the time sort of circling each other like prizefighters.'

'You haven't got to put up with this kind of thing, you know.'

'Yes, I have.'

'You could tell someone. The gardaí . . .'

Molly gave a hoot of laughter. 'Oh, yes,' she said. 'I'm sure they would be very interested in me going in and complaining about my grandmother giving me a good hiding. They'd be likely to tell me not to be so bold and to run away and play. And in the unlikely event they did take it slightly more seriously, then it would be even worse for me. Just think about it for a minute.'

Cathy didn't need a minute. 'I just wish I could do something to make things easier for you,' she said.

'You do, by being my friend. Going to your house every week helps me keep my sanity and now if I can come to Buncrana every fortnight it will be even better. Come on, I can put my own money in the post office today and I'll keep some back to buy sweets. What do you say?'

Cathy saw that the subject of the beating was now closed, and she gave Molly's arm a squeeze and said, 'I say that you are the nicest friend a girl can have.'

'And I say that that is cupboard love,' said Molly.

A fortnight later it would have been Molly's mother's birthday, and Tom knew why the girl was feeling so dispirited and low, because he remembered the day his wee sister was born. He was sent off on the horse, not Dobbin then, to alert Maggie Allinson, who did as a midwife for them all around, and he recalled he was nearly been blown right off the horse, and more than once, for the wind was nearly fierce enough to raise the thatch on the roof.

Maggie had come back with him astride the horse, holding him tight around his waist, for she said she wouldn't risk to take the trap and her smallish pony out in such a gale, and it wasn't long altogether till the wails of a newborn filled the cottage. Suddenly the wind howling and moaning and hurling itself about like a creature in torment ceased to matter.

Only moments later, Tom had gazed with awe at the tiny, perfect and oh so beautiful little baby and that is what he told Molly that day in the cowshed.

'A baby is a wonderful thing,' he said. 'Like a little miracle

174

that seems to get into your heart straight away somehow. I had to leave the room and I went out into the teeth of that storm and cried my eyes out.'

Molly's eyes were moist too as she said, 'I am glad you told me, Uncle Tom. Granddad used to tell me tons about Dad as a wee boy and when he was born and everything, but Mom . . . I suppose because this home was closed to her, she cut her early life from her memory, saying only that she was spoiled. Anyway, she said once that it made her unhappy to think how it had been, so I never asked again.

'Dad's birthday was the day after the funeral,' she went on. 'Mom was so pleased thinking she would be out of hospital in time for it and then it sort of passed in a blur of sadness. Anyway, when I sad this to Granddad, he said we should use their birthdays as a time to remember their lives, which were happy and fruitful, and not concentrate on the day or way they died, I think that is a good idea, don't you?'

'I do,' Tom said sincerely and then added gently, 'Molly, when did he tell you this?'

Molly clapped her hand to her mouth. Too late she remembered that Tom knew nothing about the letters. So many, many times, going or returning from the McEvoys, she had nearly mentioned the content of the letters, nothing earth-shattering, just some amusing incident her grandfather had mentioned, or a funny expression Hilda had used, and always she had stopped herself in time. And now this! What a stupid fool she had been. She groaned as she covered her face with her hands.

Tom peeled her hands away and held them between his own. 'Look at me, Molly. This is me, your Uncle Tom, who means you no harm, who only has your good interests at heart, and nothing you tell me here will I tell another living soul, unless you give me leave to do so.'

Molly lifted her eyes and knew that Tom spoke the truth, and so the story of the letters unfolded and Tom was amazed, and annoyed with himself for not thinking up his own plan to foil his mother. But when he said this, Molly told him it was better this way.

'No one connects the letters to me at all, for they are addressed to Cathy, and knowing the postman to be curious, for they want to know all your business here, Nellie let on that Cathy has two English pen friends.'

'You needn't worry that I will betray you, Molly,' Tom said. 'But how do you go on for stamps and paper and all?'

'Jack McEvoy—' Molly got no further.

'Well, that at least I can do for you,' Tom said, glad he could have some involvement. 'You can tell Jack McEvoy that your uncle will deal with it from now on. In fact, I will tell him myself when we go to Buncrana today.'

Molly nearly told him about the money then, but she didn't. That was her assurance that one day she would be free of this place and she could not risk that being compromised in any way. She knew Jack would say nothing to her uncle about the postal orders, because he had given his word and she trusted him.

She did feel bad, though, when Tom said, 'I'll tell you what I feel so awful about too, now that I have given myself time to think about it, and that is the fact that when I demanded a wage for myself that day coming back from the town, I never gave you a thought at all. I know what it is to have no money. I was that way for years and from now on will give you sixpence every week.'

'No, it's all right, Uncle Tom, really.'

'Of course it is not all right,' Tom said, and with a smile went on, 'and don't think I can't afford it. I have plenty to buy enough Guinness to pour down my throat, as my mother is fond of saying every Saturday all the way home in the cart and when we both get in on Sunday evenings, and enough to buy baccy for my pipe. What she doesn't know is I have a club I pay in to each week in the draper's for my next suit for Mass, the first I will ever choose for myself, and some left over that I put in a Post Office account for a rainy day, so sixpence is neither here nor there, and this too will be a secret between us.'

Inside the house, Molly's grandmother was waiting for her. She, of course, knew full well what day it was, but she had said nothing about it and Molly imagined that it was going to be a nonevent, not mentioned at all.

In this she was wrong, though the first thing Biddy growled out at them was that they had taken their time over the milking. Then her eyes slid over to Molly's and she said almost as a challenge, 'You know what day it is today, I suppose?'

'Of course I do.'

'I'm arranging for the nine o'clock Mass tomorrow to be said on your mother's behalf,' Biddy said. 'I am seeing the priest in Buncrana today.'

Only Molly's eyes betrayed her surprise and her grand-mother went on, 'Course, it might already be too late. Where d'you think she is now, Molly, your wonderful mother? Roasting in the flames of hell alongside your father, the pair of them screaming in agony each and every day, or did Jesus have mercy on her soul and cast her into purgatory, where she will languish for ever until there are prayers enough said to get her out?'

Biddy saw the look on Molly's face, the raw pain of loss, and she smiled as she sneered, 'I'm surprised that loving her as much as you say you did, you are not on your knees nearly all the night through, praying for the repose of your mother's soul.'

Sheer willpower kept Molly's voice steady as she said, 'Mom was the best mother to myself and Kevin that she ever could be, and a good wife to our dad, who she loved with all her heart. They died together side by side and if there is anything good to come out of that awful day, then it is that, for one wouldn't have ever been truly happy without the other.'

'Do you think the Good Lord cares one jot about what sort of mother Nuala was to a godless man or mother

177

to the children she should never have born him?' Biddy screeched.

'Do you know,' Molly said, 'my God is nothing like yours. Mine is good and kind and just, not hateful and vengeful like yours seems to be, and I think He cares about each and every one of us.'

'Isn't there something in the Bible where Jesus says He cares about the lilies in the field?' Tom asked his mother. 'Surely to God, some higher being who cares about a few flowers would care just as much or more about people, all people, I should think.'

Biddy surprisingly had no answer to that and Molly was grateful for her uncle's intervention for she had been near breaking point and was surprised that he had seemed aware of that.

Despite this, though, she was very nervous at the accent the priest would put on the Mass the following day. She needn't have worried. Father Finlay saw the white-faced Molly in the church and his heart went out to her. He spoke only positive things about the family, and Nuala and Ted in particular, and went on to talk of the tragedy that this loving couple and devoted parents, with so much life yet to live, should have been taken from it, leaving their children orphans and their relatives and friends devastated.

Outside the church, Biddy was not allowed to scurry home, driving Molly before her, for so many surrounded them, the men shaking Molly by the hand and many women, whom Molly saw had been crying, hugging her.

It was not the service Biddy had expected or asked for, and neither was the response afterwards, and she noted not one person had commended her for taking Molly to live with her. At one time she would have made Molly pay for that – a good thump or box on the ears would make her feel a whole lot better – but somehow, since that last beating, something had changed between them.

She had thought then the girl would be so cowed and

frightened, but that hadn't happened. Molly had continued to stand up to her and Biddy hadn't any idea how to cope with that.

Molly had no idea of Biddy's thoughts and when she roared at her later because she said the cabbage was inadequately drained, she flinched for the expected blow, and when it didn't come she was more than surprised.

As the first anniversary of the deaths and funeral of Nuala and Ted approached, Molly felt her spirits plummet. She remembered each minute of the terrible day they both died, as sharply as if it was engraved on her heart, or at least she remembered it until the doctor's tablets had done their job.

But because she hadn't actually seen her parents' bodies after their death, their funeral had affected her just as much. It was then she felt she had said goodbye to them properly and she had hardly been able to bear the sight of their coffins being lowered into the earth. She couldn't seem to prevent the memories seeping into her consciousness, so vividly at times that she would gasp with the pain of it.

She knew her grandmother, watched her with a measure of satisfaction and she wondered anew about the woman's mental state. Surely it wasn't normal to take such pleasure in another's misery?

Tom couldn't seem to help her and as the day Nuala and Ted had both died drew near, he did ask Molly if she didn't want to talk about it. But, she said talking would not help, it was just one more thing she had to live through. She got through it too, though she worked like an automaton, spoke only in answer to something someone asked her and that night Tom heard her crying for hours.

In fact, she was finding she was unable to sleep properly and if she did drop off, the lurid and upsetting dreams would soon wake her. Each day she felt worse and totally alone to deal with the dreadful memory of it all.

Tom was glad that that year the 26 April, which was the

anniversary of the funeral, fell on a Sunday, knowing that Molly would at least have the love and support of the McEvoys for part of that day. He made it his business to make Nellie aware of the significance of the date.

That Sunday morning, everyone who saw Molly knew there was something grievously wrong with her. Not indeed that many did see her, because she entered the church with Biddy just as the Mass had begun and left before the last response. Nellie, who had hoped to have a quiet word with the girl, was prevented from doing this and was heartily glad she would see the child later that day.

Molly hadn't really cared. By Sunday morning she had had no sleep for days and was too tired and downhearted to function properly. The pain in her head was so bad and she had the desire to curl up in a ball, her arms wrapped around her aching body, and howl like a wounded animal might.

Nothing touched her, not even Biddy's ill humour, worse that day than ever, but she set off with her uncle as usual in the afternoon. Once they were away from the house, though, she said, 'I don't think I will go to Cathy's today.'

'Why not?' Tom said. 'They will be expecting you.'

'I am too tired to make the journey,' Molly said. 'And I will be no fit company for anyone today.'

'Listen to me, Molly,' Tom said. 'I could go up and explain to the McEvoys and yes, they would fully understand, for they know what day this is. True friends are there for you through the dark times too, and I think you need Nellie, Cathy and even Jack more than ever today. Their true and sincere sympathy might soothe you.'

'I don't think anyone can do anything to help me today,' Molly said. 'I just want to sink down into the grass here and let the world go on without me.'

Tom shook his head sadly. 'Molly, if I could share any of this burden for you, I would gladly do so, for I see plainly how you are suffering at the moment, but I am

180

certain that trying to hide away from this is not the way to deal with it.'

'How d'you know that?' Molly cried.

'Molly, Nuala was my wee sister.'

'Oh, yes,' Molly said sarcastically. 'Of course she was. I forgot, like you conveniently forgot about her. Some big brother you turned out to be. You didn't even know my mother.'

'D'you think that makes me feel any better?' Tom demanded. 'Do you not think that I am heartsore about the past years that now I can do nothing about? I can't roll back time and have another go at it, though I wish with all my soul that I could, for in abandoning Nuala, I abandoned all of you. Whatever I do now, I could never make it up to you for that. How do you think that makes me feel?'

Molly looked at her uncle and saw, as well as sadness, there was guilt lodged in his eyes and even in the very set of his shoulders. 'You must feel awful,' she conceded, sorry for her outburst.

'Sometimes,' Tom admitted, 'I almost despise myself for my weakness.'

'You can't expect to overcome years of dominance in five minutes,' Molly pointed out.

'No,' Tom said, 'I suppose not. But you know it is hard to look back on your life as a grown man and see what a fool you have been throughout most of it. And now,' he said, 'we are nearing Buncrana. Do I go on alone and make your excuses to the McEvoys or are you going along to tea, as they will expect?'

Molly knew she had to go. She couldn't let her good kind friends down and knew uncle was right, they wouldn't expect her to be sparkling company. And so she nodded her head, 'All right then, I will go on to the McEvoys'.'

Nellie told Cathy to say nothing to upset Molly that day as they washed up after dinner, and Cathy was incensed that her mother thought she even had to mention it to her.

181

'D'you think I would?' she retorted. 'What sort of friend do you think I am? If I was Molly I wouldn't want the 23 or 26 April to exist on the calendar at all, but she is one of the bravest people I know, and she just might want to talk about it.'

'Well, that is all right if she leads the conversation,' Nellie said. 'God knows, the child has plenty to put up with anyway.'

Cathy, looking at Molly a little later, thought there had been no need for her mother's warning at all, for she could see clearly how sorrow-laden she was.

Nellie saw it too and she was also aware that she almost shrank from her embrace and Cathy's and guessed that the only ones Molly needed that day were those of the people who had gone through it with her. Nellie couldn't bring those people together, but she had the next best thing and she said, 'I have letters for you, my dear, as you weren't in Buncrana yesterday. Would you like to go up to Cathy's room now and read them in peace?'

Nellie couldn't have said anything better. Normally, Molly left the letters until she was alone at home, but that day she didn't want to leave them to read, and she didn't want anyone with her when she read them either. However, she knew that that was a rude thing to do in someone else's house and she could hardly ban Cathy from her own bedroom, so she heard herself saying, 'No, it's all right.'

'No it isn't,' Cathy retorted. 'And we can't make it all right. I think that you need to read those letters now. Don't worry, I shan't mind a bit.'

And so Molly read the words from those she had left behind, and tears dribbled down her cheeks. She knew it was right to cry and she felt their love and compassion for her, and she knew, though the letters had been written a few days before, Granddad, Kevin and Hilda would all be going through it the same as she that day and she was suddenly overcome with sadness.

182

When Cathy heard the anguished sobbing coming from her bedroom, she got to her feet to comfort her friend.

'No,' Nellie said. 'It is neither of us Molly wants right now and she badly needs to shed those tears.'

Nellie was right. Molly needed no one. She keened aloud with her arms wrapped around her body, racked with sobs and she rocked backwards and forwards in her distress. Memories of her parents flitted across her mind and tears streamed from her eyes like a torrent, as she felt the aching loss of them anew.

Later, when all had been quiet for some time, Nellie crept upstairs to see Molly spreadeagled and fast asleep on Cathy's bed. She had tear trails still on her cheeks and the letters were scrunched in her clenched hands. Nellie eased the letters from her and left them on the little cabinet by the bed, then fetched a blanket to put over Molly.

She slept deeply for three hours and as she struggled to wakefulness she realised that it was the first dreamless sleep she had had for days. Her heart felt strangely lighter, though she was mortified at falling asleep in someone else's house. Nellie waved away her apologies and encouraged her sit up to the tea they had saved for her and eat her fill. Molly hadn't felt hungry in days either, and suddenly she realised she was ravenous and she attacked the meal with gusto.

When she finished eventually and sat back with a sigh, Cathy said, 'Feeling any better?'

'Yes,' Molly said. 'Sort of lighter, you know?'

'I know all right,' Cathy said with a grin. 'Don't understand it, though. After the tea you have put away I would have said that you would have to feel a whole lot heavier.'

Molly found herself smiling at her friend, something else she hadn't done in days. 'You are a fool.'

'I know,' Cathy said with a sigh. 'Didn't we establish this early in our friendship?'

'Yeah, we did.'

'Well then, it's old news you're telling,' Cathy said as her mother came into the room and beamed when she saw Molly's empty plate.

'That's what I like to see,' she said. 'How do you feel now, Molly?'

'Better,' Molly said. 'I don't really understand why though, because nothing's changed. To tell you the truth, I have dreaded this day arriving.'

'That is quite understandable,' Nellie said. 'But I would say that it will never be quite as bad for you again as it has been this first year of that terrible, awful tragedy.'

'How can you be so sure?'

'Because I know you,' Nellie said, 'and I have come to know the strength of your character. I'm not saying that you will never miss your parents and that tug of loss will never leave you, but you have survived it and you should be proud of yourself.'

THIRTEEN

Molly took Nellie's words to heart and they helped her cope in the days that followed and the next Sunday she was able to talk of it with just a hint of Sadness.

'We used to make a big thing of birthdays,' Molly told Nellie and Cathy the following Sunday afternoon. 'On Dad's birthday, the year before Mom was sick, we went to the Alex Theatre in Birmingham to see a variety show. Kevin didn't go because he was too young, so Granddad looked after him and it was just me and my parents, and there was a man called Max Wall as the star of the show. What a comedian!

'I remember laughing so hard my stomach ached and then to put the tin hat on it, though we'd had this party tea and all before we left the house, we bought fish and chips on the way home and ate them out of the paper. It was the perfect end to the perfect day, and nothing can ever erase my memory of that. What hurts me a bit is that Kevin won't have many memories at all. I mean, what can you really remember clearly from when you were five?'

'Not a lot,' Cathy and Nellie admitted.

'Sometimes I think because he was so young, eventually he will probably forget what our parents looked like,' Molly said.

'It must be terribly hard for him right enough,' Nellie said with sympathy, 'and I often think it was wrong to part you. You really needed each other and please God you will be together soon.'

'There is still a part of me, like a nagging tooth, that asks why?' Molly said. 'That was the question Kevin asked the priest on the day of the funeral. But of course he didn't know either. I think Kevin thought he had a sort of hotline to God and could come up with a host of reasons why He needed our parents more than we did at that time.'

'I really understand your bewilderment,' Nellie said. 'And I haven't any answers to give you either. It was a dreadful and terribly tragic accident. To be honest, there are many things in the world that I don't understand, but I have to live life the way it is.'

'I do see what you mean,' Molly said. 'And you are right. We all hear of horrible things happening to people every day of the week. And now that this has happened to me, and I can do nothing to change it, the only way to deal with it is to go on, look forward and live my life as my parents would want me to.'

Both Nellie and Cathy were astounded by Molly's stoicism and courage. Nellie gave her hands a squeeze as she said gently, 'Well done, my dear. Now, how about tea and cake all round?'

'I'd say about time too,' Jack said, coming into the room at that moment. He had a large grin plastered to his face as he went on, 'And be quick about it too, woman. Tom will be here soon and we don't want the Guinness spoiling.'

'Don't you "woman" me, Jack McEvoy,' Nellie said in mock indignation, though she got to her feet as she spoke. 'And as for the Guinness spoiling, you never leave it in the glass long enough to spoil. And I wasn't talking to you, anyway. It was Cathy and Molly I was speaking to.'

Cathy raised her eyes to the ceiling, and Molly bit her lip to prevent a laugh escaping as they heard Jack's indignant voice as he followed his wife out of the room, protesting, 'Well, I like that, not talking to me, not considering me at all and me the head of the house . . .'

Molly felt a surge of happiness that she could count on

this family, who were so at one with one another, as her friends. She said, 'I do think your parents are lovely.'

Cathy pretended to consider this and then said with a grin, 'They're not so bad, as parents go. I think I have done quite a good job of knocking them into shape.'

Molly laughed. 'I wonder what your mother would say about that, Cathy. Maybe we should ask her. Isn't that her voice calling us now?'

Cathy left school that summer and began work in the shop full time. To mark the occasion, Nellie bought her new clothes, including a couple of brassieres to accommodate her quite large and pendulous breasts. Molly was so envious of the brassieres that Cathy showed her the Sunday after they were bought, but even more envious of the size of Cathy's breasts, which would fit in them, for hers were small in comparison.

'Don't worry about it,' Cathy said, when Molly said this. 'Anyway, with your build wouldn't large breasts look a bit stupid?'

'I suppose,' Molly agreed, for she was very fine-boned.

'They are not much use to me either,' Cathy went on. 'I mean, think about it. Look at the figure you have, and the skin and hair I would die for. It isn't as if I can take out my breasts for everyone to have a look and remark on how big they are, is it?' And then there was a slight pause before she said, 'Not just yet a while, anyway.'

'Cathy!'

'Why are you so shocked?' Cathy said. 'Someone will be entitled to take a look at them one day. And,' she added with an impish grin, 'more than a look if I know anything.'

'Do you ever think about things like that?'

'Don't you?'

'I asked first.'

'Well, course I do,' Cathy said. 'It's natural, isn't it, to wonder?'

'You don't think it's a sin?'

187

'How could it be?' Cathy said. 'The priests would probably say it was but, God, don't they see sin everywhere? If you got out of bed one morning and blew your nose, they would find probably find some sin in there somewhere.'

'So you don't confess it?'

'I do not,' Cathy said emphatically. 'And you won't either if you have any sense. What Mammy told us last month, did you think that a sin?'

'No,' Molly said definitely. 'Anything but, and less than a fortnight later, I was more than grateful.'

Seeing the girls developing into young women, Nellie had taken them aside and explained about periods, and just a scant two weeks later Molly started. She knew without Nellie she would have thought she was dying. As it was, she had been able to go into the farmhouse without any fuss, and ask her grandmother did she have any cotton pads for she had started her periods.

If her grandmother was surprised by her calmness, she made no comment about it. All she did growl out as she passed her the pads was, 'Period or not, there is to be no slacking. It happens to every woman every month and so there is no need to make a song and dance about it. Fill yourself a bucket of water to leave in your room to soak the used ones in and that should be all there is to it.'

Molly did as her grandmother told her and despite the messiness and the griping pains in her stomach, she welcomed her periods for they meant she was growing up, one step nearer to the time when she could leave this place.

The letters from Birmingham brought Molly up to date with things going on in the world beyond her narrow existence, like the civil war that had begun in Spain in the summer of that year, though Molly couldn't see why Tom was so concerned about it.

'But, Uncle Tom, Spain is miles away from us, and haven't there always been little wars or rumours of wars happening

188

in these types of countries?' she said, as they walked side by side one bright and pleasant Sunday afternoon.

'I have a very uneasy feeling about it, that's all.'

'But why?'

'Molly,' Tom asked, 'have you ever stood dominoes in such a way that when you push the first one it knocks into the next and so on, until they all topple over?'

'Oh, yes,' Molly said. 'I used to spend hours doing that for Kevin.'

'Well, I can't help feeling that what is happening in Spain is the first domino,' Tom said. 'Only time will tell if I am right.'

Molly, though, thought he was just being an old worry guts. She was more concerned with the Olympic Games in Berlin that summer, which she read all about in the papers at the McEvoys'. She was incensed by the fact that Hitler would not honour the black American athlete who beat all before him and, as Tom said, the action showed the whole world just how racist Hitler's government was.

There were other things in the paper closer to home too, like the poverty in England, which even the Irish papers occasionally reported on.

'Granddad says it's as bad as ever,' Molly said. 'It was bad when I left but I sort of hoped it would have begun getting better by now and not just go on year after year. Granddad said if something isn't done soon, he can just see the unemployed taking matters into their own hands and Hilda says more or less the same.'

It seemed there were many around who thought that, though, for by the time the harvest was completed and all stacked away for the winter, there came news of two hundred men walking from Jarrow in the North-East, where unemployment was nearly seventy per cent to bring their plight to the government in London.

The gesture captured the imagination of Ireland too, and there were many pictures in the papers of the weary marchers with thin, wasted faces, walking behind their battered bus containing all their provisions and cooking facilities rolling along beside them. Some towns and villages welcomed them and they were brought into church halls and fed, while other places were barred to them.

'Afraid of riots amongst their own townsfolk, I imagine,' Jack said at the tea table after scrutinising the paper. 'Mind,' he added, 'it is one hell of a way to travel on empty stomachs.'

It was. Molly hadn't been that sure where Jarrow was and Jack had shown both her and Cathy on a map. It *was* one hell of a way to travel, whichever way you looked at it, whether your stomach was full or not, Molly thought. It was gratifying to read that in the towns where the men were officially barred from entering, often church organisations and even ordinary people took on the task of feeding them.

'My mother would do something like that,' Molly said. 'She bought pies for our dinner one day in the Bull Ring and then gave them away to this barefoot woman and her clutch of children. She said that the woman was so, so grateful, like as if she had given her the crown jewels. We had to have bread and dripping that day and she said we had to be grateful for that, for those children looked as if in all their short lives they had never had full stomachs.'

'Point is, though,' Jack said, 'it shouldn't have to happen that way. There should be jobs for the people. Seems to me Ireland wasn't the only one let down after the Great War. And there is no good this chap Mosley trying to blame it all on the Jews, and inciting people to rise up against them.'

In the end, though, the Jarrow March was all for nothing, for the Prime Minister refused to see or speak with the men and, defeated and demoralised, they had no option but to return home with the situation unresolved. It seemed the last straw when King Edward abdicated, because the nation would not accept the American divorcee he had taken up with as their queen.

'Deserting the sinking ship or what?' Tom asked as they made their way to the McEvoys, the Sunday following this announcement on 11 December.

'I think it's what,' Molly said. 'Our old neighbour never liked him much. She thought the fact that he was handsome was the only thing he had in his favour, and that could be a handicap in a way, because if he was as ugly as sin, King or no King, I don't reckon old Wallis would have looked the side he was on.'

'You could be right,' Tom said with a grin.

'Anyway, it may be just as well,' Molly said. 'My granddad has been worried about Edward as King for ages because he says he's too keen on Germany and the German government. And with all we hear about them all the time, isn't that the last nation in the world you would like to be on friendly terms with?'

'I would say so.'

'And so would I,' Molly said, then added, 'This has been an unsettled year one way and another, hasn't it?'

'Aye,' Tom said in agreement. 'Let's hope 1937 will be better.'

Molly thought it just might be when, for her fifteenth birthday, her grandfather sent her a silver locket. When she carefully opened it, she found a photograph of her mother one side of it and her father the other. Her granddad couldn't have sent anything that could have pleased her more, and she placed it around her neck immediately, knowing she would never remove it, that she would wear her mother and father next to her heart, which was their rightful place, but beneath her clothes lest her grandmother see.

There had been little snow in the winter of 1936/7 and few truly gale-force winds, but the frost had been a hard one and the days bone-chillingly cold. Molly wasn't the only one to feel glad when the warmth of spring began stealing into the days. It matched her more optimistic outlook. She had good friends, the support of her uncle, her savings were building up and her letters kept her in touch with what family she had.

The 19 April was a Monday that year and, mindful of Nellie's words the previous year, Molly did not allow herself to dwell on the events of that dreadful day two years before. It was a beautiful day anyway. The sun shone from a sky of cornflower blue and Molly felt almost happy as she hung the washing on the line, knowing it would be dry in no time and she could have it all ironed and put away before the day was out.

The following week, Tom had to go into Buncrana and when he came back he told them of the bombing of the Basque town of Guernica. Jack had saved the papers for Tom to see for himself.

'German planes were used,' Tom said, 'and hundreds were killed, because it was market day and all, and no warning of any sort.'

'I am sorry, really sorry about all the people dying,' Molly said later as they milked the cows together, 'but it can't have anything to do with us here, or England either, can it?'

'It might,' Tom said. 'I imagine it was Hitler's way of showing the world what he is capable of.'

'Right, so now the world knows,' Molly said. 'But it was directed against the poor people of Spain, not us.'

Tom opened his mouth, but said nothing more. Molly was not ready yet to hear of his concerns. If he was right and he hoped to God he wasn't, then before too long there would be plenty to worry about. What was the point of meeting trouble halfway?

Anyway, Molly told herself as the year rolled on, she was right not to fret over Spain. Britain and Ireland were islands and safe, surely. England had a new King on the throne too, for Edward's brother had been crowned George VI. Her granddad had said in his letters that the celebrations had been muted somewhat because of the scandal surrounding Edward's abdication. Anyway, whoever was on the throne was ruling over a country that had its own severe problems, and in Molly's opinion the war to put an end to poverty was a far better battle to fight.

In January 1938, Biddy had news of her son Joe, from America. His mother-in-law had finally died and as soon as arrangements were finalised, Joe would be leaving.

'Is he coming here?' Molly asked Tom that evening as they milked the cows.

Tom smiled and shook his head. 'Joe left here with big ideas. Told everyone he was off to the New World to make a fortune, that he would come back with gold dripping from his fingers, and he can't face coming back here with his tail between his legs.'

'So what is he going to do?'

'He intends making for England as soon as he can, only the winter is not the best time to be travelling the Atlantic. He is looking to the spring to sail. I offered to send him the fare, for I know things have been tough for some time and the funeral must have been expensive, but he said he has some pride left. Gloria intends selling her mother's rings to raise the money, apparently. Hers have already gone the same way to keep them alive this far. Anyway, he has a job of sorts now that keeps them just about surviving until they are ready to leave.'

'What will he do in England?'

'Anything he can turn his hand to,' Tom said. 'One thing neither myself nor Joe is afraid of is hard work. Once he is in England, I shall cease worrying so much about him.'

Biddy didn't see it that way, of course. 'Going to England is madness!' she declared. 'Why England, when he has a place ready and waiting for him here? He belongs here. They can have Molly's room and she can sleep in the barn.'

'Thank you very much,' Molly commented sarcastically.

'And it is more, far more, than you deserve,' Biddy snapped. 'Write and tell him, Tom.'

'I will do no such thing, Mammy,' Tom said. 'Joe is a grown man and knows he can come back here and welcome at any time, and without relegating Molly to the barn either. But he has made the decision to make for England.'

'I might have known I couldn't count on you,' Biddy snarled. 'I will write to him myself and demand he comes here. I haven't seen him in years and I am getting no younger. Joe will be home before long, mark my words.'

'Will he, do you think?' Molly asked Tom later.

He shook his head. 'I doubt it, unless his character is changed totally. I told you, he never leaped to do Mammy's bidding like muggins here did.'

Joe and his family arrived in England in early March where they found lodgings in Tottenham in London, and Joe soon got a job in the docks.

Biddy, of course, blamed Gloria for Joe's staying away. 'Thinks we are not good enough, that's what it is,' she said. 'Don't know why he had to take up with a Yankee trollop in the first place.'

'She is Joe's choice,' Tom said quietly, 'and that is good enough for me.'

But not apparently for Biddy. Watching her, Molly gave a shiver of apprehension for the unknown American woman. She knew Biddy would always blame her for their decision to stay in England, and the longer time passed, the greater her bitterness would be. She sincerely hoped the two never got to meet.

As Molly passed her sixteenth birthday, she remembered the promise she had made to Kevin that she come back when she was sixteen, but as the time drew near she was hesitant to do this. Part of the reason was money, for although Paul Simmons had been more than generous, and a postal order had come every week, most of which she deposited in the post office, she knew she would be in need of a fair bit when she set off back to Birmingham. There were the fares,

194

for one thing, and perhaps lodgings and money enough to keep her until she got a job, because there was no way that she was going to live off her granddad.

Then Nellie told her that she thought Biddy might well have the right to bring her back if she was under the age of eighteen. 'I mean, she will hardly agree to you going back and consorting with the people she sees as heathens,' she said to Molly.

Molly gave a wry smile. 'I wasn't thinking of telling her, Nellie,' she said. 'I was going to slip away without a word. I know she wouldn't agree to it, and not just for the religious aspect of it either. She has had me skivvying in that house and farm since the day I arrived. When I do leave here and she has to do some of these things herself she is going to have one almighty shock.'

'So,' Nellie said, 'wouldn't it be better to put off leaving for a while until you are older and she will have no more jurisdiction over you? She could easily get the police to help her trace a runaway, especially a girl. When you leave here, you don't want to think that that old besom has any sort of right at all to haul you back again.'

And wouldn't she make me suffer for that act of defiance if she did? Molly thought, and a shiver ran through her. 'It would give me a chance to save more,' she conceded. 'But . . . well, eighteen is another two years away and there is that promise I made to Kevin.'

'You didn't know the set-up of the place when you made that promise, Molly,' Nellie reminded her. 'Nor just how bad your grandmother could be. Write to the child and give him some reason why you can't come just yet.'

Knowing that Nellie spoke good sense, Molly wrote to her brother that very night, but because she had never told them in Birmingham how bad her grandmother was, she just said she hadn't enough money saved to leave Ireland yet, but she would be with him as soon as she possibly could. That night, she lay in bed and went over the letter in her mind, knowing she had made the right decision.

One of the first things she had to do when she left this place was buy new clothes, for she had grown out of those she had brought with her. She now had definite breasts developing, though she would never have the figure of the more voluptuous Cathy. This, together with the muscles in her back, which had been strengthened by the work on the farm, had made her dresses for Mass very tight, and her coat she struggled to fasten at all. She had also grown taller, so that the dresses she had brought with her three years before were several inches above her knee and she could barely walk in her shoes that pinched her feet so badly.

Eventually and begrudgingly, Biddy declared she needed new clothes. Molly was as pleased as any other young girl at the thought of new things and she thanked her grandmother, not something she was wont to do often. It was as she saw her grandmother's lips curl as if in amusement that she felt the first tingling of apprehension.

Buncrana was well served with dress shops, but Biddy marched past them all and instead took Molly into the drapers. Molly's heart sank when Biddy selected cloth in the dullest of grey and navy blue for the dressmaker to make up into two dresses for Molly. She didn't hear what was discussed, for she was sent outside the shop after the dressmaker had measured her, so she didn't see the dressmaker trying to remonstrate with Biddy and try to change her mind.

'After all, I have a reputation to keep up,' she told Nellie later. 'What that woman wants me to do is not something I approve of at all, at all. She wants no decoration, not even shiny buttons, or a collar and cuff of a contrasting colour. And what in God's name is the point of it? It's like throwing some old bag over a beautiful flower. I tell you, Nellie, I thought of refusing to make the dresses at all, but,' and here she gave a shrug, 'times are tough. I can't really afford to turn business away.'

The following week, when Molly saw the dresses, her heart sank. There was no adornment of any sort about them and they went right up to the neck and down to the wrist and ended halfway down her calf.

'Ah God, Nellie, if you could have seen the look in that poor girl's eyes when she looked at herself in the mirror,' the dressmaker said to Nellie afterwards. 'And the grandmother enjoying it, so she was.'

'Yes,' Nellie said with a grimace. 'She would be.'

In fact, Biddy was far from finished. She bought Molly a couple of liberty bodices too. Molly had worn these before as a child for extra warmth in the winter, but they were nothing like these ones, which pressed her breasts down uncomfortably and had suspenders attached to them. Biddy bought thick black stockings to attach to them and voluminous knickers.

'Take that look off your face, girl,' Biddy said, as they left the shop. 'This is what you are getting. Like it or lump it, it makes no odds to me. Now for the coat and boots.'

The boots were second-hand, a pair the cobbler had left on his hands after repairing them. 'They are more a boy's boot than a girl's,' he told Biddy doubtfully.

'A boot's a boot, isn't it?'

'Yes, but these are hobnailed to make them hard-wearing. That's why the mothers buy them for the boys.'

'They look just fine to me,' Biddy said. She turned to Molly and said, 'Try them on. If they fit you, we will take them.'

Molly thought of the ugly clothes and the ugly underwear and now the ugly boots, and she wanted to weep, especially when she remembered the pretty clothes her mother had bought her, which she took such pleasure in wearing, and the patent shoes that she could almost see her face in.

197

However, she knew her grandmother was already enjoying her discomfort and would be delighted to see tears. She would not give her that satisfaction. She lifted her head at this resolve. The movement was barely perceptible, but Biddy spotted it and it enraged her. By God, she thought, I will knock that pride out of her if it is the last thing I do. The shabby black coat she bought in the second-hand shop was one the proprietor thought he would never get rid of. It was far too big for Molly too, and so long she knew it would reach the top of her boots, but Biddy told him to wrap it up, they would take it.

The next morning, Tom could hardly believe her eyes when Molly came out of her room dressed in her new clothes for Mass. He understood now why she hadn't been excited at getting new things like Nuala had always been. She would be showing him this and that in the cart even, and once home insist on putting the new things on and parading in front of them all, his mother looking on dotingly at her darling child.

His eyes slid to his mother's now and he saw the gleam of satisfaction there. He thought her a malicious old cow and he knew the best thing to do was not to mention the clothes at all.

So he smiled at Molly and said, 'You ready then?'

Molly was grateful to Tom and when she got to the church no one commented either, but Molly couldn't altogether ignore the looks of pity that were shot her way. She didn't want pity. It was no earthly use to anyone. She had money of her own now to buy what clothes she wanted. The five shillings had grown over the two years, especially as most weeks Tom remembered to give her sixpence, which she usually saved to pay for stationery and stamps. But she would not touch a penny piece of that money. It was to be her gateway to freedom, when she would be able to dress in any way she chose.

* * *

198

Just after they had news of Joe's safe arrival in England, Molly heard of Germany's invasion of Austria.

'Uncle Tom, you don't just march into another person's country and take it over,' Molly said as they walked home from the McEvoys' one Sunday evening.

'Well, that's what Hitler did all right.'

'And they just let him?'

'That's about the strength of it,' Tom said. 'Course, he was Austrian by birth. That's maybe why. Anyway, they say without a shot fired he is now in charge of Austria. They call it the Anschluss. It means joining up, I suppose, like a merger.'

'But I don't understand,' Molly said. 'I mean, why did he want Austria? Isn't Germany enough for him?'

'Ah, Molly! If it was just Austria.'

'What do you mean?'

'I mean that I think this is the tip of a very big iceberg.'

'But it doesn't have to be,' Molly said. 'If Hitler wants Austria for some reason, and Austria doesn't mind, then let him have the damned place if it matters much to him.'

'I think, Molly, that that is what the world will be forced to do,' said Tom.

Then in late September of that same year the Prime Minister of Britain, Neville Chamberlain, had gone to see Hitler in Munich and worked out a deal, and there was a picture of him on the front pages of the paper waving the piece of paper and declaring, 'I believe it is peace for our time.'

Molly, as usual, followed the news stories at Cathy's house. 'That's good news, at any rate,' she said.

'Um, I suppose,' Cathy replied.

'What d'you mean?'

'Well, it's just that Daddy said that Chamberlain had to give Hitler a piece of Czechoslovakia to get him to agree.'

Molly pondered this for a moment and then she said, 'Well, I don't see that that is right. I know what problems there are taking away part of a country, and Ireland knows

199

that maybe better than many. I also don't see what gave Britain the authority to take land from one country and give it to another just because they wanted it, and I have no idea how the Czechoslovakian government or its people feel about it either. But I can't help feeling if the alternative was war they would probably agree anyway.'

'You're right, of course,' Cathy said. 'It is what anyone with any sense would want. Anyway, I'm grateful that all the fretting and anxiety is out of the way. Maybe now everyone can stop going around with doleful faces.'

'Oh God, Cathy,' Molly cried with a smile, 'do you really think that is likely? It is adults we are talking about here, and the age of miracles is past long ago.'

'Cathy says her father thinks Chamberlain a fool,' Molly told her uncle one Sunday evening in early February 1939, as they walked home from the McEvoys'.

'He does,' Tom said, 'and so do I if he actually trusts Hitler and believes that bit of paper he was shaking so importantly has any credence at all. I don't want a war, Molly – no one in their right mind would – but somehow we seem to be balanced on a knife-edge, like we are waiting for something.'

They hadn't long to wait, because the following month, though the Spanish Civil War eventually drew to a close, the dictator Franco was the victor and the leader of the country, and that same month Hitler's armies marched into Czechoslovakia.

In May, Joe wrote to tell them of the Territorial Army recalled and mobilised, and the call-up begun of young men of twenty and twenty-one years. For the first time, Molly faced the fact that Britain at least was walking the path to war, and she wrote an impassioned letter to her grandfather and Hilda, telling them to look after themselves and keep safe at all costs.

Stan, probably thinking to reassure his granddaughter,

told her of the corrugated iron shelters that would be delivered to every house with a garden big enough to take them.

It will be the end of me growing my taters and my onions, at least for now, because we will have to dig a big pit to put it in. Kevin will help me – you would hardly know the lad now for he is growing up fast. Anyway, when the pit is dug and the thing assembled and fitted into it, you pile earth on the top. People say if there is enough earth then you can still grow your vegetables.

So don't you worry your little head about us, for won't we be as safe as houses in there? If war does come, it will not be another Guernica here, so don't fret.

It didn't make Molly feel any better at all. The thought of her grandfather and her little brother, and possibly Hilda and her husband too, burrowing into the ground like animals, while bombs rained down on them from the sky, horrified her. Her grandfather's reference to Guernica bought to mind the pictures she had seen of that blitzed town, the buildings reduced to piles of smoking, smouldering rubble, its many dead or dying, others dreadfully injured.

The savagery of it had shocked the world and now that same thing perhaps might be afflicted on them or those belonging to them. God, it didn't bear thinking about.

The talk of war was everywhere and couldn't be escaped as the spring rolled into summer. Tom told her, going home from the McEvoys one day, that not all Irishmen felt that the war should affect them or their country at all.

'Why not?'

'Well, you see, many feel that this is England's fight, not theirs, and they should keep well out of it. I think they are remembering England's promise of Home Rule as thanks for Ireland's support in the Great War, where our brother Finn lost his life.'

Molly nodded. 'Mom told me about that and also that the promise wasn't kept.'

'That's right,' Tom said. 'And of course that led to years of unease and almost civil war raging through the land. People here don't want to be dragged in again.'

'I can see they have a point,' Molly said. 'How do you feel?'

'I think the past should stay in the past,' Tom said firmly. 'What's done is done, and it does no good to be rehashing it all the time. I think if Britain goes to war we could well be dragged into it whether we like it or not. And though I am essentially a man of peace, I could do my bit as well as the next man if I had to.'

'Yeah, I think that is the best way to look at it really,' Molly agreed.

'But I think it would do no harm to get a wireless in,' Tom said.

'A wireless! Oh, Uncle Tom!' Molly hugged herself with delight.

Tom smiled at her. 'Joe was after advising me to get one; keep abreast of things,' he said in explanation. 'Seems a good enough idea to me.'

'But how will you work it?' Molly asked. 'I mean, we had a wireless at home, but it ran on electric.'

'These have something called an accumulator in the back,' Tom said. 'The man in the shop in Buncrana was showing me. He said it has to be charged up every so often and I can do that in Buncrana when I go in on a Saturday. Anyway, he has one on order for me and I am picking it up next Saturday.'

'Oh, it will be grand to have a wireless,' Molly said. 'Ooh, I can't wait.'

Biddy didn't think it was grand at all. 'Waste of more money,' she growled out as Tom proudly carried it indoors. 'Boy, money must burn a hole in your pocket.'

'I am no boy,' Tom snapped back. 'And when I ask you to give me something towards anything I buy, then you may express an opinion. This was bought with my own hard-earned money and we have already established that what I do with that is my own business.'

Molly smiled. For her money, Tom could go for a drink every day of the week because he could always cope better with his mother when he had sunk a few pints of Guinness with Jack and the rest of the men. And anyway, she thought, nothing could take the pleasure away from actually having a wireless in the house again.

FOURTEEN

England at least was preparing for war. Molly's grandfather told her of the trenches dug in Birmingham parks and the reinforced brick-built shelters that were going up everywhere. Even the children got involved, and Kevin wrote and told her of the hundreds of bags they had spent ages filling with sand through the hot summer days.

Hilda explained to her about the blackout and the issuing of gas masks.

> Not a chink of light to be seen outside and if it is, you face a fine of £200, think on that? And the ruddy gas masks is just horrible. They smell to high heaven, and everyone has a box to put them in that they must carry around their neck in case of gas attacks, they say.

'What are these gas attacks like, Uncle Tom?' Molly asked one day in the cowshed.

'Well,' Tom said, 'I can only talk about the last war when the Germans used mustard gas on the soldiers. It buggers up, I mean, damages the lungs so that a person can't breathe.'

'Does it kill?'

'Aye, I believe it can do,' Tom said. 'I suppose all these measures are to protect the civilian population. They are sending the children away too, so Joe said. Did your grandfather tell you that?'

Molly nodded. 'Doesn't affect them,' she said. 'Erdington obviously isn't considered a high-risk area.'

'Tottenham is,' Tom said. 'But Joe says that Gloria won't even consider Ben going anywhere.'

'I don't blame her either,' Molly said. 'But it is scary, isn't it?'

'All war is scary,' Tom said. 'Only a fool wouldn't be scared, and though the raids and all won't happen here, because Ireland has declared itself neutral, we have loved ones to worry about in England that I am certain will soon be in the thick of it.'

'I know,' Molly said, and her heart felt as heavy as lead.

On Friday, 1 September, the day many children from England's cities were travelling to unknown destinations, Germany invaded Poland. Molly's eyes met those of her uncle as the voice on the wireless told them what this meant. Everyone with a grain of common sense knew already.

Molly was glad the following Sunday that her grandmother wasn't the kind to linger after nine o'clock Mass. There was going to be an address by the British Prime Minister, just after eleven, and Molly wanted to have the opportunity to listen to it, although she knew what it was going to say.

She wasn't disappointed either. By 11.15 a.m. on Sunday 3 September 1939, she heard that Britain was at war with Germany, and she felt suddenly numbed with fear.

Everyone, both in Ireland and Britain, expected raids from the air once war between Britain and Germany was official, but it didn't happen. In fact, nothing did. There were battles at sea and ships sunk which were often reported in the Irish papers. Though Molly could feel sorry about the sailors who had lost their lives, that didn't adversely affect her loved ones at all.

In fact, what seemed to affect them most was the blackout. As Hilda put it,

Telling you, Molly, you ain't seen dark like it. You can't see a hand in front of you. And there's accidents, of course. I mean, stands to reason. Some of them have been little, like slipping off kerbs and that, and you do feel right daft when you find yourself apologising to the pillar box, or lamppost you have just walked into. But, some of the accidents have been more serious and people have been injured, or even killed on the roads, because the cars and buses and stuff are unlit too. In fact, my old man says he wonders who the enemy is, for Germany has been quiet since the balloon really went up. Calm before the storm, I dare say, but if the government don't do summat about this here blackout soon, there won't be the people left to fight Hitler off if he does try to take a pop at us.

Her granddad hated it as much as anyone else, but he was also dreading the rationing that was being introduced in the new year.

I know, though, it will be a fairer system and much better than the last war when the rich bought all before them, so that in some places there was little left in the shops for the rest of us. Anyway, I suppose I must put up with it like everyone else. If you utter a word in complaint about any damned thing these days you are reminded there is a war on. I mean, as if you are likely to forget.

I've had word that we are having our Anderson shelter delivered next week. We have the pit already dug and once the shelter is up I will make it as snug as I can for the two of us. Then Hitler can do his worst and we'll be as safe as houses.

Now, Molly, I want you to listen to me. I never wanted you to go to Ireland in the first place and I know that you would be well aware of that. And you also know that in the normal way of things I would welcome you back tomorrow, but you are safer where you are and I want you to stay put until this little lot is over. Me and Kevin are all right, but you would be put to work in a munitions factory or something like that, and those are the places that will be right in the firing range if any attacks come. I couldn't bear it if anything happened to either of you children.

Molly could understand her granddad's concern and was glad too that he was having the Anderson shelter delivered at last. She might not be that ecstatic about the two of them burrowing inside a tin shack buried in the garden but she had to admit that if the raids came, it had to be a safer place to bide than out in the open with no protection at all.

Spring came early in 1940, and, even though she longed to go back to Birmingham, by May Molly thought the countryside had never looked better. The sunshine lent a glow to everything, and many of the trees were heavy with fragrant blossom. Added to this, all the crops were ripening very satisfactorily in the fields. The war seemed a million miles away.

And yet just the previous evening she had heard a man on the wireless tell them of the bombing of Rotterdam that left nine hundred people dead. Molly felt sick, for she knew that this was Blitzkrieg, or lightning war, which the Germans had promised was coming and she also knew what had been done in Rotterdam could be achieved just as well in Birmingham, London or anywhere else they chose.

No one was surprised when Belgium and Holland surrendered, and then towards the end of the month they heard of the defeat of France, the Allied troops trapped on the beaches of Dunkirk and the frantic efforts to rescue them.

'Don't the people in Birmingham tell you any of this?' Tom asked Molly one day in early June as they did the milking together.

'If they try, like they did in the beginning, then the censor cuts it out,' Molly said. 'Now they stick to general things like how hard it is to make the rations stretch and how they have food programmes on the wireless every day and between films in the cinema, and there are hints and tips in the newspapers and magazines. Granddad has taken on an allotment with Hilda's husband, Alf, though he says he now has a fine crop of potatoes growing in the earth he piled on top of the Anderson shelter.'

'Which they haven't had any occasion to use yet.'

'No, thank God,' Molly said fervently. 'It is bound to come, though. The government have recommended putting tape crisscrossing the windows to prevent flying glass in the event of an attack, and the blackout is as stringent as ever, though they are now allowing shielded torches and shielded light on cars and other vehicles.'

'That must help.'

'Yeah,' Molly said with a wry smile. 'It would, I think, if the batteries for the torches were easier to get hold of. Granddad said he reckons that he could get hold of the crown jewels with less bother. I mean,' she added, 'there isn't much light to be had from the stars and the moon in the smoky Birmingham skies.'

'And that might be just as well, when all is said and done,' Tom said.

Molly looked at Tom, but didn't say anything. She was no fool and knew exactly what he was meaning, for a full moon shining brightly in the sky, as she had often seen it in Ireland, would surely light the way for any enemy planes determined to empty their load over Britain.

Tom saw the look on her face and wished he had kept his big mouth shut.

In mid-July, platoons of soldiers from the Irish Army arrived in Buncrana. It was strange to see soldiers thronging the streets, filling the marketplace and a fair few drinking at the hotel where Molly would meet up with her uncle on Saturday before walking back into the town.

'Do you know what they are doing here?' she asked Tom as they set off the first day.

'Aye,' Tom said. 'Me and Jack had a fine chat with them. Apparently, they are here to guard Ireland's neutrality.'

Molly stared at Tom open-mouthed. 'You can't be serious?'

'That's what they said.'

'Yes, but, Uncle Tom, Hitler's armies have goose-stepped throughout half of the world and emerged victorious. What earthly chance have a few soldiers got against such an army?'

Tom shrugged. 'Better than doing nothing, I suppose,' he said. 'Anyway, it is even more important now.'

'Why?'

'Because the navy has commandeered Derry and that's awfully close. They say Lough Foyle is filling up with naval craft, and the docks at Derry are now known as HMS *Ferret*. The soldier we spoke to said the British are building new airfields all over the six counties.'

'For what, exactly?'

'Well, I think it is all hush-hush,' Tom said. 'These soldiers weren't told it chapter and verse or anything, but these things get about. One fella says they will be doing convoy duty, trying to protect the merchant ships that will sail up to meet them. Good thing too, I'd say, especially as the southern ports are having a time of it just now.'

They were too. Night after night they heard on the wireless of the blitzing of those coastal towns. Molly felt sorry for the families suffering from such a battering, and Hitler massing his troops just across the channel.

Churchill claimed 'the Battle of Britain' was about to begin, which he said would be fought mainly in the air. He warned those in Britain to brace themselves for he was certain the whole fury and might of the enemy must very soon be turned upon them. Molly knew that was right, for

209

though the threat of invasion seemed less, almost every night Hitler's bombers began attacking London and other areas.

'Birmingham isn't mentioned,' Tom said one night as he turned the wireless set off. 'It just mentions a Midland town and that could be anywhere.'

'I am pretty certain that it is Birmingham,' Molly said. 'Remember the raid last month that the newscaster said took the roof off the Market Hall in the Bull Ring in the city centre, and the later one that did damage to the church there, St Martin's? Well, Birmingham's Bull Ring has both places and it would be too much of a coincidence for another Midland town to have exactly the same buildings, I would have thought. Believe me, Uncle Tom, Birmingham is getting its share too.'

The nightly raids seemed to increase through October, and then the letters from Stan and Hilda ceased. At first, Molly wasn't that bothered. Nellie told her that the shifting of letters might not be a priority for a country in the grip of war and to have patience. October gave way to November and Molly's letters to those in Birmingham had a frantic edge to them. Deep anxiety dogged her from morning till night and invaded her dreams while she slept.

'I don't care what Granddad said,' Molly declared as she walked home with Tom one Sunday in early November after telling him of the lack of the letters she so relied on. 'I must go and see if they are all right. It's the not knowing that gets to you after a while.'

'It's not a country I would be choosing to visit just now.'

'Nor I, by choice.'

'How will you manage it?'

'The same as everyone else, I suppose.'

'I mean . . .'

'I have money, Tom, if that's what you are worrying about,' Molly said, and she told him about the fund set up by Paul Simmons. 'Apart from the paper, stamps and envelopes, which I often saved your sixpences for, the money has been untouched for years.'

Tom's face was one beam of relief. 'You don't know how good that makes me feel that you will have a bit of money behind you. It is one less thing to worry about.'

'Next Saturday in Buncrana I will buy the tickets and make preparations,' Molly said. 'All I ask of you is that you cover for me on the morning I leave.'

'I will help you in any way I can, you know that.'

However, before Saturday they heard of the massive raid on Coventry on 14 November, which began just after seven. Coventry had been attacked before but that night it was, according to the wireless, the fiercest yet.

Biddy gave a grim humourless laugh and said to Molly with gloating satisfaction, 'Hah, there will be none of your precious country standing when the Germans have finished.'

'Do you know,' Molly said, 'I think you are seriously unhinged. Why d'you think the Germans so wonderful? What d'you think would have happened to us all if the Germans had invaded? I tell you this much, they would have made short shrift of you. And don't even think about that,' she warned as she saw her grandmother's fist raised. 'You touch me and you'll get twice as much back.'

Biddy was incensed, but saw that Molly meant what she had said. She had once told her grandmother that she could get away with hitting her only because she was bigger and stronger and said that it wouldn't always be that way. Now, while Molly hadn't grown terribly tall, she was hardened through the work on the farm, while the years had aged her grandmother, who had developed a slight stoop. Because of the indolent life Biddy had adopted when she had Molly to skivvy for her, she had become quite plump.

Biddy knew she was no match for Molly now and she lowered her clenched fist and contented herself with snarling, 'I bet they'll be none belonging to you left alive in that

211

godforsaken place after this little lot is over. They will be burned to a crisp like those in Coventry.'

Molly didn't even bother replying to this, knowing there was little point, and the following evening she found out the true extent of the damage to Coventry. In a raid that had gone on for over nine hours, the city was pounded by 500 bombers that destroyed over four thousand houses, three-quarters of the factories and annihilated the tram system, leaving nearly six hundred dead and countless others injured. The euphoric German papers were claiming to have invented a new word, *Koventrieren*, which was to signify the razing to the ground of a place. Molly knew with a dread certainty that Birmingham would be in line for some of the same.

That thought, however, only strengthened her determination. The next day being a Saturday, she visited Buncrana. Tom had barely brought the cart to a stop outside the Market Hall before Molly had jumped out of it. She was in too much of a tear to get things in motion to wait to set up the produce as she normally did and Tom knew this.

'Away then,' he said, and Molly needed no further bidding.

'Where's she off to?' she heard her grandmother ask peevishly.

'Running an errand for me,' Tom replied.

'What sort of errand?' Biddy asked, and though Molly by then was too far away to hear Tom's answer, she didn't care what he said anyway. She had things to do here and no one was going to stop her. She made her way to Main Street and the post office. She had arranged with Nellie already that she would remove all the money from her account bar one pound, as she didn't know how much things might cost. Cathy and Nellie were both waiting for her when she burst through the door. 'You have a letter,' Cathy cried.

Molly felt relief flood all through her. 'Oh, thank God!'

Her relief was short-lived, however, for she saw at once

that the letter was from Kevin, the address almost illegible as it had been written in pencil. The note inside had jagged edges as if it had been torn from a pad, but even so, the cryptic plea for help was clear enough: 'Molly, come and get me. It is horrible in this place – luv Kevin.'

'What is it?' Nellie asked, seeing the blood drain from Molly's face. Silently she handed the note over.

'What does it mean?' Cathy asked. 'Where is he?'

Molly shrugged. 'I have no idea. But it is even more important now for me to go over there and find out what has happened.' She remembered the promise she had made to her young tearful brother before she left, and knew whatever the risks to herself she could afford to lose no time in going to Birmingham and finding Kevin, however long it took.

'If anything major had occurred that meant for some reason your grandfather couldn't look after your brother, your grandmother would have been informed as next of kin,' Nellie said.

'Well, she hasn't, has she? I mean, she hasn't said.'

'Did she tell your mother when her own father died?'

Molly went cold. 'But she knows how much it matters to me?'

'Would that concern her?' Nellie asked. 'And she has no idea you would ever know, or at least for years, because she doesn't know that you have been receiving letters from them.'

'Oh God!' Molly cried. 'Well, have official letters come for her that you can remember?'

'I don't know, Molly, really I don't. There is such a volume of mail now – more since the war began – and I couldn't say, hand on heart, that your grandmother has received official letters or that she hasn't. Can you remember, Cathy?'

Cathy shook her head sadly. 'No, sorry, Molly. I haven't a clue. Why don't you ask her?'

'Because I would have to explain how I know and that

would bring in the letters and involve you, and I would rather not do that,' Molly said. 'And it would achieve nothing, because she wouldn't tell me.'

She looked from Cathy to her mother and admitted plaintively, 'I am scared. More scared than I have ever been in the whole of my life.'

'I know,' Nellie said. 'I don't know what you will find in Birmingham, and I wish to God you hadn't to face it on your own, but there is no help for it. Even without that heart-rending note, you have to go. And now the die is cast, as it were, we must turn our minds to practicalities.'

'Like what?'

'Like your clothes, my dear.'

'My clothes?'

'My dear girl, you cannot arrive in Birmingham with just two dresses,' Nellie said, drawing Molly into their living quarters as she spoke. 'You are smaller than Cathy, so you can have her old things. Don't worry, I have discussed it with her and she is in agreement. I have bought you some pretty underwear as well and a couple of brassieres, though I had to guess your size.'

'Nellie, you mustn't do this.'

'My dear girl, all the years you have been coming to our house I have never bought you a thing,' Nellie said. 'Not even on your birthday and at Christmas. I have felt bad about it too, at times, though it has been deliberate, because I didn't want to make things worse for you at the house and I was pretty certain anyway you wouldn't be allowed to accept things from us.'

'I wouldn't,' Molly said. 'I know I wouldn't. In fact, she would probably take them from me at the door and throw them straight into the fire.'

'I thought as much.'

'But you don't have to buy me anything,' Molly said, 'though I am incredibly grateful.'

'Listen to me, child dear,' Nellie said. 'You are going to

a country in the grip of war and you do not know what you will find, or where you will lay your head tonight or maybe many nights yet to come. You may have great need of clothes. Now, about those hobnailed boots . . .'

'I'm not taking them,' Molly said. 'I know that much. Whatever the weather I am wearing these shoes that Uncle Tom forced his mother to buy for me.' Molly well remembered the row when, as springtime really set in, Tom had declared that Molly had to have shoes for Mass and that his mother couldn't expect the child to go along in hobnailed boots any more.

'You are not shaming Molly, Mammy, but yourself,' Tom had cried. 'And if you refuse to have her decently shod, then I will shame you further and take her to Buncrana and buy her some shoes myself and let it be known why I am having to do it.'

And so Biddy was forced to buy her shoes, but they were summer-weight sandal-type shoes.

Now Nellie said, 'Take them with you by all means but you really need to travel in boots. 'What good timing that Cathy grew out of her boots only a couple of weeks ago. Your feet are so slender I know they will fit you.'

'Nellie, I . . .'

'All you need now is a nice case to put it all in,' Nellie said. 'And I have a lovely smart one that you can have a loan of.'

'I don't know what to say,' Molly said. 'Thank you seems so inadequate.'

'It's a pleasure, my dear girl,' Nellie said. 'I will worry about you every minute you are away, and though you have a fair bit of money, you will in all probability have to pay for lodgings. At least if you take plenty of clothes it will be one expense spared.'

'Nellie, you are so kind and generous,' Molly said. She felt her eyes well up with tears. 'I will miss you so much –' she said brokenly – 'miss all of you – and I am so very grateful for everything you have done for me. Thank you so very, very much.'

Cathy and Nellie were crying as much as Molly as they embraced. When Jack took her in his arms too and said, 'Look after yourself, bonny lass,' Molly felt such despondency her heart was like a solid lump inside her.

FIFTEEN

'Now are you sure you have everything?' Tom whispered to Molly as she made ready to leave.

'Everything,' Molly said. 'And there is no need for you to go with me.'

'There is, and I would prefer it,' Tom said, helping Molly through the window and following after her. 'Anyway, I want to talk to you.'

'Oh?'

'Aye,' Tom said. 'Put your bag on your other shoulder and I will have your case, and we will walk arm in arm because it will be warmer, and I will tell you all about Aggie.'

'Who's Aggie?' Molly said, glad enough to cuddle into Tom as they walked together through the raw, wintry night.

'She was the eldest of the family.'

Molly wrinkled her brow. 'Mom never mentioned a sister. In fact,' she said surprised, 'no one mentioned another girl. Did she die?'

'I don't know,' Tom said. 'I really don't know what happened to her. She ran away from home when she was fifteen.'

Molly stopped dead and stared at her uncle. 'Seriously?' she asked. 'She actually ran away from home?'

'Yes,' Tom said. 'Your mother was only a year old at the time, and as we were forbidden to mention her name ever after it, she never even knew about her. That's why, when your mother sent that letter to Mammy, it was probably

217

like a double betrayal. Two daughters gone to the bad, as it were – not that that excuses her behaviour in any way.'

'Did Aggie want to marry a Protestant too then?'

'No,' Tom said. 'As far as I am aware she didn't want to marry anyone.'

'But . . . Uncle Tom, she was little more than a child,' Molly said. 'Where did she go and why?'

Tom shrugged his shoulders. 'If she ever sent a letter to give any sort of explanation then I never saw it, or was told of it,' he said.

'Now,' Molly commented, 'why doesn't that surprise me? But . . .'

'Come on,' Tom said. 'We must walk before we stick to the ground altogether and it would never do for you to miss your train.'

Molly saw the sense of that, but her head was still teeming with questions about the unknown Aggie she had just found out about. She wondered why her grandmother hadn't made enquiries of her whereabouts, get the Gardaí involved as Nellie had thought Biddy might if Molly had tried to leave before she was eighteen.

'Did Aggie's life with her mother just get that difficult?'

'You could say that,' Tom said gently. 'Poor Aggie. As the eldest she had no childhood at all and was run off her feet in much the same way you were. Look,' he went on, 'though I can tell you nothing of what befell Aggie after she left here, and I was then only thirteen and not in a position to help her at all, that's why I wanted it to be different for you.'

'There is no comparison,' Molly said. 'I have a good case full of nice clothes and a money belt full of cash, even food for the journey, and that fine torch and a rake of extra batteries, as it will be dark by the time I reach Birmingham. Every eventuality is catered for and, look, I can see the lights of the station from here. You need come no further.'

But for all Molly's brave words, Tom heard the quiver

in her voice and knew she was perilously near to tears. For the first time, he put his arms around her and held her tight.

'Don't think the worst,' he said. 'Wait and see.'

'It isn't thinking the worst, Uncle Tom,' Molly said, taking comfort from her uncle's arms around her. 'It is being realistic.'

Tom, who now knew Molly well, was aware she was very near breaking point, and though he could hardly blame her, it wouldn't help for her to go to pieces now. He released her and said, 'Come on now. You have to stay strong for young Kevin. If you are right – and I hope and pray that you are not – then how must he be feeling?'

Molly straightened her shoulders and wiped her eyes, for her uncle was right and if some second terrible tragedy · meant that they were left alone in the world, then it was down to her, because she was eighteen, almost an adult, and old enough now to see to her brother. As soon as she reached Birmingham, she intended to seek him out.

Tom saw with relief that Molly had recovered herself and said, 'You will write? Even if you have no permanent address for me to write back to, let me know you are all right. Nellie will hold any letters you send me?'

'I will be glad to write to you,' Molly said. She stood on tiptoe and kissed her uncle on the cheek. 'Thank you for your kindness to me over the years.'

Tom's face was flushed crimson with embarrassment and his voice gruff as he said, 'Everything I did for you was a pleasure, and you may as well know that I will miss you greatly, more than I ever thought possible. But now you must go, for the train will not wait.'

Tom watched Molly walk away until the darkness swallowed her up. Burned into his memory was the day many years before when Aggie had climbed out of the window to make for England and to the very city that Molly was making for. From the night he'd watched her climb into the cart at the top of the lane, he never saw or heard from her

219

again and he knew he wouldn't rest until he got a letter from Molly saying she was all right.

Molly knew the train she would travel to Derry on would be a goods train really, but she would be comfortable enough in the passenger coach they attached to the end. When she booked her ticket, the stationmaster warned her the journey would be slow with plenty of stops, but this was the only convenient train. The other passenger trains didn't go out until too late for Molly to catch the mail boat when it sailed with the tide at about ten to eight.

That early winter's morning, Molly entered the carriage with a sigh. She could hardly credit that she was here at last, on her way to Birmingham, and on this date, Tuesday, 19 November, more that five years after she had left it. Had she just been going home in the normal way she would have been in a fever of excitement, but the nagging knot of worry about the safety of her loved ones had crystallised into real alarm at the arrival of Kevin's note and she wished the journey was over and she was safe at the other end.

She stacked her case in the rack above her and sat back in the seat. Thanks to Nellie and Cathy's generosity she was warmly and respectably clad for the journey. She had delighted in the feel of the soft underclothes against her skin and the brassiere that cupped her breasts so comfortably as she had dressed that morning, and she had chosen to wear the tartan skirt and the red jumper that Nellie and Cathy had insisted she had. The thick black stockings were her own, but the fine boots had once been Cathy's and she smiled at her reflection in the mirror as she unplaited her hair and coiled it into a bun, which she fastened at the nape of her neck. It was the way Nellie wore her hair, and Molly knew that immediately she looked more grown up.

It was a shame she thought that she had to cover her fine clothes with the old black coat, which was as drab and shapeless as ever, though even that looked better when

220

teamed with the tam-o'-shanter and scarf that Tom had bought her that first Christmas.

The journey was, as she had been warned, very stop and start, and so slow that sometimes she had an urge to get out and push. One half of her was in a fever of excitement to get to Birmingham, to find Kevin and bring him some measure of comfort, and yet the other half of her recoiled from the idea of what she might find.

By the time the train had chugged its way into Derry, she felt as cold as ice and burdened down with sadness. The night was still dark as pitch on the train to the docks at Belfast, and though the sky had lightened a little by the time she was aboard the boat, it hardly affected Molly's mood.

The pearly dawn had just begun to steal across the sky when she stood on deck and watched the boat pull away from the shores of Ireland. She remembered doing the same thing in Liverpool when she vowed to return, and she also remembered the promise she had made to her little brother, which she was now going to keep.

This time, although her stomach did churn a little, she was able to eat and keep down some of the food that Tom had packed for her, and she bought a cup of nice hot tea to wash it down, but it didn't chase away the cold, dead feeling inside her, nor stop her imagining the tragic and devastating scenario waiting for her at the end of the journey. Many spoke to the young and very pretty girl travelling alone and looking so sorrowful, and although she was pleasant enough, she wasn't up to a long, in-depth conversation with anyone. She wanted to keep herself focused on what she had to do once she reached Birmingham, because that helped keep the tears at bay and she had shed quite enough of those.

Although the day was grey, overcast and bitterly cold, Molly was glad it was daylight when they reached Liverpool and she followed the other passengers as they made their way to the station. The train south had passed three stations with the names blacked out before she mentioned it to a fellow passenger.

'It's to confuse the enemy,' the woman said. 'You know, in case there are spies travelling about the country.'

'But how do people manage if they didn't know the area?'

'Have to manage, and that's that,' the woman said. 'I mean, my dear, don't you know there is a war on? God, if I had had a pound every time someone said that to me since this whole shebang started, I would be a rich woman by now.'

'Yeah,' said another. 'As if you couldn't know. Even if a Martian landed I would say he would be aware of it, and in short order too. And the government treat us like imbeciles. I mean, look at that poster.'

The train had drawn to a halt at another nameless station and Molly saw that on the wall was a poster showing a man and woman standing beside a train ticket office that looked closed and the poster asked, 'Is Your Journey Really Necessary?'

'It's because they want trains left to move the troops, my old man said,' the first woman told Molly. 'But I ask you, with this stop-start nature they have at the moment and the way trains never run on time, because "there is a war on", you understand, if your journey wasn't necessary, then I'm sure you would stop at home.'

'This is all new to me,' Molly said. 'I was born in Birmingham but was taken to my grandmother's in Ireland when my parents died five years ago.'

'Ah,' the first woman said, 'how lucky to have one of your own willing to take you in, in such awful circumstances.'

If only you knew, Molly thought, but didn't give voice to it.

'Why come back now?' asked the second woman.

Molly told them about her young brother staying with his grandfather and the absence of letters that prompted her to come and see for herself what had happened to them.

'Well, I hope you find them both safe and sound,' the first woman said. 'But you will see Birmingham is very changed from the place you remember, and the two women regaled Molly with tales about the raids on Birmingham and the great swathes of the city laid waste, until the train drew up at a station they said was Crewe, where they had to change trains. Molly remembered it well, but for all that, was worried about missing Birmingham when she eventually got there. She was glad the two women were travelling on with her as they said they would make sure she got off at the right place.

They were true to their word, and when Molly alighted from the train, despite herself, she scanned the platform. She would have given anything to see her grandfather waiting for her, to see his eyes light up when he saw her, feel his arms go around her tight. She would smell the smoke from the pipe he always left in his jacket pocket, and she would kiss his dear, weathered cheek and tell him how glad she was to be back.

Tears stood out in her eyes at the realisation that she might never see him again, and she suddenly felt very lost and more than a little scared. She had no plan of action. She had money and knew she had to find lodgings, but she had no idea where to start. The almost sleepless night and the long and wearing day had begun to take their toll.

Two men had been watching Molly. They saw she was young and noted that there was no one to greet her. She was just the sort of girl they were interested in. Their eyes met, but they didn't speak; there was no need. They waited until the platform virtually cleared of passengers and the girl still stood there in an agony of indecision, trying to batten down her rising panic and decide what to do first.

'Can we be of any assistance to you, miss?'

Molly had no sense of alarm or unease, rather relief that someone had actually spoken to her, especially when the two men looked so respectable, dressed in suits and shirts

223

and ties. The man who had spoken had actually doffed his hat, which had been a novel experience. Who better to ask advice of than these two men?

She had actually opened her mouth to say this, but she was prevented by the wails of the air-raid sirens and she looked at them, her eyes standing out in her head and intense fear displayed in every line of her body. Ray Morris, the man who had spoken to her, knew that he was on to a winner, for the girl was stunning, absolutely stunning, and he knew Vera would pay a good price for one who looked like this – when he had broken her in a bit, that was. She liked them broken in, did Vera.

But that was for later. Now there was the air raid to deal with, a raid that the girl was obviously scared rigid of. He took her arm, saying firmly, 'Come, we must seek shelter. My name is Ray Morris and my friend here Charlie Johnson. Don't worry, we will look after you.'

Molly was only too glad to let the two men take charge, and they led her from the station. Outside was a hive of ordered activity, for everyone seemed to know where they were going. Molly and her escorts followed the stream of people. The strains of the siren died away and the dull thumping sounds of the first explosions, as yet some way away, could be heard.

Powerful searchlights lit up the sky and men with tin hats on their heads and armbands circling their upper arms urged people to hurry. Molly was never so pleased with anything as she was at the feel of Ray's arm through hers, while his friend Charlie came behind carrying the case. They went into a brick building, which seemed surrounded by sandbags. It was cold and dank, and very dim as the only light came from a couple of swinging paraffin lamps. The place looked very uncomfortable, the only seats bare wooden benches fastened to the walls. Yet Molly was glad that Ray sat her down on one of those, with him and Charlie beside her, because there wasn't enough seating for

224

all the people crowding into the place and some had to make themselves as comfortable as possible on the floor.

Molly had inadvertently arrived in Birmingham at the start of the worst raid that the city had suffered so far, though none was aware of that yet, of course. Inside the shelter, people talked and smoked and played cards, and some sang while others prayed. However, as the raid went on hour after hour, the crashes, bangs and booms becoming relentless, accompanied by the ringing of the bells of the emergency services, Molly wasn't the only one giving small yelps of terror or shaking like a leaf. The heart-rending screams and cries from the frightened babies and small children rose above everything.

The air grew muggy and stale, and Molly wasn't sure how long they had been entombed when just above them there was one terrific explosion. Even the seasoned Brummies, well used to raids, began to wail and whimper in fear. The wardens played their torches around the roof and walls and Molly saw that the walls were bulging in an alarming way, while the roof was creaking ominously. She suddenly felt her eyes gritty and tasted brick dust in her mouth, and by the light of the warden's torch she saw the mortar seeding from between the bricks holding up the roof trickling down on those below.

Suddenly the shelter door was opened and a warden popped his head through. 'Get everyone out,' he cried, 'and quick. This place is in danger of collapse.'

There was pandemonium and panic. People were shouting and shrieking as they fought to get out first, elbowing others out of the way. Ray, however, took hold of Molly's arms and pushed his way through the fear-driven crowd until they were out on the street, where the air smelled of smoke and gas, and scarlet flames licked the night sky. It was no safer, of course, and the warden was trying to direct the distressed people to the nearest alternative shelter. Molly stood a little way from the sinking, collapsing shelter and saw nearby buildings that seemed to crumple to the ground in a mass of rubble and masonry. The tramlines were lifted and buckled, and there were great craters in the road.

Above, the planes were all around her like menacing black beetles, flying in formation, droning like thunder, and the barking of guns, which she presumed were trying to bring them down, was incessant. She actually saw the bomb doors of the first planes open, saw the black harbingers of death toppling from them before Ray took one arm and Charlie the other as they hurried her through the streets after the warden trying to lead them to a place of safety.

Molly noted with some surprise the devastation around her as they leaped over masonry that had spilled onto the pavements, and avoided potholes, dribbling hosepipes and bleeding sandbags. By the time they reached the nearest shelter, which was in a cellar, Molly felt rigid with fear and quite surprised that she was alive and in one piece. She felt she would always be grateful to Ray and Charlie because she knew she wouldn't have managed half so well without them.

Throughout the rest of that raid, Molly trembled and shivered in abject fear, jumping with any louder than usual bangs, and she bit her bottom lip until she tasted blood. In the end Ray put his arms around her. In fact she snuggled in further, seeking comfort, and Ray held her shaking form and encouraged her to tell him what she was doing in Birmingham.

'It might help,' he said. 'Take your mind off things.'

Ray had another reason for asking. Molly had all the hallmarks of a runaway – there had certainly been no one waiting for her with arms outstretched at the station – and yet there was something about that theory that didn't quite gel. He had to be sure there would be no marauding father after him, no policeman feeling his collar.

'I doubt there is anything that I can say or do that would take my mind off what is going on,' Molly said, flinching at the noise of an eruption too close for comfort, 'but I will tell you if you like.' She intended to tell him a diluted version of what had happened to her, but Ray was too skilful at asking questions for her to do that unless she had been downright rude, and how could she be to someone who had been so kind to her? When she began it just spilled out of her, particularly the concern she had for her little brother and how important it was to find him as quickly as possible.

'Don't worry,' Ray said. 'I will help you do that, if you like. Though you were born and bred in Birmingham you were a child when you left it five years ago and the place is so different now.'

'I think you are one of the kindest men I have ever met,' Molly said sincerely. 'And I thank God I met up with you this night. And I would be grateful for any help you can give me.'

Ray smiled to himself, but he had noticed the slur in Molly's voice and how her eyes were glazed with fatigue. He said, 'You look all in, if you don't mind me saying so. Why don't you lie against me and try to sleep?'

Molly didn't argue. She was very tired, though she doubted she would sleep, but it was a relief just to lean against Ray and close her heavy eyes, and quite soon afterwards the exhausting events of that very long day overcame her and she fell into a deep sleep, despite the noise of the continued bombardment.

Ray, watching her sleep, told himself he was on to a winner this time. This Molly had no mother, nor father either, in fact no one but a young boy to miss her at all. It was just perfect, especially when he found out where the boy was and ensured that he wouldn't pose any sort of problem to them.

Molly was woken with a jerk by another ear-splitting siren and, seeing her alarm, Ray gave her shoulder a squeeze. 'That's the all clear, sweetheart,' he told her. 'It's all over, at least till the next time.'

Molly hadn't been the only one who had fallen asleep.

Around her, others were waking stiff and cold, and began making their way to the door. Molly felt sorry for the mothers trying to rouse still drowsy children, or soothing fractious ones while they gathered their belongings around them.

And then, she suddenly realised, apart from the bag that she had hung from her shoulder, she had nothing with her at all. After a cursory look around she said, 'Where's my case?'

Though it had always been part of the plan to dispose of the case, like they always did, Charlie looked contrite. 'I'm sorry, Molly. When they told us to get out of that shelter and fast, the case just went out of my head.'

Molly could quite see how that would be. She had been frightened witless herself, but everything she owned was in that case. 'It's all right,' she said. 'Really, I do understand, it's just . . .'

'We'll go back that way,' Ray promised, 'and see if we can salvage anything, if you like, but just now I could murder a bacon sandwich.'

'So could I,' Molly said. 'But where will you get one of those?'

'WVS van,' Ray said. 'Course, they don't always have bacon, but toast and tea would fill a corner, I bet.'

'You bet right. Lead me to it,' Molly said.

She found it just as Ray said. Only a street away was a van where two motherly, smiling women dispensed sympathy and humour with the tea. They were doing quite a trade, both with the weary homeless and the rescue workers. The orange sky lit up the early morning like daylight and Molly could see that almost all were covered with a film of dust, on their faces and in their hair. She guessed she was the same, and that her hat was probably ingrained with the stuff. They did have bacon butties, quite the nicest Molly had ever tasted, and these were washed down with hot, sweet tea. After, Molly, who had been feeling quite frightened and tearful, was more in control.

That was until she surveyed the mound that had been

228

where they had taken shelter earlier that night and knew she would have been killed if they hadn't got out. What was her life in comparison to a caseful of clothes? Nothing, of course, but what was she to wear – and in fact where was she to sleep off what was left of the night?

Ray surveyed the mound with satisfaction, knowing the case would be crushed beyond recognition. And he knew the site would remain untouched: there wasn't the manpower to clear mounds of rubbish that were no danger to anyone. It was all they could do to rescue those trapped, and so this time Ray didn't even have the bother of throwing the case in the cut, like he'd had to do a couple of times.

He said to Molly, 'So, what are your plans now?'

'I haven't any,' Molly said. 'Not now, I mean. I had intended looking for lodgings just for a few days while I found out a few things and, I hoped, located Kevin, but then there was the raid and all, and now I don't really know.'

'Well, you can't go looking for lodgings at this time of night – or morning, I should say,' Ray said, 'because it isn't yet five o'clock.'

'I know,' Molly said. 'Maybe I should go to the police station. They could probably direct me to a rescue centre, or something.'

That was the very last thing Ray wanted her to do, but he showed no alarm. Instead, he draped an arm around Molly's shoulder and said softly, 'Look, around you, Molly. This sea of rubble used to be streets and streets of houses, and the people that once lived in them are filling the rescue centres. They are bursting at the seams. The raid you witnessed tonight was one of many. The city has been pounded since August.'

'What, then?' Molly asked helplessly.

'Well,' Ray said, 'I am looking after a flat for a friend who can't live in it at the moment. It's the first floor of a house not far away and the place is completely empty. It would be somewhere to lay your head down for tonight, at least.'

How Molly longed to do just that, but maybe it wasn't wise – not that the men had said or done anything remotely suggestive or improper, and Ray in particular had been kindness itself.

'Neither of us has designs on you, so don't think that,' Ray said, and he spoke the truth for he was not attracted to women, men and boys being more his scene. And as for Charlie, though he would sample both, he liked his woman older, far more experienced and willing to indulge in fairly kinky sex. Girls like Molly did not interest him in the slightest.

When Ray said, 'We won't even be there; we both have our own places,' the last of Molly's reservations fled.

'All right then,' she said. 'I would like to have the use of the flat for tonight at least.'

The house Ray took her to was on the end of a terraced row, and next to it was a wide entry bordered on the other side by a high wall that had once been part of a factory, until it had been decimated by the bombing. The house had been converted into two flats very skilfully, and both were completely self-contained.

Beyond the front door, stairs led to the flat on the first floor while the door underneath the stairs led to the ground-floor flat. In the flat itself, just inside the door, was a hallway. Charlie helped Molly off with her coat, and she took off her dusty hat and scarf too. As she pulled her money belt over her head, she said, 'I had all my money in there. I was advised that it was the safest way to carry it.'

'Quite right too,' Ray said, putting it in the drawer of the cupboard next to the coat stand. 'There are all sorts of strange people about today. Come on in and see the place.'

Molly was amazed when she saw the opulence of the flat, which even the blackout curtains couldn't entirely spoil. The floor of the very large living room was carpeted and lit with two glittering chandeliers. And if that wasn't luxurious enough, two maroon settees and an armchair, which

Molly was sure were leather, were grouped around the gas fire with a shining brass fender. Two bureaus of dark wood were in the chimney alcoves, on top of one a fancy wireless, which it bore little resemblance to the one Tom had bought in Buncrana. Against the far wall was a shining, dark wooden dining table, and tucked beneath it were six chairs, again upholstered in maroon leather. And the whole place was heated by radiators.

'It is absolutely marvellous,' Molly said. 'But, Ray, won't your friend mind me just moving in like this?'

'No, Molly, he'll be pleased,' Ray said. 'And that is the honest truth. You wouldn't know the way your old city is now. Empty properties are either occupied by squatters, who have been bombed out, or commandeered by the military. My friend has only got away with it so far because this is on the first floor. Anyway, it's only for a few days.'

'Yes, that's right,' Molly said. 'He must have a fine job, this friend of yours.'

'I wouldn't know what he docs,' Ray said vaguely. 'A bit of this and a bit of that.'

Molly thought it a funny sort of job, but she reminded herself that he was Ray's friend and it really was none of her business. She contented herself with exploring the rest of the flat. There were two doors from the living room. One led to a sparkling kitchen that Molly knew it would be a pleasure to work in. At the other side of the room a door opened on to a small corridor with two further doors leading off that. The first was a bathroom and it had all manner of beauty products left there: body creams and lotions, even some cosmetics, as well as shampoos and soaps such as Molly had never seen in her life before. She wondered at the manner of woman, for it must have been a woman, who would leave all this behind, as if she had left in one hell of a hurry.

She shrugged. That wasn't her problem and she was more than glad the things were available when she caught sight

231

of herself, for her face was coated with dust and dirt, which was even gilding her eyelashes. Feeling a little daring, she filled the basin with water, which was piping hot, washed her hands and face with the delicious-smelling soap and dried them with the soft, fluffy towels left behind the door. Then she tidied her hair with the comb that she found in the little glass-fronted cabinet on the wall.

Feeling better and more refreshed, she went from there to the bedroom. The bed was very large and she noted the sheets were silk. The fact that they were black with cream edging was unnerving enough, but what really threw her were the mirrors on the ceiling and down the length of one wall. Then she knew that however lavish this place was, she would breath easier when she was away from it.

Back in the main room, the men had opened a bottle of brandy that they said they had found in the cabinet part of the bureau and they had a glass filled for her too, diluted with lemonade. There was something else added to Molly's glass, which would make her sleep like the dead, for Ray said he didn't want to come back and find the bird had flown, though he would take the precaution of locking the door.

Molly's heart sank. She was incredibly tired and would have preferred to seek her bed, even with the black silk sheets, but she knew Ray and Charlie only meant to be kind.

'I have never tasted alcohol,' she said, lifting the glass and sniffing apprehensively.

'Bout time you did then,' Charlie said. 'What age are you, anyway? Sixteen? Seventeen?'

'I was eighteen in February,' Molly said.

'Then the brandy will do you no harm at all, and once you have it drunk you will sleep like a top.'

'I think I would sleep well enough without the brandy.'

'It'll be better with, trust me,' Charlie said. 'Isn't that right, Ray?'

'It's right,' Ray said. 'And when you have it drunk then

we will leave you to sleep the sleep of the just. So let us toast the fact that we met up with you tonight.'

Oh, Molly had no trouble toasting that. She didn't dare think of what might have happened to her if she hadn't met up with these lovely men. 'Down the hatch,' Charlie said as the glasses chinked. Molly took a large swallow and found she liked the taste, and accepted another when she found her glass empty.

But when she had finished that one, she felt very peculiar. She knew Ray and Charlie were talking, but she wasn't able to register what they were saying. Her head had begun to swim quite alarmingly and when she tried to speak, her voice was befuddled and she couldn't remember what she had wanted to say.

'I would say you are a wee bit drunk,' Ray said with a smile.

Molly tried to say she was sorry but her tongue seemed to have swollen to twice its normal size and what came out was just gobbledegook. Ray and Charlie laughed.

'Come on,' Ray said. 'We'll help you to bed and be on our way.'

Molly tried to say she didn't need help, but she was unable to form the words, and when she tried to stand, she found she couldn't do that either. It was as if her legs belonged to someone else. The two men carried her to the bedroom and laid her on the bed, where her eyes closed of their own volition.

'What are you doing?' Charlie asked as Ray began easing Molly's jumper up.

'Undressing her.'

'But, why?'

'Well, I don't want to leave her in her clothes all night,' Ray said. 'She won't remember any of this. If we were that way inclined, we could both take her now and she'd be none the wiser. But she is more valuable to us as she is because I am positive she is a virgin and I have Collingsworth looking for just such a girl. He is willing to pay and pay well if the girl is untouched.'

'So what are we doing this for?'

'Because when she wakes tomorrow under the sheets and in a slinky nightdress, and we say we left her fully clothed, she won't remember a thing about it and I have a feeling that will unnerve her a bit and that's what I want.'

Charlie shrugged. 'You are a queer kettle of fish, mate,' he said. 'But I won't argue with you because I think we are sitting on a little goldmine with this one, if we play our cards right.'

'That is what I am counting on,' Ray said. 'So you just look in those drawers and get me the slinkiest, sexiest nightdress you can find.'

And Charlie, with a grin, did just that.

SIXTEEN

Molly woke with a raging thirst. Her head felt as if it were made of cotton wool, and Ray was standing beside her bed, holding a cup of tea.

'How are you feeling?'

'Awful,' she said, and her voice came out like a croak. She struggled to sit up and suddenly realised that she had a nightdress on that she had never seen before. 'How did I get here and undressed and all?' she asked, taking the very welcome cup of tea.

Ray looked confused. 'What do you mean?' he said. 'I told you to choose and left you to it.'

Molly took a long gulp of the tea, for all it was so hot, before saying to Ray, 'I can't remember anything, not even getting undressed.'

Ray smiled. 'That doesn't surprise me,' he said. 'Let's say you were not yourself last night.'

'Was I drunk?'

'A little, I think,' Ray said. 'But that was made worse by tiredness and the upset and distress you suffered in the raid.'

'I'm sorry.'

'Don't be,' Ray said. 'It happens to the best of us. Now, are you hungry?'

Molly suddenly realised she was. 'Starving,' she said, 'and when I have eaten, I will start the search for Kevin.'

'Too late for that today, my dear.'

'What do you mean?'

'It's already turned five o'clock.'

'You don't mean in the evening?'

'I do indeed.'

'I can't have slept all that time.'

'You did, and all I can say is you must have needed it.'

'Maybe I did,' Molly said. 'But I am still annoyed with myself. Can we not go out afterwards, when I have eaten?'

'Out in the blackout with a full moon shining in the sky?' Ray said. 'How would it be if we were caught in a raid that went on for hours and we were unable to get home? Trust me in this, my dear.'

'All right,' Molly said with a sigh. 'To tell you the truth, I still feel tired and not myself at all. I don't think I would be up to it anyway.'

'It is quite understandable,' Ray said. 'You sit and rest yourself and drink your tea, and I will rustle us up something to eat.'

When Ray had gone, Molly put the drained cup down and got out of bed, padded across the room and immediately caught sight of herself in one of the many mirrors. Her face was the colour of lint and her hair tousled about her head because she hadn't plaited it and it had come adrift from the Kirbigrips that had held it fast. Her eyes looked puzzled and were screwed up in pain.

She was wearing the most beautiful nightdress, which she was sure she had never seen before. It was made of silk, and a deep azure blue with a white lace trim, and though it was floor length there was a split either side to her thigh. There wasn't much to the bodice at all. It seemed to be made entirely of lace and it was so low cut it barely covered her nipples. Her face flushed with shame for, by her standards, the nightdress was almost indecent. She suddenly realised with alarm that her locket was gone. Scanning the room a little frantically, she spied it on the little table by the bed. But she never took it off. Then she told herself she

236

couldn't remember taking anything else off either, and she felt ashamed of her behaviour.

Ray didn't seem bothered about any of it, though, and he brought her broth in on a tray. 'Come back into bed,' he said, 'and eat this up. Then maybe you would like a bath?'

'Oh, I would love one. Will anyone mind?'

'How could anyone mind? There is only you and me here. I'll have to find you something else to wear; the things that you had on last night are covered in dust. There are plenty of clothes here, and for all you are a bit on the small size, I'm sure I will find something to fit you.'

'I can't wear someone else's clothes.'

'Well, you sure as hell can't go round in your birthday suit,' Ray said with a grin. 'It's too cold, for one thing. Anyway, it didn't bother you last night when you put on that nightdress.'

'But who do they all belong to?'

'Don't you worry your pretty head about that,' Ray said. 'Eat up now. You'll feel better afterwards.'

And Molly did. She was unaware of the white powder that Ray had mixed in with the broth. Afterwards a bath seemed a wonderful idea, and a few minutes later she was luxuriating in a hot bath full of fragrant bubbles. She washed her hair too with creamy shampoo.

Eventually, she stepped out and, wrapping herself in a towelling robe, she went through to the bedroom when Ray had laid some clothes on the bed. They were not at all the sort of things she was used to and she was not at all sure she wanted to get used to them either. She had virtually lived in dungarees and shirts for over five years, and though she had longed for something prettier and more feminine, she had never envisaged wearing clothes like those Ray had laid out. The lacy underwear and sheer silk stockings were nice enough, but the blouse was so clingy, none of her shape was left to the imagination and the neckline plunged so low it showed a fair bit of cleavage. The skirts were far too short too.

237

Fully dressed, she surveyed herself in one of the many mirrors. She looked like a different person and she knew without doubt that if there had been a person dressed as she was in Buncrana, people would assume she was fast, up to no good. Molly's cheeks grew hot at the thought.

When Ray knocked on the door she was almost too embarrassed to open it, feeling sure she was showing too much flesh altogether. He obviously didn't feel the same way, though, for she saw his eyes widen in appreciation.

'Do I look all right?' she asked tentatively.

Ray knew that Molly would have no idea how fetching she was. Her skin was fresh and glowing from the warm bath, her cheeks pink-tinged, and her hair was wrapped up in a towel, turban-style but some of her curls had escaped the turban and framed her pretty little face. For a moment Ray regretted that girls as beautiful as this one did not stir him in the slightest.

Molly's eyes were troubled, but when Ray said, 'You do not look just all right, you look wondrous,' they cleared a little.

She looked doubtfully at her reflection. 'Are you sure?'

'Quite sure.'

'You don't think I look a bit, well, sort of fast?'

'Molly, believe me, you are the picture of loveliness,' Ray said. He caught up her hands and turned her round to face him, and added, 'You also look seductive and extremely sexy, and what's wrong with that?'

'I . . . I don't know that I want to be sexy,' Molly said. 'And these clothes feel strange on me.'

'They don't look strange.'

'Well,' Molly said with a shrug, 'they'll do, I suppose, till I can get something more suitable.'

Ray pulled Molly towards him and put an arm around her shoulder as he said gently, 'Listen, sweetheart, Britain is at war. Making clothes in vast quantities is not considered important for the nation's survival and most places

238

that make clothes have been converted to making uniforms anyway, so there is little in the shops to buy. You were not the only one, either, to be left with just the clothes on your back. No one can afford to be too choosy these days. So these things may not be your choice, but there is little alternative.'

Molly knew Ray was probably right. After all, what did she know of war restrictions? And she had no desire to upset the man who had been so kind to her.

'Anyway,' Ray went on, 'you have a lovely body. Never be ashamed of it.'

'But it's wrong to show yourself.'

'Who said? The harridan of a grandmother?'

'No, well, I mean she didn't need to. I just knew.'

'Why?'

'What do you mean?'

'I mean why is it wrong to show your body?' Ray said. 'The female naked form can be beautiful. Look at some of the paintings.'

'I . . . I haven't seen paintings like that.'

'There are many of them in the art gallery in the town, or were before the war.'

'But in real life . . .'

'Someone had to pose, don't forget.'

'I couldn't do that,' Molly said with a shiver of distaste.

'Why not?' Ray said, and without waiting for a reply, went on. 'Look, my darling girl, you are no longer in a little tin-pot Irish town. You are eighteen years old and in a thriving city. Let yourself go a bit. And you do want to, even if you won't admit it. Look at the nightdress you chose for yourself. It's nice, very nice. You chose well and the fact that you can't remember doing it is neither here nor there – you still chose it. Be honest with yourself. You wanted to look sexy.'

Did I? Molly wondered. She couldn't seem to think straight; her head felt woozy. It wasn't unpleasant, in fact it was quite a nice feeling, but it did mean she couldn't seem to hold a thought in her head for long.

Molly was not to know how expressive her face was. Not that Ray scrutinised her closely and had a very good guess at what went on in her head.

'So let's have no more complaints about the clothes then,' he said, leading her by the hand into the living room and sitting her down on the sofa.

'No, Ray,' Molly said. 'I'm sorry. It was very ungrateful of me. But who did those clothes belong to?' She was curious about the type of woman who would leave all her things behind in such a way. 'Do they belong to your friend's wife?'

'He has no wife,' Ray said. 'And the things don't belong to one person.'

'Oh,' Molly said, perplexed.

'This flat belongs to a friend of mine, as I said,' Ray said. 'There is no need for you to know his name,' he went on, because by the time Molly was given over to Collingsworth for his pleasure he definitely didn't want her on her guard in any way. 'He is away at the present time, as I said, but he often entertains ladies here, and he likes them to feel clean and comfortable – hence the toiletries in the bathroom – and then to dress up for him because it pleases him, and the ladies like to please him in all ways.'

'Oh, oh, I see.'

'You're shocked, aren't you?'

Shocked was an understatement. Molly wasn't a fool and she knew what the girls would be doing to please him. She thought of the bedroom with the mirrors, and privately considered it one of the most disgusting things she had ever encountered. But she tried hard to cover that disgust as she cried, 'No . . . no, not at all.'

'Don't deny it,' Ray said with a smile. 'You are shaken right down to the core of your good little Catholic soul.'

'It's just that I have never heard of such behaviour.'

'And you think it wrong?'

'We are taught it is wrong.'

'What harm are they doing?'

'Well, if they are . . . if they do . . . What I mean is, sex before marriage is a big sin, just about the biggest, and these people will go to hell when they die.'

Ray burst into a gale of laughter at this before asking, 'For what? For bringing a bit of comfort and pleasure to one another?' That maybe was a little exaggeration, for the girls didn't always like it at first. They put up with it, though, as Molly would in time. The powders, their love of gin and the fear of being beaten virtually ensured their compliance until they got over their initial distaste.

No one had ever spoken to Molly of the pleasure to be had from sex. In fact, no one talked about sex much at all. Molly remembered Nellie telling her that her husband would tell her all about it on her wedding night. And she had wondered at the time how her husband would find out if it wasn't up for any sort of discussion at all. Nellie had never mentioned any pleasure to be had, but made it sound more of a duty that a woman had to do for her husband.

Here Ray spoke openly of men and women bringing pleasure to one another sexually. It was all alien to Molly. Yet Ray was right in one way, for they were hurting no one. She wasn't sure, though, that she could act that way, or even want to. She had never even been alone with a boy, let alone held hands or, heaven forbid, kissed.

She had allowed Ray to hold her tight when she was scared of the raids and had no objection to him draping an arm around her shoulder when he was explaining something, but he did those things as a brother might. Molly had never felt the slightest unease with Ray, but she didn't know that she would like anyone else to be so intimate.

Ray watched her face and smiled to himself. Molly didn't know what pleasures were in store for her.

'Time for a drink,' he said.

'Oh, no, after yesterday—'

'Nonsense,' Ray said, surreptitiously tipping the white powder into Molly's glass before adding the lemonade. 'Brandy is good for shock and, protest as you might, I have shocked you to the core this evening, so I am afraid I must insist.'

Molly sipped the drink, which she did like the taste of. But within minutes of finishing it she felt lethargy beginning to creep over her.

Ray felt the sag against his body and said, 'Come on, bed for you, before you are too far gone again.'

Molly wondered why she was so tired, but she definitely was, and she staggered as she got to her feet. Ray had to help her to the bedroom, and there she sat on the bed and tried to summon up the energy to get undressed. However, it proved too much for her and she slumped on the bed just as she was. Ray found her in a deep sleep a little later, so deep that when the sirens went off she didn't stir. Ray smiled as he undressed her, leaving her clothes scattering the floor and this time rolled her into bed and under the covers completely naked.

In the living room, he stood for a moment listening, but the raid was some distance away and he decided to risk going out. He had to see Charlie anyway, but he took the precaution of locking the bedroom door as well as the front one, and pocketing both keys before he set off into the night.

Ray found Charlie in his local. He sipped his drink while Charlie told him what he had found out that day of the people that Molly had come to Birmingham to find.

'Nothing on that Hilda,' he said. 'I mean, the people in her house didn't know anything, so I reckon she has kicked the bucket and a neighbour of the granddad's told me he had pegged it too and the kid was in an orphanage. She weren't sure which one, but thought it was probably Erdington Cottage Homes.'

'Molly is never going to know this,' Ray said. 'In fact,

with the powders and brandy I am tipping down her neck she'll barely be able remember her own name by the end of the week, let alone the reason she came back to Birmingham.'

'But why brandy?' Charlie asked. 'She will get nowt but gin at Vera's.'

'Yeah, but I prefer brandy,' Ray said. 'Don't worry, by the time she goes to Vera's, she will drink anything going, and be willing to sell her old grandmother for the price of a fix.'

'Hear hear,' Charlie said, and they chinked glasses as the all clear sounded.

When Molly realised she was naked in bed the following morning she was filled with mortification. Never in her like could she remember going to bed in such a state, and she looked at her clothes littering the floor with horrified surprise, for she had always folded her clothes neatly, even the hated dungarees, before getting into bed.

She also felt ill, really ill. Her head was pounding and she felt as if she had weights pulling at her, dragging her down. She knew that day she had to look for Kevin, but she didn't know whether she had the strength even to get to the bathroom unaided. There was a knock at the door and as Ray entered with a cup of tea, Molly swiftly pulled the clothes to her neck.

Ray smiled as he laid the tea on the side table and surveyed the floor. 'You went a little wild in here last night,' he remarked. Then he picked up the nightdress Molly had worn the previous night and said, 'Did you choose another nightdress for yourself?'

Molly's eyes were like circles in her head as she shook it slowly from side to side, dislodging the sheet as she did so and displaying her bare shoulders. Ray cried, 'You have nothing on at all, have you?'

'No.'

'Well, now, you brazen little hussy, you try and tell me

now that you are not trying to break out of the prudish prison your upbringing and the Catholic Church has put you in.'

'I don't know. Maybe,' Molly said. 'I feel so confused, and my head is spinning. I feel really ill, Ray.'

'Have your tea,' Ray advised, handing her the cup and saucer. 'I've put a wee drop of brandy in it to guard against the cold. That will put you right.'

'Good,' Molly said. 'Because I have to get up then. I have to look for something.' For a moment her eyes were troubled and her brow puckered as she tried to remember. Then her eyes cleared and she said, 'No, not something, but some people: my brother, Kevin, Granddad and Hilda.'

'Not today I don't think,' Ray said.

'Oh, but—'

'Look,' Ray said, and he drew aside the blackout curtains. Molly saw rain teeming down outside. 'You couldn't go out in this,' he said. 'And anyway, do you feel up to it?'

'No,' Molly said in a small voice. 'Ray, what is happening to me?'

'I'd say you were exhausted and you might have caught a chill or something on the way over. Nothing a couple of days in bed won't cure.'

'You think so?'

'Yes, I think so,' Ray said reassuringly. 'Now, I'll see if I can rustle us up some breakfast and you needn't lift a finger. What do you say?'

'I say that sounds just fine,' said Molly.

Molly spent the day in bed, getting out of it only to use the bathroom, not even bothering to dress so that Ray laughingly called her his little wanton, but the next day she felt worse instead of better, and was only helped by the especially laced tea that Ray brought her in.

The weather had improved slightly by the afternoon, and as Ray drew the blackout curtains he noted the clear skies and the half-moon visible in the dusky sky, and knew that there could easily be a raid that night. In her drug-induced sleep, Molly had slept through the light skirmish on Wednesday night and there hadn't been a raid on Thursday, but in case there was one that night, he gave Molly an extra ladle of brandy and more powder than usual to ensure she would sleep through it before he left the flat.

However, Molly had a nightmare, and in the middle of it she began to scream and woke with a jolt, panting with fear, which increased when she realised it wasn't her screaming at all; it was coming from outside and it was the air-raid siren.

She felt disorientated and strange, and she struggled out of bed, calling for Ray. Her legs felt very wobbly and, holding on to the bed and the bedside cabinet, she made a staggering lurch to the door and was alarmed to find it locked. She hammered on it and shouted until she was hoarse, then faced the realisation that she was alone in the flat. Then total terror took hold of her. She sank to the floor and sobbed while all around her was the drone of planes, the whistle of descending bombs, the crump and crash of explosions, the barking of the ack-ack fire and then the ringing bells of the emergency services.

The hours ticked by and there was no let-up in the bombing. Time lost all meaning. There was no sign of Ray returning either, and surely now, she told herself, he couldn't return in the teeth of a raid. Shaking like a leaf, Molly gingerly pulled herself up and stood swaying and holding on to the bedpost for dear life, waiting for the room to stop its listing. She was going to watch what was happening outside, face her fear like her father had always told her to do.

There were two windows in the bedroom, one overlooking the factory and the other on to the street, and she made for that one because she could hold on to the bed all the way round. Then with the blackout curtains pulled wide, she stood and watched as Birmingham burned.

Pockets of fire were everywhere, littering the skyline, spitting and crackling into the night with flames of yellow, orange and red vying with the arc lights raking the sky. Molly heard the bombs descend, saw buildings crumple in balloons of dust, some bursting into flames. Firemen valiantly played their hoses on them and ambulances streaked through the night. She watched for some time, mesmerised by it all, until in the end she cried at the sight of her city being destroyed and for the innocent men, women and children who had to try to live through it. She knew many would be injured or killed before the raid was over.

Suddenly, a bomb fell close, so close it shook the building. Molly felt the tremor beneath her feet and she fairly leaped onto the bed with a howl of anguished fear. Her whole body was quivering and her teeth chattering as she sat with her knees meeting her chin, her arms wrapped around herself and her head down, and waited for the building to collapse on top of her and for her to die.

Ray found her there the next morning. He had sat out the raid in a public shelter and then gone back to his own place after the all clear had sounded in the early morning to grab a few hours' sleep. When he first saw Molly curled as she was on the bed, she was so still and the room so quiet he thought for a moment she had died of fright. The thought passed through his mind that Collingsworth would not get the virgin he craved, nor would he and Charlie get the money he had promised them.

However, Molly was not dead. As Ray took hold of one of her arms, he felt the pulse and he peeled her hands away from her knees. Molly's eyes were open. That had startled him at first, but he realised they were seeing nothing. She was in some sort of trance and he caught hold of her shoulders and shook her a little.

When Molly came to and saw Ray's face before her, the one face she had longed to see, she, who didn't hug and kiss easily, was so overcome with joy and relief that she

246

threw her arms around his neck and began kissing him all over his face.

He pushed her away and she began to babble, 'Oh, please, don't leave me, Ray. I can't bear it when you do. Please stay with me. I will do anything, just about anything, if you stay with me.'

Ray smiled. He knew now that Molly would be putty in his hands and he put his arms around her and said, 'All right. Stop this now. You are trembling like a leaf. I'm here, aren't I, and not going anywhere?'

'Oh, thank you, Ray, thank you.'

'You are a silly girl to get into such a state.'

'It was the raid, Ray,' Molly said. 'I was so scared and I called for you, and the door was locked.'

'Of course it was,' Ray said. 'It always is when I leave, to keep you safe.'

'But where do you go?'

'To my own flat,' Ray said. 'I told you from the start that I have my own place.'

'Did you?'

'Don't you remember when I offered you this place first?'

Molly shook her head. She concentrated hard, but when she tried to remember, all she saw was deep blackness, and the effort of trying to break through that made her head ache. The absolute terror she had felt during the raid, which she had been sure she would never survive, plus the powders Ray was feeding her, had obliterated her memory.

'I remember nothing but the raid last night,' she admitted at last.

'Nothing?'

Molly shook her head. 'All that went before is a blank. I don't even know what I am doing here.'

'We were in a shelter together because of the bombing, me, you and Charlie, my mate, and you said you had nowhere to go and I offered you this place.'

'I don't know who I am.'

'Your first name is Molly, you told us that much,' Ray said. 'But I don't know your surname. Does it matter? Are you unhappy?'

'No.'

'Well, then?'

'But my memory—'

'Will probably return all the quicker if you don't worry at it.'

'You think so?'

'I know so,' Ray said. 'Trust me.'

'Oh, I do totally, Ray,' Molly said and added, 'Will you stay here tonight?'

'There is no bed but yours,' Ray reminded her.

Molly remembered how intense her fear had been the night before and feared she would die of fright if she had to experience that again alone.

'You can share it with me,' she said.

'Do you know what you are saying?'

Molly swallowed deeply and then looked Ray full in the face and said, 'Yes.'

Ray knew then that if he had been a proper red-blooded male he would have taken the girl up on the offer and to hell with the consequences. The fact that he had no interest that way was one of the reasons he had been employed to collect up the runaway girls and those escaping council care, and groom them for the whorehouse, so his emotions were not moved in any way by Molly's offer.

However, it would never do for her to know this and so he said, 'I think you are not really yourself, Molly, or you would never have said that. And if I were to do this you could well regret it and resent me afterwards.'

'I would never resent you,' Molly said firmly. 'I couldn't. I think I love you.'

'And I am fond of you too, Molly,' Ray said, draping an arm casually about her shoulder. 'That is why I can't do what you ask.'

'Oh, but, Ray, I can't bear to be alone, really I can't.'

'I can give you something to help,' Ray said. 'Do you trust me?'

'I do, Ray. Truly I do.'

'So if I say that I can give you something that will make you sleep like a baby till morning, when I will be back, you'll take it?'

'I'd rather you stayed.'

'We have been through this,' Ray said, tight-lipped.

'Oh, please don't be cross with me,' Molly cried, distressed. 'I will do anything you want.'

'Right, then,' Ray said. 'Now we know exactly where we stand.'

SEVENTEEN

Molly was entering a shadowy period in her life when she was only half alive, though most times she was unaware of this. At first there were times when people's faces would float before her, but when she tried to hold them in her mind, they seem to shroud over with mist and disappear.

When she was eventually worried enough to talk to Ray about this he said, 'You are thoroughly washed out, Molly, and your brain has shut down a little to enable you to rest and get really fit again, that's all it is.'

'You really do believe I will recover eventually?'

'Of course, and the thing to do is not worry about it,' Ray said. 'Sit back, relax and let me look after you.'

Molly gave a sigh. How good that sounded. She felt too utterly exhausted to care for herself. 'I'd like that,' she said, 'but haven't you got to go to work sometime?'

'Don't you concern yourself with that.'

No, Molly didn't want to concern herself with anything. She hadn't enough energy, for one thing. And she didn't want to risk offending Ray, for he was the one she saw every day – the only person, in fact, apart from a couple of brief visits from Charlie. She no longer minded Ray locking her in for her own safety whenever he had to go out. She had no desire to leave the flat herself, because she felt safe in there.

She hadn't to worry about anything, Ray said, not even cooking the meals, because he would deal with all that –

not that she was eating much, but she liked the brandy and the gin that Ray had introduced her to and the white powders he gave her, which he said were a tonic, always made her feel better.

Every few days, Ray would take away her dirty clothes and a few days later they would come back clean and pressed. The first time this happened she had asked Ray who dealt with the clothes and he said she hadn't to concern herself with things like that. And so she didn't, because it really didn't matter. In fact she was finding very few things did matter, and it was better once the half-remembered shadowy figures faded completely from her consciousness.

'So when are you going to give Molly a try-out?' Charlie asked Ray one day towards the middle of December. 'She's been here over three weeks already. You've never kept anyone longer than a fortnight before.'

'Yeah, I know,' Ray said. 'Collingsworth's been away, though, hasn't he? He's back now and I have set it up here for this Saturday night. I tell you, Molly is as ripe as a plum, just ready to be picked. Timing's good, anyway, because the older couple below us have gone to their daughter's for a while to escape the bombing, so Collingsworth can make all the noise he needs,' Ray said with a leer. 'If you know what I mean.'

Charlie gave a humourless laugh. 'Oh, I know all right,' he said. 'I should say the dirty old bugger is going to have some fun that night. You've done the work on Molly, though. God, she'll be led like a lamb to the bleeding slaughter.'

'If she knows anything about it, you mean,' Ray said. 'Some days she is not aware of much, but in any case, I will prepare her. She will do as she is told, don't worry.'

'She certainly thinks the sun shines out of your arse,' Charlie said. 'She just does everything you tell her to.'

'Like she will on Saturday night,' Ray said confidently. 'And if she is a really good girl, then I may buy her a specially nice Christmas present.'

Unaware of what was planned for her, Molly accepted it when Ray sat on the sofa and told that he had to go to a special dinner with Edwin Collingsworth, the man who owned the flat she was occupying.

She didn't remember that he was the man Ray had spoken of before, who'd had girls entertain him in the flat, so all she said was, 'Does he want me to move out?'

'No, don't worry,' Ray said. 'He has another place he lives in most of the time, but he does want to meet you, though.'

'Why?'

'Sweetheart, you are living in his flat, and rent-free as well. Isn't it natural that he is curious about you?'

'Oh, yes, of course, Ray.'

'He is also my boss, in a way, and it is very important that everything goes well tonight.'

Molly looked at him with a dreamy expression in her slightly glazed eyes. 'Yes, Ray.'

'I want you to help me in this.'

'You know I will,' Molly said, because she owed such a debt to Ray and would never forget it. 'What do you want me to do?'

'I will be bringing him back here after the meal, and if you want to continue to live here and also please me, it is important that you are very, very nice to him, when I pop out for a little while. You do understand what I mean by being nice, don't you?'

'Yes, of course,' Molly said. She knew what nice was, and she was hardly likely to be less than that to a friend of Ray's who was also her landlord.

'So you do whatever he wants?'

'Whatever he wants,' Molly repeated, and Ray was pleased to hear the slur in her voice from the effect of the drugs that he had given her a little while before. 'I will do anything he wants because I am to be nice to him.'

'Good girl!' Ray said, and Molly basked in his praise.

252

'Now, while I am away I want you to have a long bath and wash your hair, because I want you to look your best,' he said, hauling her to her feet. 'And I will go and choose the clothes I want you to wear afterwards.'

Edwin Collingsworth had not been in the house five minutes when Molly made up her mind she didn't like him. There was nothing even remotely attractive about him, for he was an undersized man, with an extremely sparse head of mousy brown hair surrounding a very large and definite bald patch. His wrinkled face was thin and he had a long, pinched nose and lips so lean and narrow they made his mouth look mean and cruel.

His eyes, though, were his worst feature. They were small, too close together and glittered as cold as two pieces of blue flint as they raked over Molly until she felt as if she was stripped naked before him.

He stepped forward and said in a sharp, nasal voice, 'I am delighted to meet you, Molly, and I must say you are just as beautiful as Ray said you were.'

Molly took Mr Collingsworth's proffered hand and then wished she hadn't, for it was limp and clammy. She imagined, as she shook it, that it was like shaking hands with a warm, wet fish. But, for Ray's sake, she didn't show any aversion in her manner and just told the man that she was pleased to meet him. Ray at least looked satisfied with her response.

She offered tea, but Ray said he had something Mr Collingsworth would much prefer and produced a bottle of whiskey. He was so obviously right, for it brought the ghost of a smile to the man's face, which wrinkled it up more than ever and made him look worse, if possible.

'Ah,' he said. 'Bushmills. Nothing beats a drop of Irish malt.'

Mr Collingsworth claimed he couldn't enjoy the drink unless Molly joined them, which she was more than happy to do, and Ray knew a few drinks, mixed with the powders, would make her like putty in the man's hand. Collingsworth had already paid Ray highly for providing a virgin, the balance to be paid when Molly had satisfied his desires, whatever they were.

'We must celebrate this day, don't you feel, my dear?' Collingsworth said, chinking his glass against hers.

Molly was puzzled. 'Why? What's special about today?'

'It's the day I have met you, my dear,' Collingsworth said. 'And the day you and I are going to get to know each other better.'

Molly's eyes sought Ray's, but she could read nothing in them that she could understand and he had a smile on his face that made her uneasy.

Edwin Collingsworth had never had much luck with women. He knew that most found him repulsive, but his money and influence ensured he had the means to pay prostitutes to satisfy his frustrated lust, and also offer any other sexual deviation he wanted. However, the women he paid were usually older, and had done it many times before, and what he really liked was an untried virgin. He wanted his hands to be the first to explore a young girl's body and possibly awaken the sexual awareness and arousal wrapped up inside her so that if she allowed herself it could be an enjoyable experience.

Ray was one of the best at finding girls to fulfil his needs and using the powders, which Collingsworth also supplied, together with alcohol, would soon have the girls compliant and eager to please. Now here was another little beauty, and though his penis had throbbed almost painfully at the nearness of her, he told himself to go slow with this one, take his time, and the pleasure would be all the sweeter for it.

The only stipulation Ray had made was that he wasn't to hurt her physically. He knew that was because she was destined for Vera's place the following week. Her knocking

254

shop would have a lot of new punters over Christmas, drunk, many of them – not that the girls minded that. They always said the drunks tipped better. Vera said the regulars liked a bit of new blood, but they were no good to her if they had been smacked about a bit. Collingsworth had no desire to hurt Molly, however, just shag her over and over in the long night before them.

Yet he sensed her unease and, in his experience, most women were more amenable after a drink or two, so he said to Molly, 'Come on now. I said that this is a celebration, so you just drink up that drink and I will pour us each another, and you can sit here beside me and tell me all about yourself.'

Molly had no desire to get any closer to Collingsworth than she had to. He made her skin crawl and there was a sort of aura of unwholesomeness emanating from him. She looked to Ray for help, but his eyes were harder than she had ever seen them, and he gave an almost imperceptible jerk of his head towards Collingsworth so that Molly knew that this was part of being nice to him. Surely, to please Ray, she could do this one small thing? He had never asked her to do anything before, and after tonight she probably wouldn't see much of Mr Collingsworth at all. So she downed the contents of her glass, welcoming the ensuing dizziness, and Ray took it for a refill as she sank down beside Collingsworth on the sofa and tried not to show her distaste when he pulled her close against him.

She caught Ray's eyes upon her, shining in approval, so she took a large gulp of the drink he gave her and let her body sag against this man she had to be nice to.

As Collingsworth felt her warmth and closeness, his excitement mounted.

Ray said. 'As you two seem to be getting along so well, I will leave you now.'

'Yes,' Collingsworth said. 'We will be fine, won't we, Molly?'

Molly felt anything but fine, but she knew to say that would make Ray angry. She had never seen him angry and had no desire to, nor did she want to disappoint him, and so she gave a brief nod, but when she heard the front door slam, she drank deeply again, hoping it would chase away the nervousness coursing through her veins.

'Tell me about yourself, my dear,' Collingsworth said.

'What d'you want to know, Mr Collingsworth?'

'It's Edwin, my dear. Can you call me Edwin?'

Molly shrugged. 'If you like.'

'Now I would like to know all about you,' Collingsworth said.

'But I don't know anything,' Molly said. 'My past is like a big black hole.'

Collingsworth smiled because Ray had done his work well. It was far better that the girls destined for the whorehouse remembered as little of their former lives as possible.

'I used to worry that I was losing my mind,' Molly admitted.

'Oh, no, not you, my dear girl,' Collingsworth said firmly. 'I think that you maybe have suffered a trauma or tragedy of some kind and these memory lapses are in the nature of delayed shock. It is quite common, and temporary too, I believe.'

'You are so understanding,' Molly said in slight amazement. His attitude had surprised her and she thought for the first time that she might have misjudged the man. She snuggled in closer so that she felt his breath between her breasts.

Later, when Molly recalled the events of that day, she could hardly credit that she had allowed the man such liberties. In some sort of dreamlike trance, she felt his hand stroking her leg, and she just thought it felt lovely and wasn't even alarmed when it went higher and higher.

Hearing her contented sigh, Collingsworth felt himself harden in anticipation.

256

'I'll never hurt you, you know that, don't you?' Collingsworth said as he released her stockings from their suspenders and rolled them seductively down her legs, to drop on the floor.

'Of course I do,' Molly said, her head lolling against him drunkenly, but she suddenly felt incredibly tired and said, 'I think I am drunk and I need to go to bed.'

'And so do I,' Collingsworth said, his voice husky with desire.

Molly giggled. 'You can't get into my bed, though. You will need to go home to your own bed.'

'I don't think so,' the man replied.

He hadn't realised just how drunk and drugged Molly was, and she staggered so much when she was at last upright that the pair of them nearly landed on the floor. This amused Molly no end, and she began to giggle. Collingsworth was just glad that Molly was small and slight, or he would never have managed her, and he half hauled, half dragged her to the bedroom. He lowered her onto the bed, where she lay with an inane smile playing around her mouth.

Collingsworth, however, wasn't looking at Molly's mouth. He was aching with desire as he began unbuttoning her blouse.

'You are so very beautiful, you know,' he said.

Molly said nothing, for it was as if these things were happening to someone else. She felt as if she was looking down on her body lying on the bed, and watching the man who was stroking her sensually sending her into a stupor-like sleep, and she closed her eyes and sighed. She dreamed someone had their hands on her breasts and it was so beautiful, she never wanted to wake up.

Collingsworth though, was in a fever of anxiety to take the prize before him that he had paid dearly for and he began tearing his clothes off, too aroused now for gentleness. Naked, he launched himself on top of Molly.

He nearly knocked the breath from her body and thoroughly woke her. He clamped his mouth on hers roughly, and when he thrust his thick tongue into Molly's mouth, she felt as if she was going to choke, and she thrashed her head from side to side to try to dislodge it. But it was when Collingsworth pulled her knickers down and pummelled one hand between her legs brutally, and his mouth filled with saliva, that Molly fully realised what was happening to her.

When Collingsworth heard Molly groan and thrash about on the bed, he thought she was overcome by the same passion that was consuming him, and he guided his pulsating penis to his goal at last. By God, he was going to enjoy every last second of this.

For the life of her, Molly couldn't understand, or remember, how she came to be on her bed semi-clad, with a naked man on top of her. But Collingsworth was filled with lust and totally unprepared for her suddenly wrenching her lips from his and pushing him with all her might so he fell from the bed in a heap.

In a second he was up, but Molly, even in her semi-drunken state, was quicker and was making for the door.

Collingsworth caught her by the arm.

'Leave go of me.'

'You must be joking,' he said angrily. 'What the bleeding hell are you playing at?'

'How can you ask that?' Molly cried. She wished her head did not feel as if it was filled with cotton wool and that the room would stay still, for she had the feeling that, to counter this, she needed to have her wits about her. She faced the man and said accusingly, 'You were going to . . .'

'I know what I was going to do, and so do you, you drunken whore.' Collingsworth was so incensed he shot spittle from his mouth as he spoke. 'So what is all this about?'

Molly was mortified with shame, and she thought that he had every right to be angry and upset. The way she had behaved he must have thought she was offering herself.

Hadn't she gone a good distance down that road? Unbidden, Ray's face swam before her, charging her to be nice to this man but she fastened her brassiere and blouse before saying in a conciliatory way that she was far from feeling, 'I am sorry, sorry that you have been upset and disappointed, and I do understand how angry you felt, but I am not that sort of girl and if I hadn't drunk so much I wouldn't have allowed things to get this far. Shall we get properly dressed now and we'll say no more about it?'

Collingsworth jerked at Molly's arm with such suddenness she cried out as she spun in front of him, and, holding her roughly by the arms, he slammed her so hard against the mirrored wall that the room swam. 'Listen to me, you moronic slut,' he ground out. 'I know exactly what type of girl you are, what you are going to be, and that is a whore in one of the knocking shops in Birmingham from next week, so don't come all innocent with me. You must have known the score.'

Molly was completely bemused. 'What are you on about? What score and what do you mean? I am not a whore.'

He gave a grim and humourless laugh that sent a shiver down Molly's spine as he said, 'Maybe you're not yet, but you soon will be.'

'I will not!'

'Jesus Christ, did you come over on the banana boat or were you born half-witted?' he demanded. 'Why d'you think Ray took you in, eh? Thought he was a bleeding charity, did you?'

'I don't know what you mean?' Molly said, though her body seemed to be filling up with dread. 'Ray has shown me nothing but kindness.'

'Course he has, darling,' Collingsworth said in a voice dripping with sarcasm. 'Heart of gold, has our Ray, and a few days ago out of kindness he sold you to me for tonight.'

'Don't be ridiculous.'

'Ridiculous, am I?' the man sneered. 'I speak the truth,

259

and I bought you for my own use tonight because you have something that is prized and that I wanted and that is your maidenhead. I take it you are a virgin?'

'Of course I am.'

'There is no "of course" in this business.' He pressed himself so close to her that he was spitting in her face as he spoke. She noted his eyes seemed to shine with a demonic light as he said in levelled tones that were as cold as ice, 'And let me tell you another thing: I intend to have that prize that I paid for and you can be accommodating or not. Either way, it makes no odds to me.'

Molly was so frightened her heart seemed to be jumping about in her chest as she ground out, 'I don't think so.'

'Well, I do,' Collingsworth suddenly bellowed. Rage that he had been duped, made fun of, took hold of him. Someone would pay. Molly was unprepared for both the suddenness and the power of the punch that knocked her to the floor and caused blood to pour from her nose.

Collingsworth looked at her coldly. He had promised Ray he wouldn't hurt her physically, for it was well known that he sometimes liked to rough his woman up, and he would have been banned from many a whorehouse for it if he hadn't been such an influential man, whom they all depended on. He hadn't had any intention of hurting Molly when he had arrived that night, but that had all gone by the board now. She deserved all he was prepared to mete out to her and he powered a kick into her side as he said, 'Get to your feet and let's get down to it because I always get what I pay for.'

Molly gave a groan as the man's foot caught her, and she curled up instinctively. Through bloodshot eyes she lay and watched the blood drip from her nose and pool on the carpet, as her assailant said, 'Get up unless you want some more of the same.'

She heard his voice and saw the foot raised, and then she saw an old woman as if through a window in her mind.

This image was not misty or hazy, though. The old woman's cold eyes, like Edwin Collingsworth's, were filled with malice and hatred, and her fists were raised. The image engendered such anger in her that she leaped to her feet and threw herself at Collingsworth with a shriek, like some sort of screaming virago.

Collingsworth was unprepared, both for the attack and for the strength of the girl, who looked as if a puff of wind would blow her away. He threw her against the wall, but as he came towards her, she kicked him between the legs.

She had no shoes on, however, and so, although he doubled up at first, he had recovered enough to be after her as she made for the living room. She wondered where Ray was and how long she had been with this mad man, and knew she had to get out of the place, out into the street and shout for help.

Collingsworth, who had thought Molly would be easily subdued, was taken aback at first and then he seemed to increase in strength. Chairs and small tables were overturned, and vases and lamps crashed to the floor as he crossed the room in pursuit of Molly until he had caught her by the arm and smacked a hard hand across her face so that for a moment she was blinded. In that moment he had her against him, his fingers pulling her knickers to one side. She gave a yelp of terror and punched him to each side of his head with her fists, which were as hard as little hammers. Then she tore herself from his grip, hearing her blouse rip but paying no heed as she made for the door.

But when Collingsworth caught hold of her again, she felt despair fill her being and she knew this was it. She was spent. He would have his way with her and there was nothing she could do about it because she had no strength left.

He kicked her to the floor, and she saw he had the heavy base of a table lamp raised to crash down on her head. She dived under a coffee table. Before her were Collingsworth's legs, and in a split second she had hold of them and jerked

261

with all her might. Collingsworth had been unbalanced, ready to smash Molly's skull, and before he was able to recover himself he fell heavily. His head hit the table with a sickening thud as he went down so when he hit the floor he was already unconscious, and blood was seeping from a gaping wound, staining the carpet crimson.

For a moment Molly sat and looked at him. She was petrified and didn't have a clue what to do, but she knew one thing: if he came to again he would kill her as easily as swatting a fly. She had to get him to the door, bolt and lock it against him and wait for Ray to come home. He would tell her what to do.

Ordinarily, Molly wouldn't have been able to move even a man of Collingsworth's stature, but that night she managed it although she was both sweating and crying with the effort when she eventually heaved him outside the door of the flat. She couldn't leave him there – he was too close – and she rolled him to the top of the stairs, pushed him with her foot, watched him topple down the first couple of steps and then disappear into the darkness. She heard him hit every step.

She gave a sudden shiver and realised that, while she was scantily clad, Collingsworth was naked. She ran into the bedroom, collected up his clothes and threw them down the stairs. Shaking from head to foot, she bolted and barred the door behind her. Then, overcome by nausea, she fled for the bathroom where she vomited over and over into the toilet.

Now that the fight was over, she was aware of aching pain everywhere and she could plainly see why when she stood before the mirror. Her body was a mass of bruises, but her face had borne the brunt of Collingsworth's anger and she sported two black eyes, her face was smeared with blood from the shattered nose, and her bottom lip was split wide open. She wanted to lie on the floor and weep but she knew that that would achieve nothing, so she forced herself to run a bath. She sank with a sigh into the perfumed waters, knowing everything would sting and throb afresh, but she felt defiled and dirty and she needed to try to wash that feeling away.

EIGHTEEN

Molly tossed and turned on the bed, in too much pain and far too upset to sleep, but as she played the scenes over and over again in her head, she became horrified by what she had done and she began to wonder if it had been her fault in some way and if she could have handled it better. The point was, she had drunk too much to behave in any sort of logical way and that *was* her fault. And was it really necessary for her to push Collingsworth down the stairs, especially as he had already passed out and had a head wound seeping blood?

She hadn't been thinking straight. She had just wanted the man as far away from her as possible, where he couldn't hurt her any more, but what if she had killed him? He was rich and influential, Ray had intimated, and she knew she would never get away with killing or even maiming such a person. What would happen to her when it was discovered what she had done? She ran her trembling fingers around her neck, imagined the hangman's noose tightening there and felt sick with fear.

Ray would know what to do when he came back, though she faced the fact he might be less than pleased with her at first, because pulling Collingsworth's legs from under him so that he was knocked unconscious and then rolling him down the stairs could not be construed as being 'nice' to him by any stretch of the imagination.

But then when she told Ray what Collingsworth had

wanted to do, surely he would see that she had little alternative? When he saw the mess that the man had made of her face, she imagined that he would be incensed on her behalf, because she knew that he couldn't be involved in any of this, whatever the odious man had said. If he had been, wouldn't he at the very least have tried to take advantage of her before this?

She had offered for him to share her bed. She was sure she wouldn't have minded too much, not if it had been Ray, but he had been too much of a gentleman to do that. Instead, he had cared for her and certainly had never laid a finger on her in an inappropriate way.

However, Ray wasn't there, so it was down to her. She knew she had to find out exactly what she had done to Edwin Collingsworth. Her nerve ends quivered and she wished she could curl up in bed and pretend that the naked man, maybe lying dead at the bottom of the stairs, was nothing to do with her.

She shivered as she pushed the covers back, for the place was like an ice box and her head pounded as she lifted it from the pillow. She felt as if she was going to be sick, but she fought the nausea and slid her feet thankfully into slippers. She wished the silky wrap she tied around herself was a cosy woolly one, for though it looked fine, it was not made for warmth.

She doubted, though, that anything could warm her up properly, for it was terror that was filling her veins with ice. She padded across to the front door and, once there, it took all her reserves of strength to slide the bolts back and ease it open. She had picked up one of the torches Ray always left in a cupboard in the hall, and by its light, dim though it was, she saw there was nothing at the bottom of the stairs. There was no body, no clothes – nothing.

However, she had to be certain, and she descended the stairs, her senses on high alert, ready to flee at any moment. But, the stairwell was completely empty except for the little pool of blood at the bottom. Then her torch showed up something gleaming on the floor. She bent to look more closely and saw that it was a pair of gold cufflinks. Collingsworth's she presumed, which must have fallen out of his cuffs when she threw his clothes down the stairs. She put them into the pocket of her wrap.

She should have felt relieved, but she wasn't. What if someone had found him and summoned an ambulance, or maybe he had regained consciousness enough to dress himself before stumbling into the street to get help. Either way, it wasn't necessarily good news for her.

She went back to the apartment, not bothering to slide the bolts now that Collingsworth was no longer at the bottom of the steps. In the kitchen she made a cup of tea, hoping it might stop her teeth chattering. And that was where a furious Ray found her a little later.

Collingsworth's chauffeur, Will Baker, had brought Ray and Collingsworth to the apartment the evening before. His instructions were then to take Ray wherever he wanted to go, return to the apartment, and wait outside it until his boss might need him. However, it had been cold sitting in the car, and after an hour, the chauffeur had got out to walk up and down, slapping his arms to his sides and had stepped out of the wind into the entry just below Molly's window to light up a cigarette.

When he heard the commotion, he had grimaced to himself, for he guessed the little quirk his employer had of occasionally beating up young girls and women had got the better of him again. There could be trouble over this if he had done her harm, because Ray had told him he had warned him not to hurt her in any way. He knew why too: the girl was lined up to go to Vera's whorehouse the following week. 'Installed before Christmas and working like a good 'un by the New Year,' was the way Ray put it, and if she was damaged in any way, he knew full well

266

Vera wouldn't want her, or pay for her, till she was healed and could be of some use.

The chauffeur moved round to the front door of the house, though he knew that it was more than his life was worth to interfere. That was, until he heard the unmistakable sound of someone falling down the stairs. He knew then that his employer might have killed the girl. It wouldn't be the first time either, he knew, and it had sickened him when he had heard his heavies boasting about it.

Anyway, he decided, whether Collingsworth liked it or not, he couldn't leave someone who might well need help at the bottom of the stairs so he waited till all was quiet beyond the door before he cautiously opened it. Mindful of the blackout, he had to shut it behind him before he could turn on his torch and then his heart skipped a beat, for it was no young girl there but the battered and bruised body of his employer, and though he was as naked as the day he was born, his clothes lay in a heap on top of him.

Had the girl done him in? Fought for her honour, like? Dear Christ, she was in one heap of trouble, whichever way it was. Will leant across, felt for the pulse in his employer's neck and was relieved that he was alive at least, so it wouldn't be the gallows for that young girl, whoever she was.

But the man was still unconscious and the wound Will saw on the back of his head was bleeding profusely. He tried to stanch that with his handkerchief before shaking him gently and whispering, 'Mr Collingsworth, sir. Mr Collingsworth. Wake up, sir. Wake up.'

He was relieved to see his employer's eyes flutter open, even though he did shut them straight away, growling out irritably, 'Turn that bloody torch away from my face, you fool. Nearly damned well blinded me. And where the hell am I anyway?'

But the chauffeur didn't have to answer that, because the events of that evening had begun to seep into Collingsworth's

267

brain and consummate rage filled his entire body. 'Help me into my clothes, man. Don't just stand there,' he commanded.

Will did most of the dressing, for Collingsworth was disorientated and badly co-ordinated. Though the chauffeur thought he should go to hospital to be checked over, particularly for the head injury, which was still seeping blood and matting in his sparse hair, even through the handkerchief, he said nothing. He knew that these people from the underworld seldom visited doctors or hospitals in the normal way. They had their own people to attend them, who were paid well to keep their mouths shut.

Will Baker didn't like the colour of Collingsworth's face at all and noted how he had to help him to his feet once he was dressed and then prevent him falling flat on his face as, taking almost all his weight, he semi-carried the man to his car.

'Where to, boss?'

'Home. Where else, you bloody fool?'

In Collingsworth's house, in full light, the man looked worse and the chauffeur was worried enough to say, 'Shall I ring the doctor, sir?' knowing that he had a special doctor attend him.

But his employer brushed the suggestion away impatiently. 'It's not a doctor I want but that man Morris. Find him and bring him here.'

'Yes, sir.'

The chauffeur had taken Ray to the casino, so he was likely spending the money Collingsworth had given him that evening.

It had been Ray that had put Will in line for a job with Collingsworth after meeting him in a pub one night. They had been at school together, though not special friends, but that night they caught up with news of one another. Will, feeling very sorry for himself, told Ray of being invalided out of the army after his lungs were buggered up after the rout at Dunkirk.

Ray, on the other hand, never specified what he actually

268

did for a living, or how he had evaded the call-up, but he did tell Will that he might be able to do him a favour.

'My boss is in need of a chauffeur and general dogsbody since the last one was called up. You can drive, I suppose?'

'Well, yes, but with petrol rationed I wouldn't imagine there will be much work in that line at the moment.'

'Don't you believe it,' Ray had said. 'This man, as well as being incredibly rich, has his finger in so many pies. Rationing of anything doesn't seem to apply to him. Anyway, no harm in having a chat.'

Will agreed there wasn't, but when he met Edwin Collingsworth he hadn't liked him at all. The more he knew about him, the more his dislike and unease grew. Yet a job was a job, and better than no damned thing at all.

His fear, when he had been made aware of the extent of his injuries, was that he'd be unable to provide for his wife, Betty, and he knew she had been frightened of that too. It was even more important now that she was expecting their first child. It always gave him pride when he placed his wage packet into her hand on a Friday night and saw that special smile on her face. He would go to hell and back in order that she and the child would not go short.

Collingsworth paid well, Will had to admit, though sometimes he demanded more than his pound of flesh and his Betty would kick up about it though he never discussed his work with her. He knew she would disapprove of most of it, and if she just had a hint of some of the things he had seen done, the things he had been asked to cover up, or provide an alibi for, she would probably demand he give it up. And just where would they be then? Up the creek without a paddle, that's where. Anyway, it was far better for Betty, and much safer for her, to know nothing and to think he had a regular sort of job.

Ray was surprised to hear that Collingsworth had returned home before the morning, for it wasn't even midnight, but ask as he might, Will said he knew nothing about anything.

All he knew was that he was told to fetch him and that was what he was doing. Ray knew he was lying, though he didn't blame him because it was always safer for a person to keep their head down. He had seen Collingsworth in a temper and it was a frightening spectacle.

In Will's absence, Collingsworth had called his doctor, who had come round immediately, shaved the hair around the head wound and then cleaned and stitched it so that the first thing that Ray noticed was the large white bandage encircling the man's head.

'Good God, Edwin! What happened to you?'

'You might well ask, and the answer is being fool enough to be left in with that she-devil.'

Ray's mouth dropped agape. 'Molly?' he said incredulously. 'Molly did that to you?'

'What do you think?' Collingsworth spat out.

'But how? I mean, there is nothing to her.'

'That is neither here nor there,' Collingsworth snapped. 'You said she would be ready and waiting, that she knew the score.'

'She did,' Ray said. 'I mean, I told her she had to be nice to you, very nice, and I asked her if she knew what I meant and she said that of course she did.'

Surely, Ray thought suddenly, she wasn't so naive as to think that being 'nice' was offering him a cup of tea and a biscuit or two?

'Oh, she was nice all right,' Collingsworth snapped. 'So nice that not content with knocking me out, she pushed me down the bleeding stairs.' He went on to recount to Ray what had happened in the apartment. 'She bloody near killed me,' he said at the end. 'She might have succeeded if Will hadn't found me and brought me home, and I want to know what you are going to do about it.'

'What do you want me to do?' Ray demanded. 'I'll have a word, put her straight, give her a good hiding if you like, so she will remember.'

'I have done that already,' Collingsworth said. 'And that is not good enough. No one gets away with doing this to me. And I want every penny back from the money I paid you this evening.'

'I haven't got it,' Ray said. 'I mean, not all of it. I spent some at the casino. I had a bit of bad luck.'

'That is not my problem.'

'You have to give me time.'

'I have to give you nothing,' Collingsworth snarled.

'I was going to sell Molly on to Vera,' Ray said. 'I would have some cash then all right.'

'Well, now you will have to think of another way to earn enough to pay me back,' Collingsworth said. 'And remember, I am not a patient man.'

'I can't pay you what I haven't got.'

'You are not listening to me, Morris, and I don't like that,' Collingsworth snarled. 'You pay me what you owe or I turn you over to my heavies and then you will be lucky if you ever work again.'

He let this sink in, then went on, 'There is a way around this, because if you kill the girl, and in a way that can never be traced back to me, the debt will be cancelled.'

Ray gasped. Outside the door, Will, who was eavesdropping, felt his blood turn to ice.

'I haven't ever killed anyone, Edwin, never,' Ray said. 'Or even come anywhere near it.'

'So?'

'What if I make a mess of it?'

'Then I suggest that you get on a slow boat to China,' Collingsworth said with a sardonic smile. 'Because wherever you try running to, I will seek you out and hunt you down, and make you wish that you had never been born. I do hope that I have made myself clear?'

Will melted away from the door as Ray opened it. He went out into the street, his senses reeling. He could barely believe that he had just heard two men discussing killing a

271

young girl with so little feeling. He had never listened in to what went on behind Collingsworth's door before, preferring to keep well out of the man's business, and he wished to God he hadn't listened that day either, but finding his boss the way he had had made him curious.

And now he had heard they intended to kill a young girl and in cold blood for the simple reason that she had objected to Collingsworth shagging her. He could hardly blame her, for the man had surely been at the back of the queue when good looks were dished out. He was also a nasty piece of work and likely old enough to be her grandfather. No wonder the poor girl had fought like a tiger. The whole thing was obscene, grotesque.

All the way back to the flat, Ray was raging. He wanted to tear Molly limb from limb. Over three weeks he had kept her and fed her and cared for her, waiting for Collingsworth to return from wherever he had been, knowing he would pay well for a virgin. And then when Collingsworth had taken his pleasure, Ray would sell the girl on to Vera and pick up a wad of money to keep him until the next girl chanced along.

All he had asked Molly to do was toe the line, to repay the way he had looked after her so well, but she had screwed up every bloody thing. And yet the thought of what he had to do to prevent Collingsworth's heavies reducing him to pulp frightened the life out of him. He wasn't averse to giving a girl a good hiding if she stepped out of line, but killing – that was a different league altogether and not one he was keen on joining either.

Christ, whatever way you looked at it, it was a bloody mess and it was all Molly's fault.

Molly felt a flood of relief when she heard Ray come in, confident that he would know what to do. She looked up as he entered the kitchen and watched him survey her face.

Molly had never seen such a look in Ray's eyes before, though she recognised that it was not sympathy or pity for the mess Collingsworth had made of her. Even so, she was unprepared for what he said.

'Well, I just hope that you are bloody proud of yourself.'

Molly was totally confused. 'Ray, I . . .'

Ray dragged her to her feet by the neck of her night-dress, and with his face inches from hers, he ground out, 'I told you to be nice, didn't I?' He gave Molly a shake. 'Didn't I?'

'Yes, but, Ray, I tried, but he wanted to go with me, you know. He tried to make me . . . well, you know.'

'Well, of course he did, you silly cow. That is what he came for,' Ray snarled at her, throwing her from him with such force she had to catch hold of the table she fell against to steady herself.

She was hardly aware of this, however, because she could scarcely believe the words that Ray had flung at her. 'What are you talking about?'

'I mean, my dear, stupid bitch, that Collingsworth wanted a virgin and I had one that he paid dearly for.'

'I can't believe that I am hearing this,' Molly said, aghast. 'You know that I wouldn't do anything like that. Surely to God you didn't expect . . .'

'But I did,' Ray said wearily. 'Fool that I was, I did. I told you to be very nice and I asked you if you knew what I meant and you said yes.'

'I didn't mean . . .' Molly began through the tears seeping from her eyes.

'I told you to do whatever he wanted, didn't I?'

'Yes, but . . .'

'And what did you do, but bugger all except near kill the man.'

'Is he . . . is he all right?'

'Yeah, no thanks to you,' Ray said. 'I suppose I don't have to tell you that you are not his favourite person at the moment. In fact if you were before him this minute he would kill you with his bare hands and I wouldn't do a thing to stop him.'

Molly shuddered in sudden fear of this man for the first time. 'Don't say things like that.'

'Even if they are true?'

'But they are not. Normal people don't go on like this.'

'Collingsworth isn't normal. Even on your limited acquaintance you must have been aware of that.'

'I don't know a thing about that man, nor do I want to,' Molly said. 'But I thought I knew you, that you cared.'

Ray gave a humourless laugh and his eyes glittered with dislike. 'Cared?' he said sardonically. 'Cared for you, my dear? Wrong again, I am afraid. To me you were just a commodity, something to sell to make money from. I wouldn't touch you with a bargepole.'

Molly was shaken by Ray's words and she felt cold and lost inside. 'And I thought that you were just being a gentleman,' she said sadly.

Ray shook his head. There was no danger in telling her now. He didn't intend to leave her alive long enough to pass it on to anyone. 'No, I am not a gentleman, my dear. I prefer gentlemen.' He laughed at the confusion in her eyes and went on, 'To have sex with, I prefer men. Or to be more specific, boys, and the younger the better.'

Molly was so appalled that her lips retracted from her mouth in an expression of total contempt.

'Don't you sodding well look at me like that, you bloody excuse for a woman,' he yelled at her. Then his punch knocked her to the ground and the kick rendered her unconscious.

Ray hauled her into the bedroom and laid her on the bed. He could finish her off he thought, put a pillow over her head now, and it would all be over. He actually picked up the pillow, but couldn't bring himself to do it and he put it down again. He needed Charlie, because he would have no qualms about finishing her off when he knew what she had done, and he'd have some idea where to hide the body too.

He checked his watch. He wouldn't find Charlie at home at this time, though he had no idea where he would be either. He probably would not be home till the morning. Ray yawned suddenly, worn out with the events of the evening, and decided to make for his own place and grab a bit of kip.

It was as he was about to go out the front door that he remembered the money belt they had taken from Molly that he had put in a drawer and forgotten about. He took it out, opened it and stuffed all the notes and coins into his pocket before going out of the door, locking it behind him.

Will was still walking the streets, too churned up to return home, and when he saw Ray coming towards him from the direction of Collingsworth's flat he wondered if Ray had killed the girl already. He had to know, and so though he would far rather have spread Ray's length on the cobbles, he greeted him.

'You still about?' Ray said.

'Yeah, but I'm off home now,' Will answered, struggling to keep the disgust for the man from his voice. 'Where you making for?'

'Back to my own flat for a bit of a kip,' Ray said. He had no idea that Will had listened in to the conversation he'd had with Collingsworth and yet he knew that it had been the chauffeur who had found the man at the bottom of the stairs because Collingsworth himself had told him that much, so he said now, 'Bet you would like to know what it was all about, that shindig?'

Will shrugged. 'If you like,' he said, and added with a grim smile, 'I have found Mr Collingsworth in many strange places, but that was about the most weird and, of course, being stark naked as well put the tin hat on it, as it were.'

'Was he naked as well?' Ray said incredulously. 'Christ, he dain't tell me that.'

'I bet he didn't,' Will commented. 'Well, what was it all about?'

He listened to the potted version of events that Ray fed him, but he made no mention of getting rid of the girl. What he did say, though, was, 'Course, I was bloody mad, furious. I mean, what did she think she was there for? I gave her a good smacking, though Collingsworth had made a bloody mess of her first anyway. I knocked her clean out in the end and now I have locked her in the bedroom to stew. After I have grabbed a bit of shut-eye, I will have to run Charlie to ground because there is a little job I want him to do with me.'

Will knew exactly what that job was, and he felt sick. He couldn't stand the man's company any longer. 'I'm away.' he said. 'I am bushed and chilled to the marrow.'

He swung away from Ray as he spoke. He knew he would have to walk home, for there were no trams running at that time of night, but it wouldn't be the first time he had the long tramp home after a day's work. Anyway, that night he almost felt glad of it, and hoped that by the time he reached home his mind would have stopped its leaping about and allow him to sleep.

His house was in darkness and he was glad of it as he tiptoed up the stairs. In the light from the landing he surveyed his sleeping wife, with her cheeks flushed pink and her brown hair spread out on the pillow, noting how sleep made her look so very vulnerable. As he slipped in beside her he thought of that young girl, just as vulnerable, who was unaware what was being planned for her and felt his whole body recoil in distaste.

He faced the fact that he wasn't totally innocent either and it was no good pretending he was. Though he hadn't known when he began working for Collingsworth, he was soon aware that Ray would pick up runaways at bus and train stations and then sell them on to the knocking shop, after keeping them at the flat, doping them up with the

276

white powders and gin till they were so addicted to the stuff they would do what they were told, because if they didn't their supplies were withheld.

He had never seen the girls concerned and had always told himself that it was none of his business. Now he listened to his wife's even and untroubled breathing and, though his eyes were gritty with tiredness, he was far too emotionally charged to sleep. He knew that not far away this dreadful thing was going to take place and there was nothing he could do to stop it.

NINETEEN

Will turned off the alarm before it rang, because he had been just lying awake anyway.

Betty opened her eyes sleepily as he was dressing by the light of the lamp and said, 'You look awful.'

'Thanks,' Will said with a sardonic smile. 'I love you too.'

Betty sat up in the bed, awkwardly, because of her bulging stomach, and supported herself on one elbow as she scrutinised her husband. 'I mean it, Will, really,' she said. 'Your eyes are all bloodshot and you have grey bags underneath them.'

'Don't worry. I didn't sleep too well, that's all. I had things on my mind.'

'I'll say you did. You tossed and turned so much you kept waking me up.'

'I'm sorry,' Will said. 'Why don't you snuggle down now? Get the sleep in while you can.'

Betty ignored that and commented instead, 'You were in powerfully late last night.'

'Yes, I know.'

'Doesn't that man think that you have a life of your own?'

'You know what the rich are like as well as I do,' Will said. 'Never a thought in their head for the people that work for them.'

'Yeah, well, I think it is a bit much expecting you to go

in so early this morning when you were so late last night. I mean, it's barely six o'clock.'

'Don't worry, I'll live,' Will said, anxious to reassure his wife and be on his way. 'And the wages are good, you have to admit. We are going to need every penny before too long, as you well know. Now, do you want me to make you a cup of tea before I go, or are you going to grab a bit of shut-eye?'

'Hmm, I know one thing, Will Baker, and that is that you are a dab hand at changing the subject when it suits you,' Betty said.

'Tea or not, then?'

'No,' Betty said. 'I will give it a miss. I'll likely be asleep again before it's cool enough to drink.'

'Come on, then,' Will said solicitously. 'Snuggle down and I'll tuck you in and you'll be as snug as a bug in a rug.'

With a sigh and a smile, Betty did as Will bade her.

As he gazed at her lovely, dark brown eyes, he felt his heart turn over with love for his young wife, carrying their much-wanted child. He would die if anything happened to her. Maybe that young girl, about to end her life by Ray's hand, had been loved by someone too once upon a time, in an earlier and less depraved life.

'What is it? What's wrong?' Betty asked in sudden alarm, seeing the discomfort Will was feeling flood over his face.

'Nothing,' Will said. 'What could be wrong?' He kissed his wife gently on the lips and went on, 'Come on now. I have to be on my way and you have to look after my son and heir, so that he is born fine and healthy.'

Betty said no more but she knew that something was troubling her husband. She could read him like a book. Worry lurked behind his soft grey eyes, furrowed his brow and brought a tight look to his ashen face. She heard him moving about in the kitchen, the pop of the gas as he put the kettle on and the rattle of crockery as he got some breakfast for himself. He didn't take long over it, and only a few minutes later she heard him go out and she knew he would be making for the tram. She snuggled down in the bed, closed her eyes and tried to sleep, but she was so tormented about what could be wrong with Will that it drove all drowsiness away. In the end she gave a sigh, got to her feet wearily and, shivering with cold, began to dress quickly.

Collingsworth had taken to his bed on doctor's orders and wouldn't be needing the services of a chauffeur that day at least, Will was told at his employer's door. He stood in the road outside, knowing he could just go home now and pretend he knew nothing. Betty would be glad to see him – he had little enough free time to spend with her – and by tomorrow it would all be over and things could go on as they always had.

On the other hand, could he just ignore what he had overheard and which he knew to be true? Could he go home to his young wife and enjoy himself, knowing that it was that young girl's last day on earth? And how in God's name would he ever live with himself if he did?

There wasn't a choice in this, he knew. There was just the one right thing to do, and he made for home, where he had a set of ladders in the shed.

Betty had poked the fire into life, shaking some nuggets of coal onto it, and had put the kettle on when she heard a noise outside. She turned off the light, lifted the blackout curtains aside and peered through the glass, but she could see little, though she had the idea that she could make out a vague grey shape moving around.

She knew she wouldn't rest until she found out if there was someone in her yard who shouldn't be there, so taking her coat from the hook behind the door, and armed with her large shielded torch, she opened the kitchen door stealthily and stepped outside. When she suddenly turned the torch on, it lit up her husband in the doorway of the shed, carrying the ladders. She heard him give a groan of dismay as he spotted her watching him.

'Will, what are you doing home? And what on earth do you want with the ladders? Are you going to clean the windows in the dark, or what?'

'Ssh,' Will hissed urgently. The last thing he wanted was to have his Betty involved in this sordid business, but he realised he owed her an explanation. If she then decided the risk was too great, that would be that.

'We need to talk,' he said.

'Yes, we do,' Betty answered grimly as she turned and made for the house. 'And, I would say, about time too.'

Once inside, Betty saw just how shaken her husband was. She made tea, and put a cup before each of them.

'Well?' she asked finally.

Will ran his fingers through his sandy hair distractedly. 'I hardly know where to start.'

'Well, you could start by telling me what you want ladders for at this hour of the morning, and it dark as pitch out there?'

Will shook his head. 'No. Oh, by Christ, it goes much further back than that. God, Betty, you don't know the half of it.'

'Nor likely to either if you don't tell me.'

'I'm afraid.'

'Of me?'

'Yes,' Will said. 'I am afraid that you will despise me when you hear some of the things I have done.'

Betty looked at him amazed. 'Will, I love you. You are my husband and the father of our child. I would never despise you.' She reached for his hand across the table and held it tight. 'Tell me what it is that is distressing you so much,' she said. 'I have the feeling that you have kept it to yourself long enough.'

Will started at the very beginning, with meeting Ray in the pub that night, though Betty already knew some of that. She knew nothing of the rest, though, and listened in horrified amazement as Will spoke about his slide to the edge of the corrupt and perverted life that his employer and those around him enjoyed.

His ravaged eyes, racked with guilt, looked into hers and he said, 'Normal rules don't apply to these people, nor does the law. And if someone gets in the way, they get rid of them.'

'Get rid of them?' Betty repeated. 'You mean . . . ?'

Will drew one finger across his neck and Betty, hardly able to believe it, said, 'Kill them? They kill people?' She removed her hand from Will's and looked him full in the face as she said earnestly, 'Tell me that you have had no hand in that?'

'Of course not,' Will said emphatically. 'What in Christ's name do you take me for?'

'A fool, Will Baker, that's what I take you for,' Betty spat out. 'A weak-willed and gullible fool who allowed himself to be sucked into such evilness and debauchery in the first place.'

Will accepted the censure, knowing he deserved that and worse. If he was honest, he had shocked himself. It was one thing going along each day and doing things alien to him, or just plain wrong, especially when he was mixing with people to whom those things were commonplace. It was quite another to sit before his wife and confess those things. It was the very first time he had put into words the things he had had to do, and if he was so disturbed, he could just imagine what it was doing to Betty, whose life up until then had been serene and unsullied. He was bitterly ashamed that he had brought disgrace into it and he told her this.

Betty looked at the man she loved with all her heart and soul – or at least she loved the man she thought he had been, the one she had considered honest and trustworthy – and felt a shudder run all through her.

Will saw it and his heart sank, but he knew he had to go on and tell all, and so he said, 'I haven't finished yet and this will explain why I needed the ladders.' He went on to tell her what he had overheard and his meeting Ray after it.

Betty was astounded. 'Why are you sitting here with such information?' she demanded. 'Go to the police.'

Will shook his head. 'I can't do that, Betty.'

'Why not?'

'Haven't you listened to a word I have said?' Will said. 'If I did that your life wouldn't be worth tuppence, and it isn't as if I would be here to give you any sort of protection.'

'Why not?'

'Look, Betty, if I just trot into any police station and say I know of a girl that is about to be murdered and I have the address and all the details, what d'you think would happen then? Do you think that they thank me for the information, rescue the girl and that would be the end of it? Don't you think it far more likely that they will haul me in and find out how I knew all this? Then everything would come out. By not speaking sooner about some of the other nefarious things I have been involved in, I am as guilty as the perpetrators, or that is probably how the police would see it. Face it, Betty, if the police ever got wind of any of this I would be looking at a hefty prison sentence. Far more important than that, though, what concerns me is what the boss would do to you as soon as the police began ferreting out their information. These people don't mess around, you know.'

'No, I don't know,' Betty snapped, but she realised with sudden clarity that Will spoke the truth. If he admitted to any of this then he would be locked up, and that thought sent cold shivers down her spine. Why the hell had he got involved in something like this?

She was suddenly blisteringly angry with him. 'How would I be expected to know people like that or how they would behave?' she burst out. 'A short while ago, I would have said I knew you inside out. Now it is as if I am married to a stranger.'

283

'Look,' Will said, 'Ray told me where the girl still is and I want to have a go at getting her out. That's what the ladder is for.'

'And won't anyone watching think it strange to see a ladder up to a window?'

'No one will see,' Will said. 'That's part of the beauty of it. The side of the house is down a sort of alleyway and the bedroom window overlooks the yard of a factory. That's how I can pinpoint the bedroom. I stepped into that alleyway for a bit of shelter and to light my fag out the wind, like, and I heard the first struggles and shouts. The factory is deserted now, though, because it was caught in a raid in the autumn and is not rebuilt yet. But there is a fairly high wall still standing and I will be able to hide the ladder behind there once I get the girl out of the building.'

'Thought it all out then?'

'Well, I only thought of it when I was given the day off,' Will said. 'I mean, I wanted to do something when I heard it first, but I didn't then know how I could achieve it. I've been hatching the plan all the way home. What d'you think?'

Betty nodded slowly. 'It could just work,' she said. 'And then what?'

'What do you mean?'

'According to you, they are out to kill this girl.'

'They are. D'you think I would make up something like this?'

'How would I know?' Betty snapped. 'But if you are right there are two major problems I can see. How will you release her and not have them come gunning for you? And if you should succeed in letting her go free, what will you do with her?'

'The first point is easier to answer,' Will said. 'I am sure that I can cover my tracks so that it looks as if she got out of that place on her own, but after that I don't know. I mean, I can't bring her here. It would be far too risky for you.'

Betty nodded slowly. 'Maybe not here, and not just for

284

the risk to me either. I mean, they could search here,' she said, 'But what about my mother's? Those thugs don't know where she lives.'

'Will she mind?'

'Not when I explain it all,' Betty said. 'And as I will move in as well, she'll probably be pleased. And it will satisfy the neighbours because what could be more natural than me staying with my mother now that I am seven months gone? Mom will likely be glad of the company anyway, because she has been lonely since Dad went two years ago. Always said she'd sell the house because she didn't need all the space, but the war put paid to that and I'm glad of it now, for it is the safest place to hide that girl if you do manage to release her. And you could come up for your dinner at night and keep us abreast of things.'

'Yeah, I can just see this working,' Will said. 'And it won't be for ever. I mean, she must have plans and some reason why she came to Birmingham in the first place.'

'How d'you know she did?'

'Ray said,' Will told her. 'Him and Charlie picked her up at the station. It's their usual haunting ground. He also said she came from Ireland.'

'Ah, poor girl!' Betty said. 'You know I will have nightmares about those girls sent to the whorehouses.'

'There is little we can do about those now.'

'I know that,' Betty replied. But here is one that we might be able to save. Come on, we haven't got much time, because it will start getting light in an hour and things will be riskier then. Get going, and I will go along to my mother's and alert her, even if I have to get her out of bed to do it.'

There were no blackout curtains drawn, or shutters at the windows of the house, Will noted, but it didn't matter because the room was in darkness. Perched at the top of the ladder, he rapped on the glass quite loudly and saw an indistinct grey shape move slightly in the room. It came no closer, though, and Will couldn't risk drawing attention to himself by shouting. After a minute or two he rapped again, thinking it would be a tragic irony if the plan failed because the girl was too afraid to come to the window.

The point was, really he couldn't blame her. Why should she trust a strange man on a ladder outside her bedroom window rapping at the glass? Who would? Yet it was desperately important that she did trust him, came nearer and then maybe he could convince her that he meant her no harm.

Molly had woken in a lather of sweat and she had had the shakes ever since. She thought something was seriously wrong, that she was dying, and she felt so wretched that she wouldn't have cared. She had no idea it was her body reacting to the absence of drugs it had become so used to over the weeks.

When she heard the rapping on the glass, she turned her head to the sound but did nothing further. She wasn't totally sure she hadn't imagined it, because strange things had been happening to her mind of late and she felt too ill, in too much pain to move. But the rapping came again and she decided to see what it was. She struggled from the bed and then had to hold on to it as her head swam and the room tilted and swayed in front of her. When she felt able to move again it was with the shambling gait of a very old and sick woman.

When she saw the man's face the other side of the glass, she recoiled in horror. To her, men meant pain and suffering, and she had had enough of that to last her a lifetime, so when the man beckoned to her to open the window she shook her head wildly. Did he think her mad altogether?

Then she heard his voice. It was gentle, soothing, and it said, 'Open the window. I swear I mean you no harm. I am here to try and help you.'

Oh, how Molly wanted help, someone to tell her what to do, because she hadn't a clue. What have you got to lose? her mind screamed. Ray might be back any minute and he might start on you again. At the thought of that, she stepped

286

forward and threw open the window, wondering if she was going from the frying pan into the fire, but too dispirited to care much.

Will was inside her room in seconds, pushing the haversack he carried through first. Though he couldn't see the full extent of the injuries to Molly's face, what he could make out made him feel physically sick. He could never raise his hand to a woman and couldn't understand how any man could. And yet he told himself if he didn't get this girl away from here, a battered face would be the least of her worries. He must make her see that.

'Listen,' he said, putting his hands on her shoulders, 'your life is in grave danger.' And when she didn't answer he tried again, 'Do you understand what I said?'

Molly nodded, and then was sorry because her head began thumping again. She said through thick lips, 'You said my life was in danger.'

'It is,' Will insisted. 'It is because of what you did to Collingsworth.'

He felt the shudder run all down her body and he added, 'Believe me, I am his chauffeur and heard him talking to Ray. He wants you killed.'

Abject and absolute terror took hold of Molly then. 'But . . . but what am I to do?'

'I have come to get you out.'

'But that won't help. I have nowhere to go.'

'Let me worry about that,' Will said. 'Will you trust me?'

Molly looked at Will's open face and what she could see of it was full of concern for her. For that reason she knew that this man was an honest one. She said, 'I don't know why, but I believe you.'

Will sighed in relief. 'Now, listen,' he said. 'You can escape from this room via the ladder, but it has to seem as if you got out on your own. If they were to think otherwise, my life, as well as yours, will be in danger. Do you understand that?'

Again there was that nod, as if it was too much effort for Molly to speak.

'So,' Will said, 'we must tear the sheets up until we have enough to reach the ground, or near enough anyway, and as quickly as possible because time is against us.'

Molly needed no second bidding to do that. She took pleasure in tearing those black sheets into sizeable strips, which Will tied together, fastening one end of the rope to the leg of the bed.

'That's about it,' he said at last, tipping the tied sheets from the window where they dangled just about a foot from the ground.

Then Will unpacked the haversack and inside was a woman's coat, a scarf, hat and gloves and a pair of boots. He smiled at Molly's puzzled expression.

'They are from my wife,' he said. 'She thought you may have need of them and I'd say she was right.'

'You're married,' Molly said, because to be married seemed a very safe and ordinary thing to be.

'Well married,' Will said. 'My wife is seven months pregnant and that was her favourite coat, but it won't go near her now. Mind you, it would fit you three times over. There isn't much of you, is there, and the boots will probably be like boats, but they will be better than those fancy slippers. Mind you, we must take everything with us, because you wouldn't leave without clothes. In fact, it might pay us to take some things from the drawers, as well, just to allay any suspicions they may have.'

Eventually they were ready and Will went onto the ladder first and guided Molly down gently. She was glad of it, for everything ached and the wind blew with such intensity it threatened to pluck her off it.

'Won't the ladder sort of give it away?' she said to Will when she reached the ground, and she heard him give a throaty chuckle.

'You leave the ladder to me,' he said, as he lifted it and

288

dropped it the other side of the factory wall. 'It can bide there until it is safe to come and fetch it. Now we must be away from here, and as fast as we can.'

It wasn't very fast, because Molly was in pain with every step and Will was soon aware of it. He knew it was a tidy walk to Aston, where Betty's mother lived, and they daren't risk a tram. They hadn't set out far when it began to rain, icy, sleety rain with the gusty wind behind it. Will was glad of it, for it meant the streets were virtually empty, though the sky had begun to lighten and those that were out had little inclination to linger.

Molly had the hat pulled well down and the scarf pulled up, so it was when they arrived at 8 Albert Road, the little terrace house of Ruby Mitchell, Betty's mother, and Molly took off her sopping things, that they saw the full extent of the injuries to her face. For a while they were all struck dumb, and then Will almost ground out, 'God Almighty!' He had seldom seen such savagery and knew without a shadow of a doubt that he had done the right thing. So did the two women.

'I'll make us all a drop of tea,' Ruby said, knowing that it was the panacea for every ailment known to man.

'Not for me, Ma,' Will said. 'I had better head back.'

'Take a drop of tea at least.'

'I daren't,' Will said. 'When the balloon goes up it will be better for me if I am in my own home, with my coat and boots dry, so I can convince any that are the slightest bit interested that I have not left my own fireside since I was given the day off.'

The three women knew what sense Will spoke, for the safety of them all hinged on Will acting Mr Innocent and covering every angle.

There was consternation when Ray and Charlie turned up at the flat that afternoon to find the bedroom empty and the sheets dangling from the open window.

289

'Christ, she's done a runner,' Ray said as he strode into the room and pulled in the knotted sheets.

'Thought you said you had slapped her about a bit.'

'Yeah, I did.' Ray slammed the window shut. 'Wouldn't have thought she was in any fit shape to run off.'

'Obviously you didn't hit her hard enough,' Charlie sneered at him, and added, 'When I teach women a lesson, they really are ready to go nowhere for some time.'

'Yeah, I know.' Ray was opening and shutting drawers as he spoke. 'I have seen the results of your handiwork. You really are one vicious sod.'

'You be glad I am,' Charlie said. 'I was the one you came running to when you wanted help to do the girl in and what do we do now when she ain't even here?'

'We find her, what else?' Ray said, flinging open the wardrobe door.

'Better let Collingsworth know she's gone walkabout.'

'Are you mad?' Ray cried. 'Jesus, my life would be worth nothing if he got to know I had lost her. He'd turn me over to his bullyboys to beat me to pulp without a second thought and then probably feed me through the mincer.'

'It will be worse if we don't tell him.'

'It couldn't be worse,' Ray said with a shudder. 'Not for me it couldn't.'

'But what if we don't find her?'

'Course we will,' Ray said confidently. 'She has no money, and though she has taken most of the clothes from here they will hardly keep her warm. She has no coat or proper shoes and the day is raw. I expect that we will find her wandering the streets aimlessly and, by God, when I do find her, I will make her pay for this.'

'And what if her aimless wandering leads her to a police station?'

'What can she tell them if it does?' Ray said. 'She can hardly remember the days of the week. She wouldn't be able to tell them where she came from, nor what she is doing in Birmingham. And she won't have a clue where this house is because it was dark when she came and she hasn't left it at all since she came into it, so it will be highly unlikely to be able to pinpoint where it is, and she has no idea of the address.'

'Even so . . .'

'She'll be wandering the streets, I tell you,' Ray said. 'Come on, we're wasting time and we have only got an hour or so of daylight left.'

They hadn't been back out long when icy sleet began to fall again, and they were soon wet to the skin and freezing cold as they toiled through street after street. They checked out alleyways and entries, and any other places where a person might hide, and their anger and annoyance increased at every step.

When the short winter day ended and the murky dusk turned into black night, the temperature plummeted further, and they were no nearer finding the girl. 'We haven't a snowball's chance in hell of finding her now anyroad,' Charlie said. 'Not in the bleeding blackout.'

'No,' Ray agreed. 'Mind you, if she is out in this, dressed in the type of clothes she had, she will be a stiff by morning.'

'Yeah, and while that will save you a job, don't you think it will raise questions if they find the frozen corpse of a girl dressed like a prostitute and with a bashed-up face?' Charlie said. 'Dead or alive, that girl has to be found.'

'Not in this.'

'Hardly,' Charlie said. 'When you can't see a hand in front of you. But at first light – and I know how you feel about Collingsworth, and with reason I'd say – he has to know. We'll need him anyway, because there is a limit to what the two of us can do.'

Ray knew what Charlie said made good sense, but he was dreadfully afraid of facing Collingsworth after the last time and admitting that he had let escape the girl he had been charged to kill. And he was right to be afraid, for his rage that day was frightening.

Ray thought that he had witnessed Collingsworth in a temper before but what he had seen then had been nothing to how the man reacted to the latest news. His face turned puce with anger, his eyes bulged, and spittle formed at the corners of his mouth as he listened to Ray's bumbling tale.

When he had finished he looked at him with wild eyes that shone with a strange, almost demonic light and spat out through his thin lips, 'You stupid, useless bastard!'

Ray had begun to shake. He couldn't ever remember being so scared.

Charlie could sense his fear and, watching Collingsworth, knew he was aware of it too. Even Ray's voice shook as he said placatingly, 'Yes, but—'

'You're nothing but a sodding arsehole who can be trusted to do nothing.'

'Give me another chance?' Ray pleaded. 'We'll find her easily in the morning because she has no money and no contacts, and little more than the clothes she stood up in. Christ, she might be dead already and if she isn't I'll finish her off, promise.'

'Like you did before?'

'Yeah, I know, but—'

Suddenly, Collingsworth lost patience with him and clicked his fingers. Immediately, two heavies, who had been flanking the walls, stepped forward. Ray took one look at them and tried to make a bolt for the door, but he knew it was useless. One caught hold of him, easily lifting him and then set him down on the floor and held him with his hands behind his back.

'Edwin, please?' Ray implored frantically. 'Give me another chance? I'm begging you . . .'

His voice ended in a scream of terror as the other heavy powered a punch that snapped his head back and caused Charlie to wince. He continued to thump his fist into Ray

292

and Collingsworth watched it all impassively. Charlie was sure they intended to kill Ray as his cries gave way to whimpers and then moans until in the end he lost consciousness. Only then did Collingsworth snap his fingers, and the sickening thuds into the bloodied man stopped.

The man holding Ray let him slump to the floor, as Collingsworth growled out, 'Dump him in one of the bedrooms for now and lock the door. We don't want any more escaping.'

Charlie looked at Collingsworth nervously as he wondered if some of the same treatment was to be meted out to him, but Collingsworth had no problem with Charlie. 'We will lead a search for the girl as soon as it's any way light at all,' he said, 'so you be back here at seven or so and we will go over what everyone is to do.'

'What about Ray?' Charlie said, feeling bound to ask.

'What about him?' Collingsworth replied. 'He won't be going anywhere for some time, and really that is just a foretaste of what will happen to him if he screws up again. If we find the girl alive then he will deal with her, and if he fails this time . . .'

He didn't need to say any more. At his words and the expression on his face, Charlie felt as if an icy finger had trailed down his spine and he knew he wouldn't change places with Ray for anything he could name.

TWENTY

'We have them completely flummoxed,' Will told Betty the next day. 'As Collingsworth said to me today, it's like the girl has disappeared off the face of the earth. They are convinced too that she had to have help, but they don't know who, or what or anything.'

'They don't suspect you?'

'My dear girl, this lot would suspect their own mothers,' Will said. 'Oh, they have been round to the house. I know their tactics: one keeps you talking while the other has a good poke around, but of course he found nothing.'

'Why you?' Betty asked in alarm.

'Why not me?' Will said. 'I shouldn't imagine that I was the only one. Anyway, you say the girl isn't well?'

'Ah, Will, that girl has gone through it,' Betty said. 'Her name is Molly. She told us that much, but she doesn't know her other name. In fact, she doesn't know much. She is so doped up she was near climbing the walls, shaking and crying all the time, begging and pleading for us to get her that muck that Ray was pumping into her. She didn't sleep at all last night. Mom has been great, but we took it in turns through the night because she can't be left. If we have to leave her for any reason we have to lock her in.'

'She wouldn't be crazy enough to go out, surely?'

'Will, when she is in the throes of this addiction she is crazy enough to do anything,' Betty said.

Betty was right. Molly felt as if she was going mad. Hammers banged inside her head and griping cramps in her stomach doubled her over and caused her to groan and cry out with the pain. She was unable to control her limbs and she shook constantly, and though she was tired, incredibly weary, her mind was jumping about too much to allow her to sleep. She couldn't eat either, and whatever she tried was vomited straight back. It was gin she craved, or whisky, and the white powders that made her feel better. She begged and pleaded for those.

Added to this, her body either ached or throbbed or stung from the beatings she had received, and she could feel her face was a pulpy bloodied mess, though neither Ruby nor Betty had let her look at herself. She wondered if life was worth living. She was a girl with no past, a very uncertain future and she was bloody scared stiff.

However, Molly did improve, though it was slow, and it was a week later before she realised that her symptoms were easing. She went downstairs for the first time, but only in the evening because it wasn't safe for her to be up in the day when a neighbour might catch sight of her and start asking awkward questions.

She was frustrated that she could still remember nothing of her past, but Betty told her not to worry about it. 'Maybe you are trying too hard,' she said. 'Let it all sort of fester in your head, like, and then it might come back in a rush.'

'I really wish that would happen,' Molly said. 'You know, Ray must have had me drugged up to the eyeballs most of the time, because I had no idea so much time had elapsed. I was living a sort of half-life. And I thought he was wonderful, you know. That is what I can't get over.'

'Don't think about that any more,' Betty advised. 'That was the way he wanted you. Will says you are not the first he has virtually abducted in the guise of being friendly, and the others were all sent to whorehouses. You weren't to know he was a perverted bully.'

'Yes, I know, but here you are preparing for Christmas, and I have sort of lost a big portion of my life.'

'Don't think about it any more,' Ruby said. 'You can give us a hand making all the festive stuff, if you are up to it. Mind, it will be a bit of a frugal Christmas, with rationing biting as tight as it is, but we'll do our best.'

Molly knew that everyone only got just so much food each week and by living there she was taking someone else's share. She said, 'I should get my own ration book. It's wrong to take your allowance.'

'Maybe in the New Year,' Will said. 'You couldn't go out with your face looking like that anyway, and it is too soon to be taking to the streets. Remember, if you are spotted and identified, the rest of us are in danger too.'

'I do see that,' Molly said. 'And I would never do that to you – I owe you too much. But how are you managing?'

'I get extra rations,' Betty said. 'I have a special green ration book because I am pregnant and I have extra milk and am entitled to more eggs. Then Mom bought in tinned stuff long before war was declared. She knew that war was inevitable – well, we all did really, after Munich – and she remembered the last war when the gentry bought nearly all the food up in some shops. So every week she would buy a few extra items and put them away. Don't worry, we get by all right.'

And with that Molly had to be content.

'Wakey, wakey, Molly.'

Molly had been in an unusually deep and dreamless sleep, and as she struggled to wakefulness she saw Will beside her bed, with Betty and Ruby behind him, big smiles plastered across their faces, and carrying parcels wrapped in brown paper.

'What's this?' Molly asked, though she too was smiling. 'I am too old to believe in Santa Claus.'

296

'No one is too old to believe in Santa Claus,' Will declared. 'Look at this special delivery that was waiting for you downstairs this morning.'

'I know what manner of delivery it was, and it was from no man in a red suit,' Molly said. 'And really, you shouldn't have. I already owe you so much and haven't two halfpennies to bless myself with to buy any of you anything, even if I could get out to take a look in the shops.'

'It's not worth it,' Will told her. 'The shops have little stock now. If you ask me, clothes will be the next thing to be rationed.'

'Well,' said Betty. 'I will hardly notice that, but I'd say it might be harder when the baby comes because one thing babies are good at is growing.'

'You're right there, girl,' Ruby said with a chuckle.

Will put in, 'Well, I'd say Molly has done growing.' He placed the parcel on the bed beside her, adding, 'These are things you will need and they are not new, but bought at the Rag Market down the Bull Ring. Open it. Go on.'

Molly unwrapped the parcel to reveal a matching hat, gloves and a scarf in a warm russet colour and of the softest wool.

Will said, 'Happy Christmas, Molly.'

This sentiment was echoed by the others, but Molly barely heard them for a memory was tugging at her brain. There was another time when this had happened, when someone had wished her Happy Christmas and had given into her hand a parcel containing a hat, scarf and gloves set. The image came into focus and she shut her eyes tight, unwilling to let this memory go. She saw herself receiving the gift, reacting with pleasure and surprise, and she suddenly said, 'Uncle Tom.' She had no idea where the name had come from at first and then his dear open face appeared before her and she said, 'He gave me a set like this for Christmas years ago.'

Will was very excited. It was nice to know that Molly

wasn't completely alone in the world. 'And where is he now, this uncle of yours?'

Molly shook her head; there was no more.

'Likely in Ireland,' Ruby said. 'From your accent I would say that is where you come from.'

'Could be right,' Will said. 'And Ray would have probably picked you up at the station.'

'I can't believe that you were mixed up with people like these,' Betty said.

'We've been through that, Betty,' Will said, 'And Christmas Day is not the time to discuss it further. Give Molly your parcels.'

Betty had bought Molly a winter coat. It was dark brown, very stylish, and fitted with a half-belt fastened at the back. The collar and cuffs were trimmed with velvet the exact same shade as the things Will had bought. Ruby gave Molly a pair of fur-lined brown boots.

'I haven't been so well dressed for years,' Molly said in delight at the lovely things chosen just for her. This was true, for through the day she was also wearing Betty's clothes that she was too big to fit into now.

All through that wonderful Christmas Day and days following, the memories, so long hidden from her, began to flit across Molly's mind. They weren't in any order or sequence, and she struggled to make sense of them, but she rejoiced in each one and stored it away. It was New Year's Eve before she had them in some order and could tell Will, Betty and Ruby about her earlier life.

She told of why she had been forced to go to Ireland and of the years there, and the note from her brother that had sent her scurrying back. She told them how she had met Ray and Charlie at New Street Station, and the raid that so unnerved her.

'Ray, in particular, seemed so kind and terribly considerate of my fears. The first shelter we were in was caught in the blast of a bomb. It was utter mayhem and I ended up leaving my case behind with everything in it. It was crushed when the shelter collapsed. Without Ray and Charlie that night I would have been lost and so I sort of marked them down as good people, you know?' She sighed and went on. 'That allayed any suspicions I might have had about them. After that, it all gets a bit hazy. I suppose that was the drugs, wasn't it?'

Will nodded. 'I'd say so. It's how they usually work. I know little about that side of things, but from what I hear, the girls taken to the whorehouse are often unaware of where they are until it is too late. It is Ray's job to get them hooked on those powders and gin so they will do anything it takes to get the money for their next fix, or next drink.'

'And I was nearly one of them,' Molly said. 'I didn't know what I was doing in that flat, and I didn't care until the night Collingsworth came. I remember him saying he paid dearly to get a virgin and he got so mad when I said I couldn't do that sort of thing.'

'How did you get the better of him?' Will asked. 'I wondered at the time, and more since I have met you, for you are just a dot of a thing.'

'Ah, that was just a lucky chance and I took it,' Molly said, and she went on to explain how she had felled Collingsworth.

'But how did you get him outside the door?' Will asked.

'I was so angry and frightened by then,' Molly said, 'I think I could have shifted a steamroller if I'd had to. And then I just rolled him down the stairs.'

'To the day he dies he will never forgive you for that,' Will said, and a tremor ran all through Molly at his words.

'Shut up, Will,' Betty said sharply. 'Can't you see you are scaring the poor girl to death? I for one don't blame her in the slightest, and I would have done the same or worse in her shoes. Finished off the old bugger, I would have.'

'I thought she had,' Will said. 'Honest, my heart near stopped when I saw him there. Might have solved one

299

problem as well, Betty, but it would make a hundred more. People like that are too influential for folk to be able to bump them off and get away with it. The man isn't worth ending your life at the end of a hangman's rope. I was bloody glad the man was still alive, I'll tell you. Molly,' he turned to her, 'I know you lost your case, but have you anything of value at all, because to get away from here you will need money?'

'I have just this,' Molly said, withdrawing the locket, 'though I would hate to part with it.' She clicked it open and showed him the picture of her parents inside.

'You wouldn't get much for it either,' Will said. 'It's gold they are after.'

'There is nothing else,' Molly said. 'I had money, but Ray took it from me – to keep it safe, he said – and I never saw it again. But no, oh, wait,' she cried suddenly, leaping to her feet with a cry of excitement and pounding up the stairs. 'I wasn't sure they would still be there,' she said when she returned. 'I had them in the pocket of the wrap I had on.' She opened her hand to reveal the cufflinks.

'Those are Collingsworth's, and solid gold,' Will said. 'Where did you get them?'

Molly told him and he whistled in astonishment. 'God, that was jammy. He hasn't missed them. He was in no fit state to notice much that night, but even afterwards he's not said anything. Point is, he owns so many pairs and yet he knows every one. You'll get a pretty penny for these.'

'D'you mean someone will buy them?'

'To pawn them would be best.'

'Pawn them?' Molly said, wrinkling her nose. 'I've heard of people pawning things but I have never done it myself. How does it work?'

'The pawnbroker sort of buys things from you, but gives you a ticket that you can redeem to get the stuff back within a certain time, only you have to pay him more than he gave you. If you don't redeem it, then he is at liberty to sell it.'

300

'Well, we'll do that then.'

'Yeah, but not around here,' Will said. 'Collingsworth is too well known in these parts and all around the town. Need to go maybe as far as Sutton Coldfield to be safe.'

'Oh, I know where that is,' Molly said. 'That won't bother me.'

'And I can't be involved in this,' Will said. 'If ever these are recognised by someone I cannot risk them being traced back to me. With a bit of luck you might well be out of it by then, but we will all still be here.'

'I know, Will,' Molly said. 'You have done more than enough and I would ask no more of you.' She meant every word and yet she recoiled at the thought of entering a pawnbroker's. But she knew if she was ever to leave Ruby's and press on with what she had come to Birmingham for, she had to do it.

Will was still nervous about Molly going out and about, but knew that she really did need to register for a ration book and identity card because everyone did, and they couldn't manage to feed her without one for much longer. Molly understood Will's concern, and it wasn't only Collingsworth she had to be careful of, but the neighbours too.

Early in the New Year, Molly and Ruby were up and out well before it was light, easy enough to do in those dark and dismal winter days, but both women were tired, for there had been a raid the night before and they had had to seek shelter in the cellar and so were feeling very jaded. As they scurried for the tram, Molly heard the frost crackling beneath her feet. The piercing wind cut through her like a knife, despite her good thick coat, and the air was so raw it almost hurt to breath.

And yet she knew the bleak weather conditions worked to their advantage because, in the inky blackness with her hat pulled well down and scarf wrapped around her mouth,

301

Molly felt quite safe, especially as they met few people on the road and those they did were similarly clad. Everyone seemed to be in a rush to get some place too, and she couldn't blame them one bit. She imagined they were too anxious to be about their own business and under cover as quickly as possible and had no time or inclination to worry about other people on the road. Certainly no one gave them a backward glance, and it was far too chilly for anyone to linger.

The swaying clanking and very draughty tram dropped them at Colmore Row, and as they walked up that wide road towards the Council House, Molly had great sympathy for the citizens of Birmingham. She could see in the gloomy half-light, the gaping holes, often filled with piles of masonry, charred roof beams, slates and other assorted debris where once buildings had stood.

Such indiscriminate and brutal destruction made her think again of her young brother and her grandfather, and she wondered what had happened to them. The tug of worry had never left her since her memory had returned, and she was frustrated that she was unable to try to find out anything and maybe be a measure of comfort to her young brother, She wondered too how long it would be before Will should decide that it was safe enough for her to leave. She knew she had to listen to him, though, and however worried she was about her family, she would never dream of defying Will and maybe putting his family in danger, though it was very hard to do nothing at all.

'Now, remember you are my niece newly over from Ireland to help Betty with the baby,' Ruby said.

Molly nodded because it was what had been decided the night before. But the official who listened to her explanation said, 'Funny time to come, when the country is at war.'

'That's why,' Molly said. 'Betty is worried about coping with the baby in the raids and all.'

'My daughter is living with me at the moment, you see,'

Ruby said, 'but once the baby is born and she is returned to her own home, I am registering for war work and so Molly has come to give her a hand until she is properly on her feet again.'

'And what do you intend to do then?' the man asked Molly. 'Will you return to Ireland?'

Molly shook her head. 'I very much doubt it,' she said. 'I think I will look for a job here.'

The man seemed happy enough with that and he stamped the ration book and handed it over, saying as he did, 'You have to register with a grocer, greengrocer and butcher to get your allotted rations. I suppose your aunt has explained all that to you already.'

Molly had been surprised when Ruby had said she was going to look for war-related work because she had not said a word about it to anyone, though Molly knew the country had a desperate need for women to enter the workplace. She asked her about it as they made their way home.

'It's not something I have just thought of,' Ruby said. 'It started when I read about the need for woman workers in the papers before Christmas. I mean, they even had vans with loudspeakers touring the areas, urging woman to do their bit. I know if my Harold had still been alive he would have encouraged me to go for it.'

'Well, I think it's wonderful,' Molly said.

'Point is, Molly, we have got to win this damned war,' Ruby said. 'There is no doubt about that, and so I would say it needs every man jack of us women that can to set to and not only free as many men as possible, but make sure they have the arms they need to fight effectively.'

Molly knew Ruby spoke the truth. 'You are right. I only wish I could do something worthwhile.'

'You need to have patience,' Ruby said.

But Molly was worried because she knew she couldn't stay with Ruby for ever. In fact, every day she stayed there she was jeopardising them all, but she hadn't a plan in her

303

head about how she was to support herself once she left the house.

The new year of 1941 was just over a week old when Collingsworth decided to redouble his efforts to find Molly. As he confided to Will, she couldn't be dead.

'If she was, her body would have fetched up somewhere by now.'

'Not if she jumped in the canal.'

Collingsworth thought about this for a minute or two, then said, 'No, all right, if she jumped in the canal her body might never be found, though with the traffic using the canals since the war began it might well be. But I ask you, why would she go to the trouble of escaping just to do herself in? It don't make sense. No, I feel it in my bones that she is alive and well, and to be in that state someone has had to be helping her. When I find out who that person is, they will wish they had never taken their first breath.'

Will tasted fear in his mouth that caused it to go suddenly dry, while his heart hammered in his chest, and not for himself alone, but for Betty and the gutsy Ruby. For a moment he wished he had never overheard that conversation between Collingsworth and Ray. If he hadn't heard it, the deed would have been done and he would have known nothing about it. Molly could have been counted as one more casualty in a war that had already claimed many innocent victims. Hearing about it, however, meant that because he was an ordinary, decent human being, he had to do something, and in doing so endangered the lives of those dearest to him.

There was no course open to him but to go on with it now. Ray, when he had recovered sufficiently, had readily told Collingsworth all he knew about Molly that she had recounted to him in the shelter, and the things that Charlie had checked out, and so Collingsworth learned about the grandfather, who Ray found out had died, and the brother who was probably in Erdington Cottage Homes in Fentham Road.

'She doesn't know this?'

'Well, I didn't tell her, and when she left she would have no memory of a brother or anything else much. If she has recovered herself sufficiently now, and her memory has returned, she will easily find out, as Charlie did.'

And so a watch was put on Molly's grandfather's house and another was sent to keep an eye out at the entrance to the Cottage Homes. Will knew of this, but told no one at the house in case it alarmed them. He told Molly only that she wouldn't be able to make a move just yet a while.

A month later they were no further forward and the search was called off in the middle of February, though Collingsworth said he could feel in his bones that the girl was alive and somewhere in the city. Of course, he told himself, they wouldn't have had to go to all this bother if Morris hadn't screwed up so badly in the first place, and his frustration turned to anger directed against the man. He wished he had let the heavies go on and finish him off that time. Well, that could be remedied he thought; Ray Morris was nothing to him.

Ray was no fool and he knew the way the wind was blowing with Collingsworth. When he saw his heavies outside his flat, just after the search was called off, he shook with fear. He had barely recovered from the first beating that Collingsworth had authorised and he guessed that if he stayed around for this one, then it would be the end for him, and he climbed out of his window, down the drainpipe and was away.

Once in the streets, he had no idea where to go at first. His flat was closed to him now, so he just had the clothes he stood up in and the money in his pocket. He also knew too much for Collingsworth to just let him walk away. The bullyboys would be after him and he needed to put some distance between him and them.

To do that he needed money, and the only way he knew to get ready cash, without putting himself in much risk, was to head for his home in Sutton Coldfield. His mother was always pleased to see him and he could wheedle money out of her with no bother at all – he had done it often enough in the past – and then he could put real distance between Collingsworth and himself.

Collingsworth didn't know straight away that Ray had done a runner, because there had been nothing packed up in his flat to indicate this and he had no idea that he had caught sight of his heavies at his door. He thought he was going about some business of his own, so it was over a week later when he tumbled to it.

Will was unaware of this, but he did know that they had given up the search for Molly at long last. He told her he thought it was safe for her to travel to Sutton Coldfield to try to pawn the cufflinks.

He had drawn a map for her of where the pawnshop was in relation to the train station. 'You come down Station Road here,' he said, pointing to the diagram with the pencil, 'and you will be in Mill Street. You go along Mill Street to Victoria Road, and that's where you will find the pawn-broker. I don't know the name of it and couldn't ask without raising suspicions, but you can't miss it, because there are three balls hanging outside.'

Molly had no desire to go into a pawnbroker's shop and get money for something that wasn't even hers, but there was no alternative. She knew she would have to leave very early in the morning before most people were abroad to avoid being seen by many, and not return till after dark.

She said to Will, 'When I am rid of the cufflinks, as I will have time to spare, I will see if I can find out anything about Kevin and Granddad as Erdington is so close to Sutton Coldfield. I promise I'll keep a low profile.'

306

'Oh, Molly!'

'You can't expect me not to do this, Will,' Molly said. 'That is unreasonable. You know how anxious I have been.'

'I know,' Will said. 'But it is just when people start asking questions . . .'

'I'm only asking the neighbours to start with,' Molly said. 'And you said the search has been called off now.'

'It has, but . . .'

'Will I can't stay here for ever,' Molly said gently.

Will sighed. 'I know. But you will be careful, won't you? Keep your eyes peeled.'

'Course I will, and try not to worry so much,' Molly said, but she knew that Will would fret every minute she was away.

TWENTY-ONE

The interior of the pawn shop was just as dark and dingy as Molly had expected, and she was heartily glad the place was empty. The door had pinged as she had entered the shop, and from the back an oldish man shambled out. He was dressed all in black in a suit that had probably been smart at one time, but was definitely shabby-looking. His face was lugubrious and long, and he reminded Molly of the man in the Jewish baker's shop not far from her old house, where her mother might send her for fresh bread on a Sunday morning.

'Can I help you?' the man asked.

In answer, Molly withdrew the cufflinks from her bag and placed them on the counter. She saw the man's eyes gleam. 'What would you give me for these?'

The man took up an eyeglass to scrutinise the links more intently, though he hardly needed it. He knew that they were solid gold and worth a small fortune.

When he lowered the glass, he said, 'Where did you get these from? Did you come by them honestly?'

How glad Molly was that she was wearing Betty's best outfit – a coat with a fur collar and a hat of the same fur, and boots with high heels. For all they were a little big for her, she looked eminently respectable. She hadn't wanted to take them at first and Will had told her not to be so silly. 'If you go in dressed any old how they may think you have stolen the links and give you nothing.'

She was glad she had seen the wisdom of that in the end. Those clothes gave her the confidence to draw herself up to her maximum height, look the man straight in the eyes and without hesitation say, 'Of course I came by them honestly. They were left to me by my father, who passed away recently, and now I need the money.'

Her face was so honest and open, the pawnbroker believed her totally. Molly wondered if her character was flawed in some way that enabled her to lie so easily and so well, for the pawnbroker said, 'I'm sorry, miss, but we have to be so careful. I don't want the police to come sniffing around.'

'No, I'm sure.'

'The cufflinks are very fine. Your father must have been a man of good taste.'

'He was,' Molly said, glad that she could say that so truthfully. 'And my mother was too.' And then she added, 'They were killed together in a car accident.'

'How tragic for you, my dear.'

'That's why I need the money. Will you take the cufflinks?'

'I most certainly will,' the pawnbroker said, mentally rubbing his hands with glee. 'I can offer you six pounds on them.'

Six pounds was a fortune and Molly gave a gasp of pleasure. 'I'll take it gladly.'

'I shall just write you out a ticket in case you should want to redeem them.'

'I won't, honestly,' Molly said firmly.

'Even so, my dear, who knows but that your circumstances will change tomorrow and you would want to redeem the keepsake your father left you.'

Molly let the man write out the ticket, for it was easier than arguing, though once outside the shop, she screwed it into a ball and threw it in the gutter.

She didn't notice the man who had ducked into an entry as he caught sight of her. It was Ray, and he had the urge to leap on Molly straight away and strangle the life out of her for all the trouble she had caused, but he could hardly do that in the middle of the day in the open street.

He wondered what Molly had been doing there, so well dressed and respectable-looking, and what the hell she had to pawn. A few minutes later he was picking up and unfolding the docket he had seen her throw away. He didn't associate the cufflinks with Collingsworth, though he knew that she must have stolen them from someone, and he pocketed the docket until he decided what to do about it.

He also wondered what to do with the knowledge that Molly was in Sutton Coldfield. If he told Collingsworth, it wouldn't be enough that he had seen the girl. He would only want to know when he was going to do her in. On the other hand, if his mother would stop acting so tight he could be away out of this, ready to start again at something else, and he would prefer that to killing anyone and so he let Molly walk away.

Molly decided to go first to Hilda's as it was nearest to the station, and then Gravelly Lane and see if she could find out what had happened to her grandfather. She was well aware what she might find out that day would hardly be good news, and she alighted from the train at Station Road with some trepidation.

There was a stranger in Hilda's house, who knew nothing of the previous occupants, or where they had gone, or even if they were alive or dead, and Molly turned away dispirited. There were strangers in her old home too and Molly found it slightly unsettling to see different curtains fluttering at the window.

The woman of the house, seeing Molly standing staring, came to the door. 'Can I help you?'

'Yes, I mean no,' said Molly flustered. 'I mean, I used to live here.'

'Here?' the woman repeated in surprise and then suddenly said, 'Oh yes, I remember now, the neighbours have

310

mentioned you. I mean, I suppose it was you if you lived in this house. Did you lose your parents sudden, like, a few years ago?'

Molly nodded. 'In a car crash.'

The woman nodded sagely. 'Dreadful they said it was and then Hilda next door they said you was so pally with, like.'

'Dead?' Molly repeated. 'Hilda is dead?'

'Well, I don't rightly know,' the woman said. 'She was real poorly, I know that well enough, and they came and took her away in an ambulance. The husband wasn't coping, for all we did our best, and in the end one of the daughters came and took him away to live with them. I never knew what happened to Hilda.'

Molly felt a sudden sense of loss because whether Hilda was alive or dead, she was as good as dead to her. She could weep when she thought that she would never see that lovely round face again with the eyes that twinkled with amusement.

The distress was plain on her face and the woman said, 'Sorry, must have been a shock, like, hearing it like that.'

'It was,' Molly said. 'And yet . . . I thought that I had prepared myself for this sort of thing. Only now I know that you can never prepare yourself, not really.'

'No, you can't,' the woman agreed. 'Why don't you come in a minute and have a hot drink at least? It's cold enough to freeze a penguin's chuff today, as my old man would say.'

'No, thank you,' Molly said, 'It's very kind of you but I need to see about my brother and grandfather.'

'Well, I'll not keep you if you are certain about not wanting that drink.'

Molly wasn't sure when she started crying, she only knew that she couldn't stop once she had begun. Two people asked if she was all right and if they could help, and she just shook her head and walked on, still crying.

At the door of the house that had used to belong to her

granddad, Molly took a grip on herself and scrubbed at the tears with her handkerchief before she lifted the knocker. There was no answer and she waited a few minutes and then knocked again. Then the woman next door came out.

'No good you keep knocking, they are all at work . . .' she began to say, and then as Molly turned to look at her she squealed. 'Eeh, Molly. What a bloody sight for sore eyes you are, girl.'

'What's happened, Mrs Hewitt?'

'Lots, duck and not good, most of it,' Nancy Hewitt said sadly. 'But we can't talk on the pavement. Come in. I'll make a brew and tell you anything you want to know.'

Molly didn't say a word until the tea was before her and then she said, 'Granddad's dead, isn't he, Mrs Hewitt?'

Nancy gave a brief nod and Molly gasped, and then, despite the shards of pain stabbing at her heart, she asked, 'How did he die?'

'He was killed while he was fire watching on top of a factory,' Nancy said. 'I had Kevin in with me. Stan always left him in whenever he was on duty and when the news came, oh, dear me, Kevin was bereft, quite distraught. The doctor had to be sent to give him something in the end.'

'So where did he go then?' Molly asked.

'Well, I kept him for a few days, but with my own four and my mother-in-law here as well I just hadn't the room for anything permanent,' Nancy said. 'When I told the Welfare people about you going off to live in Ireland with the maternal grandmother they were pleased and said they would contact her. They thought, well, we all thought, that she would take Kevin on too, with your granddad dead and all. I mean, he was family just as much as you were, and I agreed to look after Kevin in the meantime.'

'But she didn't?'

'No. A woman from the Welfare told me the day of the funeral. They'd had a letter just that morning. And the grandmother had not only refused to take him in, but said

312

you both wanted nothing to do with him at all, no communication whatsoever. I tell you, this woman from the Welfare said she had seen some things in her line of work but she said the tone of the letter fair shook her up.

'Anyroad that was that, and a few days later, the Welfare told me to take Kevin to the Children's Receiving Centre in Summerfield Road. Must admit, it gave me a pang when I left him.

'But, you carried on writing, Molly. I knew because I had the key for next door, 'cos I was sort of looking after the place until the new tenants took over. I used to collect the post and knew your handwriting. It did make me wonder if you had been told anything at all.'

'No, I hadn't.'

Nancy gave an emphatic nod of her head. 'Thought as much. Downright wicked, that. Anyroad, I collected all them letters together and asked Social Services where he had ended up so I could send the letters on.'

'What do you mean?'

'Well, see, the place in Summerfield Road is just where the kids is sent first off. They don't stay there, like.'

'So where do they go from there?'

'Wherever they has space, I s'pose,' Nancy said. 'They did tell me he might be sent to Erdington Cottage Homes in Fentham Road. That's what I told the man who came asking too.'

'What man?'

'Said he was from the council, seeing that the children were being cared for properly,' Nancy said. 'He were right respectable, nicely dressed and well spoken and all, and yet I felt . . . I won't say exactly uneasy, but odd, like, that he didn't know where the kid was sent and he had to ask a neighbour, and I said as much too.'

Molly had a cold feeling in the pit of her stomach and she said, 'Can you remember when he came, this man?'

'Yeah,' Nancy said. 'It was after that big raid, just after

313

Coventry copped it, the nineteenth, that were and he came the day after.'

Molly knew then that it had been either Ray or Charlie checking up on what she had told them about her brother, seeing that he was well out of the way and wouldn't pose any sort of a problem.

She gave a shiver of distaste at the memory of what they had planned for her, but she didn't really want to think about them and so in an effort to change the subject, she said, 'So did you send the letters to Erdington Cottage Homes then?'

'No, Molly,' Nancy said, 'I sent them nowhere, because I wasn't let.'

'Why ever not?'

'Because in that letter your grandmother forbade it.'

'D'you know, Mrs Hewitt, Kevin must have felt totally abandoned.'

'I know,' Nancy agreed. 'And that grandmother of yours must be a very wicked woman.'

'She is,' Molly said with feeling, leaping to her feet 'But now isn't the time to go into it. I must go and see Kevin.'

'Not without a bit in your mouth you don't,' Nancy said, pushing Molly back in the chair. 'It is too cold to go traipsing about the streets on an empty stomach.'

Molly stood before the large ornate gates, which was the entrance to the homes, her stomach in knots and her mouth so dry it hurt to swallow. Even knowing of the callous and cruel nature of her grandmother, she could scarcely believe that she hadn't told her of her grandfather's death, that she hadn't been allowed to grieve for the loss of him and attend the funeral to pay her deep respects to the man that she had loved so much.

But then, she reminded herself, hadn't her grandmother done the selfsame thing with her own mother, Nuala, when her father died because she considered her responsible for

314

his death? She knew full well why she had reacted as she did towards Kevin, though, and that was because she would consider him a sinner now, a heathen. Molly didn't know whether her grandfather insisted that Kevin go to Mass or not, but she guessed not, for if the Church had any input in their lives, Kevin wouldn't have been put in a cottage home, but in one of the Catholic homes, probably Father Hudson's. She didn't care about all that, and she remembered guiltily that she hadn't been near a church herself since she had arrived in Birmingham.

But what mattered now, in fact the only thing that mattered, was Kevin and letting him know that she was still around and that she loved him and would do all in her power to care for him as much as she was able. She pulled on the bell rope to the side of the gates. There was a large building just inside, a sort of lodge place, Molly presumed, and a man emerged from that and approached the gate, which he unlocked and opened.

'Can I help you?'

'Yes, I am here to see my brother, Kevin Maguire.'

The man's sombre expression didn't alter at all and he asked in flat tones, 'You got an appointment?'

'No,' Molly said. 'I have only just found out that he is probably in here.'

The man appeared to think about this for a minute or two before saying, 'You had better come in and see Mr Sutcliffe, the superintendent, and the matron.' He threw the gate fully open as he said, 'Follow me.'

The man took Molly into the Lodge and left her in a little room off the hall with a curt, 'Wait here.'

Molly looked round the unprepossessing room and thought it a dismal place, with its beige walls and brown paintwork, and just bench-type seats around the edge to sit on. But then she wasn't there to judge the décor, she told herself, and turned at the sound of footsteps approaching.

The superintendent was quite a small and dapper man,

315

with thinning brown hair slicked back and sporting a trim moustache on his upper lip. He looked even smaller beside the stout and rather formidable matron in her starched uniform.

However, the man smiled at Molly and shook hands as he said in his precise way, 'Good day, Miss Maguire. I suppose it is Miss Maguire?'

'Yes, Molly Maguire.'

'And you are here about your brother, Kevin?'

'I am here to see him,' Molly said insistently.

'Shall we go into the office where we can be more comfortable and discuss this fully?'

'Yes, but can I see him?' Molly asked.

'All in good time, my dear,' the superintendent said. 'And perhaps, Matron, you could organise some tea?'

The woman left and Molly followed the superintendent and took the chair he indicated at one side of the desk.

He withdrew a file from the filing cabinet and scanned it before saying to Molly, 'Why were you split up after your parents died?'

Molly hesitated. The last thing she wanted this man to think was that she was paranoid and given to hysteria. Maybe then they would not let her see Kevin at all, and she knew few would really understand how evil her grandmother was. They would think Molly was exaggerating or even that it was a total tissue of lies. To gain access to her brother she had to appear sane, sensible and mature, and if that meant lying through her teeth, then she would do so.

'We weren't going to be,' Molly told him. 'We were both due to go to Ireland, but Kevin became ill. The doctors said to take him away from all that was familiar would be harmful at that time.'

'Yes, I see that,' the superintendent said. 'But then when your grandmother was informed of your grandfather's death she not only refused to care for him, but also said she wanted

316

no communication with Kevin and neither did you. I have her reply here on record.'

'She had no right to speak for me,' Molly said. 'But I suppose she did it with the best of intentions.'

'What do you mean?'

'Well, my grandmother was very sick at the time,' Molly said, thinking: sick, right enough, but hers is an illness of the mind. But for the benefit of the superintendent she told an alternative story. 'Grandmother said that Kevin had seen enough of illness and death to last a lifetime and she also knew that with me having to nurse her, I would have little time or energy to deal with a young and distressed child. I wrote to him, but by the time Granddad's neighbour found my letters in the house and took them to the receiving centre where she had left Kevin, he wasn't allowed to have them because of that letter. I knew nothing about that until I came to Birmingham when grandfather's neighbour filled me in with a lot of things.'

After a pause she went on, 'There is something else as well. You see, neither my father nor grandfather were Catholics, and because Kevin was left here I think my grand-mother assumed that he would be raised as a non-Catholic and that was probably another reason why she thought it was better that he stay in Birmingham.'

'Letters wouldn't have hurt, though.'

'She didn't have that long when she was well enough to write them,' Molly said, assuming a sad expression.

'I am sorry, my dear,' the superintendent said. 'I had no idea.'

Molly refused to feel like a heel. This was for Kevin. 'As for me,' she went on, 'I was too busy. And then of course I had written and had no replies and so I didn't know if the letters were getting through or not. And then when it was all over, I found the letter you sent in my grandmother's effects and here I am.'

The matron came in bearing a tray of tea and Molly said

impatiently, 'Is that all you need to know, because I came here to see the brother I haven't seen in five years?'

'Kevin is at school with all the others,' the matron said, handing Molly a cup of tea and fixing her with a hard stare. 'And all that Mr Sutcliffe is trying to do is ascertain that it will be good for Kevin to see you after all this time. The child has been traumatised and hurt enough.'

'I don't intend to hurt him,' Molly burst out. 'I love him. I always have.'

'And you are rather young too,' the matron said. 'What age are you?'

'I will be nineteen tomorrow,' Molly said, 'over eight years older than Kevin, who won't be eleven until March.'

'I must say I thought you much younger,' the superintendent said, 'didn't you, Matron?'

The matron nodded. 'I thought you were not long out of the schoolroom.'

'It's because I am small,' Molly said. 'I am well used to a reaction like that, but I take after my mother. She was the same.'

'This puts a different complexion on the matter entirely,' the superintendent said. 'You are almost an adult and of course you must see Kevin. Could you come back this afternoon?'

Molly nodded eagerly and then, because she wanted no misunderstanding, she said, 'I can't take Kevin away, not yet. I need to find a job to support myself first and a place to live, though ideally I would like somewhere where I could look after Kevin totally eventually.'

'I understand perfectly,' said the superintendent and, thinking she was newly arrived from Ireland, asked, 'Where are you staying now?'

'In lodgings in Aston,' Molly said, thinking there was no harm in telling them that. 'But I can't stay there indefinitely. Anyway, now that I have located Kevin, I want a place close by so I can see him as often as possible.'

318

'Have you any line of work in mind or don't you care what you do?' the matron continued.

'I will do anything that pays me enough money to live on,' Molly said simply.

'So you would try hotel work?'

Molly remembered Cathy telling her how her sisters thought hotel work was great because you got a uniform, and your board and lodging, and were paid too.

'That would be perfect,' she said. 'Do you know any hotel locally wanting people?'

The matron smiled. 'Not locally, no,' she said. 'But I have a cousin who works in Four Oaks in a large hotel called Moor Hall. Do you know Four Oaks at all?'

'I sort of know where it is,' Molly said. 'My parents used to take me to Sutton Park quite a few times. I remember the Four Oaks gate.'

'That's right.'

'Isn't it a distance from here?'

'Not on the train,' the matron said. 'There is a direct line.'

And quite far enough away from Collingsworth and his cronies, Molly thought. There I would feel safe.

'The point is,' the matron went on, 'they have had a few girls leave and they are recruiting now to train them in time for Easter when the hotel will start to fill up.'

'Should I write to them, d'you think?'

'I should take yourself up today,' the matron said. 'You have time to fill anyway before Kevin gets in, and the day is too cold for you to walk about much. The hotel will be easy to find. You just get off at Four Oaks Station and anyone will tell you where it is.'

Molly saw the sense of that and took her leave, promising to return and asking them not to tell Kevin where she had been, she wanted to surprise him later.

She hadn't left the Cottage Homes long when the matron asked permission to use the phone.

319

'Yes,' said the superintendent in surprise, for she had never made such a request before. 'Who do you want to phone?'

'My cousin in that posh hotel,' the matron said. 'She has a lot of clout with the manager. He listens to her, and right now I think that young girl could do with a bit of a helping hand.'

Posh was not the word Molly would have used to describe Moor Hall Hotel when she walked up the gravel drive and saw the stupendous house before her, set in its own grounds. The magnificence of it all rendered her speechless.

She knew enough of such places to realise that she did not go up the marble steps and in the front entrance, but when she knocked at the door at the back and explained who she was and why she had come, she was very well received. The manager had been told about the girl, whom he agreed to see almost immediately, and Molly told him the truth as far as it went – that after her parents died she went to her maternal grandmother in Ireland and Kevin stayed with his paternal grandfather in Birmingham. After her grandfather's death, Kevin had had to go into a home and Molly had moved to be closer to him so that she could see him as often as she could.

The manager liked Irish girls. He had employed many and most had been well used to hard work. Though Molly was small, he could bet she was as strong as the next.

'I need waitresses, in the main,' he said. 'But there might be other duties when the hotel is full, chambermaiding, for example. Have you any objections to that?'

'None at all,' Molly said. 'I will do whatever is needed.'

'And when could you start?'

'Immediately,' Molly said. 'In fact, the sooner the better.'

Afterwards, she had the urge to turn cartwheels on the lawn. Nothing – not the bleak, cold day, or the thick dark clouds – had the power to dampen her spirits, for she felt that this was a new chapter of her life opening up, a new job, new place to live and a chance to get to know her brother all over again.

Kevin at first hadn't quite believed that his sister had let him down. He had had to steal the paper, the envelope and the stamp from the office to write that last note, for when he asked for these things he was told Molly wanted no further communication with him. He didn't believe it and he wrote to her in desperation, but she didn't come, didn't even reply, and he eventually came to the realisation that they were right after all, that she really didn't want anything to do with him any more. He was on his own, he felt lonely and afraid, and he was terribly frightened of the future. For a time, his nightmares had returned and he became so withdrawn he had to go to see a psychiatrist.

He had told him all his fears and doubts, and the psychiatrist talked him through them. In the end he had told him that, harsh as it appeared, the reality was that he had to learn to stand on his own two feet and look after himself because that is what he would have to do when he left the home. Kevin knew that really, and said it was probably as well because everyone he loved had eventually been taken from him, but inside he ached for the sister he remembered so clearly.

That day, as he returned from school, he was asked to go down to the Lodge.

'What you been and gone and done, Maguire?' another boy asked, giving Kevin a punch on the shoulder, for the Lodge was where reprimands and punishments were meted out.

'Gerroff me,' Kevin said, giving the other boy a push. 'I ain't done nothing.'

'That's what they all say,' another commented sagely. 'You'll get six of the best, I reckon.'

321

'Oh, shurrup!' Kevin snapped, but as he walked to the Lodge, he examined everything he had done over the past few days and couldn't think of anything bad enough to be caned for. He knew, though, adults were a funny breed and could sometimes get mad over very little, and so he was full of trepidation as he knocked on the door.

The superintendent opened it. 'Come in, Kevin,' he said almost jovially. 'Don't look so scared. No one is going to eat you. There is someone here to see you.'

Kevin suppressed a sigh. He knew that it would be another doctor or psychiatrist because those people were all he ever saw, but when he went into the office, and the woman turned to greet him, he felt as if his heart had stopped beating for a moment or two.

'Molly?' he said uncertainly, not sure she wouldn't just vanish if he spoke her name. 'You came?'

Molly saw that the little boy she had left behind was gone and the boy before her stood straight and tall, looking more and more like his father as Molly remembered him. But he was still a child and in need, and Molly smiled as she said, 'Of course I came. I promised you I would.'

Kevin remembered that smile so well, and he was across the room in two bounds. He threw his arms around his sister and when he felt the tears running from his eyes, he didn't bother wiping them away because he felt as if the loneliness was dripping from him.

It was even better when Molly, breaking off the embrace, said, 'Go and get your coat, Kevin. I am taking you out for tea.'

Kevin's eyes were alive with excitement. 'Out to tea. Oh boy!'

'Well, you and I have a lot of catching up to do, don't you think?'

'Not half,' Kevin said. 'I won't be two ticks.'

'Where you going, Maguire?' asked a boy, seeing him lift his coat from the peg in the cloakroom.

'Mind your own business,' Kevin said. 'And for your information I weren't caned neither. Me sister has come to see me.'

'You ain't got a sister.'

'I have, and she's taking me out to tea, so there,' Kevin said, and with that parting shot he was away and running like a dervish down the drive towards the Lodge.

'Why did you take so long to come and see me?' Kevin asked later, between mouthfuls of fish and chips.

'Well, I had things to see to first,' Molly said evasively. 'Anyway, you didn't put an address on the letter.'

'I had to write it quick before they caught me,' Kevin said. 'Anyroad, I thought you would know the address, that the social workers who brought me here would have told you.'

'They may well have told our grandmother,' Molly said, 'but I never got to hear of it.'

'Why not?'

Molly shrugged. 'I really don't know, Kevin,' she said. 'Between you and me, I think the woman is crackers. She seemed to delight in making my life a misery. She never even told me granddad had died.'

'Dain't she?' Kevin said, totally shocked that one person should keep such a thing from another. 'That's horrible, that is – but she was horrible, weren't she? When they said she dain't want anything to do with me, I was glad. They said you dain't either and I didn't believe that. Well,' he added more honestly, 'I didn't at first. It was just when you didn't come and that, but it's all right now 'cos I can come home with you, can't I?'

'I haven't got a home, Kevin.'

'What about our granddad's house?'

'That's long gone to other tenants,' Molly said. 'But even if I had somewhere to live, I would still have to work at a job that paid enough to support us both.'

'So I've got to stay at the home then?' Kevin said morosely.

'Yes, I am afraid so for now,' Molly said. 'I will be working at Moor Hall Hotel in Four Oaks and I will be able to come and see you in my time off and we can go out places.' She saw the disappointment in Kevin's eyes and said, 'I know it probably isn't what you hoped for. But it is really the best I can do for now. Is it really horrible?'

'It's not so bad now,' Kevin admitted. 'I hated that Receiving Place that Mrs Hewitt took me to first. I was there for three days totally on my own before I met the other kids, and we all wore the same type of scratchy clothes and I was real lonely. I hated it.'

'How long were you there for?'

'Nearly thee weeks,' Kevin said, 'and then a group of us was taken here. A man took us and said we had to stay in the Lodge for a bit before being moved into a cottage.'

'Why?'

'Search me,' Kevin said. 'They tell you nowt. You see the doctor and everything to make sure that you ain't picked up anything infectious in the other place, Mother Jenkins said. She's my housemother and that's what we have to call her. Anyway, it was there, in the Lodge, that I wrote that note and stole the envelope and stamp and I posted it on my way to school. I go to Osbourne Road now.'

'Not the Abbey?'

Kevin shook his head. 'I never went back there once I was out of hospital. Granddad said I didn't have to if I didn't want. I don't believe in God and all that, not since Mom and Dad died, and Granddad said he dain't blame me one bit. Father Monahon came, of course. We sort of expected him, like,' Kevin said, and a ghost of a smile played around his mouth at the memory. 'They had one hell of a bust-up, him and Granddad, and in the end Granddad sent him running up the road as if his bum was on fire and he never come back. I don't half miss our granddad, Moll.'

'I know,' Molly said. 'I'm still coming to terms with his death, myself. But at least we have got each other.'

'Yeah,' Kevin said. 'And you take bloody good care of yourself. I'm fed up losing people.'

Molly didn't chide him. She knew by his face how much he still suffered. She just asked, 'Where is Granddad buried?'

'Witton Cemetery.'

'We'll go up next time, if you want,' Molly said. 'I'd like to go. I'll get some flowers and that, and at least make his grave look nice.'

Kevin nodded, but Molly knew by the glitter of tears in his eyes and the forlorn look on his face that he was probably remembering the funeral. It must have been dreadful for him all on his own.

In an effort to distract him she said, 'How many children live in the cottages?'

'Sixteen, mainly,' Kevin said. 'There is in ours, anyroad. There are only boys. The girls have their own houses.'

'So if you had to stay there a bit longer, you'd cope with that?'

'I'd have to, wouldn't I?' Kevin said. 'One thing I have learned is, it ain't any use wishing things were different to the way they are.'

'That is a good lesson to learn,' Molly said.

'S'pose it is,' Kevin said. 'D'you think I could have a piece of cake now?'

'Two if you can manage them,' Molly smiled. 'You have certainly got your appetite back.'

'Oh, I eat all before me now,' Kevin said. 'Granddad used to say I have either got worms or hollow legs, one or the other.'

Molly could just hear her granddad saying that, but she didn't want to go down the road of remembering and feeling sad, so she said, 'Come on, let's see what cakes they have in today.'

TWENTY-TWO

It was as Molly was on her way back to Aston that she decided she wouldn't tell any of them about her job, which she was starting in the afternoon of the following day. They would be glad for her and probably relieved, she knew, because it would be better for them all if Molly went her own way now. But what they didn't know about the name or location of her employment they couldn't let slip, even inadvertently, and Molly would feel safer that way.

Betty was very near her time now and it would have been nice maybe to have waited a few days till the birth was over. However, when Molly told the hotel manager she could start immediately, he had taken her at her word and she couldn't pass up the opportunity of the job and a place to live that was also near to Kevin.

'You managed to pawn the cufflinks then?' Will said as they sat around the fire that evening. 'Did you have any trouble?'

'No, not really,' Molly said. 'He asked if I came by them honestly. You know, I think there must be some flaw in my character to be able to lie so convincingly.' She shrugged. 'Anyway, in the end, he gave me six pounds for them.'

'They are worth at least three times that amount,' Will said.

'Six pounds seemed a great deal of money to me,' Molly said. 'I was well satisfied.'

'Well, at least it will enable you to get far away from here,' Will said.

Molly shook her head. 'That isn't an option any more, Will.' She told them all what had happened to her grandfather and her old neighbour, and that she had located her brother Kevin and he was in an orphanage.

'Oh God!' said the tender-hearted Betty. 'Did that upset you?'

'A bit,' Molly admitted. 'It's not a place I would have chosen for him, but better he is cared for in an orphanage than thrown out on to the streets.'

'Yes, I suppose.'

'Anyway, he is all right,' Molly said. 'I mean, he isn't in some sort of prison. He's goes to a normal school and I took him out to tea, but now that I know where Kevin is, I must be somewhere near so that I can get to see him as often as possible.'

'Molly!'

'Will, he is ten years old and I am all he has in the world,' Molly said. 'You know what he said to me? That I had to take great care of myself because he was fed up losing people.'

'Ah God, that's sad,' Ruby said. 'You have to admit that, Will. You must see the girl has a point?'

Of course Will could see that. But just that day he had found out that Ray Morris had disappeared. 'Bet you any money he makes for Sutton Coldfield,' said the man who had told him, and then, not noting the bleached look on Will's face, went on, 'His old lady lives that way and thinks the sun shines out of his arse.'

Sutton Coldfield, the very place he had sent Molly to. Will had felt sick with fear for her and for all of them. He knew he had to get Molly alone and impress on her the danger she was in by even trying to see her brother. He would say nothing in front of Betty, especially with her so near her time and all, but he knew that Collingsworth was sending his heavies to winkle out Ray and put an end to him. If Molly hung about in Sutton Coldfield, or Erdington, they could easily come upon her first. He had to make her see that by insisting on the need to visit her brother, she was putting all their lives in danger. He knew she wasn't stupid, and he was sure she would see this herself when the facts were laid before her

However, before Will had any opportunity to speak to Molly, he came down the next morning to find a note on the table with two pound notes on top of it secured with the salt pot.

Dear Will, Betty and Ruby,
   Thank you so much for all you have done for me, but the time has come for me to move on. I used the hours I was waiting for Kevin to return from school, securing employment for myself and a place to live. It's better that you don't know where, but you don't need to worry about me any more. The money is only a small percentage of what I owe you, and not only in financial terms either, and, Betty, I have had to borrow some clothes. These will be returned to you at the first opportunity and I hope the birth of the baby goes well. I am sure it will and I'm sorry I will miss it.
   Love to you all,
   Molly

'Bugger!' Will cried, throwing the note down in exasperation. 'Damn and blast the stupid girl.'

All their lives could now be in jeopardy, Will knew, for if Collingsworth's heavies found Molly they would ensure that before she died she would say who had helped her escape. They were masters of the art of torture. They had boasted to him about things they had done to people that had make him feel sick. He knew if they found Molly, eventually she would welcome death as a blessed relief, and so

328

would he when they had finished with him. And then they would come for Betty and the child. Even Ruby would not be safe. Sweet Jesus! He tasted fear for his loved ones like a sour and acrid taste in his mouth, but knew he could do nothing about it but wait.

Unaware of this, Molly had taken the first train out to Sutton Coldfield where she had waited for the shops to open. Knowing it would look strange to arrive without luggage and, anyway, she had to have clothes to wear, she first bought a large bag to put the things in. There wasn't much in the shops but at least no rationing on clothes as yet, and she bought underwear, nightwear and toiletries, a dress and cardigan, a couple of skirts and the very practical slacks that women were beginning to wear, a couple of jumpers and a pair of shoes. With all these packed in the bag, a smile on her face and a spring in her step, she made her way to the station to catch the train to Four Oaks.

Molly had never done hotel work before, but she was a quick learner and a neat worker. Even the laying up of the tables seemed common sense when you understood the order the food was served in and she picked that up easily too. After a few days, she began at last almost to enjoy herself. In the semi-rural location of the hotel, Ray Morris and Collingsworth and their nefarious dealings seemed to belong to another life.

Now that she had a proper address, she could write to her Uncle Tom, and Cathy, Nellie and Jack, as she had promised. She knew they would be worried about her. She had thought about that as soon as she had regained her memory, had even mentioned it to Will, but he had not been keen. She wouldn't put Ruby's address on the letter, but he was concerned that, after a silence of some weeks, someone from Ireland might come to try to seek her out and would know the area she was in by the postmark.

329

It was too risky for anyone to be going around asking for the whereabouts of Molly Maguire, she quite saw that. She knew the safety of them all hinged on her having disappeared totally and so she hadn't mentioned it again.

That no longer applied, though, and now she could write to them all and set their mind at rest, but even as she drew the writing pad she had bought towards her, she hesitated. It was three months since she had left her home in Buncrana and she had no idea what excuse she could give them for her silence during that time. How could she explain to them in that sleepy little town about the shadowy time when she had nearly, very nearly, slid into the half-world, of drugs and prostitution, or hiding out in someone's house because she had nearly killed a man?

How could she hope to explain that to anyone and expect them to understand how it was? Wouldn't they be disgusted with her, think that in some way she had asked for, almost invited the men's attention? She couldn't bear that they should think that way about her. Better do and say nothing, she decided, for then at least their memories of her were left unsullied.

To the people left behind in Ireland it was as if she really had disappeared off the face of the earth.

'It's like history is repeating itself,' Tom said to Nellie one Saturday morning as both Christmas and the New Year passed with no word from Molly. 'She has disappeared just as Aggie did.'

'Well, I didn't know about Aggie,' Nellie said. 'I was just a child myself when she vanished, but I know Molly well enough and did think that she would send a card at Christmas. I told Cathy so, for she was worried sick about her, and we had our cards and letters written to send as soon as we had her address. Tell you the truth, I expected a wee note before, to say she had got there safely, but when nothing came I told myself that maybe she was waiting to

330

write until she had news and a permanent place to stay. But when Christmas passed, then New Year . . .' She looked at Tom with tension-filled eyes and said, 'Dear God, it's bloody scary. D'you think one of us should go over and see if we can find out what has happened to her?'

'How?' Tom said morosely. 'Don't you think those same thoughts are not eating me up inside, but how is that to be achieved? You have the post office that you cannot leave so easily, and I can't leave Mammy with the farm to see to on her own. God knows, her temper grows no easier, but I just can't do that to her.'

'I know you can't,' Nellie said with a sigh. 'You are that kind of man, but few would put up with what you do, and I really don't know what is the matter with Biddy, for she doesn't seem a bit concerned about the girl we are both worried to death about.'

'She was concerned enough the morning she found she had run away,' Tom said. 'Though maybe "concerned" is not quite the right word. Of course, I got it in the neck because she knew I had to have had a hand in it. I didn't bother denying it either, and I am surprised that the roars and bellows of her were not heard in the town. Jesus, she is a bloody hard woman to live with. Never a good word to say about Molly, and she was a grand girl altogether. We used to have many a chat, you know?'

'I know,' Nellie said. 'She thought a lot about you.'

'And now I feel so bloody helpless.'

'I feel the same,' Nellie admitted. 'After all, the country is at war, with raids going on all the time.'

'Don't, Nellie,' Tom said, because as the time went on, with no word from Molly, he was tortured by the image of her being blown to pieces by a bomb, for if she wasn't, if she was all right, wouldn't she have written to one of them by now?

He shook his head to try to get rid of the terrifying image, and Nellie wasn't surprised to see tears in his eyes. Eventually, he recovered himself enough to say, 'I know Mammy regrets ever bringing Molly to Ireland and so do I.'

'What are you saying, Tom?'

'When the child was in England I didn't know her,' Tom said. 'But here I got to know her and to love her, and I don't mind telling you, Nellie, that when she left she took away a piece of my heart with her.'

Molly wasn't totally unaware of what they were going through in Ireland. Sometimes she would imagine what they thought had happened to her and she always felt sad afterwards, though it never occurred to her that they thought she might be dead. In fact, the air raids had slowed down considerably. There were no raids at all in February and only a few light skirmishes in the early part of March.

Daisy Burrows, one of the three girls who shared Molly's room, told her Sutton Coldfield had got off lightly compared to other parts of Birmingham, for example where her family lived.

'There was whole areas laid waste there,' she said. 'Sometimes a raid is so fierce the tar is set alight, or it melts and slides into the gutters. Either way it buggers up the trams, 'cos the rails gets all buckled and twisted.

'Our Dad usually walks to work now, and you go down streets where there used to be houses and shops and small factories, all reduced to piles of rubble now, and sometimes spilled so far into the pavement you have to clamber over it and avoid the burst sandbags seeping everywhere and dribbling hosepipes, and the smell is sometimes enough to knock you out.'

Molly had experienced a little of this in the air raid the evening that she had arrived in Birmingham. She didn't share this, however, because that was the time she met Ray and Charlie, and she really wanted to draw a line under that episode.

Anyway, she told herself, that had been one night. Trying

to live a normal life under such bombardment night after night must be a terrific strain. Daisy agreed.

'Our Mom has this shelter bag,' she said. 'She has all the identity cards in it, ration books, insurance policies and lots of photographs as well because she said when you leave your house you are never sure if it will still be standing when the raid is over. That's terrible, ain't it? I mean, our house might not be much, but at least it's ours.'

'Maybe the raids are all over for Birmingham now.'

'Wouldn't put money on it if I were you,' Matty Smart, another of the girls, said. 'I think it is all part of Hitler's plan: get us all relaxed like and then wallop.'

'Whether they do or not it will not affect us at all,' Lily Pollard said. 'You can see that for yourself in the number of semi-permanent residents here, hiding out in as safe a place as they can get. All well-to-do, of course, 'cos a person has to be flipping rich to afford the prices at Moor Hall in the first place.'

'It's the way they talk to you I can't stand,' Matty put in. 'They are probably used to personal servants to attend to their every need, but it really gets my back up when they click their fingers and call, "You, girl," the way they do.'

'Gives us something to do, looking after them, though, doesn't it?' Molly reminded them. 'And what are we doing really? I mean, the country might as well not be at war as far as we are concerned.'

That changed a little the next day as, under a directive from the government and in a fit of patriotic zeal, the hotel manager said the lawns had to be sacrificed to the 'Dig For Victory' campaign, and the staff were asked to volunteer their services.

Molly was a bit sad at first, for she loved the view from the attic windows: the expanse of lush green grass with the flowerbeds at the sides and the trees at the edge.

However, then she remembered reading about the ships being sunk with tons of foodstuffs on board, even in the

333

early days of the war, and how Derry had been commandeered by the navy, and the sole purpose of the naval craft
and RAF planes was to protect the merchant ships. She
knew then that providing food for the country was far more
important than a view and she lost no time in offering her
services.

She knew she would feel better doing something useful,
and after her years in Ireland she had developed a love of
the land.

'There is nothing like the sight of a field of crops ripening
that went into the ground as little bulbs or seeds,' she told
the others, 'and the springtime is the right time for planting.'

'I'll take your word for it,' Daisy said. 'Don't have to
experience things first-hand for me to appreciate them.'

'Anyroad, what about that brother you was telling us
about?' Matty put in. 'Don't you want to see him in your
free time?'

'Course I do,' Molly said. 'But he is at school all day.
Anyway, the Homes have got times for visiting. They are a
bit flexible with me, knowing the sort of job I do and also
knowing that I am the only family Kevin has, I suppose,
but even so, there are times I am off and can't see him. I
mean, what about when we are on a split shift?'

'That's when I retire to my bed for a well-earned rest,'
Daisy said.

'Aye,' Lily said with a laugh. 'That, my dear girl, is because
lazy is your middle name. Resting is for old bones. You should
come for a mooch up Four Oaks with me and Matty – and
you, Molly.'

'I've no money,' Molly said. 'What I don't spend taking
Kevin out I save because really eventually I want a place of
my own where I can look after him properly and I'll need
every penny when that time comes.'

'Why do that?' Daisy said. 'Ain't he been looked after
all right where he is?'

'Yeah, and it is an awful responsibility,' Lily said.

'It's what my parents would expect me to do,' Molly said quietly.

No one said anything after that because they all felt incredibly sorry for Molly when they heard her tale, which was the same as she had told the manager.

And he, also feeling sorry for her, arranged her time off as she wanted, as far as possible, especially as she was willing to work so many evenings, particularly at weekends, so that she could have time off in the day. From the first Molly had been grateful to him and over that first month had visited Kevin on a weekly basis, either on a Saturday or a Sunday.

Things had not been going so well for Ray Morris since he had first caught sight of Molly in Sutton Coldfield. His mother, who used to welcome him with open arms, was different this time, rabbiting on that she didn't have any money to give him.

'You've cleaned me out with what I have given you in the past,' she said. 'I haven't got a bottomless pit. And another thing, how the hell am I to feed you for weeks on end with rationing as tight as it is? You'll have to get yourself up to Sutton Town Hall and register for a ration book.'

There was no way Ray was doing that. They would ask too many awkward questions, like how come he wasn't in uniform. His mother had gone on about that too.

'You want me to put my life on the line then?' he had asked testily. 'Thought you loved me.'

'I do, you know I do,' his mother had said. 'But it's the neighbours, you see. They will wonder. One even asked me straight out the other day.'

'And what did you say?'

'I said that you had flat feet. Couldn't think of anything else, not straight out, anyway.'

'Well, flat feet will do,' Ray said. 'So that's all right then.'

'No, Ray, it isn't,' his mother argued. 'For a start I don't think she believed me, and there are others who say nothing, but think plenty. I see it in their eyes. What if they report you? I have always been respectable and I can't have police, or whoever it is deals with stuff like that, at my door, asking questions and poking about. And at the end of it, you will get in one heap of trouble.'

Ray didn't doubt that for one minute.

'And,' his mother added, 'there is still the business of the ration cards.'

'Look, I'll sort it. I said so, didn't I?'

'Yeah, when you arrived over a month ago. It don't look to me like you are doing much about it.'

Ray knew he had to find somewhere else to live because his mother was right. One of the nosy old busybodies around the doors had only to whisper their concerns to those in authority and they would be round like a shot. But where could he go, and without a ration book?

Point was, he had a ration book and identity card that Collingsworth had got for him. He didn't ask where he had got them from – the man wasn't that keen on questions of any kind – and he had had to leave them in the flat the day he had made his escape.

He went to seek out the man he used to work for when he had been living in Sutton. The huge bear of a man, who went by the nickname of Tiny, ran an illicit and dishonest casino above a pub in Erdington. That was where Ray had met Collingsworth, who had offered him more lucrative work. Ray had jumped at the chance and left Tiny in the lurch at the time, and Tiny reminded him of it when he asked him if he had any jobs going.

'That was years ago,' Ray protested.

'Yeah? Well, maybe I am like an elephant and never forget.'

'Come on, Tiny,' Ray coaxed. 'We go back a long way.' And then, as Tiny made no comment, he grew desperate. 'Come on, I know a fair bit about what goes on here that I could spill into the right ears.'

336

Tiny lifted Ray by his lapels and almost spat into his face, 'Don't you try that on with me, mate. You ain't in any position. And if I was in your shoes now, even I would be shitting myself.' He dropped Ray with a look of contempt

Ray straightened the collar of his coat before saying as nonchalantly as he could, 'What you on about now?'

Tiny's mouth turned up in a malicious sneer. 'The word is out Collingsworth's heavies are after you and heading this way, reckoning that, as you have no dosh, you would be running home to your dear ma's.'

Ray paled and his mouth went dry. He hadn't been absolutely sure that Collingsworth's bullyboys would follow him here, but then he knew too much, far too much, and he had made a balls-up of killing the girl. That was enough to sign his death warrant, he knew.

Tiny, watching Ray's face, grinned before saying, 'So I can't touch you with a bargepole, mate. More than my life's worth.'

'They're out to do for me this time, Tiny,' Ray said. 'Nothing less will satisfy Collingsworth.'

Tiny shrugged. 'So what do you want me to do?'

'I thought we were mates.'

'So did I, until you ran out on me.'

'So just because I left—'

'No, it isn't just 'cos of that, you stupid bugger,' Tiny bawled. 'I will have nothing to do with you because I value my own skin too much. Them blokes don't mess about. I have seen what was left of a man Collingsworth thought needed teaching a lesson and the best advice I can give you is to leave town and stay left.'

'I need money, Tiny.'

'Not from me you don't. Try your old woman.'

'She won't give me any more. Says she hasn't got it.'

''Tain't your lucky day, is it?' Tiny said. Then, suddenly tired of the man, he added, 'Look, sling your hook, Morris. Just fuck off! It would never do for anyone to say you were seen round here.'

Ray had no option but to go. But he had no idea where. He bitterly regretted letting Molly get away from him when he saw her outside the pawnbroker's. He couldn't have done anything then, but he could have tailed her and found out where she was living. It was just that then he had expected his mother to cough up, as she always had in the past, and he could have been well away from this place by now.

So lost in thought was he that he almost walked into Molly leaving the Palace Cinema with a young boy, obviously the brother. So she had got her bloody memory back, Ray thought, stepping into an entry while they passed. But she couldn't be allowed to live if she could remember stuff.

Molly took the boy into the milk bar and Ray took up residence in the pub across the road. He used the money he had wheedled out of his mother that dinner-time to buy a pint, and he positioned himself in a place where he could keep an eye on the café door.

He was draining his third pint and full darkness had fallen before he saw them appear, and he slipped out after them. He guessed they were making their way to the Cottage Homes at Fentham Road, but it was where Molly went then that was important.

'Here we are then,' Ray heard Molly say as she stood before the gates and pulled on the bell. 'Same time next week.' She gave the boy a hug. 'We better make the most of this as well, because once Easter gets nearer I might not get the weekends off so easily.'

'And you are taking me to see *Pinocchio* next week?'

'I said so, didn't I? It's part of your birthday treat.'

The gates opened and a man's voice said, 'Hello, Kevin. Had a good time?'

'Yes, thanks,' the boy said. 'We're going to see *Pinocchio* next week.' Then he turned and said to Molly, 'Don't be late, Moll, will you?'

There was a laugh in Molly's voice as she answered, 'I'm

338

never late and you make sure you're ready. I will be here on the dot of half-past two.'

'We'll see he is washed and brushed up ready for you,' the man said. 'Good night, miss.'

'Good night. Good night, Kevin.'

The gates clanged shut and Molly began to hurry down Hunton Hill. As she turned into Gravelly Hill, Ray understood the reason for her haste for he could see the train was chugging into Gravelly Hill Station. He caught it by the skin of his teeth, causing the stationmaster to shake his head at him for his foolishness, but a lot he cared. Far better upset the stationmaster than alert Molly to the fact that he was tailing her.

When Ray saw her leave at Four Oaks Station he got off too, and he followed her to the hotel where he saw her go in the side door. He smiled to himself.

'Gotcha!'

He returned to the station and checked his watch. Half-past eight, and the pawnbroker's didn't shut until nine. He checked the notes in his wallet and the coins in his pocket. He regretted buying so much beer for he had barely enough to redeem the cufflinks, but for some reason he knew they were important. When he had them in his hand, he smiled to himself, for he recognised them as Collingsworth's. He put them in his pocket and made for the tram to take him to town.

Long before he reached Collingsworth's house he was spotted and marched before the man with his arms held tight behind him.

'There is no need for this heavy stuff,' Ray said. 'I was coming to see you anyway.'

Collingsworth signed for the men to release Ray's arms. 'Really?' he said with heavy sarcasm. 'When a couple of my men called round to wish you the time of day a few weeks ago, it was to find the bird had flown, as it were.'

'Time of day, my arse!' Ray said. 'They were there to beat me to pulp. Now there is no need to do that.'

'And why is that?'

'Because I have found Molly,' Ray said, adding sneeringly, 'Something none of your fine henchmen was able to do. And here is another thing.' He drew the cufflinks from his pocket and laid them on the desk in front of Collingsworth.

'I was looking for these the other night,' Collingsworth said angrily.

'You wouldn't have found them,' Ray told him. 'Molly stole them from you and then pawned them to get some cash.'

'And where is she now?' Collingsworth growled. 'God, I could tear that girl limb from limb myself.'

'This is the beauty of it,' Ray said. 'She is at Moor Hall Hotel in Four Oaks – and the place is in the middle of bloody nowhere. She has made contact with her brother and so the bitch has got her memory back and she could do for the lot of us.'

'She is not going to get the chance.'

'No, by Christ, she isn't,' Ray said vehemently.

'You mess up this time, Morris, and you'd better start saying your own prayers.'

'I won't mess up,' Ray said. 'But listen, next Saturday she is taking her brother to the pictures in Erdington. Then, if it follows the same pattern as today, she takes him for a bite to eat, then on to the orphanage place and then catches the train at Gravelly Hill Station. The train gets in at ten past eight and she walks to the hotel alone. There is not a soul about. We could have a van parked in the fields. In the blackout behind the hedge it will never be seen. I'll drive that, if you like, and all your fellows have to do is snatch Molly, bring her back here and I will deal with her.'

'Before she dies,' Collingsworth said, 'I want to know how she got out of that flat. Somebody had to help her and I want to know who that person was.'

'Don't worry,' Ray said, 'I will enjoy extracting that information from her.'

'That's what I like to hear.' Collingsworth extended his hand and as Ray shook it he said, 'Welcome back.'

TWENTY-THREE

Molly would only leave the security of the hotel once a week, and then just for Kevin's sake, because she felt completely safe there, the way she thought she would never feel again.

It wasn't entirely for lack of money that she refused the other girls' offers to go to see the shops at Four Oaks or Sutton Coldfield; it had been nervousness, certainly in the beginning. Of course, she might be being overcautious. They had probably given up the search for her by now, but she couldn't risk it – not just for her own sake, but for Will and his family, who had to be protected at all costs.

She felt a little guilty about Will and wished, despite wanting to draw a line under the whole episode, she had sent him a little note assuring him that she was fine. She could have included a message with the bundle of clothes she returned to Betty as she had promised to do. But she had shied away from that in the end, thinking that, as she didn't know how things were, it was probably safer for Will and her to have no contact whatsoever.

She had even taken care to post the clothes from an Erdington post office, because Four Oaks was only a small place and if he knew she was there and wanted to, he could undoubtedly have traced her, and so could anyone else who caught sight of the franked stamp.

She gave a sigh that night as she turned down the lane to the hotel. She had been on the go all day because she had served at breakfast as well as chambermaiding before going to meet her brother. Her feet throbbed but then she told herself she always slept better with fresh air in her lungs.

Once she would have said that she would miss nothing from her time in Ireland, but she found that she did miss the stillness that had unnerved her so much in the beginning, and that night was no different.

The blackout didn't affect Molly as much as many of the others because there had been no streetlights on the farm either. She had been unnerved by this at first, but eventually had learned to rely on the moon and the stars. Sometimes there was no moon, of course, and the stars might be obscured by clouds or by the smoke and smog in the air, but that night the moon was almost full and hung like a shimmering ball, casting its silver light down, and the stars twinkled in their midnight-blue backdrop.

'Never be afraid of the dark, Molly,' her uncle had said. 'Sometimes then you see things hidden in the day, for many wild animals are shy and use the cover of nightfall to go about their business. They won't harm you, so don't be feared.'

Dear, dear Uncle Tom, Molly thought as she walked on. He had no notion of human animals who used the cover of darkness to be about their business, and who definitely did mean harm. But not here, she thought, not in the grounds of this hotel miles from anywhere. She gave a sigh of contentment and drank in the night air as she walked up the lane, catching the smell of the dew-dampened earth the other side of the hedge that she had taken a great hand in cultivating. That brought back memories of Ireland too and working alongside Tom, and she felt a sudden pang of homesickness that took her by surprise.

But, she told herself sharply, she would have to get over it, for it was better by far that they remember her as she was. All that mattered to her at that moment was Kevin,

343

and she smiled as she remembered how he had enjoyed *Pinocchio* earlier. She hadn't been looking forward to it herself, seeing it as a film just for children, and was surprised by how much she had liked it. She wasn't the only adult either and they all seemed to be equally impressed.

She had been thinking about the future a lot recently, for she realised that she couldn't live the rest of her life fearful and constantly looking over her shoulder. She had resolved that when Kevin was finished with the home, or she managed to get him out sooner, they would take off and start a new life in another town entirely.

Barely had this thought left her when she felt herself grabbed from behind by two muscular arms. For a second she froze and then she screamed for all she was worth, her mind filled with terror, for she suddenly knew that this was no random attack: this was the sort of thing Will had been afraid of.

A man slapped his hand over her mouth, but it had been open for her scream, and she clamped her teeth down hard. He gave a cry and dropped his hand as she tasted his blood in her mouth and screamed again, louder than ever. Frantic at the noise she was making, the other man made a grab at her, but she twisted away from him and he was able to grab just the one arm. She gave a cry and pulled at her arm, trying to free herself, and when that didn't work she swung her free hand at him wildly and caught his cheek a ringing slap.

'You bleeding little wildcat,' the man growled out and gave her a sudden tug so that she almost fell against him. She raked her nails down his face, feeling the skin tear as he grabbed her so tight she could barely breathe, and she was whimpering in fear as he threatened, 'You'll pay for that, you bleeding little bastard.'

The other man's hand was still throbbing and dripping blood, and he snarled, 'Finish her off and be done with it, sodding little bitch.'

Molly gave a tug at his words and so the karate chop that should have broken her neck landed wide. He wasn't aware of this in the darkness, especially as the blow did cause her to lose consciousness, and as she folded at his feet, he gave a sigh of satisfaction.

'Job done,' he said. 'Whistle up the van and we'll heave the meddlesome bitch into it and be away. Collingsworth will reward us well for this night's work.'

A sudden bellow caused him to peer down the lane. By the light of a wavering torch they saw two figures approaching them at speed as the van began reversing down the lane.

Daisy having the evening off and a young soldier, Martin Farrader, whom she was dating, had been lying in the field on Martin's greatcoat for some time, kissing and canoodling. Martin had been trying to persuade Daisy to go the whole way with him and Daisy was resisting with every bit of willpower that she possessed. 'Go on Dais,' he'd pleaded. 'God knows when I will see you again. You know we pull out tomorrow. Give me summat to remember you by,' and he'd nuzzled her neck, sending her senses reeling. 'I thought you said you loved me.'

'I do,' Daisy had panted.

'Well, then?'

'Oh Christ,' Daisy's whole body was aching with desire, and when Martin had urged, 'Come on, Dais, if you love me, prove it,' she'd been going to give into him, wanted to give into him, when the first scream sliced through the air. 'What was that?'

Martin's mind was on other things and he said impatiently, 'Who cares? An animal or summat.'

At the second scream, the yearning passion had dropped away from Daisy. 'That ain't no animal,' she'd stated. 'Someone's in trouble. Get off me, Martin.'

'We can't stop now.'

'We bloody well can,' Daisy said, giving Martin a hefty shove and getting to her feet. 'Someone is in trouble, I tell you. Pull up your trousers, for God's sake,' she'd added, adjusting her own clothing. 'That sounded like some poor soul was being murdered.'

She wasn't sure the deed hadn't been done either as just seconds later Martin's army-issue torch showed up the shadowy figures up the lane and they saw the girl or woman slumped on the ground beside two beefy-looking men. With a shout, Martin took off towards them with Daisy not far behind, yelling like mad as she ran, for someone to, 'Help, for Christ's sake!'

Martin laid into one fellow, while Daisy launched herself on the back of the other. He was unprepared for this, and as she tugged at the man's hair with one hand, the other pulled at his nose and gouged at his eyes. The man leaped about roaring, trying to dislodge the mad woman on his back.

Suddenly, his elbow jabbed Daisy in the side with such force, she released her hold a little and the man gave a jerk of his shoulders. Daisy flew through the air to land on the ground with a thud. She lay there, stunned, feeling as every bone in her body had been loosened.

'Jesus, are you all right?' Martin cried.

His assailant took advantage of Martin's preoccupation to land him a powerful right hook, swiftly followed by a left, and Martin was knocked clean out. The van was nearly up to them, but suddenly there was a shout. In the light spilling from the kitchen, totally against regulations, the two heavies saw a body of people running up from the house. The man leading the way, and gaining on the others, held a meat cleaver in his hand.

'Jesus Christ!' breathed the ruffian who had floored Martin. 'Let's get out of here.'

The other went to pick Molly up. 'Leave her. We haven't time for that now. They will be on top of us in a minute.'

The other man saw that he was right. 'Have this to remember me by,' he said to Molly's inert form, and he drove his booted foot into the side of her body before leaping into the van.

The staff let the van go. They hadn't a hope in hell of catching it anyway, and they thought the people on the ground needed their attention more. Daisy was struggling groggily to her feet and Martin was sitting up, rubbing his chin, but the girl lay still, and when the chef turned her over, Daisy saw who it was for the first time.

'Ah, Jesus Christ,' she breathed. 'Poor sod. Is she dead?'

'Not quite,' said the head chef, who was examining her with the aid of Martin's torch. 'But her pulse is very weak.' He turned to Lily, standing at the edge of her group, her mouth wide open with shock and said sharply, 'Pull yourself together, girl. Find the manager and tell him what's happened and say we need an ambulance here, and as soon as possible.'

The chef told the manager of Daisy and Martin's involvement in the fracas that had left Molly so badly injured. Leaving the chef and housekeeper to wait for the ambulance, he insisted they go back to the hotel, for he could see that Daisy was still distraught and even Martin was shaken.

'You should be proud of yourselves,' he told them. 'What a mercy you were on hand.'

Daisy blushed as she recalled why they were on hand and what they had been at just minutes before that first scream. Still, whichever way you looked at it, it was lucky they were there.

'I would be happier if you were both examined by my own doctor,' the manager told them. 'He has been sent for and is on his way.'

Daisy said nothing, but she knew she would welcome being examined, for while her body throbbed and smarted, reaction to the whole incident had set in. She felt as if all her nerve endings were raw and exposed for all to see, and she couldn't seem to stop crying.

Martin protested, however. 'But I need to go back to the camp, sir,' he said. 'I have to be in by eleven and it is turned ten now.'

'I will phone through and explain,' the manager said. 'The police will want to see you as well as the doctor. Don't worry, you'll be all right. I will tell them you are somewhat of a hero.'

Matty knocked at the door to say an Inspector Norton had arrived and was waiting for the manager in his office, but later, facing the policeman across his desk the manager admitted that there was hardly anything he could tell him about the young waitress.

'And how did she get on with the customers, the staff? Is she a likeable girl?' the policeman asked.

'I believe so,' the manager said. 'I have certainly had no complaints about her. She hasn't been here that long really. She had come over from Ireland recently, apparently to be closer to her brother after the grandfather, who had been looking after him, died.'

'She has a brother then?' the policeman commented. 'He might be able to tell us something more.'

The manager nodded. 'He might,' he said, 'though he's only a child, ten or eleven – that sort of age, I believe, and living in Erdington Cottage Homes. I sort of had the feeling that the two were alone in the world.'

'Whereabouts in Ireland did she come from?'

'She didn't say,' the manager said. 'Maybe her room-mates know more. Daisy is waiting to see the doctor now. I'll have her and her young man sent for and she can tell you what she knows about Molly. They were first on the scene, and got involved, so you will need to talk to them anyway.'

However, Daisy couldn't help the policeman any further either. 'She never said where the place was in Ireland,' she said. 'In fact she never said much about it at all.'

'And had she had any enemies that you know of?'

348

'No, she wasn't the sort of girl to make enemies.'

'Boyfriend trouble?'

Daisy shook her head. 'She didn't have a boyfriend.'

'Are you sure?'

'Positive. For one thing, she would probably have said. Girls talk about things like that, but anyroad she never went anywhere. There was only one man in that girl's life and that was her brother. God, he will be lost if anything happens to her. Molly sees him every weekend. They only have each other, I think.'

Inspector Norton nodded. 'The manager said something similar,' he said.

'She did say once that it was her maternal grandmother she was sent to when her parents died,' Daisy said. 'And I think she must be alone in the world, apart from the brother, because I know she hasn't been here long, but she has never had a letter or anything.'

'We can check that with the brother,' the policeman said. 'As he is so young we are leaving that until the morning. In the meantime, the manager said you and your young man became involved. Can you both give me an account of that?'

'I'll be glad to do that,' Daisy said fiercely, 'or anything else that will help catch the murderous thugs who did this to Molly.'

Kevin was in line ready for the short march to the church wearing his Sunday clothes, dark grey suit, white shirt, grey tie and socks with garters to keep them up when the superintendent came to fetch him.

'There is a policeman to see you, Kevin,' Mr Sutcliffe said as they walked down together to the Lodge. Then, noticing Kevin's startled expression, he said reassuringly, 'There is nothing to worry about. You have done nothing wrong. He thinks you may be able to help him.'

Kevin's anxiety did not abate though, because he knew that policemen seldom brought good news, and they walked

349

in silence, the only sound being the tramp of their feet on the path. With each step, Kevin's trepidation grew.

The superintendent was thinking back to the news the inspector had given him when he arrived. He had been shocked and upset, but he knew Kevin would be devastated.

'Need we tell him that she was attacked?' he asked. 'Could we not say she has been taken ill?'

'I'm afraid not,' Norton said. 'The point is, Kevin might know something that he thinks is of no consequence, and which might give us some clue or other, some line of investigation to follow. It's a long shot, I suppose, but God knows we need all the help we can at the moment. Everyone I talk to speaks well of Molly Maguire, she was liked by colleagues and customers alike, by all accounts, and went nowhere except once a week to see Kevin.'

'She did that, all right,' Mr Sutcliffe said. 'Regular as clockwork and always on time. I don't know her well, but I thought her a fine young woman the times I have met her. She loves her young brother, that I do know, and her coming here has made a vast difference to him.'

Norton felt a wave of sympathy for the child wash over him and he said, 'Then I am sure he will like to help me catch the thugs who attacked his sister if he can. To be honest, Kevin is all I have got. Molly is in a coma.'

Mr Sutcliffe nodded. 'I will fetch him directly and I sincerely hope that he will be able to help you.'

When Kevin entered the sitting room, he saw a man sitting on the easy chair, who got up when he saw the boy.

'Hello, Kevin,' he said heartily.

Kevin eyed him suspiciously. 'Hello,' he said. 'Who are you?'

'I'm Inspector Norton. Why don't you sit down on the chair opposite me?'

Kevin continued to stand. He licked his lips before saying, 'You don't look like a policeman.'

'That's because I am in plain clothes.'

'Why?'

350

'Sit down, Kevin,' Mr Sutcliffe said and Kevin sat down obediently but gingerly on the edge of the seat.

'Why aren't you dressed like a policeman?' he persisted.

'That's just how it is, Kevin,' Norton said. 'I am in what they call the plain-clothes division, but I am a proper policeman.'

Kevin swallowed deeply. 'Last time a policeman came to see my granddad, it was to tell him my mother and father were dead. Why have you come?'

Inspector Norton was wondering how to phrase what he had to say when Kevin, feeling as though a lead weight had fastened to his heart, said, 'It's Molly, isn't it? It has to be really, because she is the only one left.'

Norton nodded. 'You're right. This is about Molly.'

'Is she dead?'

'No,' Norton said, 'she's not dead, but she is unconscious and has been taken to the Cottage Hospital in Sutton Coldfield.'

Kevin felt despair rising in him and had difficulty speaking, but he had to know. 'What happened?'

Norton didn't go into detail, but what he said was enough, and Kevin cried, 'Why would anyone do that to Molly? She's good and kind . . .' He couldn't go on. The lump in his throat was threatening to choke him and his voice was husky as he asked, 'Is she going to die?'

'No, I'm sure she isn't,' Norton said, though he wasn't at all sure. 'But we don't know anything about her, you see, or why she was attacked and hope you might help us.'

'How?'

'Someone went all out to badly hurt your sister last night,' Norton said. 'Someone who went to the trouble to have a van ready to get away in. It doesn't sound to me like a random attack.'

'What d'you mean?'

'I mean, it looks as if your sister was targeted, that she was the intended victim.'

351

'But why?'

'That is what we are trying to find out, Kevin,' the inspector said. 'Do you know, or did she tell you of anyone that maybe had a grudge against her?'

Kevin shook his head. 'No, never.'

'Did you ever meet anyone else on the days Molly took you out?'

'No.'

'Did she speak about other people?'

'Only them she worked with, sometimes.'

'And she got on with them?'

Kevin shrugged. 'She seemed to.'

'And what about her time in Ireland?' the inspector said. 'Mr Sutcliffe told me she went to Ireland with your maternal grandmother after your parents died, and you stayed here with your paternal grandfather?'

'That's right,' Kevin said, and a tremor passed all through him as he remembered that time, so awful anyway, and compounded by the arrival of his grandmother.

Norton saw the tremor, but did not connect it to what he had said about the grandmother, thinking only that Kevin was remembering the death of his parents, and so he went on, 'And whereabouts did she live in Ireland?'

Kevin thought about that for a minute or two. One whisper that he had a grandmother still alive, and where she lived, and she could be over here like a shot, that evil woman that didn't even tell Molly their granddad had died. He knew if it was a choice between living with her, or at the home then the home would win hands down. However, children were not given a choice. One hint of that woman's existence and his opinion wouldn't matter a jot.

'I think the woman is dead,' the superintendent murmured into the silence. 'Kevin's sister told me that the first time she came. I presumed that the old lady's illness and death, and all the formalities that entailed, were the reason she hadn't come over to see Kevin sooner.'

352

What Molly had told Mr Sutcliffe surprised Kevin, but he was glad she had said that. He confirmed, 'That's right. She died.'

'Had she a name, this grandmother of yours?'

Kevin was ready for that one. There was a boy who sat next to him at school and his name was Lenny Brannigan. Without batting an eyelid, Kevin said, 'Brannigan. Her name was Bridget Brannigan.'

'Are there any other relatives?'

'No,' Kevin said. 'We've always been short on relations.'

'And where did they live in Ireland?'

Kevin wasn't going to say the north, but he didn't know Ireland very well and so he shrugged. 'I dunno.'

Norton suddenly knew he was lying. 'Come now, Kevin,' he said with force joviality. 'You must have written to her.'

Kevin hated people talking to him in that false way and so he said, 'Yeah, course I did, but then I gave the letter to my granddad. He wrote the envelope.'

'Didn't you want to know where she was?'

'No, not particularly,' Kevin said. 'I didn't want Molly to go in the first place and she never wanted it either. I didn't really want to look on a map or owt and see just how far away she was. What good would that have done?'

Norton was well aware that Kevin knew far more than he was prepared to say, but there was no point pursuing it if the woman was dead and gone anyway. 'Was there anything there that worried Molly, do you know? Did she ever write and say she was afraid of something or someone?'

'Yeah, her grandmother that she was forced to live with,' Kevin might have said, but that wouldn't be helpful, so instead he told the policeman, 'If there was, she never told us about it, but then she wouldn't, would she? I mean, why would she tell us about summat when we couldn't do owt about?'

'And there is nothing – think now – nothing that you can tell me that might help us find the people who did this awful thing?'

'Nothing,' Kevin said, 'honest there ain't. Till Molly turned up in February I hadn't seen her for five years. I was just finding out about her. Can I go and see her?'

Norton shook his head. 'Afraid not, Kevin. I phoned the hospital before I came here and they said you have to be twelve.' Kevin wasn't even surprised. It was the same when his mom was sick. It wasn't even worth complaining about, but his voice was low and thick with tears as he said, 'Can I go now?'

Mr Sutcliffe looked across at the inspector. He knew that Kevin wanted to be away before the tears overwhelmed him, and the policeman guessed this too. 'Yes, that will be all, Kevin,' he said. 'For now, at least.'

'No need to go into the church now, Kevin,' Mr Sutcliffe said. 'The service will be halfway over.'

Kevin had no intention of making for the church. He was going to the house where the bedrooms would be empty and where he could weep out his loneliness and fear of the future laid out like a black hole in front of him.

TWENTY-FOUR

Kevin spent a restless night. He had tossed and turned before eventually dropping off around midnight, then having a nightmare in which his sister had died and he was prevented from seeing her or going to her funeral because they said he wasn't old enough. He woke up sobbing so loudly, his housemother, Mother Jenkins, came to comfort him and in the end took him downstairs, lest he disturb the others, not at all surprised he was upset. All the children had been told Kevin's sister was in hospital when they returned from church, though they had been given no details.

But Mother Jenkins told him she was in a coma, and that was the first time that Kevin had heard the word. As he sat in the kitchen, drinking the cocoa the housemother had made for him, he said, 'What's a coma?'

'Like a deep sleep, Kevin.'

To Kevin that didn't sound so bad. 'I sleep deep,' he said. 'Granddad was always on about it. Some mornings he had to shake me before I woke up proper, like. Have they tried that with Molly?'

'I shouldn't think so, Kevin,' Mother Jenkins said, feeling very sorry for the young boy. 'Though, of course, I don't know what treatment she is undergoing.'

'Nor do I,' Kevin commented bitterly, and the housemother had a measure of sympathy with him. Kevin and Molly were tremendously fond of one another – anyone

355

with half an eye could see that – and the over-twelve rule seemed incredibly harsh and inflexible. After all, the lad was turned eleven. However, she knew to say this would not help him and so she said instead, 'Never mind, Kevin. Let's hope she is fully recovered soon, eh?'

'Yeah,' Kevin said morosely. 'That's all I can do, hope.'

It was the next morning, on the way to school, that the resentment caused him to rebel. 'Tell them I was took bad on the road and went back home,' he told the boy beside him.

'You bunking off, Maguire?' the boy asked. 'You'll get the cane if they find out.'

'I'm going to see my sister.'

Everyone knew that Kevin couldn't see his sister because he wasn't old enough. He had told them that himself. The boy said, 'Thought you said they wouldn't let you?'

'I'm not going to ask them. I'm going to try and sneak in.'

'They'll murder you for this.'

Kevin shrugged. 'Don't care. I want to see her. Don't think it's asking a lot. I mean, 'tain't as if I'm a little kid or owt. Anyway, all you have to do is say I was took bad on the road. Afterwards, you can always say you really thought I was feeling ill. You won't get into trouble for it.'

'All right,' the boy said. 'And you needn't worry, Maguire, I ain't no sneak anyroad.'

Kevin knew he had to take the train to Sutton Coldfield. He had the dinner money he had been given that morning, and he also had the two pennies he had been given to put on the collection plate the day before, which his housefather had forgotten to reclaim from him.

He didn't feel bad about spending that money, though he knew that certainly his houseparents and the superintendent would not view this in the same light and that he would probably feel the sting of the cane afterwards for his effort, but he really didn't care. He wouldn't have been driven to such extremes if he had been allowed to see Molly in the first place.

He blessed the fact too that he was in school uniform and therefore not marked out as a boy from the Cottage Homes, especially when the stationmaster looked at him with a beady eye when he asked for a return to Sutton Coldfield.

'And where might you be going this Monday morning when you should be at school?' he asked.

Kevin had semi-expected this, though it annoyed him that adults would question children as to what they were doing and where they were going as if they thought, just because they were older, they had some sort of right. However, he knew too he hadn't to show his annoyance or be rude, which seemed to be one of the deadly sins, and he was amazed how easily the lies tripped off his tongue.

'I've got an appointment at the Cottage Hospital in Sutton,' he said. 'My mom's meeting me off the train.' He remembered one of the boys saying before they were bombed out and his mother killed, she used to clean offices and be back home in time to get the breakfast before school, and so he went on, 'She cleans offices in Sutton so has to leave the house real early.'

The stationmaster accepted that, knowing that many more women were working now than before the war and so he passed over the ticket without further ado and Kevin settled to wait for the train with a measure of excitement, mixed with apprehension, because travelling on a train, especially alone, was a novel experience for him.

However, he managed very well and alighted at the station at Sutton feeling quite proud of himself. A few minutes later he was looking down the hill of cobbled stone. He had asked directions of the stationmaster in Sutton Coldfield Station, and knew that once at the bottom of the hill he had to turn right and go straight on, way past the shops, and he would come to the hospital on his left-hand side.

It was quite a hike before Kevin came to the two-storeyed, red-brick building, with 'Sutton Coldfield Cottage Hospital' written on a plaque above the arched front door. However, Kevin knew that he would be given short shrift if he went up the steps and through that door in the usual way. Luckily the hospital stood on the corner of another road called Farthing Lane, and that led to the back of the building.

Once there, he didn't know what to do next and he told himself it was worse than useless to stand in the middle of the small yard, where he ran the risk of being seen and evicted in short order. The door was firmly shut, but maybe he could have a peep in the windows, he told himself. But when he tried this, edging himself along from window to window, he could see little, due to the flimsy curtaining on the other side. Eventually, having scrutinised them all and being no wiser, he leaned against the wall, chewing his thumb-nail and wondering what to do next. Although he stood outside the hospital that Molly was in, he felt as far away from her as ever.

When a van turned into the yard, Kevin leaped behind a convenient bush. The van pulled up before the back of the hospital with a squeal of brakes. A nurse came out of the door at the side the same time as the van driver, another woman, leaped out of the cab.

Laundry, Kevin said to himself, recognising the bundles they carried from the back of the van, for they had laundry delivered to the Cottage Homes too. He waited until the nurse and van driver had actually gone into the building before sidling out from behind the bush, sprinting across the yard and peering inside. A long corridor stretched before him with doors to his left, but to the right were other rooms, and from there he could hear the voices of the nurse and the van driver and so he went stealthily along the corridor.

He hadn't the least idea where Molly was and yet now

he was inside he hesitated to open the doors and look. These were sick people – they had to be or they wouldn't be in hospital. What if his sudden unannounced arrival in their room gave them heart failure? Would he be prepared to risk that?

In the end, though, he had no time to think or worry about other people. When he heard footsteps on the stairs just to the right of him, he opened the nearest door and slipped into the room, intending to hide there until whoever was coming down the stairs had gone.

He glanced around. He had thought the room empty, it was so quiet. He approached the bed cautiously, and there was Molly, looking for all the world as if she had lain down on the bed for a few minutes and dropped off.

There was nothing scary or frightening, and so he said loudly, 'Molly, wake up. It's me, Kevin.'

Kevin's high-pitched voice pierced the black tunnel Molly lay in, which neither the sombre tones of the police inspector nor the hushed voices of the nurses had disturbed.

Kevin missed the slight flickering of her eyelids, though, because at that moment the door opened and two nurses came in, astounded to see a boy in the room of a patient that had only been left unattended for a few minutes.

For a split second they stared at one another and then one cried, 'What are you doing here, you bad boy?'

Kevin shrugged. 'Nothing.' He felt deflated, completely flat. He had thought if he could see Molly and speak to her, then she would be all right again, but that hadn't happened and now he had to pay the price.

He wasn't surprised when one of the nurses sprang forward and, grasping him by the shoulders, shook him so hard he thought his head would fall off, saying as she did so, 'Nothing? I'll give you nothing, you bold strap.'

'Gerroff me,' Kevin cried, struggling with her to get her to release the hold she had on him. 'Leave me alone.'

'If you have hurt her in any way—'

'Course I haven't,' Kevin said, outraged. 'She's me sister. Why would I want to harm her?'

The other nurse said. 'Oh, I know who you are then. You're the one the policeman asked about, aren't you? They said you were too young to see your sister.'

'Yeah, well, I don't think I am, see,' Kevin declared. 'I think that's a stupid rule, that.'

'Do you?' said the first nurse. 'As if anyone cares about your opinion. And how did you get in anyway?'

'I sneaked in when the laundry van came.'

'Oh, did you indeed? Let's see what Matron has to say about all this. I'll tell you, lad, I wouldn't be in your shoes—'

'No, wait,' said the other nurse. 'Look!'

Molly had heard the distress in Kevin's voice and her eyelids fluttered almost alarmingly with the effort of trying to open them, and then slowly and painfully, she forced them apart, though even this small action exhausted her.

'Oh, Glory be to God,' breathed the nurse.

Molly looked at her in a blank and rather vacant way as she said, 'You're back with us again.' She went closer to the bed and said, 'Can you hear me? Blink your eyes once if you hear what I say?'

Molly slowly shut her eyes and then peeled the lids open again and the nurse gave a small cry of pleasure, but it was Kevin that Molly's eyes sought, and the nurse, seeing this, pulled him forward. 'Hello, Molly,' he said, and saw the answer in the recognition in her eyes.

Then as she closed her eyes again, the nurse urged, 'Talk to her again. Say something.'

And what Kevin said was, 'Don't go to sleep again, Molly. You've been asleep for ages and ages. You can't still be tired. Wake up, for God's sake.'

When Molly's eyes opened again, tears seeped from them and trickled down her cheeks, and Kevin leaped away from the bed. 'I've made her cry,' he said, horrified.

'No,' the first nurse assured him. 'Those are happy tears. See, her eyes are still glowing. It is a good sign, believe me, and I am away to tell Matron about this.'

Because Kevin was the one who pulled Molly out of the coma, the doctor who examined her maintained he had to be allowed to visit his sister because it was good for her, despite his youth, and Mr Sutcliffe at the Cottage Homes was contacted so that this could be arranged. Kevin was quite nervous of this initially, because he thought he would be in trouble. The man did take him to task over both being absent from school without permission and spending his dinner money. Kevin knew, though, that the superintendent's heart wasn't in the rebuke, that he was just going through the motions, and Kevin wasn't punished in any other way, though he was so happy he wouldn't have cared if he had been.

When Molly had first woke from the coma, she was disorientated and confused and quite frightened, and any memory she had of the reason she was in the hospital was hazy at first, floating in the recess of her mind. However, these images became firmer and more defined, until she recalled every detail of the terror of the attack. She had thought the men would kill her and when the doctor told her they nearly succeeded, that the blow to her neck had been intended to break it, she wasn't surprised, but she worried what they would do when they found she was still alive. Likely they would try again, and she was filled with a terrible foreboding that she was living on borrowed time.

When the doctor went on to say the police were anxious to talk to her, Molly sighed. She had no desire to speak to any policeman and relive the events of that night. She knew it had to be faced, however, and Inspector Norton was the one who came to see her.

Molly knew that anything she said, or even hinted about that shadowy time, could easily implicate Will and so it

361

seemed much safer to say that she could remember nothing. 'My memory comes in bits,' she said. 'I remember arriving in Birmingham.'

'Where you took lodgings in Aston?'

'Did I?'

'That is what you told them at the Cottage Homes.'

'Then it must be right.'

'But you have no idea where it was?'

'I'm afraid not.'

'Let's take you back a little further,' the inspector said. 'Your brother said that after your parents died, you were taken to live with your maternal grandmother, Biddy Brannigan, but he didn't know the address.'

Molly hesitated for just a moment, and though she covered herself quickly, Norton noticed it. She knew exactly why Kevin had not told the inspector the real name and address of his grandmother and that was because he didn't want her in any part of his life and he'd know she had a claim on him. She had the right, if she so wished, to take him from the orphanage, and though she had said she wanted nothing to do with him, he wasn't prepared to take that risk. She didn't blame him in the slightest.

She said, 'That's right, and it isn't odd that he didn't know the address. He was only five when I went away and wasn't even able to write then. He would sometimes do pictures for me, and Granddad would put them in with his letters. When Kevin was old enough to write little notes, my grandfather still addressed the envelopes. As for me, I lived almost in the back of beyond in Connemara.' She remembered the place Bernadette McCauley had once told her her mother came from, and went on, 'The nearest town was Kilvara and that was a good five miles away. My grandmother scratched a living of sorts, but she was getting no younger and was very glad I was there to help her, because there was no one else.'

'She had no other family?'

'None,' Molly said. 'She had had children, but they had all died. My mother was the last.'

'And did you or your grandmother make any enemies there?'

'Enemies?'

'Miss Maguire, I believe the attack was meant for you,' the inspector said. 'It was planned. No one else has been attacked in that way. You were targeted and if we establish why, we have a good chance of catching the people who did it. Believe me, you very nearly died and might have done if it hadn't been for Daisy and her young man.'

Molly's eyes opened wider. That was the first time she had heard about Daisy's involvement. 'Why?' she asked. 'What did Daisy do?' and listened as the inspector told her. 'I would like to see her,' she said. 'Thank her personally.'

'We'll see to it,' the inspector promised. 'What can you remember of that evening yourself?'

'Nothing of any value,' Molly said. 'I remember walking up the lane and then nothing.'

The inspector sighed, although the doctor had warned him that amnesia was common with a head injury.

'I suppose it's pointless asking you if you remember what happened to your handbag?'

'My handbag?'

'It's missing.'

'Sorry. I haven't a clue where that is either.'

'You did have it with you that night?'

'Yes, of course. I had been out with Kevin.'

'It can't be found.'

Molly shrugged. 'I really can't help you. I don't know what happened to it. Maybe the men who attacked me took it. Perhaps that's what it was – a robbery that went wrong.'

'Was there money in it?'

'Very little,' Molly said. 'Even my savings book has little in it. I hadn't been at the hotel long enough to save much.'

'I honestly don't think that people would go to such

trouble to steal the handbag of a waitress,' the inspector said.

Molly didn't either, and sincerely hoped her assailants hadn't taken her bag because her ration book and her identity card had been in there and both had Ruby's address on because that was where Molly had been living at the time. She didn't want any of Collingsworth's henchmen or police poking about around there, because if they did they might open a real can of worms. She thanked God she had kept the travel permit, which all Irish people had to have at the time, in the money belt that Ray had taken off her because there was a picture of her on it and her real address just outside Buncrana.

The mystery of the missing handbag, though, was solved the next day when Daisy came to visit.

'I just wanted to see you to thank you personally for what you did that night,' Molly said. 'The inspector said that you probably saved my life.'

'Glad I was able to help,' Daisy said, and then went on with an impish grin, 'Maybe I am the one to thank you, for letting me keep my maidenhead a little longer.'

'You mean?'

'I mean we were very close,' Daisy said. 'Your screams put a stop to that, all right.'

'Oh, Daisy.'

'Martin said more than "Oh, Daisy", I'll tell you.' Daisy smiled, and added, 'You are not his favourite person of all time. But never mind all that now,' she went on, diving into the bag she had at her feet. 'Look what the chef has sent you,' and she withdrew a large orange.

Oranges were so hard to get that Molly just gaped at it. 'Where did he get it?' she asked at last.

'He wouldn't say,' Daisy replied. '"Ask no questions and you'll be told no lies," was his answer to me. I think he has his own sources. Anyway, he has sent you some apples too, and we girls all pooled our sweet ration to get you a bit of chocolate.'

'Oh, you are so very good.'

'Aren't we?' Daisy agreed. 'Fitted up with halos, the lot of us. And I have a confession to make too.'

'What?'

'I have your handbag. I didn't want them police ferreting through your things and I didn't see how it could be relevant to anything anyroad. I went back up the lane real early the next morning to see if I could find summat, some clue about who did that to you, and when I saw your handbag stuck in the hedge I took it.'

'Oh, yes,' Molly said. 'I remember it flying off my shoulder when that thug swung me round.'

'Well, you can have it back any time you want,' Daisy said. 'That copper went all out to find it and had us all in to be questioned, but I never let on I had hold of it, like.'

Molly sighed with relief. 'That's great,' she said. 'You keep it for now. I'll have it back when the inspector has given me up as a lost cause.'

'When is that likely to be?'

Molly shrugged. 'How would I know? You know what coppers are. But I can't remember much. All I know is what the inspector told me you did.'

'Don't see what good it would be if you did remember, unless you recognised the men or anything,' Daisy said. 'I mean, I remember it all, for what good it is. With the blackout, those men could walk past me in the street, bump into me even, and I wouldn't recognise them. Sickening, though, ain't it that they are going to get away with what they did? I mean, they did bloody near kill you.'

'I know,' Molly said, 'but there is nothing I can do about that. All I can do is thank God that they didn't succeed.'

'Amen to that,' Daisy said fervently.

Inspector Norton felt in his bones that finding the handbag was of paramount importance and wanted to order a search of the grounds of the hotel. The manager was very worried about that because, though the news of the attack hadn't reached the papers, as it had been blocked by the inspector, the guests would have to be told something to explain the police searching the whole place, and he expressed his irritation over this to Norton.

The policeman looked at him coldly. 'I didn't block the newspaper's take on this for the comfort of you or your guests,' he said, 'but so as not to frighten other women unnecessarily who have to go out in the blackout. But let's not forget Molly Maguire, the young woman in your employ, who was set upon and rendered unconscious in the grounds of the hotel you run. Finding her assailant is of paramount importance and the reason I am here.'

The newspaper editors didn't mind not running the story. It was quite common anyway in wartime to suppress news that wasn't thought to be in the common interest. The papers were reduced to four meagre pages then, with paper being at a premium, and people's confidence that the war was going well was quite low anyway at that time. The papers' directive was to concentrate on the Allies' victories, like the successful battles against the Italians in Africa, and to fill the rest of the paper with heart-warming, patriotic stories to raise morale. They quite agreed with Inspector Norton that it would benefit no one to hear of the waitress knocked unconscious in the driveway of the hotel where she worked.

Norton never got his search of the grounds of Moor Hall Hotel, though. He was overruled by the Chief Superintendent, who said he hadn't the inclination, nor the manpower to do such a thing. He said Norton was not to spend any more time on the Molly Maguire case either. 'There were plenty of other things happening awaiting your investigation,' he said 'With so little to go on, you are no further forward in finding out who carried out the attack on Molly Maguire than you were at the beginning and no more police time can be wasted on it. After all, you say the girl is improving.'

Inspector Norton had no option but to close the file on Molly. The super was right in one way: Norton didn't know why the attack had happened, or who had done it, and the bugger of it was now he might never know.

The fact that the incident was not reported confused Collingsworth. 'I tell you I broke the girl's neck,' the beefy man assured him. 'Christ, I have killed men bigger than her with that same blow. There was nothing to her.'

'Don't you believe it,' Collingsworth said with feeling. 'Look how I suffered at her hands.'

'That's why we decided to finish it there and then,' the man said. 'I know you said bring her back alive, like, but Christ, she's nowt but a heap of trouble alive. She was better off out of the road.'

'I would have liked to have known who helped her,' Collingsworth said.

'Does it matter now?'

'Not if you are sure you have killed her.'

'She folded straight off,' the second man said. 'She never moved a muscle. Honest to God, she was dead all right.'

'Why wasn't it reported then?'

'They don't always, do they?' Ray put in. 'Look at the outcry when the casualty lists were printed. Probably wouldn't allow this to go to print in case it caused wide-spread panic or summat.'

'Well, I know we only hear a quarter of what is really happening,' Collingsworth conceded. 'I suppose I can't believe that she is really gone this time.'

'You better believe it, boss. Molly Maguire ain't no more.'

Collingsworth smiled as much as he was able and his eyes glittered. Molly Maguire had had her comeuppance at last. He tossed Ray a set of keys and said, 'Fetch a couple of bottles of single malt from the cellar and we will drink to a good night's work.'

When Will found out what had befallen Molly the

following day, he felt sick, and he barely reached home before the tears began. Betty, alarmed, took his hand and led him to the settee and the tears continued to roll down his face as he told her.

'They boasted about it,' he said finally, 'as if it was something to be proud of. One said that before he left, he kicked her in the stomach to make certain like. Jesus, Betty. I put you and the baby, not to mention Ruby, at terrible risk and in the end it was all for nothing.'

'Don't blame yourself,' Betty said brokenly.

'But I made it worse,' Will cried. 'If I had left well alone, she would still have died, yes, but Ray isn't a natural killer, unlike some of the others, and he would have probably drugged her first.'

'As if that makes it better,' Betty said scornfully.

'It might have been for her,' Will retorted. 'I can't imagine her panic, or the terror she must have felt. Anyway, this has finished me with Collingsworth and his mob. I can't work for him again after this.'

Betty paled. 'I thought you said that it was hard to leave if you know as much as you do.'

'It is, unless it's official,' Will said. 'Even Collingsworth can't argue with the War Office. I have a confession to make. When I was invalided out of the army, they offered me a desk job and I was so mad with them at the time that I refused it. I was feeling sorry for myself that night I met up with Ray Morris in the pub. Well, tomorrow I am going down the recruiting office in Thorpe Street Barracks and ask if there is still a desk job I can do. Then I'm sure they can write a letter recalling me to duty if I ask them for one to show to my present employer. No need to tell them who it is. Even Collingsworth can't argue with that. But do you feel all right about me doing this, Betty?'

Betty's eyes were shining. 'That is the best news I have had in ages,' she said.

'There will probably be a cut in wages.'

368

'As if I care about that. At least now I can sleep easy in my bed – Hitler permitting, of course.'

'I think the guilt I feel at the death of Molly will stay with me for ever, though,' Will said.

Betty took Will's face between her hands, looking into his eyes, still bright with tears, and said earnestly, 'Listen to me, Will. We can do nothing now to change the situation and I do think it's best not to dwell on it, because our lives have to go on. I'm sure you will feel better when you are doing a more useful job, one that will help the war effort.'

TWENTY-FIVE

'Have you up out of here and back home in no time,' Molly's doctor said to her a few days later, after he had examined her. 'It was only that wound on your side that was giving me concern, but it is responding to treatment well now.'

Molly feigned enthusiasm, as it was expected, but she had no home, was fearful of the future and absolutely terrified of leaving the safety of the hospital.

That day Molly was transferred into the main ward beside a young girl, who introduced herself as Lynne Baxter. She was very pretty – her hair the colour of burnished bronze and cut short so that curls of it framed her face and her cheekbones were slightly pink and dusted with freckles.

However, it was Lynne's smile that turned that prettiness into true beauty. Few people could resist the desire to smile back at her and Molly was no exception.

'I am glad I am in the main ward now,' she said. 'I was so bored on my own.'

'I agree,' Molly said. 'I was in a side ward too. It helps the time pass with someone to talk to. What are you in hospital for?'

'I had an appendicitis,' Lynne said. 'Only by the time Mom got them to believe that it really was serious, it had burst and so I had blood poisoning as well. That's why, for a while, I had to have a room of my own.'

'Goodness!' Molly said. 'That sounds very nasty.'

'Yes, it was,' Lynne agreed. 'What about you?'

'I was attacked,' Molly said briefly.

The young girl's eyes opened wide with astonishment. 'Attacked?' she repeated. 'What for and who did it?'

Molly shrugged. 'I can answer neither question,' she said, 'because I haven't the answers and neither have the police.'

'You mean you were attacked for no reason, bad enough to land you in hospital, and the police cannot find out who did it?'

'That's it exactly,' Molly said. 'It isn't the fault of the police either, because you see I can't remember anything about it at all.'

'But that's terrible.'

'I agree,' Molly said. 'There is nothing I can do about it either, but because I don't know who it was, I will be so nervous when the time comes to leave here.'

'I'm not surprised,' Lynne said. 'Will you go home?'

'I haven't really got a home,' Molly said. 'My parents died six years ago.'

'Ah,' Lynne said, sympathetically 'That's really sad. Are you an only child?'

Molly only hesitated for the briefest minute before deciding to tell Lynne Baxter the same story she had told everyone else. 'I was just getting to know Kevin again,' she said at the end. 'We had been apart for over five years and that is a long time for a young child.'

'I'll say,' Lynne agreed. 'Five years is a long time for me. and I am fifteen, but it is an awful story really. You and your brother suffered so much and it is such a shame that there are just the two of you left.'

'Have you any brothers or sisters.'

'Just the one brother, Mark.'

'Older or younger?'

'Older. Mark is twenty-two,' Lynne told her. 'And man of

the house now that my father is in Scotland, doing something hush-hush for the war, Mom says. Not that we see that much of Mark either, really. He's in the RAF, you see, but he's stationed at Castle Bromwich aerodrome and he gets home when he can.'

'Is your brother a pilot?'

Lynne nodded. 'A squadron leader. He lost a lot of friends last year.'

'In the Battle of Britain?'

Lynne looked surprised. 'I didn't know whether you would know about that, living in Ireland and all.'

'Even there, most people took a great interest in it,' Molly explained. 'They knew that Britain's survival at that time depended on the Royal Air Force, and if Britain fell, Ireland's claim to remain neutral would probably count for nothing. I mean, they had little pockets of soldiers dotted here and there to protect Ireland's neutrality, but everyone knew they hadn't a hope of stopping any German Army intent on invasion. Believe me, we too were relying on the Royal Air Force. He must be brave, your brother.'

'He is,' Lynne admitted. 'Mom says they all are. She was ever so worried about him and still is, I suppose. She hides it well but I know. We've become even closer since the war started and we've had to do without the men around and cope with a lot of things by ourselves.'

'You are a very lucky girl,' Molly said. 'Even now, after all this time, there are few days that pass when I don't miss my mother. We were close too.'

'Sorry.'

'Don't be sorry. It isn't your fault that my parents died. Just appreciate what you have.'

'Oh, I do,' Lynne said. 'When you see the pictures in the paper of the raids and everything, and read some of the stories, it is very sad a lot of the time. I even appreciate Mark. He does tease, and yet I know that he really cares for me and I do miss him.'

'I missed my brother so much when we were first parted,' Molly said.

'Does it make you sad that he has had to go to an orphanage?' Lynne asked. 'I think it must be one of the worst things.'

'Well, the home is all right as far as places like that go,' Molly said. 'I mean, they seem kind enough. Kevin puts up with it and doesn't moan much, but ideally I would like to have someplace where I could have him live with me.'

'That would be lovely,' Lynne said. 'Would you mind if I tell my mother about you? There isn't much I don't share with her.'

'I don't mind,' Molly said. 'It isn't exactly a secret.'

Helen Baxter was very striking-looking and it was quite clear where Lynne had got her good looks from. She was both shocked and horrified when Lynne recounted Molly's whole tale to her that evening and she wished she could do something to help her in some way.

It was Kevin who asked Molly if she was going back to Moor Hall Hotel when she got out of hospital. Molly hid the involuntary shudder she gave at the thought, but when she answered Kevin her voice was steady.

'I couldn't go back there, Kevin. They couldn't keep my job open for ever.'

She knew even if they had she couldn't have taken it. She doubted she would ever have the courage to walk down that lane again because she knew Collingsworth's men would be back for another go.

When Kevin said, 'What will you do then?' she shook her head helplessly.

'I really don't know, Kevin.'

Lynne heard what Molly said and told her mother quietly when she visited that same evening. 'We've got to do something for her, Mom,' she said. 'She has nowhere to go when she leaves here.'

'Leave it with me,' Helen replied. 'Mark is coming tomorrow. Maybe he will have some ideas.'

Even if Lynne hadn't gone on and on about her brother coming that evening with her mother, Molly would have known who the man was framed in the doorway. He was the male double of his mother and sister, and dressed in his RAF uniform he looked absolutely stunning. He caused quite a stir amongst the young nurses. He looked at Molly as he passed her bed and smiled, and it was as if a light had been turned on inside him. She felt the breath catch in her throat.

He sat by his sister's bed first and had a few words with her. Molly saw how kind and understanding he was with Lynne, although she could guess he had a highly developed sense of fun, because it seemed to spark off him. She was surprised when he left Lynne talking to their mother and approached her bed. His mother had talked to him earlier that day about Molly Maguire and her problems. However, it was one thing hearing about her and quite another seeing this gorgeous, fragile-looking creature, who had already suffered so much. His protective streak was aroused and he knew he would do all in his power to help her.

'Would you mind if I sat with you for a few minutes?'

'Not at all.'

Mark pulled out the chair, sat beside the bed and said, 'My mother has been filling me in about your situation, hoping that I might be able to help.'

'I don't see how.'

'Look,' said Mark. 'As I see it, when you leave hospital what you need is a job and ideally some place where you can have your brother live with you.'

'Yes, and how likely am I to get anywhere to live in this city, which has been bombed to bits?' Molly said. 'At least somewhere I can afford – because that is another problem, of course. I need to work.'

'Doing what?'

'Anything that pays a decent wage,' Molly said. 'I will do anything. I'm not fussy.'

'And when do you hope to leave?'

'Soon. In the next day or two, they say.'

'I'll ask around,' Mark said. 'I am obviously not promising anything, but I will do my level best.'

'Thank you,' said Molly. She knew it was good of the man to offer to help, but she didn't hold out much hope that he would find a suitable job for her.

The next day he was back. This time Lynne didn't know he was coming because he had come straight from the air base and she gave a squeal of excitement when she saw him. Though he waved across to her and told her he would see her later, it was Molly he had news for.

Daisy had popped in to see Molly, which she did when shifts allowed, and she was astounded when the very gorgeous man came towards them. Molly smiled, for what Daisy thought about Mark Baxter was very apparent in the coy smile she gave him when Molly introduced him.

'Have you news?' she asked him.

Mark nodded. 'I think so,' he said. 'Could you work in a Naafi?'

'What on earth is a Naafi?'

Mark smiled. 'Just about the most important area on the air base. It's where the grub is dispensed.'

'Like a canteen?'

'Exactly like a canteen.'

'I told you that I would work anywhere, and I still mean it. But I will admit to you now that I am scared stiff of leaving hospital,' Molly told him.

'I think I can understand that,' Mark said. 'After what happened, you are bound to be nervous, but don't you see, the safest place by far is a military base? It is one place where people are not allowed to walk about willy-nilly. Everyone has to have a reason for being there.'

'But where would I live if I was to take this job?'

'That's the whole beauty of it,' Mark said. 'There is a chap in my squadron and his family have a house that nearly backs on to the airfield. On the Kingsbury Road. Do you know it?'

'Sort of.'

'Well, there are about ten houses all together and his father died two years ago and since then he has taken care of his mother and his two sisters. When the bombs started falling he was more worried for them than himself and he encouraged them all to move to his mother's sister's, who has a house in the country somewhere, and stay for the duration. Anyway, now he has a three-bedroomed house going begging because he lives on the airfield.'

'Oh, isn't that just perfect, though?' Daisy said.

Molly was very dubious. Neither Mark nor Daisy knew of the time that she had arrived on New Street Station and had stupidly accepted the offer of accommodation from a stranger she had just met, and look how that had turned out. She wasn't about to make that mistake again. 'I don't think so.'

Surprise and disappointment filled Mark's face as he said, 'Why? What do you mean?'

'It wouldn't be right for me to accept a house from a man, even if he is not living in it.'

'He is a decent chap,' Mark protested. 'Anyway, you can have your brother living with you, so you won't be alone.'

'Even so . . .'

'All right then,' Mark demanded. 'What's the alternative?'

And there wasn't a bloody alternative. He knew it and she knew it, and when she left the hospital she had to go somewhere. Helen had said of course she must stay with them until something turned up, but that would only be a short-term solution, whereas this way . . .

She nodded, and Mark cried, 'You'll do it?'

'I must, I suppose,' Molly said. 'Like you pointed out, I am not burdened with options.'

'That's great,' Daisy said happily. 'All the girls will be that pleased. They always ask after you.'

'Do me a favour, though, and don't give anyone my address,' Molly said. 'I will give it to you and maybe you could bring my things over, if you could, but the fewer people that know it, the better.'

Daisy knew why Molly said that and yes, maybe she was overreacting a bit, but surely that was understandable in the circumstances. So she said, 'Don't you worry, Molly, no one will get anything out of me.'

Mark stood up then. 'I'll leave you now to talk with your friend and I'll have a few words with my sister before it is time for them to throw me out.'

As he moved out of earshot, Daisy gave Molly a wink and said, 'Very tasty. He could do a favour for me any day of the week.'

'You're spoken for already,' Molly said. 'What about Martin?'

'What about him?' Daisy said with a toss of her head. 'We're not hitched yet. Anyway, a girl can still look. Mind you,' she added, 'I would be wasting my time with that hunk for he only has eyes for you.'

'Don't be so daft!' Molly cried.

'You can protest all you like, my dear,' Daisy said, 'but I am a woman of the world and we know these things.'

Molly thought she was loopy, but she decided to let her keep her little fantasy.

Easter had come and gone by the time Molly left hospital on Saturday 12 April – and so had the spate of air raids that began on the 7th and went on till the 11th, though none fell anywhere near the hospital. Parts of Birmingham were pounded, however, and Molly thought of what Daisy had said and hoped her family were safe.

Lynne had left hospital the day before in a taxi, and it was arranged that Molly would spend the weekend with her and her mother as Mark had time on Monday and Tuesday to help her move in to the empty house. As he wanted to take Molly to the air base from the hospital to see the Naafi where she would be working, and to meet Terry Sallinger, who owned the house, he told her he would pick her up in a car.

'Have you a car of your own?' Molly said, awed.

Mark laughed. 'No. It's my father's and has been left in the garage for the duration because of the shortage of petrol, but it has enough in to do what I want tomorrow.'

Never having ridden in a car before, Molly was excited until she saw it in the car park, and then she was struck dumb.

'What is it?' Mark cried, alarmed at the colour that had drained out of Molly's face. 'What's the matter?'

Molly had a flashback to the day her parents died. Just a few hours before that dreadful news came through, she remembered her father running his hand over the bonnet of a car the exact same as the one before her. 'Might give you a ride in it later, mate,' he'd said to Kevin, and then he had turned to Molly. 'What d'you think, Moll? Ain't she just the business?'

He had been so vibrant and full of life, laughing and chafing Granddad, and everyone had been happy.

The tears welled in her eyes, and though she tried to stop them, they spilled down her cheeks. Mark didn't understand – how could he? – and he tried to draw Molly towards the car but she shook her head so violently that he stopped. The trickle of tears had turned into a torrent, gushing from her and punctuated with little anguished sobs, and Mark, not knowing what else to do, put his arms around her and held her tight as she wept on his shoulder.

Later, she was eventually able to explain what had upset her so much and Mark felt Molly's pain as keenly as if it was seeping through the pores of her skin.

'Oh, my dear girl,' he said. 'There are no words I can say to ease this for you in any way, and I feel so crass and stupid. I knew your parents died in a car accident. Why didn't I think and come for you in a taxi? In fact, that is what I will do. I will leave the car here and ask the hospital to call for a taxi.'

'No.'

'It's no bother,' Mark said. 'I am not having you upset like this.'

'No, Mark,' Molly said. 'Don't make me feel worse than I do already. I am bitterly ashamed at making a holy show of myself, but I am over it now, really I am, and I would like to go in the car.'

'Are you absolutely sure?'

Molly swallowed the lump of dread in her throat and nodded.

It did take courage to climb into that car, and she felt a hollow feeling in the pit of her stomach. Mark knew how nervous she was and he drove the car with great care so that nothing might alarm her further.

Molly was impressed by the size of the air base. There were huge sheds, which Mark said were the hangars where some of the planes were stored. Others stood on the runway in formation. 'Those are the Spitfires that I fly,' Mark told her with pride, 'and further away is where the Wellingtons are stored. Those are bombers and need a longer runway.'

'But where do all the planes come from?'

'The other side of the road we have just driven down,' Mark said. 'There is a big factory there called Vickers. Each night they close the road and the planes are pushed across it. They turn them out at a rate of knots, I can tell you, and every one is needed.'

He drew the car to a stop in front of another large building. 'This is the Naafi,' he said. 'Terry arranged to meet us here so you can kill two birds with one stone, as it were.'

'Gosh, I thought the dining room at Moor Hall was big until I saw this place,' Molly said to Mark. 'You could get that dining room in four times and still have space.'

'Well, think of all the hungry airmen to feed and water, not to mention the ancillary and office staff,' Mark said. 'Anyway, come and meet your fellow workmates.'

They were all much older than she was, Molly noticed, but looked a friendly enough bunch and said they would welcome an extra pair of hands. 'Even better when those hands know what to do,' said one of them with a smile, and Molly knew it was her experience at the hotel as well as Mark's influence that had secured her the job.

Terry Sallinger said he would be delighted if she would take the house on.

'It will be commandeered by the military if you don't,' he said, 'and if you saw what shape the houses are in when they leave, well, you wouldn't credit the damage, and my mother thinks a lot of her house.'

Molly remembered Ray saying something similar about the flat she was incarcerated in, but there any similarity ended.

She grasped Terry by the hand and shook it as she said, 'I will always be grateful to you for this, and I know I will speak for my brother as well as myself. It will be wonderful for us to be together again. What about rent?'

'We'll come to some arrangement about that when you see what wages you're getting,' Terry said, and added with a laugh, 'Don't worry, I won't fleece you.'

'I didn't think for one moment you would,' Molly said, and suddenly any misgivings about taking the house on disappeared.

So when, later, Helen said a little anxiously, 'You are sure you feel all right about this?' Molly was able to assure her.

'Mark didn't bully you into it?'

'Maybe he did a bit,' Molly admitted, and added with a smile, 'But really it is the best solution all round. Now that I have met Terry Sallinger I feel much better.'

'How does your brother feel about it?'

'He doesn't mind anything really, as long as we are

together,' Molly said. 'Meeting once a week in artificial surroundings and after a gap of more than five years was not nearly enough. And, as might be expected, he does think that living next to an airfield is the most exciting place in the world to be. He told me only last week that he is going to join the air force just as soon as he can. I pray to God that this war will be over by then.'

'Good God!' exclaimed Helen. 'So do I. Your brother is only eleven. That would mean another seven years of this.' Her eyes looked suddenly bleak, and Molly said gently, 'You must worry about Mark. In fact, Lynne has said you do.'

'Worry is perhaps an understatement,' Helen told her. 'When the Battle of Britain was on, the average airman lasted a mere six weeks.' She stopped suddenly and Molly, totally shocked herself, saw the agonising memory of those nightmare days and nights flit across Helen's face. 'Six weeks. Did you know that?'

Molly shook her head. 'No, I had absolutely no idea.'

'And all so young,' Helen went on. 'At the start of their adult lives. I thought and prayed about Mark every minute of the day then. He was always so tired too, and tiredness can kill as easily as the enemy – he told me that himself – but all of them were the same: no time to take proper rest before they were off again. Mark would sometimes bring a few of the chaps home with him and they'd laugh and joke as if they hadn't a care in the world, but that was just to mask the fear they carried around with them daily, though they often could do little about the trepidation behind their eyes.'

'The point is, Mom, it had to be done,' Lynne said. 'Mark said so often.'

'I know that,' Helen said. 'I know that without their bravery and their skill, Britain could be under the Nazi jackboot now, and Birmingham could have been another Rotterdam, but even when you know it to be necessary, no mother wants to throw her own son into the slaughter you know is coming.'

Molly understood that perfectly. 'God, Helen, it must have been dreadful for you,'

'Even now, there are airmen shot down every day,' Helen said. 'Selfishly I always hope that one of them is not my son, that some other mother bears that pain, and I can't help feeling that way.' She sighed. 'It might help if my husband, Gerald, was here to share the burden. I worry about him too and miss him. We have never been apart so long before, but Lynne, I must admit, has been a tower of strength, for all her tender years.'

'Not that tender, Mom.'

'Tender enough,' Helen said firmly. 'And talking of tender years, how do you feel about going back to school next week when the term starts again? You can't afford to lose much time with those exams looming next summer.'

Molly knew that Lynne was a very clever girl, had passed the eleven-plus and was at Sutton Girls' Grammar School. The following year she would matriculate, followed by the sixth form and then on to university. Molly envied her for she knew such a future might have been hers once, if the cards hadn't been stacked against her.

'Flipping heck, Mom,' Lynne burst out. 'You don't need to remind me when those exams are. I know exactly.'

'And as far as I can see, the only way to get a good job when this little lot is over, is by getting a good education,' Molly said. 'I am always using this fascination that Kevin has for the air force to keep his head down over his books. I keep telling him they will take no dumb kids in.'

'Oh, I don't know so much about that,' Lynne said with a huge grin plastering her face. 'I mean, they took our Mark in all right.'

The following Monday morning, Mark took a taxi to the hotel where he collected Daisy, who had bundled up Molly's few possessions, together with, a meat pie, a loaf of bread, butter, fresh milk and, remarkably, four eggs, as a present from the chef. Then the taxi took them to the Erdington Cottage Homes, where they picked up the ecstatic Kevin, who had had his case packed since six o'clock that morning and could barely believe that he was going to live with Molly again as she had once promised him. Molly was already at the house, staring about her in amazed wonder, when they arrived.

The front door opened on to a hall, the stairs were to the right and one door led into the large lounge.

'It used to be two rooms,' Terry said, 'but my father had it made into one just the year before he died, with that arch as a feature.'

Molly thought it a beautiful room and attractively decorated, with large rugs covering much of the lino on the floor. The kitchen, off the hall to the back of the house, she knew many women would give their eyeteeth for. It had plenty of storage space, including a pantry, the gas boiler was fairly new and the cooker was of the latest design.

Added to that, there were three bedooms upstairs, two doubles and a single, all decorated beautifully and a bathroom with a bath, washbasin and toilet. Molly could hardly believe that she was mistress of such a place and vowed that Terry would never regret his decision to let her and Kevin live there.

They soon settled in. Molly registered with the grocer, greengrocer and butcher in the little parade of shops on the Chester Road, not far from the house. She also arranged for Kevin to leave Osbourne Road School, as it was too far from the house, and begin at Paget Road School on the nearby Pype Hayes council estate a couple of days before she was due to start work in the Naafi.

Kevin didn't mind moving school at all. In fact, he preferred it because none there knew that he had been living at a Cottage Home. He was starting Paget Road with a clean sheet, and when asked he said that his parents were dead and that he now lived with his sister and that they had moved because his sister had a job at Castle Bromwich aerodrome. That raised his standing quite highly. He didn't say what she did, said in fact it was better not to discuss things like that – 'Careless talk and all that, don't you know' – and when they assumed from this that Molly was connected to the RAF in some military capacity, Kevin didn't put them right.

Molly liked her job in the Naafi, and being unafraid of hard work and always pleasant, she was soon very popular with her colleagues. She liked all the people she worked with, though she was most friendly with May, Doris and Edna, as she worked with them most of the time. Though Molly was by far the youngest worker, they all got on remarkably well. She also kept in touch with Helen and Lynne, and with Daisy at the hotel. As time passed she couldn't believe how contented she was. The only downside to the job was the general sadness if any of their aircrew were lost, and it was hard to see the empty chairs grouped around the tables.

The war went on apace, and Molly often asked herself if the carnage was to go on for ever. The raids in Birmingham had more or less ceased, but other cities, including London, were getting a pasting. The loss in shipping was colossal too. Not only did this mean food was not getting through, but each ship sunk meant hundreds of men also lost their lives.

The bombing of Pearl Harbor by the Japanese in December brought America into the war. It was all anyone talked about at Helen's house on Christmas Day, where Molly and Kevin were just two of the party of people invited, including her parents and many of Mark's friends that couldn't get home for the festive season.

'Enough war talk,' Helen said eventually. 'It's frightening enough to turn a body off their food, and I haven't been slaving away in the kitchen all morning to produce a meal fit for a king and see it all go to waste. Mark, will you pour everyone another drink, and Molly and Lynne can help me dish up in the kitchen?'

As soon as the kitchen door closed behind the women, Molly heard the conversation between the men start up again. 'They're still at it.'

Helen smiled wryly. 'They won't once I put their dinner before them,' she said as she transferred roast potatoes to a serving dish. 'I'll see to it that they don't.'

'Kevin, of course, is hanging on to their every word.'

'Yes, I noticed that,' Helen said with a smile. 'He's a nice boy. Still enjoying the Boy Scouts?'

'Oh, he's keener, if anything,' Molly said. 'And he is incredibly busy, because besides the Scout meetings, he has also learned how to operate a stirrup pump and is practising first aid. He's always out collecting salvage and newspapers, or on digging duty in Pype Hayes Park, as well as weeding the garden at home, which Terry cultivated and now has little time to see to. It reminds me of Ireland, to eat potatoes and cabbages and the like that have just been lifted from the ground. Terry is always immensely grateful that Kevin hasn't let the garden go to rack and ruin.'

'Do you see much of him then?'

'Hardly anything,' Molly said. 'I mean, I put the rent up every week and it might be three weeks or more before he calls to collect it.'

'Good job you are not the sort to borrow it back,' Lynne put in.

'No,' Molly said. 'Mug's game, that.'

'You're right there,' Helen said. 'Now let's get this food on the table before it gets cold. My stomach thinks my throat's cut.'

Singapore was impregnable, everyone knew, so it was a great blow when it fell to the Japanese on 15 February after thousands lost their lives and thousands more were taken prisoner. But life had to go on – another battle, another day – and by Easter, American servicemen had moved on to the base. There were a fair few in Sutton

385

Coldfield, according to Daisy, and a great attraction they were proving to be.

'You know what they say about them?' Daisy said. 'Overpaid, oversexed and over here, and maybe they are, but that is one invasion I would more than welcome.'

'Daisy!'

'Oh, don't go all stuffy on me and tell me to think of Martin,' Daisy said, 'because I am only looking. Mind you, they are really good to look at. We go more often to Sutton Coldfield now because some of them are based at St George's Barracks, billeted with locals, so I heard. You can bet our manager wouldn't offer any of our empty rooms for their use. Shame really. I'm sure all us girls would make sure they had every creature comfort.'

'You are awful, Daisy,' Molly said, but she was laughing herself.

'Well, you should see them, Moll,' Daisy said. 'When they go marching up and down the road, even the customers in the shops come out to watch; they even come from behind the counter.'

'What for, to see a company of soldiers marching?'

'No,' Daisy said, laughing at the memory of it, 'to see the little Gl at the end. He always wangles to be at the back, so the officers don't catch sight of him, I s'pose, and he doesn't march, he jitterbugs up the road, and doffs his cap right and left and always has a dirty great smile on his face. He is a real card.'

'Hm,' Molly said, 'I doubt that his commanding officers would see it in the same light.' But even as she said the words she remembered Helen telling her of the pilots laughing and joking as if they hadn't a care in the world, yet she had seen the fear in their eyes. Maybe this was the young Gl's way of coping.

'Well, let's hope they never catch sight of him then,' Daisy said. 'And that jitterbugging looks fun.'

'The American lads here say that too.'

'Maybe we should think about taking lessons and go to a dance a time or two.'

'No, I don't think so.'

'Why not?'

'Well, there's my job – and Kevin, of course.'

'We all have jobs, Molly,' Daisy said, 'And we are not at them twenty-four hours a day, seven days a week, and Kevin is a big boy. You are twenty years old, not sixty or seventy.'

'I know that.'

'Well, then,' Daisy said, and when Molly didn't go on to explain further, she suddenly exclaimed, 'You have someone special. That's it, isn't it?'

'No, it isn't.'

'Well, why isn't it?' Daisy demanded. 'It flipping well ought to be. You have a camp full of men to choose from and not one has touched your heart yet. You watch it, or you will end up on the shelf.'

Molly shrugged. 'Maybe that's just where I want to be.'

Daisy shook her head over Molly, and she wasn't the only one. Helen too said she should get out more. The woman she worked with in the Naafi could have told her that it wasn't that the men weren't interested in her; they buzzed around her like bees round a honey pot, the Americans being the most persistent. Her colleagues had all expected that Molly being so absolutely gorgeous-looking and so pleasant into the bargain would be snapped up fairly quickly, and yet she seemed to hold her admirers at arm's length. As Edna put it, 'It's like 'er has a barrier up.'

'Maybe she does right, though,' May said. 'What if she was to lose her heart and he didn't make it?'

'Ah, there is that and all,' Edna conceded. 'Bloody war. Hard for the young ones to have any life at all.'

Molly could have told them that one man already held her heart and that man was Mark Baxter. She went weak at the knees every time she saw him, and worried terribly about him when his squadron was operational.

She knew he felt something for her too because she had said seen it in his eyes, but he hadn't said anything to her. He probably thought she was an ice maiden. She knew that was what some of the boys called her; she had overheard them and couldn't altogether blame them. She couldn't bring herself to trust men any more, not even Mark, and so she battened down her own feelings and built a wall around herself. She told herself she was doing Mark a favour because he had no part to play in her future. No man had, for the thought of any sort of intimacy made her feel physically sick.

TWENTY-SIX

There had been three air raids at the very end of July, the first one taking everyone by surprise as it had been a full year since the last raid of any significance. The sirens were late coming and the people slow to take cover, as many felt it to be a false alarm, so the death toll was quite high. When there was an even more intense raid the following night, many, including Molly, feared that this was a forerunner of another blitz.

After that, there was nothing, though it was a long time before people began to relax a little and sleep easy in their beds. At the air base, it helped that the Naafi staff were so busy at work with the influx of the Americans. Molly often applied for extra shifts, knowing that total exhaustion was the only way that she could have even a chance of a decent night's sleep.

One dinner-time in mid-October, they were as busy as they usually were and Molly was serving mechanically, almost without looking at the people's faces. But then, as one man neared the front of the queue, she caught sight of who it was and she staggered and would have fallen but for Edna beside her, who caught her arm.

'You want to take more water with it, duck,' she said, and then she caught sight of Molly's bleached face and said, ''Ere, Molly. Are you all right?'

The man looked up and as his eyes locked with Molly's,

he too looked as if he had seen a ghost. For a second or two he stood stock still, staring, and then he began pushing his way through the crowds, apologising as he elbowed people out of the way, until he reached the counter. Molly had stood in the same spot since she had first recognised the man, only her eyes had followed him.

She felt as though she had been kicked in the stomach. She had been tracked down again. Was nowhere safe? The man was looking at her with puzzled eyes and his brow was puckered into a frown as he asked, questioningly, 'Molly, is that really you?'

Molly sighed. She was tired of running and so she said, 'Yes it's me. Hello, Will. How did you find me?'

'I didn't,' Will said. 'That is . . . dear Lord, I was told you were dead.'

'I nearly was. But what are you doing here?'

'Nothing to do with you, Molly,' Will said, seeing the trepidation on her face and understanding the reason for it. 'Look, we need to talk. Is there somewhere?'

'Out the back,' Molly said with her jerk of her head. 'Go through and wait for me,' and she turned to Edna. 'Can you hold the fort? I just need a few minutes.'

The woman was intrigued but she also knew that Molly was one of the hardest workers there and so she said with a smile, 'Go on then. Someone from your distant and murky past, is he?'

'Something like that.'

May approached just as Molly was lifting the counter flap and said, 'Watch yourself, lass. I hear tell he's married.'

'He is,' Molly said, 'Once, in another life, I knew his wife.'

May was nonplussed. She turned to Doris beside her. 'Did you hear that? What did you make of it?'

'Nothing,' Doris said, 'I have given up trying to understand the young people of today.'

At that moment Molly was saying to Will, 'Collingsworth's

390

thugs nearly killed me. The doctors said I was lucky to survive.'

'Well, when there was no report of an attack in the paper, they presumed you had snuffed it,' Will said. 'It was Ray who found out where you were that time and betrayed you to save his own skin, or so I heard.' He shook his head and went on, 'Anyway, that was the finish for me. I went to see them at the army barracks and they offered me a job in the stores and then sent a letter to Collingsworth, explaining that I had been recalled.'

'But this is an RAF base.'

'I had noticed that,' Will remarked laconically. 'It was the planes that gave it away.'

'Fool,' Molly said with a smile. 'You know what I mean.'

'I have been seconded,' Will said. 'Apparently, the store manager here has hurt his back and I am filling in until he is better. I have already been here a couple of days. It is amazing that we haven't met before.'

'I was working in the kitchens, probably. We take it in turns,' Molly said. 'Let me get this straight now. You have no connection with Collingsworth or the others?'

'None whatsoever, haven't had for months now and have never been happier.'

'And as far as you know, they have stopped looking for me?'

'Why would they look? They think you are dead.'

'Then it is over?' Molly cried, her eyes glowing with excitement. 'I am free.'

'As a bird, my darling girl,' Will said.

Molly felt the heavy weight she had been carrying around for ages slide off from between her shoulder blades. So overcome was she that, despite how she felt about being touched, or intimacy in general, she threw her arms around Will's neck as she cried, 'You don't know how good that makes me feel.'

Will hugged her back in delight that the girl he had

thought murdered was alive and well. However, Mark, who had been making his way to the Naafi, had witnessed that embrace and, knowing how Molly felt about anyone touching her, could only conclude that the man was special to Molly in some way, though who the hell he was, was anyone's guess.

Now he had to stop that hankering after her once and for all. Molly had made her choice and it wasn't him. It was time to draw a line under Molly Maguire.

Will was waiting for Molly after her shift, as arranged, and she took him to the house, for they had much to talk about. Kevin was at Scouts and so Molly took Will through to the kitchen and put the kettle on, saying as she did so, 'Do you mind if we sit here? It is warmer at this time of day. With us both out all day I don't light the fire in the sitting room until the evening.'

'I don't mind where I sit,' Will said, 'but tea would be very welcome.'

'I want to know everything,' Molly said as she filled the kettle and put it on the gas. 'But first about Betty and the baby.'

Will was puffed up with pride as he said, 'Not so much of a baby now. She had a wee boy, the day after you left, and we call him Sam.'

'I'm pleased for you, Will,' Molly said sincerely. 'And so glad you left that set-up.'

'And me,' Will said. 'I was suddenly sickened by the whole thing and bitterly ashamed for my part in any of it.'

'I felt the same,' Molly said, 'I couldn't believe that I had been such a fool.'

'Betty and Ruby would love to see you again,' Will said suddenly. 'They missed you so much when you left. Betty hoped you would include a note or at least an address when you sent the clothes back.'

'I didn't dare.'

'I understood that, but Betty was a bit hurt, I think.'

'I knew she'd feel that way,' Molly said sadly. 'I did feel bad about that, but I was too frightened to let anyone know where I was. I would love to see them both now that it's safer. Why don't you all come to Sunday lunch? It's my day off this week. Have you to work?'

'Only till one o'clock,' Will said. 'Betty and Ruby can bring young Sam up on the tram and we can meet here.'

And so it was arranged.

It was wonderful to see Betty and Ruby again. The two women hugged Molly in delight, and Sam was as cute as a button, twenty months old with a mischievous glint in his dancing brown eyes and a smile that would melt a heart of stone. The adults doted on him, and little wonder.

She introduced them all to Kevin, saying only that they were people she had lodged with when she had first come to Birmingham, and she had bumped into Will again as he worked at the base. Kevin accepted this and liked the family, although he was completely bowled over by the baby, who insisted on following him around the house. Over the meal they discussed only general matters, and Will asked Kevin many questions about Scouts, which he loved so much. Yet Molly knew there was something wrong, a sort of constraint.

After dinner, Kevin was on digging duty at the park and little Sam was put down in Molly's bed for a nap. When Will said he wanted to talk to her, she suddenly decided she didn't want to hear anything he had to say.

'I don't want to talk about Collingsworth,' she said. 'I never want to hear his name again. You must see why that is?'

'Of course I understand,' Will said. 'What happened to you might have turned the brain of a lesser person, but I know you to be strong and brave, and I think a person who would always do what they thought was right.'

'Oh, yes,' Molly said sarcastically. 'Like I went off with two strangers in the middle of the night. Really wise move, that.'

'You were eighteen, in a strange place, and terrified by the worst air raid Birmingham had ever seen. It was the very early hours of a dark November morning,' Will said. 'I said you were brave, not fearless. It wasn't your fault and you must tell yourself that.'

'Will, why are you saying all this now?'

'Because I want to put a stop to it once and for all,' Will said. 'I want us both to go to the police and tell them.'

Molly looked at him aghast. 'Are you crazy?' she cried. 'Didn't you always say that if those villains heard a whisper, they would pay you a visit one dark night and silence you for good?'

'I know what I said, but—'

'One of the reasons I told the police nothing about my attackers was because I was thinking of you and Betty and Ruby. I didn't want you involved.'

'But I was involved,' Will said. 'And now I want to make a clean breast of it and see these people who prey on vulnerable young girls are put behind bars and kept there for a very long time. Don't worry, I have talked it over with Betty and Ruby, and they both agree.'

Molly looked across at the women and Betty said, 'It really is the only thing to do, Molly.'

'But why now, all of a sudden?' Molly asked.

'Well, I could have gone and told my story at any time,' Will said, 'but it would hold more credence if you came too and said just what had happened to you.'

Molly shook her head emphatically. 'I can't do that. I am surprised you even thought to ask me such a thing.'

'I want to show you something,' Will said, and he went to take a copy of a newspaper from the pocket of his topcoat and spread it out on the table. There was a picture of a young and pretty girl who had apparently gone missing after a row with her parents.

'Her name is Christine Naylor, a London girl evacuated with her school to a place in Wales. There she met up with a couple of girls from Birmingham that she became great friends with,' Will said. 'In early October the girls from Birmingham hit fourteen and went home. Christine Naylor wanted to do the same thing, but her parents were adamant that she should do the school cert first before she got any sort of job and she returned home a week ago to have it out with them. The result was a row and the following morning they found her bed hadn't been slept in and many of her clothes and her savings book were gone. They could only assume that she has come to Birmingham in search of the girls.'

'But she might not have done,' Molly cried. 'She could have gone anywhere. And even if she did come here, her disappearance might have nothing to do with Ray and Charlie.'

'I saw them with her when I was shopping in the town when it was just coming on to dusk,' Betty said. 'I sort of knew Ray because I have glimpsed him once or twice, but I couldn't remember at the time why his face was so familiar and I didn't know the other chap at all, but I recognised the girl. As soon as I saw her picture in the paper I remembered where I had seen that Ray before and I told Will.'

'That doesn't prove anything,' Molly protested.

'Molly, she was dead upset, the girl,' Betty said. 'Crying fit to burst, she was, the poor sod. And that Ray had his arm around her and I heard him say that he knew of a nice place where she could stay the night. And you are so right, Molly,' she went on turning to face her, 'Ray looks so respectable and sounded so understanding and concerned, anyone would be taken in by him. The girl was, anyway, and they went off together. I should imagine that you wouldn't need fifty guesses to know what will happen to her and where she will end up.'

Molly felt sick and Will put in, 'And this girl is not yet fifteen.'

Fifteen! Younger even than Lynne, Molly thought. What if she had a row with Helen and just disappeared? God, it was unthinkable. What despicable people these men were. And if she did nothing, the practice would just go on and on. Could she live with herself, knowing that she had the power to change things?

She took a deep breath and said, 'You're right, this vile trade must be stopped. But there is Kevin. I don't want him at risk.'

'We'll talk to the police about that,' Will said. 'They will look after you and Kevin. You will be the star witness in this and they won't want to lose you.'

'What about your family?'

'Me and Mom are taking Sam to some relatives in the Cotswolds for a bit,' Betty said. 'They've been asking us to go for years.'

'I'll have to see my commanding officer too,' Will said. 'I may lose my job, may even be imprisoned for my part in it. Who knows? But one thing I do know is that I just can't stand by and condone this any more. The girl's whole family is distraught. There was a picture of her parents the following day.'

When Molly looked at the photograph of the saddened couple, beaten down with anguish at the loss of their daughter, she felt guilt flood her being. She knew she had inflicted exactly the same pain on Tom and Nellie, Jack and Cathy, all those who had cared for her, and tears of shame seeped from her eyes and trickled down her cheeks.

'Don't cry, Molly,' Will said, 'I know it's scary, but—'

'It's not that,' Molly said. 'It's looking at the girl's parents and seeing their suffering, because I have done that to my uncle and friends I had in Buncrana.'

'What do you mean?'

'I've not written to them, not once since I arrived in Birmingham.'

'They probably think you are dead then,' Will said. 'Killed

in a raid or something. You should write to them, Molly. Surely they deserve that?'

'Yes, of course,' Mollie said. 'But for God's sake, Will, how do I write an account of all that has happened to me?'

'Better you do it that they read about it in the papers.'

'Will this make the papers?'

'It may do. A lot depends on what is happening with the war at the time.'

'Oh God,' Molly breathed. 'I can't risk that. I will have to give them some account of why I have been silent for two years, won't I?'

That question didn't need an answer. Molly looked at Will's face and said, 'It will be the hardest letter I have ever written in my life.' But she knew in her heart of hearts it had to be done.

Inspector Norton – Molly had insisted that it had to be Norton they told first – listened to the tale Will and Molly told him with open-mouthed incredulity, especially when Will explained how he had rescued Molly and then hid her for some weeks. Norton had known that Molly had kept something back about the attack, and learned now she had done it to protect William Baker and his family, and no wonder after all he had risked on her behalf. He didn't doubt a word of what either said. Molly's account was told so matter-of-factly, her eyes fixed on the rain lashing the windows, though Norton saw the terrible memories lurking behind her eyes.

He knew the man and woman in front of him probably had no idea that they had handed him the golden egg. He had been after the gang for some time, had a dossier already prepared, but he had never found anyone brave enough to speak out before.

And then, as if Molly had guessed the inspector's thoughts, she said, 'We are putting ourselves at great risk telling you these things, and the one I worry about most in all this is my brother, Kevin.'

'Would it be possible for him to live elsewhere for a few weeks?' the inspector asked.

'Inspector, I have just had him back from the Cottage Homes. I can't send him away again,' Molly said emphatically. 'He would never forgive me, and likely refuse to go anyway.'

'Has he friends?'

'Well, yes, but with me working and all I don't know who they are, and nothing about their families. Oh,' she said suddenly, 'he does go to Scouts. He loves that.'

'Maybe the Scout leader could take him on for a while?'

'I don't know him either.'

'Leave that to me,' the inspector said. 'You just prepare Kevin.'

'I just don't know where to start telling all this to a young boy.'

'I prefer you not to tell him anything. Nor anyone else either. I would prefer no whisper of this to get out.'

'My commanding officer needed to know,' Will said.

'Yes, of course, but these people are used to keeping mum about things. Have you told anyone, Miss Maguire?'

'No, not a soul,' Molly said. 'I did start writing a letter to my family and friends in Ireland, but gave up. It was just so difficult to explain.'

'Keep it that way,' Norton advised. 'Baker, haven't you a wife and child?'

'Yes, sir, but they are well out of this in the Cotswolds.'

'Good man. As for yourself . . . ?'

'I'm all right, sir. I will keep my wits about me.'

'Wits are little defence against a couple of men jumping you, as they did Miss Maguire, or a gun shot in your chest,' Norton said. 'Now, Miss Maguire is to have a police bodyguard and—'

'Am I?' Molly said in surprise. 'Is that really necessary?'

'I think so,' the inspector said grimly. 'And as for you, Baker, I would like you to stay at the camp for now.'

'I can't do that.'

'Course you can. I will talk with whoever I need to to get this organised. Look,' he said to them both, 'I don't think you realise the importance and implications of this case. You are star witnesses and without either one of you, the case might fall apart and put the life of the other person on the line.'

'And when it is all over,' Will said, 'will you come for me? Will I get into trouble for my part in this?'

'That depends on the chief superintendent,' Norton said. 'But I will put in an application that no action is taken. Yes, you should have come forward earlier but you have explained how hard it was to leave the man's employ once engaged, and you are risking all coming to us now. Then, it would have been your word against his. Because of your rescue of Miss Maguire and co-operating with the police now, as long as the two of you do as you are told and we keep you safe till the trial, we are virtually guaranteed a conviction of this man and his many associates that we have wanted to nail for years. That has got to go in your favour.'

'So you are hopeful that there will be no charge?' Will asked, hardly daring to hope that he might be able just to walk away from this.

'Hopeful, but I can make no promises,' Norton said, and with that Will had to be content.

'Why don't you just go and arrest them all now?' Will asked Inspector Norton a few days later when he called at the camp to see him and Molly and check how they were.

'All in good time,' Norton said. 'And while you know your side of things, there is a big organisation involved here – big money and influence – and we want to catch them all in the one swoop. They are all under surveillance, but we can't risk moving too soon and alerting the others to disappear. Not only might we fail to take in the ringleaders, but your lives would then be in severe danger.'

399

Molly shivered and said, 'I want to get my life back on track as much as you do, Will, but I can't bear the thought of anyone involved in this business getting away with it, and to be honest I am fed up to the back teeth with looking over my shoulder every five minutes.'

'How is Kevin bearing up to it?' Norton asked.

'He is fine,' Molly said. 'I don't know what you said, but both he and the scoutmaster think that I am working undercover for something to do with the war effort, and in a way he is delighted to be associated in any capacity.'

'I didn't say that,' Norton said with a smile. 'I was just very vague and they assumed the rest.'

'Well, whatever you said it worked. Kevin is in this for as long as it takes. In fact, he's far more patient than I am.'

However, neither of them had to wait much longer because it was less than a week later that a jubilant inspector came and told them that the swoop had been successful and all the people had been apprehended, charged and were now in police custody. 'And, what's more, the girl is safe,' he said.

'I am glad of that,' Molly said. 'It's more than I hoped for. Can we tell people now? I don't mean put it over the public address system or anything, but there are people close to me, namely Daisy, who you will remember, and Lynne, who I was in hospital with, and Helen, her mother, who has been so kind to me. They know that I am hiding something from them and can't understand why.'

'I don't see that there should be any problem with that,' the inspector said. 'Tell them to keep it all under wraps for now, though.'

'You might even be able to get those letters written to Ireland,' Will commented when the policeman had gone.

'Maybe,' Molly answered shortly. 'But first things first.'

Molly came into the room with the tray of tea and looked at Daisy, Helen and Lynne, sitting together on the settee as if assembled at the end of a Miss Marple mystery. They were intrigued, not sure why Molly had summoned them, and Molly herself was terribly nervous, for she knew she had to tell them things she would rather not even think about.

But then she knew she soon would have to do that in a court of law and so she cleared her throat and said, 'I am sorry that I had to ask you here tonight, but I have something to say that might surprise, shock you even, something that concerns me. I have broken my silence now, partly because of this young girl here.' She took up the newspaper Will had given her, recounting the story of the missing schoolgirl, Christine Naylor.

'I remember that case,' Helen said. 'I remember feeling for her mother.'

'Christine has been found alive and well,' Molly said, 'but she might not have been and I might not have been either. I would like to tell you what happened to me when arrived at New Street Station in November two years ago.'

As she began her tale, a hush fell and the women and girl listened horrified to the terrifying things that had happened to Molly.

When she got to the incident with Collingsworth, how she had scuppered his plans and rendered him unconscious before tipping him down the stairs, Daisy burst out, 'Good for you, Molly.'

'I thought I had killed him, Daisy.'

'No loss if you had, I'd say.'

'No court in the land would agree with that.'

'They couldn't blame you, though,' Lynne said.

'They could, Lynne,' Molly said. 'He was a powerful and influential man. Take it from me, if I had succeeded in killing Collingsworth, I would have hanged for it.'

That shocked the women into silence again as Molly went on to describe Will Baker's intervention and then the way he had rescued her and hidden her as Collingsworth had issued a vendetta against her.

'So the attack . . .' Daisy began.

'Were thugs employed by Collingsworth, I would imagine, though I didn't really see their faces any more than you did,' Molly said. 'I didn't tell the police, because it would have implicated Will and his family. I'm sure you understand why I couldn't do that.'

'I do indeed,' Helen said. 'Do you know where this man is now?'

'That's just it,' Molly said. 'He is on the air base. When he was told I had been killed he was sickened and he applied to the army for a desk job, which they had already offered him after he was invalided out of active service following Dunkirk. To be recalled by the Forces was the only safe way to leave Collingsworth's employ. He was given a desk job at St George's barracks and just a few weeks ago he was seconded here. It was such a shock seeing him, I'll tell you.'

Helen smiled and remembered her son coming to see her to tell her that Molly had got someone special in her life after all.

Helen had looked at her son's doleful face. So that's it, she thought, he is sweet on her after all, and she had said, 'I don't think so. She would surely have told me.'

'Mother, she was hugging and kissing this man as if her life depended on it,' Mark had replied glumly. 'This is a girl that never lets a man anywhere near her. To tell you the truth, I was plucking up the courage to ask her out myself. Obviously I have dithered too long. Serves me bloody right, I suppose.'

Now the matter was cleared up Helen thought for she was certain that the man Mark had seen hugging Molly was this Will.

She was more certain of this when Molly went on, 'When Christine went missing and we knew that Ray and Charlie were involved with her disappearance because Will's wife saw them with the girl, we knew we had to go to the police and tell them what we knew.'

So this Will was married, Helen thought. That puts Molly right out of the frame, I would say, because she appears too honest to begin any sort of relationship with a married man.

'I know you don't want this shouted from the rooftops, as it were,' Helen said, 'but would you mind awfully if I was to tell Mark?'

Yes, Molly did mind. She particularly didn't want the one man she cared so much about to hear what had happened to her, dreaded to see the disgust in his eyes. However, she knew she couldn't protect him from any of it. Inspector Norton said that the trial would be too big to hope to keep it from the papers, and Molly knew they could put any slant they liked on it. Far better, surely, to hear it from Helen.

So she said, 'Tell him by all means, if you want to. After all, it will be public knowledge before long.'

'So what comes next?' Daisy asked.

'A trial to see if we can get them locked up for a good long time, with Will and I as witnesses.'

'Oh, my dear! Won't you be terribly scared?'

'No, Helen,' said Molly. 'I will be bloody terrified, but it is something that has to be done.'

TWENTY-SEVEN

The trial was set for Friday 6 November. Molly was surprised at the speed, for in her limited experience anything to do with legal matters went ponderously slowly. When she said this to Inspector Norton, however, he said that though that was usually the case, in this instance they had been collecting data on Collingsworth and his nefarious dealings and those who worked for him for some time. Speed was also essential, he went on to say, when the safety of the witnesses was at stake.

Molly knew she had to tell Kevin something, but in view of his age, she thought there was plenty of time for him to learn about prostitutes and drugs, and so the version she told him was extremely potted, saying only that she arrived in the middle of an air raid and let him assume that it had been one of the raids in the early part of 1941. She went on to say that she had accepted the offer of accommodation from two strangers who had been so kind to her in the air raid. However, she soon realised they were not good men at all and were up to all sorts of illegal things, and so she had left them and gone to stay with Will's mother-in-law, just before she had set out to look for him.

Kevin, however, was no fool. He said, 'Was all this anything to do with why you were attacked?'

Molly nodded. 'Yes. But I really didn't see their faces in the blackout, so I would never be able to identify them.

There seemed little point then in telling the police. I was sort of hiding out at the hotel because I knew they hadn't wanted me to leave, because they were afraid I would go to the police, but I could never do that, because it might have implicated Will and his family.'

Kevin remembered the quietly spoken man who had come to Sunday lunch a few weeks before, and his wife and mother-in-law and the little baby.

Molly went on, 'See, Kevin, these people don't operate under the same rules as everyone else. They tend to take the law into their own hands as they did with me, and I couldn't risk any harm coming to the people who had taken a risk to help me. Do you see what I mean?'

'Course,' Kevin said. 'We have a few bullies at our school who go on like that. They leave me alone, like, but I have seen them in action. But the men who hurt you, the police know who they are now?'

'That's right,' Molly said. 'That's why I have to go to court.'

'That's why I was sent to live with the scoutmaster, wasn't it?'

'That's right,' Molly said. 'And I wasn't able tell you or anyone until all the men had been arrested in case word slipped out and they were alerted in some way.'

Molly was glad Kevin seemed satisfied with her answer, but she knew those in Ireland wouldn't be so easy to fob off. She wondered if Will was right, and they thought her dead. She was glad they now would know she wasn't, though in her bleaker moments she did wonder if they would prefer her to be dead to behaving in the depraved way she had.

Because Molly hadn't been in touch with those in Ireland, she wasn't aware that Hilda Mason was not dead. In fact, just a few months after Molly had arrived in Birmingham, Hilda had recovered sufficiently from the heart attack to be allowed home, and she joined her husband at her daughter's place in Perry Common. Shopping in nearby Erdington

405

Village, she met Nancy Hewitt, who had no idea Hilda had survived. Nancy told Hilda that Molly Maguire came a few days before, enquiring about her grandfather and Kevin.

Hilda's mouth dropped open. 'Are you sure it was Molly?' she asked.

'Course I am,' Nancy said. 'D'you think I wouldn't know Molly? I tell you, she was here, large as life. She hadn't changed that much, and for all she is older, she isn't much bigger, and proper cut up about the old man and then finding that Kevin had had to be sent to an orphanage. I told her what I knew, and that Kevin was likely to be sent to Erdington Cottage Homes, if they had room for him, and she said she would try to find him there first, but I haven't seen hide nor hair of her since.'

And neither had Hilda, although she had searched high and low. The superintendent at Erdington Cottage Homes wouldn't even tell her whether they had a Kevin Maguire on their books, never mind let her see him, as she could claim to be no blood relation. She had the same response from the Josiah Mason's Orphanage on Orphanage Road, and the Princess Alice Home at the end of Jockey Road in Sutton Coldfield.

In the end, feeling that perhaps Molly had taken the child back to Ireland, Hilda had contacted Tom and Nellie to ask for information, and was horrified to learn Molly had not been in touch with them at all. Those in Ireland were pleased that she had not been killed in the raids as they had thought, but that had been a while ago and there had been raids aplenty after February 1941 that she could have been caught in, because it was as if Molly and Kevin had disappeared into thin air.

Tom was absolutely bowled over when he was hailed by an excited Nellie when he went into the post office on 31 October. 'Tom, I received a letter today from Molly, and so did Cathy.'

The shock was so great, Tom's mouth dropped open and

the blood drained from his face as he breathed, 'Ah, glory be to God.'

'Don't be so quick thanking the Almighty,' Nellie said. 'Our little Molly has been through the mill, if you ask me.'

'Why? What's happened to her?'

'You'd had better read it for yourself,' Nellie said. 'It's what she doesn't say that is so worrying.'

Tom agreed, for there were large gaps in his letter too. Molly said she was sorry for not getting in touch sooner, but gave no explanation as to why that was. She merely told them how her grandfather had died, and that she had found Kevin in an orphanage. Though she didn't go into details, she did say that he was now living with her.

'Whatever happened to her that she is not telling us about?' Tom asked Nellie.

'Heaven knows,' Nellie said. 'She said a little more in Cathy's letter, and to be frank, Tom, I am that worried about her.'

'Well, we can't write back and ask her anything because she didn't include her address on the letter,' Tom said. 'I need to go over there and see for myself she is all right. Shame about the grandfather dying and all, for all she semi-expected the news would not be good. She was right fond of that old man.'

'Aye, and that brother of hers,' Nellie said. 'I bet it cut her to the quick, finding he had been put into an orphanage.'

'Aye,' Tom said sadly. 'No alternative, I suppose. It's grand that they are together again at last, but I will not rest easy till I find them and see that they are all right.'

'What about the farm?' Nellie asked. 'Is Joe able for it yet?'

'Aye,' Tom said, for Joe had been badly injured in a raid in London and had brought his family to live on the farm until he should recover fully. 'He is almost fighting fit again now. That son of his, Ben, is no slouch either, for all he is not nine years old until next year.'

407

'Aye, he is a fine wee boy, all right.'

'It isn't Joe holding me up. It's Mammy.'

'How is she?' Nellie felt bound to ask.

Tom shook his head. 'Not good!' he said. 'The doctor said that it is a matter of weeks. Before Christmas, anyway. And bad as she is, I can't leave her now. When it is all over and I see her decently buried, I will be off.'

'But where will you go?' Nellie asked.

'I have that Hilda's new address, haven't I?'

'Yes, but think about it, Tom. She is Birmingham born and bred, and she couldn't find Molly either, don't forget. That is why she wrote that time, to see if we had any information.'

'Aye, well, maybe the two of us will have better success,' Tom said. 'And she might at least know a place I can stay for a wee while. We have Kevin to find as well. That might make it easier, for the child must go to school someplace.'

'Tom, have you any idea the number of schools there probably are in Birmingham?' Nellie asked him. 'It isn't a bit like Buncrana, you know.'

Nellie thought he was heading for further heartache and yet she knew too that neither she nor anyone else would be able to dissuade him.

Tom confirmed this when he said, 'Nellie, I know you mean well but I need to see Molly and Kevin with my own two eyes.'

'All right,' Nellie said. 'I see you are determined on this course of action and I will say no more about it, but if you let me have that old neighbour's new address, I will write to her today and get it away with the post.'

'How are you getting to the court?' Helen asked Molly.

'The police are collecting both Will and myself – insisting on it, in fact. Inspector Norton said it wouldn't be the first time a witness was nobbled on their way to court and he doesn't want that happening to us.' She shook her head, then went on, 'It's all alien stuff to me. Inspector Norton has been very good, finding us a solicitor and all, and warning us of the type of questions that the other side might throw at us. It was harder for Will, of course, because he was worried that he might lose his job, or even be imprisoned, and he only found out last week that neither is going to happen.'

'It must have been a terrific load off his mind.'

'It was,' Molly said. 'And he was able to write and reassure Betty, who must have been worried herself, though she never nagged Will about it or anything. She is a lovely person and so proud of Will doing the right thing that nothing else seems to matter. Will misses her something awful, but he can write and tell her to come back now. After all, Kevin came back home a week ago. Will was just more cautious and would never allow them back while there might be the slightest risk.'

Molly was extremely fond of Will and they had drawn closer together as they were both filled with dread at the ordeal before them. She had never been attracted to him sexually, however, and wasn't now, and so she tried to ignore the pointed nudges made in her direction, though no one openly said anything to her that she could refute.

Helen, knowing how her own son had misconstrued things, said to Molly, 'I bet many people think he is your fancy piece.'

'Oh, I am a complete *femme fatale*, don't you know?' Molly said with a smile. 'After all, there is me canoodling with Will all the day long and him a married man and all, and then until recently another man had been walking me to and from work each day, and he used to stay the night. The neighbours, I know, assumed he was my boyfriend and it was safer for me not to deny that. They thought it scandalous, of course. I heard them talking about it when I was filling a bucket of coal from the bunker before work. I was intended to hear. My neighbours either side were shouting to one another about how morality has gone to the wall since the war, and then one said she can't abide this practice of living together. Disgusting, she called it, and the other agreed and said it was worse when there was a child involved, seeing all this laxity.'

'Oh, my dear,' Helen said with sympathy. 'What did you do?'

'Oh,' said Molly with a grin, 'I wished them both good morning and took myself and the coal bucket back to the house.'

'Don't you mind?'

'Do you know, I don't,' Molly said. 'However, I will mind very much getting up and telling perfect strangers about my behaviour and letting them judge me.'

'You are not the one on trial, Molly.'

'And you know as well as I do that regardless who is in the dock, I will be judged as harshly, maybe more harshly, than them, especially as Inspector Norton says their prosecution will go all-out to prove what a harlot I am underneath. Set against that, what does it matter if workmates and neighbours have got the wrong end of the stick?'

'Yes,' Helen said. 'I understand exactly what you mean.'

Inspector Norton knew how Molly and Will were feeling. He hadn't been joking either when he talked about a witness being got at in one way or another on his way to court because he knew that if there was some person on the loose who didn't want Molly and Will to testify, then this was their last chance to see that didn't happen. So, early that morning, because they were on the stand first, he came to accompany them in the back of a squad car while another officer sat beside the driver in the front.

Molly watched the neighbours' curtains twitch as she walked down the path to squeeze into the back of the car, followed by Inspector Norton. She knew the neighbours would note the heavy police presence and probably conclude that she was a hardened criminal, a mass murderer at least.

But she refused to think of them and instead tried to concentrate on what Inspector Norton was saying to them both.

'Tell the plain truth,' he said. 'Just as you did to me that day when you first came into my office. Imagine that you are there doing the same thing again, for the way you spoke that day will stay with me for a long time. Sometimes,' he warned, 'you might be interrupted and sometimes the other barrister will try and cast doubt on your evidence. If that happens, keep calm, answer any question asked and reaffirm what you said before.'

Molly was remembering that as the car drew up before the large red-brick courthouse in Corporation Street, and she looked at the huge flight of steps leading up to it and shivered. She was so pleased that Helen, Lynne and Daisy had come to give her moral support, though she could hardly bear to meet Mark's eyes, terrified that she would see the revulsion in them.

He so wanted to lift her head and tell her how he felt about her, but it was neither the time nor the place, and anyway, the solicitor was by her side now.

The hardest thing was facing the people grouped in the dock: Edwin Collingsworth, Raymond Morris, Charles Johnson and two heavy-set men she had never seen before. It took every inch of courage to stand before them and take the oath. Her barrister told her first to tell the tale in her own words and Molly nodded and, fixing her eyes on a point above the wall just above the jurors' heads, she began.

All in the courtroom heard of a young life that had already tasted so much tragedy and then of the men that had befriended her at New Street Station, and all she had suffered under their hands and that of others involved. Sometimes she faltered, as if almost afraid to go on, and once she stopped altogether, consumed by shame for the words she had to say. Tears welled in her eyes and trickled down her cheeks. However, when the judge asked her if she wanted an adjournment to compose herself, she shook her head. She was offered a glass of water, which she sipped gratefully, and then she reminded herself why she was there and continued her account in a low voice, full of pain and anguish.

Even in the throes of war that had claimed many lives and much heartache, Molly's tale seemed particularly poignant, and all were affected by it. Many of the women on the jury dabbed at their eyes. As for Mark, although his mother had told him everything, his heart ached to hear from Molly's own lips how she had suffered.

He realised too in that moment that he loved her before any other, and quite understood why she had refused to get involved with men. An experience like that could put many off men for life, but he somehow knew that wouldn't be the case with Molly. She had such strength of character, and he would be ready and willing to wait until she was ready.

All their friends congratulated Molly and Will warmly afterwards, and Mark shook Will by the hand, and said he had seldom seen a braver man. As for Molly, he wanted to take her away somewhere quiet and show her how much he loved her, but Molly was surrounded by people. He envied his mother, sister and Daisy, who could hug Molly with such ease, but he knew she would pull away if he tried, though he would give his eyeteeth for the chance to hold her in his arms.

'You were both sensational,' Norton said as the car took them away from the city. 'God, we've waited for this opportunity for years. We'll really nail the bastards now.'

'When will sentence be passed?' Will asked.

'Not for some time,' Norton said. 'They are both wanted for a whole heap of other crimes – murder, drug-running, robbery . . . the list is endless. Saying that, though, we should have the whole thing wrapped up well before Christmas, but for you the ordeal is over. Put it behind you.'

412

'If it wasn't for Hitler,' said Will, 'I would say the future looks rosy.'

'Don't worry about Hitler,' Norton said. 'He's just a bit player and we will soon kick him into touch.'

They were laughing as they neared Molly's house and she saw the curtains twitching again.

'Wonder what they make of this now,' she said. 'You have obviously released me and I have returned laughing my head off. Goodness, it will keep them going for weeks.'

Norton smiled. 'Everyone will likely know all about it soon enough.'

The inspector was right, as Molly found out a good few hours later when a furious Kevin came home, waving the *Evening Mail*.

'Read that,' he said, thrusting it in front of her.

Molly's horrified eyes saw a picture of her and Will, and a full account of what she had said in court.

'Bet you're in the *Despatch* too,' Kevin commented morosely, 'and you treated me like I was five years old again and only told me half of what had happened to you.'

'I was only trying to protect you, Kevin,' Molly said.

'Oh, yeah, it protected me all right,' Kevin said sarcastically. 'Reading about what happened to my own sister in the bloody newspaper and in front of all my mates was real protection.'

'All right then,' Molly burst out angrily. 'You want the truth so you will have it. I was ashamed – yes, bloody ashamed – and for myself I would rather have gone and hid my head in the sand than put myself through what I did today. I took no pleasure in it at all. I only did it to stop other girls going down the same road. As you are such a reader of newspapers, maybe you will remember the case of Christine Naylor, who left home after a row and virtually disappeared.'

'I think so.'

'Well, the people who are in prison now had her too,'

Molly said. 'That was the real spur that made me go ahead. She wasn't even fifteen, younger than Helen's daughter, Lynne, and for her sake and to keep others safe from the depraved clutches of those men, I spoke out today. If you are going to be all sniffy and narky with me for not telling you all this sordid stuff, you must get over it on your own. I've had about as much as I can take today.'

Before Kevin had time to answer this, there was a knock at the door. Curiously and a little cautiously, for they had few visitors, Molly went to open it. Mark stood the other side with a parcel wrapped in newspaper under one arm.

'Mark,' Molly said in surprise, really pleased to see him. 'Come in.'

Mark's heart had leaped at the smile in Molly's eyes, and as he stepped into the hall he said, 'I came to see how you are feeling now. Then, as I passed the fish-and-chip shop on the Chester Road, there was a queue forming and a woman told me there was word that there was some fish in, so I joined on the end. I thought I would be queuing until tomorrow morning, but I got to the counter in the end and I have three portions of fish and chips here. Could you and Kevin do it justice?'

Molly's mouth watered and she realised she hadn't eaten all day, she had just existed on cups of tea.

'Thank you, Mark,' she said. 'That will be just the job, and a sight better than the whale meat I got last week. I'll get the plates. Maybe you can go in there and talk some sense into Kevin, who is sulking because I didn't tell him the whole story and he had to read it in the newspapers.'

However, before either of them could move, Kevin came into the hall, tears streaming down his face. Molly hadn't seen her young brother cry since the time she had arrived at the Cottage Homes for the first time, and she wrapped her two arms around him.

'I'm sorry, really sorry,' he said, his voice thick with unshed tears. 'I should never have said those things to you. It was just that . . . well, you always said that we were in this together and I felt that you were shutting me out. When I read all about what you went through and that, I was bloody scared at what might have happened to you.'

Molly held Kevin away from her so that she could look in his eyes and said, 'Listen to me, Kevin. I promise you here and now that I will never ever keep things from you. You are growing up and I need to recognise that. Is that OK?'

Kevin's grin was a bit wobbly, but his voice was firm. 'OK.'

'Just two more things,' Molly said.

'What?'

'The first is, if you keep swearing, young man, I will wash your mouth out with carbolic,' Molly said.

Kevin had a fleeting memory of his mother threatening his father with the same thing, though he himself had been very small at the time, and he smiled and said in a singsong voice, 'OK, OK. What's the second?'

'The second,' said Molly, 'is that from the sounds and smells coming from the kitchen, the fish and chips Mark brought are on the plates and ready to eat.'

'Oh boy!' Kevin cried, for shop-bought fish and chips was a real treat.

'How hungry are you?' Molly asked.

'Are you kidding?' Kevin cried. 'For fish and chips I'm starving,' and then with a sideward glance at Molly and a grin he said, 'Absolutely bloody ravenous, in fact.'

Molly cuffed him over the side of the head playfully as he passed and they entered the kitchen laughing.

Mark's heart nearly stopped beating as he saw Molly, her face alight with laughter, a Molly he hadn't really seen, he realised, for this was a Molly released from tension and fear and the Molly he knew he would love until the breath left his body. However, he betrayed none of this. Instead he threw the tea towel over his arm to resemble a waiter, gave a bow and said, 'If madam and the young master are ready now, dinner is served.'

'Thank you,' Molly said, sitting down in the chair he pulled out for her. 'Won't you join us?'

'Don't mind if I do,' said Mark. And the three sat and ate together, talking and chatting and laughing, completely comfortable with each other at last.

Kevin was not the only one to see Molly's picture in the paper and hear the account of what had happened to her. So also did Hilda Mason. Just that day she had received the letter from Nellie saying that Molly had been in touch.

> We were grateful to get the letter, though it makes
> grim reading. I am enclosing it for you so you may see
> it for yourself. We feel so helpless over here, and Tom
> is bound to the farm just now, for his mother is dying
> and he doesn't want to leave her until the end . . .

Hilda read Molly's letter and was disturbed by it. Then that same evening she unfolded the *Evening Mail* and saw Molly's picture on the front page, and read her account of what had happened to her. Hilda's mouth dropped open. She realised what a watered-down version she had given to those in Ireland and knew that she had to go and see the girl.

Molly's address wasn't printed in the paper, but in her account she said she worked in the Naafi at the RAF base at Castle Bromwich. The very next morning Hilda decided she would go out to the place and see if she could see the girl, if only for a few minutes.

Paul Simmons was another who read the paper in open-mouthed astonishment. It put him in such a rage he attacked Tom in a blistering letter, which Tom opened in the cowshed.

416

What in God's name were you doing letting Molly, a young and defenceless girl, go alone to Birmingham, a city that has been bombed to blazes? Your irresponsibility in this matter beggars belief. When your mother took on guardianship of Molly, I consoled myself that at least the child would be cared for adequately and now I find you have failed in that duty too. You are an absolute disgrace and I would be surprised if you could sleep in your bed at night.

And just in case you think I am overreacting and possibly Molly has not kept you up to date, I am sending you the cuttings of the trial. There were reports in the *Despatch* and the *Evening Mail*, which you can read for yourself, while I shall make arrangements to contact Molly without delay.

Tom read all the cuttings and then, unable to believe it, read them again. He imagined Molly standing there, having to say these things, his little Molly, who would never harm a fly, and for these dreadful things to happen to her.

He didn't blame Paul Simmons for the tone of his letter; Tom felt he deserved that and more. He had failed Molly, and failed her badly, and he was still failing her. He sank back onto the milking stool, put his head in his hands and sobbed.

He couldn't even seek Molly out either, while his mother chose to cling to life.

The doctor was baffled at Biddy's resilience. 'I would have said she wouldn't have lasted so long,' he'd confided just the other day. 'She might go on till after Christmas at this rate.'

Tom wondered why she didn't just die and get it over with. Despite her age, her eyes were as bitter and malicious as ever and her voice as recriminatory. It was Gloria that she really seemed to have it in for, whom she was really vicious with. She had no patience with the boy, Ben, either and would scream at him constantly and often administer the odd sharp slap, for all Joe remonstrated with her.

Tom knew that much as he wanted to drop everything and run to his young niece's side, he would be unlikely to be able to leave the farm until at least the New Year.

TWENTY-EIGHT

The next morning Molly knew from people's reactions that many had read the papers. Her neighbours, for example, greeted her quite pleasantly, though this was done in a patronising way and using a conciliatory tone, as if she had just recovered from a long illness, or was mentally defective, and Molly was left wondering if their previous silences hadn't been preferable.

Many greeted Molly in the camp, but that was normal, and the consensus of her friends in the Naafi seemed to be that she was incredibly brave and it was disgraceful that such things happened in this day and age.

Molly didn't want to rehash the whole thing again. She had done all the talking she wanted to do in the courtroom; she just said she was glad it was over and she could get on with her life. In fact, what was filling Molly's mind at that moment was her feelings about Mark, for she could no longer deny the attraction she had felt for him and yet the thought of any man touching her still filled her with abhorrence. She didn't know what to do about that.

While she was still wondering, one of the guards from the gate tapped her on the shoulder. 'Woman at the gate asking for you,' he said. 'It's strictly against orders but I can let you have a few minutes.'

Molly frowned. 'But who is she?'

'She says her name is Hilda Mason.'

419

'Hilda!' Molly shrieked. 'Are you sure?'

'That's what she said.'

'Oh, Almighty Christ, she's alive,' Molly cried. She put her hands to her face and wiped away the tears that had seeped unbidden from her eyes. 'I can't believe it.'

'I take it you want to see her then,' the guard said.

'You bet I do,' Molly said, tearing off her overall as she spoke. 'I mean that's if . . .' and she looked to the others.

'Go on,' said Edna. 'Good friend of yours, by the sound of it.'

'Our neighbour. She was like a second mother,' Molly said, sticking her feet into her boots and struggling into her coat as she hurried after the guard.

Hilda was shabbily dressed in a shapeless grey coat and scuffed boots, a scarf covering her grey hair, but to Molly she looked beautiful and she waited impatiently for the guard to open the gate. Then she was in Hilda's arms with a sigh of contentment.

'God, girl, but you are a sight for sore eyes,' Hilda said, wiping her damp cheeks.

'And you,' Molly said. 'The neighbour said you were dead, or said she thought you were dead. I didn't think I would ever see you again. This is wonderful, just wonderful, and we have so much to say and no time to say it because I can only take a little time. They are rushed off their feet in there.'

'What time do you finish?'

'Five tonight,' Molly said. 'But I live close at hand.' She gave Hilda directions to her house.

'Right, bab,' Hilda said, giving Molly a kiss. 'I will up this evening and we'll have a proper old chinwag.'

It was as Hilda was walking away that she passed the well-dressed man walking towards the air base. His face was familiar but she didn't realise who he was straight away.

'Mr Simmons,' she said suddenly.

Paul turned and looked at Hilda quizzically and she knew

that he didn't recognise her. 'Hilda Mason,' she said, extending her hand. 'Neighbour to the Maguires.'

'Of course,' Paul said. 'I'm sorry.'

'No need to be,' Hilda said. 'Why would you remember me? Are you hoping to see Molly?'

'Yes, if it's possible.'

'Not a chance, I would say,' Hilda said. 'But I have her address and I am going there this evening when she finishes her shift. Why don't you come too?'

'That's a very good idea,' Paul said with a smile. 'And you can give me the address while you share my taxi for the journey home,' Paul said. 'How does that suit?'

'It suits very well,' Hilda said with a chuckle. 'And now I know why Ted Maguire said you were always a true gentleman.'

To say that Molly was surprised to see Paul Simmons with Hilda at her door later that evening would be untrue, for she was much more than surprised: totally amazed, in fact. She hadn't thought of Mr Simmons in years and Kevin could never remember seeing him at all.

However, Paul soon put them at their ease, and when Molly confessed that she still felt shame about the whole Collingsworth episode, he took hold of her agitated hands.

'Listen to me, Molly,' he said. 'If you believe nothing else in your life, believe this: you were not to blame, not in the slightest, and never forget that.'

'It's just that—'

'Enough,' Paul said firmly. 'The perpetrators of this business are base and corrupt, and totally without either morals or a conscience. If it hadn't been for the courage of that other chap, Will, you could have easily lost your life. I would very much like to meet him and shake him by the hand, and when this little lot is over, there will be a place for him in my firm if he wants it.'

'I'm sure he will be delighted,' Molly told the man. 'You

are as good and kind as my father always said. I am sure that I can arrange a meeting with Will if you want one, but as for me . . . do you know, they don't even know in Ireland? I couldn't bring myself to tell them everything.'

'Well, that uncle of yours knows now,' Paul said. 'I sent him the cuttings from the newspaper, along with a letter. I'm still so angry with him. I can't believe he let you come on your own.'

'He couldn't have prevented me,' Molly said emphatically. 'There wasn't a person living who could have done that, more especially after the cryptic note from Kevin asking me to come and get him.' She faced Paul and said, 'What would you have me do, Mr Simmons? I know I couldn't have taken any other action than the one I did and it is my fault it turned out badly. No blame here can be attached to my uncle, who had a farm to run and a crabbed old woman to see to, and I will write and tell him so – Nellie and Cathy too, because if my uncle has told anyone, then it will be them.'

'I'm sorry,' Paul said. 'I see now that you had no other course open to you and—'

There was another knock at the door and Molly said, 'Well, I don't know who that is, but I had better see to it. Can you talk to Kevin? He doesn't remember you at all and maybe you can tell him about Dad. I'm sure he would like that, because he can't remember everything. That terrible day blotted a lot out for him.'

'I'll do that with pleasure,' Paul said. Molly watched him make his way over to the young boy, who was chattering nineteen to the dozen with Hilda.

It was Will at the door. Molly was surprised to see him, for he didn't make a habit of visiting her in the evening.

She drew him into the hall, out of the bleak winter's night as she said, 'There's someone here wants to see you, shake you by the hand, in fact. Anyway, take off your coat or you will not feel the benefit later.'

422

'Who wants to shake my hand?' Will said, doing as Molly bade him. 'I'm not averse to a little commendation now and again.'

'Bighead,' Molly teased with a smile. 'The man in question is my father's ex-employer, Paul Simmons, and I think I told you how good he has been to us all.' Will nodded and Molly went on, 'He told me that he may have a job to offer you after the war.'

'Did he?' Will said. 'I would be interested in that.'

'Right,' Molly said. 'But since you didn't know there were people in my house waiting to tell you how marvellous you are and offer you employment, what are you doing here?'

Will smiled, 'Well,' he said, 'as I didn't see you at the Naafi today, I came to tell you that I am leaving at the weekend because the other chap will be back.'

'Oh, it will be strange not seeing you around the place.'

'We were a good team, Molly,' Will said, 'better than you think. Norton came today and said numerous people are coming forward now and saying things against Collingsworth and his cronies. He came to see if I had any information on some of the claims people are making and I was able to help him a bit. He said all of Collingsworth's lot are looking at hefty prison sentences.'

Yet another knock at the door caused Molly to raise her eyes to the ceiling. 'Go in and see Paul,' she said to Will. 'He is dying to meet you.'

This time Mark stood outside the door. Molly willed her voice not to shake as she said, 'Come in.'

'I came to see if you were all right.'

'You did that yesterday,' Molly said with a smile, hoping he was unaware of her heart thudding against her ribs. 'No fish and chips tonight?'

''Fraid not.'

'Never mind. Come on in and join the party.'

Paul and Will were dispatched for beer, though Molly intended to stick to tea and ensure that Kevin did the same, and it was as she was making the tea that Hilda caught up with her and, being Hilda, got straight to the point.

'Who's Mark?'

'Just a friend, like I said when I introduced him.'

'My eye he's just a friend. I wasn't born yesterday, you know.'

'Honestly, that's all he is,' Molly said. 'I was with his young sister in the hospital and, with visiting and all, I got to know her mother, Helen, and her brother, Mark.'

'Maybe all that is true,' Hilda said, 'but I am telling you that that young man is eating his heart out for you. Don't you feel the same?'

'I don't know,' Molly cried. 'No, I am kidding myself. I feel something deeply for Mark. I don't know if it is love. How does anyone know?'

'Well, how does he make you feel?'

Molly thought for a moment and then said, 'When I opened the door to him tonight I trembled all over and my heart was going ten to the dozen. It was hard to act naturally. Sometimes,' she admitted, 'when I look at him, my legs feel as if they are made of water. Does that sound like love, Hilda?'

'I'd say so,' Hilda said with a chuckle. 'And a bad attack of it too. So what are you going to do about it?'

Molly shrugged and Hilda burst out, 'What's up with you, girl? He's a fine young man.'

'I know.'

'Then what's the problem? He ain't got a wife tucked away somewhere?'

'No,' Molly said with a smile.

'Well then, is he a nancy boy?'

'No, definitely not.'

'Come on, girl, help me out,' Hilda cried. 'There you are, two young unattached people and he loves you and you love him, so what in God's name *is* the problem?'

Molly struggled with herself because she had never told anyone the revulsion she felt when a man tried to become

424

even slightly physical, but eventually she confessed, 'The problem is me, I can't let a man touch me in that way.'

'What way?'

'You know.'

'Tell him how you feel, ducks,' Hilda advised. 'He looks the understanding sort.'

'I can't, Hilda,' Molly said. 'However understanding he is, he will want to do more than hold hands eventually. I mean, I could manage that, but anything else reminds me of Collingsworth and that awful, dreadful night.'

'I can't believe this. You are letting that louse of a man pollute the rest of your life.'

'Maybe I am, but how can I do that to Mark?' Molly cried. 'What if I was never able to let him near me? I care for him too much to do that to him. It would be better if he found another girl who could show her love properly.'

'Shouldn't I be the judge of that?' said a voice from the doorway.

Molly spun around. 'Mark,' she breathed, 'you heard?'

He was across the room in two strides. 'I want no other girl,' he said. 'I only want you. I heard you say that you care for me. Is it true?'

'Oh, yes, Mark, it's true.'

'D'you think you could love me?'

Molly hesitated, then slowly nodded. 'I think I could, but it wouldn't be fair. You see . . .'

'Oh, darling, I love you, heart, body and soul,' Mark told her. 'I think I have from the first moment I saw you. I know why you have been so reticent with men and quite understand it. Never fear me, for I will never ask you to go further than you want to, or at a faster pace.'

That was so exactly what Hilda had said that she looked back to find the room empty except for the two of them. 'When did Hilda leave?'

'I don't know,' Mark said, 'but maybe she thought we needed time on our own.'

425

'Hilda,' said Molly, 'was always a very wise woman.'

She gazed in this new realisation that she really and truly loved Mark and she was filled with the newness and the joy of it. Carried away with emotion she suddenly said. 'You can put your arms around me, if you like.'

'Are you sure?'

Molly was anything but sure, but she wanted to please Mark and so she nodded anyway and waited to feel her body tense up and the bile rise in her mouth, as Mark's arms encircled her. But nothing happened, and in fact it felt quite wonderful. She sighed and laid her head on Mark's chest and he felt her heart beat and tentatively held her tighter.

'Oh, Mark,' she said in utter contentment and just the way Molly spoke his name made Mark's heart beat faster

It was evident that something of major importance had happened in the kitchen between Mark and Molly as they came out hand in hand and slightly embarrassed. Hilda smiled her approval and Kevin looked them both up and down and then his eyes slid to Hilda's beaming face and then back to Molly and he said, 'You two going out, dating, like?'

'We will be,' Molly said. 'Will you mind?'

'Are you kidding?' Kevin said. 'It will be great having a pilot in the family, and when you get married—'

'Hey,' Molly protested, 'who said anything about getting married?'

'No one,' Kevin admitted cheerfully. 'But you will in the end, won't you? Otherwise what's the point of it all? All I wanted to know is, where am I going to live after?'

'I think that is quite a reasonable question,' Hilda said.

Molly did too. It was obvious Kevin might be anxious about that. 'With me,' she said determinedly. 'Wherever that happens to be.' And she saw her brother's shoulders relax with relief.

*   *   *

426

The news flew around the camp of the courtship of Mark Baxter and Molly Maguire, and it got the seal of approval there too.

'At least he's a free agent,' May said in relief. 'I did think she might have fancied the other fellow, for all she claimed he was just a friend.'

'No, she's too sensible a lass,' Edna replied.

'Sense has little to do with it when a girl fancies herself in love,' Doris commented.

Edna gave a chuckle. 'I can just remember feeling like that myself,' she said, 'and you are right, sense, and everything else to come to that, does go out of the window.'

'Aye, and faster than the speed of light too,' May agreed.

Molly was glad her friends were pleased, but she worried over Helen's possible reaction, knowing that many mothers resented their son's girlfriends. However, Helen kissed Molly and told her that all she desired for both her children was happiness. She admitted she had known how Mark felt about her for some time anyway, and Lynne said she hoped Molly joined the family because she would love a sister.

Molly wrote to her uncle, telling him he had not to blame himself for her decision to return to Birmingham, and explaining about Mark Baxter. She also wrote to Nellie and Jack, and a separate long letter to Cathy, opening up her heart to tell her about her feelings for Mark. Cathy replied by return confessing her love for one of the soldiers in Buncrana and as she wrote just as if she was in the same room, Molly realised how much she had missed her, missed them all and longed to see them all again.

In early December, Biddy Sullivan, in the throes of one of her famous tantrums, suffered a stroke and Tom wrote to tell Molly.

It is a bad one, the doctor said, and he confessed to me that he has been expecting something like this for years.

427

At the moment she has virtually no movement below her neck and she cannot speak. He said it is impossible to say whether further movement will return or not, and advised us to keep her warm and comfortable and pray the situation does not go on indefinitely.

I certainly hope it doesn't because most of the care of her falls to Gloria, although Gloria finds it easier to see to someone who was not yelling at her or slapping out. In fact, the old place is quite quiet now.

It is quite sad, I suppose, though she only has herself to blame and no one seems to feel sorry for Mammy. The general feeling is that she has got her just deserts and only the doctor and priest still visit. But still she clings to life, and though Gloria says Mammy is often in pain, she refuses to take the doctor's medication.

We are all just waiting for her to die.

Molly could feel no pity for her grandmother. Like the neighbours, she thought Biddy had brought her illness upon herself with her ill temper, and was reaping her just deserts now for what she had put Molly through. When she told Mark just some of the ways she had suffered at her grandmother's hands he quite understood.

Their courtship was well established now, and they saw each other as often as their shifts allowed. Sometimes Kevin went out with them, for Mark knew how close he and Molly were and, anyway, he liked the boy and got on well with him.

But whether Kevin was with them or not, their lovemaking had never gone past holding hands, and occasionally a chaste kiss on the cheek.

Biddy died in agony at the very end of January.

'Will you go over for the funeral?' Mark asked when Molly told him of the telegram that had arrived that morning.

'I will not,' Molly said adamantly.

428

'Oh, but surely—'

'No, Mark,' Molly said. 'The only reason I would go to the funeral is to dance on that foul woman's grave and I would never shame the family by doing that. I am pleased that my uncle can now come and see me, but just at the moment I am looking forward to seeing the film *Casablanca*.'

Mark knew that was Molly's way of saying that the subject was closed and he had no wish to fight with her.

Tom had hoped to come over for Molly's twenty-first birthday, but he had been delayed and Mark told her not to fret about it, that he had a treat for her. It was a wonderful day from the start, for there were a wealth of cards on the mat when she got up, including ones from Nellie and Jack and Cathy. Tom had sent a card and she even had one from her Uncle Joe, whom she had never seen, signed, 'With love from your Uncle Joe, Aunt Gloria and your cousin Ben'. There were also cards from Daisy and Martin, Helen, Lynne, Will and Betty and even Terry. When she reached the Naafi it was to find everyone had cards and presents for her, and she left later laden down with flowers. Kevin had given her a beautiful brooch, which she wore on her coat when she went to meet Mark that night to see the musical *South Pacific*.

Over a pre-theatre dinner at the Grand Hotel, one of the few buildings left standing in Colmore Row, Mark presented her with a watch with a golden strap. It was so beautiful she was rendered speechless for a while and she so wished she could have thrown her arms around Mark and shown her gratitude properly.

'It's beautiful, Mark, truly beautiful,' she gasped eventually. 'I never had anything half as fine. You are spoiling me.'

'You deserve to be spoiled,' Mark said and he reached across the table, took her hand and, looking deep in her eyes, said, 'it is the only way I have to show you how much I love you.'

Molly's stomach did a somersault. 'I love you too, Mark,'

she said, speaking the words aloud for the first time. Mark's spirits soared as she went on, 'There aren't enough words to tell you how much I truly love you. But I can't . . . you know what I mean. I'm sorry that . . .'

Mark stopped Molly's stumbling apology as he said, 'Hush. Don't be sorry about anything, and certainly not on your birthday. You love me and I love you, and that is all that matters.' He kissed the tips of Molly's fingers, sending a delicious thrill all through her body. 'You'll see,' he said. 'Everything else will fall into place in time.'

TWENTY-NINE

Mark was on three weeks of night ops. Now that Molly had actually admitted her love for him, it was harder not to be filled with fear every night as she heard the planes taking off. How well now she understood Helen's fears.

'You will learn to live with it, my dear,' Helen told her when she said this, 'but it will never totally leave you.'

It wasn't just the airmen at risk, of course, though sometimes the air tragedies had a more immediate effect and each airman lost would leave the other pilots a little subdued. Mark was particularly upset if the man missing was from his squadron. Molly knew he felt semi-responsible but there was nothing she could say to ease that for him.

She understood more now of the pilots' need to live one day at a time, their need to let off steam and the way they often tried to squeeze every bit of life into their off-duty hours. Mark was the same as the rest, though sometimes his eyes were glazed and bloodshot with tiredness, and Molly did worry more about him at those times, for she remembered what Helen had said about tiredness being a killer.

Then, one dreadful night, when Mark's stint was very nearly over Molly was roused from her sleep by a pounding on the door. She turned on the light and looked at the alarm clock to see that it was three o'clock in the morning. The pounding came again and with a sigh, she swung herself out of bed, wrapped her dressing gown around herself and pushed her feet into slippers as quickly as she could. As she descended the stairs, she heard Terry's frantic voice.

'Molly, open the door, for Christ's sake.'

She slid the bolts top and bottom, and Terry almost fell in through the door. He was still in his flying gear and his eyes were wild as he cried, 'Mark didn't make it back.'

'Didn't make it back?' Molly repeated in an appalled whisper, while the realisation of what those words meant were screaming in her head.

'We hit heavier resistance than we were prepared for, and Mark wasn't the only one, but Christ, I'm real sorry, Molly.'

'Oh God!' Molly cried. 'How can I go on without him?' She felt her legs crumple beneath her, and Terry caught her and led her to the settee. He was crying too and he shook his head helplessly as he sat down beside her.

'I don't think I want to go on without him, Terry,' Molly said. 'I love him so much.'

Terry had tasted the sorrow of losing good friends and comrades since he had joined the Royal Air Force in 1939 and he said, 'Hush, Molly. You must go on because it is what Mark would want of you, expect of you. He was a grand man. There will never be another like him and we will all miss him.'

'I have lost so many people in this life that I love, Terry,' Molly said. 'How much can one person take?'

Terry couldn't answer, his heart was too full of sorrow, and when Molly began to cry he put his arms around her and she needed the comfort of those arms too much to push Terry away. Tears rained down his own face.

Despite the embrace, Molly felt bereft and alone, as she tried to accept that never, ever would she see Mark's beloved face again, never feel his lips kissing her properly, his arms enfolding her, his hands exploring her body.

Much later, when her tears were spent and she was weak

from crying, Terry left her on the settee with a rug to cover her.

'I need to go back to the camp,' he said. 'Will you be all right?'

Molly knew she would never be all right, that she would never recover from this, but she nodded her head because she wanted to be alone. When Terry had gone, she was too churned up to rest and she paced the floor back and forth until the pain in her heart became so great she slumped to the floor, wrapped her arms around her chest and rocked backwards and forwards as she keened in anguish and despair. She knew she would never love another as she had Mark and she bitterly regretted allowing Collingsworth to sully that beautiful relationship, which had scarcely begun before it was snuffed out.

By the morning, Molly was feeling empty, completely drained inside and light-headed with the tears, but she needed to go to work, to keep active, to be too busy to think, or she would sit and cry all day. She had to get Kevin up for school as well, but before she did that, she would have to try to repair her face, for she didn't want to tell Kevin yet.

Kevin knew something was up with Molly because she was sort of distant and she had been crying. Loads, as well, it looked like. Yet when he asked her what she'd been crying about, she said she hadn't been crying, that she had a cold, like he was some little kid who would believe that stuff. He knew, despite her promise, she was shutting him out again. Molly knew it too, but she felt she wasn't strong enough to answer his questions and deal with his grief when she hadn't come to terms with her own.

The women at the Naafi knew something was up with Molly. You only had to look at her ashen face and blood-shot puffy eyes to see that she was far from well.

'D'you think she is sickening for something?' May asked.

'Looks more like sickness of the soul, if you ask me,'

Doris said. 'Poor kid looks as if she has been crying for bleeding hours.'

'She does and all,' Edna said. 'Hope nothing's gone wrong with her and that young airman.'

'Well, they haven't had time to have a row or owt,' May put in. 'Didn't he say a few days ago he was on night ops?'

'Yeah, he did,' Edna said, 'and Molly was all right yesterday, weren't her?'

'Yeah.'

There was a pause and the women looked fearfully.

'What if summat's happened to him, like?' Doris said.

'Can't be that,' Edna said. 'She wouldn't know yet.'

'Well, summat's drastically wrong,' May said. 'When I was in the kitchen just now she was moving around like a zombie, and often didn't register that I was speaking like. She was sniffing too and said she had a cold, but I reckon she was still having a little weep. I asked her if she was OK and if she wanted to go home and she said she was fine and she would rather stay.'

'She best keep in the back today, anyroad,' Edna said. 'Whatever ails her she don't want people gawping at her.'

Molly was glad to be working in the kitchen beside the taciturn chef, who didn't expect or even approve of excessive chatter. That suited her mood that day. She could not laugh, joke or chat with anyone when she was dead inside, when her world had turned upside down.

She knew eventually the news would filter through the camp of the pilots lost, but maybe by then she would be better able to cope without fearing she might sink to the floor and howl like an animal. And so by half-past eleven, when she went back out into the Naafi to help lay up the tables for lunch, the ladies on the counter knew about the four pilots lost the previous evening and knew too that one of them was Mark Baxter. They shed a few tears for the pilots and their families, but much of their sympathy was for Molly.

434

'She must have got to know somehow,' May said.

'Someone maybe called and told her,' Edna decided. 'Poor bloody cow – as if she hadn't got enough to put up with already.'

They watched Molly working slowly laying up the tables and Edna thought she had seldom seen anyone who looked so ill and yet was still on their feet.

When the door suddenly opened, it didn't register with Molly, although the three woman behind the counter were struck dumb and gazed in stupefaction at the airman framed in the door, swaying with weariness.

And then he spoke: 'Molly.'

It was the voice that Molly thought she would never, ever hear again and she raised her head slowly to see her beloved Mark in the doorway. For a moment, she thought her heart had stopped beating and then it was as if there were just the two of them in the room. Everyone else ceased to matter to either of them, and Molly threw the cutlery to the floor and was across the room in seconds. She barely took in Mark's face, grey with fatigue, or his red-rimmed eyes as she threw herself into his arms.

The tiredness left Mark as if it had never been as he held Molly tightly in his arms.

'Mark, oh darling, Terry told me . . . Oh, I thought you were dead.'

'I knew that was what you would think,' Mark said. 'That's why I had to get back. The Spit was shot to pieces and losing height, and I knew it would never make it to the airfield, but I had to find somewhere safe to land where hopefully there weren't that many people. Eventually I came down in Cannock Chase.'

'You walked from Cannock Chase?' Molly asked, because it was miles away. 'I can't believe this. It is wonderful! Magical!'

'So is this,' Mark said. 'You do realise I am holding you in my arms?'

435

Molly laughed. 'Of course I realise, and I am enjoying every minute of it. Shall we try something else now?'

'What had you in mind?'

'Would you kiss me?'

It was Molly's first proper kiss, apart from Collingsworth's bruising attempts when she thought she might choke, but the sweetness and gentleness of Mark's kiss drove that memory from her mind. It nearly took her breath away and she kissed him back with intensity. 'I love you, I love you, I love you,' Molly told Mark when they broke apart at last.

'And I you, my darling girl,' Mark said. 'And this is neither the time nor the place, but I need to know, Molly, my beloved, will you marry me?'

'Oh yes, Mark, and the sooner the better,' Molly said.

There was a collective sigh from the women and then a spontaneous round of applause from all those in the Naafi, and it broke the spell. Molly and Mark came back to the real world once more, and smiled at each other, a little embarrassed.

Suddenly there was a guard at the door and he said to Molly, 'Chap at the gate, name of Tom Sullivan. Says he's your uncle.'

'Uncle Tom!' Molly cried. 'Yes, yes he is.' She caught up Mark's hand and kissed it before saying, 'Come and meet my Uncle Tom,' and the two ran hand in hand through the airfield.

Later, with Mark rested and Molly having finished her shift, they sat and discussed the wedding plans with Tom and Kevin in the sitting room of the house. Kevin was quite pleased that Molly hadn't told him about Mark not making it back to base before he went to school that morning. He knew he would have been upset all day because he really liked Mark and would hate anything to happen to him. He was, however, very interested in the crash landing that Mark had to make and he would have quizzed him mercilessly about it if Molly hadn't put a stop to it.

'When were you thinking of having the wedding?' Tom asked.

'As soon as possible,' Molly said. 'You will give me away, won't you?'

Tom grinned and said, 'You try and stop me.'

'We will have to save first,' Mark said. 'I have a bit put by, but not nearly enough.'

'I'm sure Joe and his wife would like to come over for it too, and their son, Ben, who is your cousin, Kevin, and only a little younger than you,' Tom said.

'And I would like Jack and Nellie McEvoy, and Cathy, of course, to come too,' Molly said.

'It will take some organising, I'd say,' Tom said, 'but as for paying for it, don't worry about that. Paul Simmons said he would like to do that for you.'

'It's very kind of him,' Mark said quite stiffly, 'but—'

'I know how you feel, but he would like to do this for Ted, Molly's father's sake,' Tom said.

'Hang on,' Molly put in. 'How does Paul Simmons even know?'

'I told him.'

'When?'

'This afternoon before I came here.'

'But, Uncle Tom, you don't even know the man.'

'I went to apologise to him. I promised myself I would the first chance I got,' Tom said. 'He sent me a letter when the court case was going through when he accused me, quite rightly, in my opinion, of not looking after you properly, so I went to the address on the top of the letter.'

'I told him it wasn't your fault.'

'I know, he said,' Tom went on. 'I found him a true gentleman and he only has your interests at heart.'

'I know.'

'And,' Tom said to Mark, 'you have married a woman

437

of means, for Paul Simmons put some money by in a trust fund that matures when Molly, and Kevin too, of course, are twenty-one.'

Molly had totally forgotten that, and Kevin had never known of it at all.

'Does that worry you, Mark?' Molly said. 'I would rather give the money away than have you upset about it.'

'That would be very small-minded of me,' Mark said. 'The war won't last for ever, and when it ends, Terry's family will come back here. If this money is enough to put a deposit down on a little place of our own, won't it be better than us starting out in a couple of rooms?'

'I suppose,' Molly said. 'Though I wouldn't mind anywhere as long as I am with you.'

'Well said, Molly,' Tom said. 'They are wise words indeed for home is surely where the heart is, and it will be a happy home when those two hearts are entwined together as yours so obviously are.'

Molly was touched by the words and a little later, when he had gone back to the lodging house he was staying at, for he didn't think it seemly to stay with Molly, she said to Mark, 'Isn't Uncle Tom an old romantic?'

'He's right, though,' Mark said, snuggling Molly closer. 'When two people love each other deeply they can take anything the world throws at them.'

Molly laughed. 'Don't you think the world has thrown enough at me to last me a lifetime?' she said. 'I am looking for a smoother ride now.'

'And you will get it, my darling,' Mark said.

As their lips met, Molly knew she was the luckiest woman in the world.

ACKNOWLEDGEMENTS

This book might never have been written if my agent, Judith Murdoch, hadn't suggested it. At the time, I wasn't mightily impressed, because she wanted me to write a set of connected novels. It was something I had never done before and wasn't that keen on doing either. However, the idea grew on me. She was right, thank you, Judith. This book is the first of those novels that concentrate on members of the Sullivan family who lived in a small town in North Donegal called Buncrana, which isn't that far from Derry, though it is in the Republic of Ireland.

Judith's idea was to take each member of that family and tell their story, and you must have heard it said that everyone has a story inside them? I began with the offspring of Nuala, who was married, the mother of two children and living in Erdington, Birmingham, when this book opens.

There was a terrific amount of research to be done to access the information needed to sustain four books that will span many years. First and foremost I had to visit Buncrana and not once but many times. I had informed Buncrana Library that I was coming and why and they had lots of books ready and waiting for me to read of the history of the area, with maps and photographs that I could copy. Letterkenny Library too was able to help with maps and information, as it is the County Library, and I am indebted to all at both libraries for their support and help.

The railway and station in Buncrana is long gone, fallen way to 'progress' like many others, but the old station has been made into a pub. They have retained the ticket office and waiting room, which they showed me, and then took me outside to show me where the platform would have been, so I was able to look over the golf course Molly would have seen and Rathmullen on the other side of Lough Swilley. At the Derry Railway Museum we saw the trains used at the time and Donegal Railway Museum provided the fare rates and timetables.

I bought books to aid research too, *Donegal in Old Photographs* by Sean Beattie and *Irish Men and Women in the Second World War* by Richard Doherty, which I did find to be very good.

Best of all though, was going around Buncrana, which is a bustling, thriving place, and drinking in the atmosphere of it and talking to people. In this way, I learned why the Catholic Church is so far from town, in an area called Cockhill. There is a magnificent church built in the town now though and yet people, being people, continue to use the one in Cockhill, I was told. You seem to be able to stop any Irish people in the street and they know the history of the place they live in and are quite willing to share it. Two men, out for a stroll, were able to tell us that the massive structure in Swan Park on the banks of Lough Swilley was built in Napoleonic times to guard against French invaders. I knew about the soldiers that were deployed there in the Second World War to guard Ireland's neutrality. The men knew too, of course, and said the camp had been further round but there was nothing left of it now, so we didn't bother going to look.

It was easier to gather information about Erdington as I lived in Pype Hayes, which is not far from it, when I was growing up and went to the Abbey School. I also lived in Sutton Coldfield for some years after my marriage and I know Sutton Park very well. Yet I still found *Sutton Coldfield in the Forties* by John Bassett very helpful and I am grateful to Optima for producing so many photographs of old Birmingham that I downloaded from the internet. I also used two of Carl Chinn's books, *Our Brum*, in which he brings old Birmingham to life and *Birmingham at War*, which helped me write an accurate timeline of events and told harrowing tales of the terrifying raids and the effects on people's lives.

My family are extremely supportive of me and so thanks must go to my children, grandchildren and my lovely husband, Denis, the most important one of all. A special thanks too must go to Judith Kendall, who is a dear and close friend, Judith Evans at the airport whom I will always be grateful to and Peter Hawtin, who listened to her. Hello, Peter.

There is a tremendous team that backs me and helps the manuscript I submit become a book and they are: my great agent, Judith Murdoch, my marvellous editor, Susan Opie, and Becky Fincham, my lovely and intrepid publicist. She is leaving soon for pastures new. I wish you all the very best, Becky, but I will miss you enormously. Heartfelt thanks to you all.

Lastly, but by no means least, I thank you, the magnificent readers, who buy and read the books, for without you there would be no point to any of this. And though a special thanks must go to those who write, or e-mail, or leave a message on my website, saying how much they like my work, I appreciate and am grateful to you all and I hope you thoroughly enjoyed *A Sister's Promise*.